CHERYL WOLVERTON

The Best Christmas Ever

A Mother's Love

Steeple
Hill®

Published by Steeple Hill Books™

STEEPLE HILL BOOKS

**Steeple
Hill®**

ISBN-13: 978-0-373-65271-6
ISBN-10:   0-373-65271-2

THE BEST CHRISTMAS EVER AND A MOTHER'S LOVE

THE BEST CHRISTMAS EVER
Copyright © 1998 by Cheryl Wolverton

A MOTHER'S LOVE
Copyright © 1999 by Cheryl Wolverton

www.SteepleHill.com

Printed in U.S.A.

CONTENTS

Books by Cheryl Wolverton

CHERYL WOLVERTON

RITA® Award finalist Cheryl Wolverton has well over a dozen books to her name. Her very popular HILL CREEK, TEXAS, series has finaled in many contests. Having grown up in Oklahoma, lived in Kentucky, Texas, Louisiana and now living once more in Oklahoma, Cheryl and her husband of over twenty years and their two children, Jeremiah and Christina, always considered themselves Oklahomans transplanted to grow and flourish in the South. Readers are always welcome to contact her via mail, P.O. Box 106, Faxon, OK 73540, or e-mail, Cheryl@cherylwolverton.com. You can also visit her Web site at www.cherylwolverton.com

THE BEST CHRISTMAS EVER

For the Lord loves the just and will not forsake
His faithful ones.
They will be protected forever....
—*Psalms* 37:28

To Janet Abbott for always listening.
Thanks to Anne Canadeo, the greatest editor
in the world, and Jean Price, the greatest agent!
And I can't forget Dee Pace—
who went above and beyond for this book!
Thanks! And three other very special ladies:
Denise Gray, Donna Blacklock and Cheryl Crews.

With love to my husband who is so patient and
thoughtful when I'm going crazy over computer
problems, and my kids, Christina and Jeremiah.
You guys are the love of my life.

Prologue

Dear Santa:
All I want this year for Christmas is a mommy. I know it's sorta early still to ask, but it is almost cold out, and I miss Mommy, and so does Daddy. He doesn't exactly say he misses her, but he stares at Mommy's picture a lot. I heard my baby-sitter on the phone telling someone Daddy needed to get married again. Well, that'd mean I'd get a new mommy. And if I had a new mommy, then I wouldn't have to play Go Fish with Daddy's secretary anymore when he couldn't find a baby-sitter. And I wouldn't have to take store-bought cookies on party day at school. I could have a real mommy to bake chocolate chip cookies—and make me peanut butter-and-jelly sandwiches as much as I wanted. But most of all, Santa, I would have a mommy to hug me the way the other kids do when we get out of school. It would be just too cool to have that. So, Santa, that's what I've decided I want for Christmas. I told Jesus so He can look

around for the right mommy, then tell you which
one to bring me on Christmas Eve. I know this is
going to be the best Christmas present ever.

Thank you, Santa.

Signed,
Mickie Warner

Chapter One

"Sarah?"

Sarah Connelly smiled sweetly at her brother-in-law's incredulous tone, then watched as his surprise slowly turned to cool remoteness. "Surely, Justin, it hasn't been so long that you've forgotten me," she quipped, doing her best to hide her fear that he'd slam the door in her face.

His mask fell into place just the way Sarah remembered it had in the past. His critical gaze slowly took her in. Sarah did her best not to gather the thin sweater around her shoulders against the cold wind or his icy scrutiny.

"Maybe it's just because I've never seen you in jeans," he replied indifferently. "Remember the last time I saw you—in court? That nice little blue suit you wore when…"

"Yes, well." Sarah shrugged dismissively.

"So what brings you here?" He leaned against the

door frame, blocking her way into his house. "It has, after all, been two years."

"I wanted to see Mickie," she replied, deciding that any hope she'd had of getting the baby-sitting/house-keeper job was just a dream. He was still furious with her, and she didn't blame him. Although she'd hoped it would be different.

"I don't think that's a good idea."

"I'm her aunt."

"Who hasn't been here in two years," he retorted.

"I'm sorry." Sarah shifted her chilled feet, pushing at the loose strand of blond hair that blew across her face. She was cold. Justin knew she was cold, but he wasn't going to let her in.

"Sorry?" Justin's eyes flashed. "For what? For not coming to see Mickie? Or for trying to take her away from me two years ago?"

Instead of getting angry as she would have back then, Sarah dropped her gaze from Justin's accusing one. "Both," she finally whispered. Lifting her chin, she forced a smile. "Look, I wanted to apologize and put it all behind us, but I guess that's impossible. I'll be going."

All she wanted to do was leave. She'd known it was a stupid idea to come here and apply for the job. But her friend Bill had been so certain Justin would take her on. Of course, Bill was newly married and in love. He thought all families loved one another the way he loved his in-laws. He couldn't understand the icy wall of anger and bitterness that separated her and Justin, the guilt and fears....

Justin's hand shot out and wrapped around her small arm. "Wait."

She froze at Justin's first touch, then slowly turned. Indecision and frustration etched his rugged features. He wasn't sure if he wanted her there or not. The years hadn't changed him. Justin was still as good-looking as when she'd first met him almost seven years ago. A few gray hairs she didn't remember were now mixed in his dark brown wavy hair. It was cut short in the back and longer on the top; one lock of his hair fell casually out of place over his forehead. He hadn't gained an ounce of weight. "Since when do you wear jeans?" She liked the way he looked in them.

He cocked an eyebrow in amusement.

Warmth climbed her face as she realized she'd actually asked the question out loud.

"Since I've been doing the housework," he replied evenly.

She fidgeted a moment, then stepped back. "Well, I'd better go—"

"No. I..." He ran a hand through his hair, his other hand on his hip. Finally, he sighed. "It's been two years, Sarah. Why now?"

"You already asked that," Sarah replied with the only comeback she could think of that would give her time to form an answer.

"Daddy?"

Justin's head jerked toward the stairs.

Sarah saw panic in his eyes. "Look, Justin, if you don't want Mickie to see me I'll go. I understand if—"

"No, come on in." A long, low breath escaped Justin before he stepped back to allow her in.

Turning toward the stairs, he called up, "I'll be right there, Mickie. Go ahead and put on the jeans I laid out for you."

He stepped back and allowed Sarah to enter the house. It hadn't changed since her sister, Amy, had lived there two years ago. The same overstuffed sofa filled the living room; an oak coffee table still sat in front of the sofa, with a book of scenic landscapes throughout America on it. On the mantel framed family photos were arranged with pride and loving care. Looking out through the open curtains, Sarah saw the sky was still clouded over and it looked as though it might rain or snow any moment.

"Mickie has been asking about relatives lately. I suppose it wouldn't hurt to let you meet with her. Just don't do anything to hurt her."

Sarah jerked as if she'd been slapped. "I'd never hurt Mickie."

"Then why'd you try to take her away from me two years ago?"

This was the question Sarah had not wanted to hear. The accusation and suppressed anger in his voice were as obvious as the fact that he expected her to answer. "I truly thought she'd be better off with me, Justin," she finally said.

He snorted. "I'm sure your fiancé would love having her with you now, wouldn't he, Sarah?"

Sarah stiffened. "How do you know about André?"

"Hamilton is a small town," he replied, shrugging.

Of course everyone in the small suburb well outside the Dallas-Fort Worth metropolis knew everything about everyone. She paled, wondering if he knew the rest, too. She didn't dare ask. Instead, she said, "André likes children."

That much was true.

"So, do you still work as your fiancé's secretary?"

"So, do you still take people's business away from them?" she retorted, and was immediately contrite at the look of pain that flashed in Justin's eyes. "I'm sorry. I didn't mean that." She placed her hands on her hips, her exasperation evident in every inch of her stiff body. "Why must you be so provoking, Justin? I came here to apologize, to put the past in the past. We're family. Mickie is the only blood relative I have left. I want to get to know her. I thought you might be able to forgive me for that reason alone."

It had taken two years. She'd had to hit rock bottom and turn to God before realizing how much she'd wronged this man. But once she had acknowledged what a grievous blow she'd dealt Justin by taking him to court for custody of Mickie, she'd hoped to correct it. Her only mistake was in listening to Bill and deciding to apply for the job as housekeeper.

Of course, now that she saw how Justin still felt about her, she couldn't tell him about what she'd found out from the doctor. Or how that had led to André breaking off their engagement. Nor how that had led to the sweet note in her mailbox the following week saying that Watson and Watson had to cut back staff and she, unfortunately, was the one who had to go.

André hadn't even had the guts to fire her in person. That still hurt. But she knew God had a reason for all that happened. She knew now that if she trusted Him, He would turn everything out for the good. It was His way even when she couldn't see it herself.

Justin sighed again. "You're right. I'm sorry, too."

"I really do want to try to get along."

Justin ran a hand through his hair.

"For Amy's sake," she said, then added more desperately, "for Mickie's sake."

That swayed him. "You're right. Despite how angry I am at you, Mickie needs to know you. Other kids at kindergarten have been asking about her family. The kids at school all have aunts and uncles."

She heard the silent *and a mother.*

"I think she'd really like to meet a relative. But if you hurt her or say anything—"

"I won't," Sarah cut in. Since her devastating news and resulting breakup with André she'd had a lot of time to think and pray.

She wanted to know Mickie. She'd allowed two years to pass since the court battle, and hadn't seen Mickie since. It was time to forget the past and go forward. And she wanted to do that with the only family she had left.

"Look, I have an important meeting I'll be late for if I don't get ready. I'll go up and change. I'll tell Mickie you're here."

"Will she know who I am?"

Justin scowled. "She knows she has an aunt Sarah. You can visit with her until the baby-sitter gets here. If all goes well, then we'll see about visits after that. I'd better warn you, though—Mickie doesn't take well to strangers, whether she's heard of them or not.''

Sarah nodded.

Without another word, Justin turned and headed up the stairs.

The kids at school all have aunts and uncles.

Sarah's heart ached at his words. How much had Mickie missed because of her mother's death, because of Sarah's bitterness and anger, because of the bitterness and anger between her and Justin?

Well, she was going to set things right if she could, starting now.

A sound at the top of the stairs caught her attention and she looked up. A five-year-old girl, with long brown curly hair that hung past her shoulders stood at the top of the stairs, a fashion doll clutched in her hands.

The child studied Sarah a long minute before slowly descending. ''Daddy says you're my aunt.''

Tears welled in Sarah's eyes, but she quickly blinked them away. Mickie looked so much like Amy it hurt to see her. She wanted to grab the child and hug her, never let her go, but she knew Mickie didn't remember her. ''That's right, Michelle,'' she said, trying to hide her trembling by clasping her hands.

''Daddy calls me 'Mickie.'''

Of course, Sarah thought, not even knowing why she had used the child's given name. ''That's right. Your mom said that was the first word out of your daddy's mouth when you were born.''

Mickie's eyes widened. ''Did you know my mama?''

''Yes, sweetheart, I did. Your mama was my sister.''

Mickie's wide brown eyes, the only thing she had inherited from her father, stared at Sarah as if assessing that bit of information.

"Her picture looks like you. Will you tell me her favorite story?"

Sarah reached out for the child's hand. After Mickie slipped her tiny one into hers, she led her over to the couch. "Of course I will," she said, humbled that Mickie took her in without questioning why she'd never come by or why she'd missed birthdays and Christmases. "Her favorite story was *The Littlest Angel*. Have you ever heard that?"

Mickie shook her head and Sarah settled her in to tell her the tale.

Upstairs, Justin listened to the murmuring below. He'd told Sarah Mickie didn't usually take to people, but Mickie had been so excited when she'd found out her aunt Sarah had come to visit. Knowing the sitter would be there any minute, he'd allowed Mickie to go down by herself.

It was the least he could do after telling Sarah never to come near his child again. Sarah had attempted to breach the wall between them. He wouldn't reinforce the barricade by refusing to trust her for a few minutes with his daughter. After all, what could happen?

The ringing phone interrupted his thoughts. Pulling on his long-sleeved white shirt, he crossed the room to answer it. "Hello?"

It was Mrs. Winters, the baby-sitter. "Justin. I know I was supposed to baby-sit tonight, but I just got a call fifteen minutes ago from my daughter out in Arizona.

She's gone into early labor and it's not going well. I've had to book an emergency flight and am leaving within the hour. Justin?''

Barely able to restrain a groan of dismay, he replied, ''I understand, Mrs. Winters. I'll be praying for your daughter.''

''I really hate to do this. I know I told you I'd be able to work at least three more weeks, but pregnancies just aren't always predictable.''

''Don't worry,'' he said, even as he silently went through a list, trying to figure out whom he could round up to watch his daughter on such a short notice. ''I'll find someone. You just worry about getting to your daughter's side. I'll be fine.''

Justin could hear the relief in Mrs. Winters's voice as she hung up the phone. It might be relief for her, but it was near chaos for him. He had to make that important business meeting scheduled in less than an hour with the top executives of a software firm on the West Coast. His second-in-command, Phillip, had worked out most of the negotiations over the phone. This was the only time the executives could meet with Justin to sign the papers and go over last-minute details before the merger was completed.

Why did things have to get so messed up now? If he called off the meeting, the men might lose confidence in him and go to another company. They were desperate and needed this...and so did he. His company had suffered financial setbacks the past few years, but he had finally turned things around. With this merger, his firm would again be one of the biggest producers of software components in the southwestern United States.

He finished buttoning his shirt, then grabbed his tie and draped it around his neck. After picking up his jacket, he headed downstairs. Justin supposed he could take Mickie with him to the meeting. He'd set her up someplace comfortable with books and toys and hope she'd manage to amuse herself. He'd done it before. But this meeting would last longer than most, and be more delicate. Maybe he could call Phillip, who had picked up the businessmen from the airport, and have him stall....

Coming down the stairs, he was surprised when he saw Sarah on his couch. He had forgotten she was there.

Finally continuing on, he reached the bottom of the stairs before she spotted him and her murmurs to Mickie drifted off. Justin tossed his jacket on the back of the sofa and worked his tie into an acceptable knot. "Mickie, I need you to go upstairs and change. That was Mrs. Winters on the phone and she can't baby-sit tonight. You'll have to come with me to work." Seeing her downcast look, he decided to remind her of his secretary's presence. "Christine will be there and maybe she can play with you while I work. You love to play with her." It wasn't exactly true and he was feeling guilty for suggesting it. Mickie tolerated the older woman's game of Go Fish and her comments about her pretty little dresses.

"What about Aunt Sarah?"

Justin's gaze shifted to Sarah. He still couldn't believe he'd almost forgotten she was there. That was very odd.

In the past, every time they'd been in the same room a yelling match had ensued within minutes of their arrivals and she'd stormed off in a huff. Why was she being so quiet today? Her deep blue eyes blinked and he could have sworn she was embarrassed to be caught in the family emergency. Hah! Unlikely. Sarah loved controversy.

"What about her?"

"Why can't she watch me?"

"Mickie," her father warned, surprised by his daughter's unusual show of spirit.

"I don't think your daddy would like that." Realizing what she'd said, Sarah gazed at her brother-in-law in shocked apology.

Justin didn't know what to say. He wanted to tell her, *Impossible, there's no way I'd trust my daughter with you. You despise me.* But then he couldn't get over her look of embarrassment at what she'd just said. No matter how true it was that he and Sarah didn't get along, he didn't want his daughter to know that, which made him realize just how wrong his feelings were. But it would take time to get over those feelings.

Do unto others...

The verse he'd learned as a child floated into his mind, striking him with guilt. What was he teaching his daughter by harboring this anger? And what would she think if he didn't at least try to work through his pain and forgive his sister-in-law? It was true Mickie might not understand everything that had happened, but she would understand her aunt Sarah not coming around again.

Justin finally said, albeit reluctantly, "Actually, Sarah,

if you're available for the rest of the evening, I wouldn't mind. Mickie seems quite taken by her aunt. And it'd give you a little more time to visit.''

Sarah swallowed her automatic no. She knew Justin didn't really want her there. But could she have ever, in her wildest dreams, envisioned spending an evening with her niece? She hadn't seen Mickie since her sister's funeral. Mickie had not been at the hearing before the judge. Sarah hadn't been dismayed over that. She had believed she'd have Mickie soon enough.

How absolutely arrogant she had been, and how angry when the court had ruled in her brother-in-law's favor. Now she was getting a second chance to know Mickie, to get reacquainted with her. The door had just been opened; the opportunity she had been praying for had dropped into her lap. ''I don't have to be anywhere. I'd be glad to watch her.''

An awkward silence fell as the two adults stared at each other; it was broken finally when Mickie squealed in glee and clapped her hands.

''Will you fix me dinner? I like fried chicken, but Daddy doesn't make it. I also like peanut butter-and-jelly sandwiches. And then you can help me into my 'jamas and we can read stories till Dad gets home. Is that okay, Daddy? Can we read stories until you get home?''

Sarah saw Justin's features soften and was amazed at how much younger he looked when he smiled so gently like that. ''That sounds fine.''

When his gaze returned to Sarah, the cool mask fell back in place.

''There's a list of emergency numbers by the phone.

Fix whatever you two decide you want for dinner…except peanut butter-and-jelly sandwiches.'' He cast a warning look at his daughter, who bowed her head and appeared properly contrite at the idea of allowing any peanut butter or jelly to pass her lips again in the near future. "I should be home sometime this evening. The office is about forty-five minutes away and the people I'm meeting have to leave tonight.''

He looked at his watch. Four o'clock. He would be late at this rate. Thank goodness he had arranged to meet them at a hotel closer to his home. It had been Phillip's idea to pick them up in the limo and for them all to go to the office together for the tour and business meeting. "Any questions?''

Sarah shook her head. Still he seemed unsure. "Look, Justin,'' she said, "if you want, I'll call you every hour on the hour. You don't need to worry that we'll be gone when you return.'' She didn't tell him that she no longer had a car and had caught the bus over. Call it pride, but she just couldn't admit that.

His face didn't show if that was what he was thinking or not. He finally sighed and gave a curt nod. "I'm trusting you on this. My secretary's number is on the list. Phone if you need anything.''

He kissed his daughter goodbye and headed out the door.

Sarah couldn't believe it. She was actually alone with her niece. Why had Justin allowed it?

Was it that it had been so long and he'd relegated the past to the past? She wondered if he meant to pay her. There was no way she would ask. She wasn't even sure she could take his money. She was desperate, but was she that desperate?

True, that was why she'd originally come. But she hadn't expected to feel guilty and uncomfortable around Justin. Had she thought to be that same old arrogant woman who would look at him as though he owed her for his past sins?

Closing her mind to those questions, she turned her attention to Mickie, who was tugging on her shirt.

"Can we cook now? I like to help in the kitchen, but Mrs. Winters never lets me. She says I make a mess, especially when we have chicken. You know, we wouldn't have to have peanut butter-and-jelly *sandwiches*. Sometimes Daddy lets me eat them on crackers, too."

Sarah smiled. She hadn't eaten since last night. She'd missed breakfast this morning because she had wanted to find somewhere to shower before coming over to Justin's. The only other meal she'd have a chance at was dinner at six o'clock in the evening.

Oh, no! She suddenly focused on one small fact she'd conveniently forgotten; she had to be back by eight o'clock. Would Justin be home before then? She worried her bottom lip, then sighed. Well, there was no choice now. She'd just have to hope it worked out.

"I think peanut butter and jelly on anything is out— if that look your father gave you was any indication," she said, forcing her worries from her mind. She'd have plenty of time later to worry. Right now she wanted to soak up Mickie's presence. "Come on, let's go thaw out something and you can help me make a mess in the kitchen.''

''You make a mess?''

Mickie's eyes widened in childish horror. Sarah smiled. ''It's more fun that way.'' She winked.

Going toward the kitchen with Mickie, Sarah realized that things might actually be changing in her life. Maybe the past could be just that—the past. Maybe she could forget it; let go of the ghosts that haunted her, the mistakes she had made. Perhaps she could turn over a new leaf and start back on the right path. It'd been so long...she wasn't sure if she could even find her way back on her own. How did she get rid of years of bitterness and pain and find peace again with the very person she had wronged?

She remembered then—something her mother had told her when she'd had a fight with her dear friend and they had stopped talking for two weeks. She'd been frantic that she would never see her friend again and didn't know if Sylvia would accept her apology or not. She'd prayed but wasn't sure God had answered her prayer on how she should ask forgiveness for yelling at Sylvia.

''When you turn and walk down our street it takes five minutes to reach the end, dear. How long does it take to return?''

She had answered, ''Five minutes.''

''And how do you get back? Do you cover that distance in five seconds or fifty seconds? Do you turn and take different streets to get you back to our house?''

''No, Mama,'' she'd replied.

''That's right, dear. You simply turn around and start

from the way you came, taking one step at a time. Sometimes you can make it a little faster, sometimes not. But the important thing is you make that decision and turn around and go back.''

Her mother had been right. By confronting the issue with Sylvia, Sarah had righted things, although the lost trust between them had taken a little longer to return.

Now she knew that no matter how long it took, she wanted things right again between her and her only living relative. So maybe, if she prayed—since the first step to anything was prayer, or at least that was what she'd been taught in her family—this time things would be different between her and her brother-in-law. They could get along well enough that she would again have a family.

If she hadn't turned her back and run from God when everything had happened almost seven years ago, then this mess wouldn't have happened.

She told herself to remember that this time and everything *would* work out. Put God first, not her own selfish feelings, and trust God to work the miracle.

Looking down at Mickie, she knew that no matter what happened, she had to do that. She didn't want to lose what she only now was discovering filled a void that had long been in need of filling.

Chapter Two

The click of the door told Sarah that Justin had returned. She put down the book she'd been thumbing through and stood. Even in the darkened light of the living room Justin looked good. Tired, but good. His suit jacket was thrown over his shoulder and a hint of beard shadowed his square jaw. Dark brown eyes scanned the room before landing on her.

"Mickie asleep?"

Sarah unclasped her hands. "Yes. She fell asleep about an hour ago."

Silence fell and Sarah resisted the urge to shift. It was late and for the past hour she'd been wondering how to handle Justin's reappearance. Before, Mickie had been a buffer between them. Now that buffer was gone and she wasn't sure how to act or how her brother-in-law would act. She cleared her throat. "Well, I'd better go."

She started toward the door.

When her hand was on the knob, Justin spoke. "What really brought you here, Sarah?"

She stiffened. How could she tell him that in desperation she'd come to him for a job? He wouldn't believe it. Or worse. He might. And then he'd either laugh at her or pity her. He certainly wouldn't hire her, knowing she had been let go from her job in a lawyer's office, no matter what the reason. Doubts and fears crushed in on her, making her shoulders heavy with the burden of carrying them. Sarah forced herself to stand up straight, as if Justin might actually see the weight loading her down. "I came to bury the hatchet," she quipped, without turning around to face him.

A wry chuckle escaped Justin's lips and Sarah felt a warm tingle run down her back. Had that laugh attracted Amy? She knew it certainly affected her.

"Well then," he said when silence had fallen again, "maybe I should be glad you didn't decide to bury it in my neck like…"

She knew what he would have said—*Like when you tried to take Mickie.* She stiffened. "Good night."

"Wait." Justin rested his hand on her shoulder even as she pulled open the door. "I'm sorry."

She didn't respond but stood facing the door, hiding her eyes from his scrutiny lest he see what she was feeling.

"Will it always be this way between us?" he finally asked.

"I don't know," Sarah replied.

With a sigh, he released her.

Sarah walked out the door, deciding that she was

walking out of his life for the final time. Turning down the street, she headed to where she hoped she'd be able to catch the last bus for the night, wondering why she'd ever thought she could work for the man her sister had married.

Justin leaned his head against the closed door and sighed again. He was tired. The meeting had been a lot more complicated than he'd expected. What was supposed to be a simple merger had turned into more negotiations. Years ago he wouldn't have allowed it, but because he'd seen these men making a sincere effort to protect their employees, he'd spent the extra two hours negotiating. Then they'd had to have a new contract typed and finally signed. The men had fortunately found seats on a later flight. It was almost eleven o'clock and he'd been worried about his daughter...and he'd treated Sarah badly.

Pushing away from the door, he turned, then went through the house, flipping off lights and checking windows. There had been no reason for him to say such cruel things to her. Indeed, she'd been trying to bury the hatchet. That was the longest they'd gone without snipping at each other. And then he'd had to ruin it. She was Amy's sister—the only link he and Mickie had to Amy. The least he could have done was hold his tongue. It was just that when he'd opened the door and seen her rising from the couch, the book of scenic landscapes sliding from her lap, he'd felt as though someone had punched him in the gut. He'd never noticed that Sarah was a very beautiful woman, despite her beat-up jeans and sweater. He'd always pictured her as tough and aggressive. Her soft golden hair, which she'd always worn up, had floated about her face tonight, giving her the look of innocence wronged. But he'd not wronged her. And she wasn't innocent or soft. He knew her real personality. She had tried to take his daughter away. He'd been right to fight her to keep his child. And he wouldn't forget the pain that fight had caused anytime soon, no matter how innocent or beautiful she looked.

He hadn't felt a spark of interest in a woman since Amy's death. How could that spark be ignited by the sister who had caused them both so much grief? In anger at his own reaction to her, he'd struck out.

He trudged up the stairs. After checking on Mickie to make sure she was covered, he undressed.

Because of his actions, Mickie would probably never see Sarah again. She'd be stuck with a baby-sitter all day—

Baby-sitter!

Justin didn't have a baby-sitter for his daughter, tomorrow or anytime. He collapsed on the side of the bed and dropped his head into his hands. How could he have forgotten?

Easy. Big blue eyes and a heart-stopping smile had clouded his thinking.

Well, he couldn't let them distract him now. He had to find someone for tomorrow. Justin lifted his head. Maybe this was a way to prove to Sarah that he wanted to accept her apology and make amends. He could ask her to baby-sit this weekend, since she probably didn't work on weekends, and Mickie could get to know her.

Of course his day would be short on Saturday. He only had to finish up the paperwork related to tonight's merger and make sure everything was running smoothly. Then he could invite Sarah over for dinner on Sunday as a gesture of thanks. That should smooth over the mistake he'd made tonight.

He reached into the drawer by his bed and pulled out the phone book. After finding her number, he dialed it.

He listened as the call connected.

On the third ring, instead of an answering machine picking up, he heard a message saying the phone was disconnected.

Frowning, he put the receiver down. Had she moved lately? He called Information and the operator told him she had no listing under Sarah's name.

Thinking back, he remembered Bill, from church, mentioning he'd talked to Sarah only last week. He hadn't said where he'd seen her or what they'd talked about. His friends were that way. If they met up with Sarah they only informed him that they'd seen her. Few of his friends felt the need to gossip and dredge up past pains. And, he thought, a few were still friends with Sarah, though none ever really talked about her when he was around.

Bill was the answer. If it had been only last week since he'd talked to her he would know where she was now living. Despite the late hour, Justin picked up the phone and dialed Bill's number. On the second ring, Bill answered it. Justin smiled. Bill had a thing for computers and was usually up until one or two in the morning playing around with some new software or game.

"Hey, Bill," he said. "Uh, sorry to call so late."

"Justin? No problem. I'm up. What's going on?"

"I just tried to get hold of Sarah. She stopped by earlier today and I need to talk to her. I tried the phone number I have for her, but the service has been disconnected. I figured you could tell me where she moved."

Silence followed.

Justin frowned.

Finally, Bill spoke, but it wasn't with the answer Justin had wanted.

"You say you talked to her today?"

"Yeah. She, uh, watched Mickie for me. I was in a bind—"

"You let her baby-sit your daughter?"

Why was Bill sounding so shocked? "Yeah. She came by to visit. My baby-sitter had an emergency and Mickie seemed taken with Sarah. Look," Justin said, becoming impatient, "do you know where she moved? I'd like to get hold of her." Suddenly, it dawned on Justin what had been bothering him. Her number had not been changed but disconnected. Why? Wait a minute. She had been engaged— "Or what her new last name is," he added, drawing the conclusion that she must now be married and that was why she no longer had a phone number of her own. "I'd like to…thank her," he finished, thinking that if she was married, then she wouldn't want to baby-sit on a weekend. He couldn't believe she had stayed tonight with a husband waiting for her at home. At least her marriage explained her decreased anger and bitterness since the last time they'd seen each other.

"Sarah didn't tell you?"

Confused, Justin wrinkled his brow. "Tell me what? That she had married? No, but I know she was engaged—"

"*Was* is the operative word there, buddy. You'd better sit down."

Justin stood, instead. "Look, Bill, obviously you know something I don't. Why don't you try telling me."

"I don't know all the particulars. Just that she's no longer engaged."

"Is that all?"

"No. As a matter of fact, it's not. She no longer works for her fiancé's family, either, as of a very short time ago. Nor does she live in her old apartment."

Justin sighed impatiently. "I know the latter—that's why I called you. Do you know where she lives?"

"Yes."

Restlessly, Justin ran a hand through his hair. Why was Bill acting as if Sarah's address and phone number were a national secret? Okay, so Bill felt sorry for Sarah. She had broken off with her fiancé and quit her job. Justin was sorry for her, too, but that might just work out to his best. Maybe he could hire Sarah for a week or two until she found a better job…unless she already had one. But first he had to locate her. This was all too much to take in at once. Just what did he really know about Sarah? Very little, he suddenly realized.

"So where is she?" he demanded, quickly reaching the end of his rope.

There was a hesitation, then a sigh. "Look, Justin, maybe since she didn't tell you—"

"Where, Bill?" he demanded.

"Okay, okay! But if she's mad at me—"

"Bill!"

"She's living at a homeless shelter downtown near Second Street."

Justin's legs collapsed underneath him and he sank to the bed, stunned. "Homeless shelter?" he whispered, unable to believe what he was hearing.

"Yeah. Evidently, when she lost her job, she didn't have enough money to pay her rent. She had to move out but had nowhere to go and wouldn't let me help since I'm so newly married. She refuses to collect unemployment—"

"She was fired!" Justin shouted.

"As I said," Bill continued without answering Justin's question, "she comes in twice a week, looking for a job. The law office, it seems, was overstaffed and had to get rid of a secretary."

"What's the shelter's name and number?"

"Why?"

"Because I'm going to call and leave a message for Sarah to expect me."

"Sorry, bud, the shelter closes its doors at eight. Which also means no phone calls, either."

"What do you mean, it closes its doors at eight?"

"Just what I said. Haven't you ever been around shelters? In the morning the people are fed, then put out for the day. At the end of the day the shelters reopen and the occupants are allowed back in for supper. At eight this particular one closes its doors and no one else is allowed in. The place is usually full by six or so anyway."

A sick feeling curled in Justin's stomach. "What about Sarah?"

"What about her?"

"What if she's late getting back? Would they let her in? I mean, if she had a good explanation?"

"Sarah's staying at a very good shelter, Justin. Try not to worry. She's been there a couple of weeks now. They've treated her well. They won't turn her out."

Cold fear filled Justin's heart. "You're not answering my question. If Sarah was late, would they let her in?"

"Sarah knows the rules. She wouldn't have been late."

Justin had his answer. "Thanks, Bill."

"You okay?"

How could Justin answer that truthfully? "Yeah," he lied.

Sarah, his sister-in-law, who had been here only thirty minutes ago, was living in a shelter. His sister-in-law, for pity sakes! Why hadn't she come to him?

In a flash of insight he realized she had. Today. And he'd snipped at her from the time he'd opened the door, never giving her a chance to state her true purpose in coming.

Anger replaced the guilt. Oh, he'd asked, but she'd refused to tell Justin what was going on. It'd always been that way. Amy had been heartsick when Sarah had closed herself off from her only sister because Amy had married him. Of course Sarah had had a good reason for not speaking to him.

His anger deflated. They were both at fault. But why hadn't she opened up to him tonight and told him she was penniless and living in a shelter?

Because she didn't trust him. And he didn't trust her. And she knew that.

Yet despite that, Justin admitted to his feelings of earlier today. True, he'd felt shock and anger when he'd seen her, then experienced a need to prove that he held nothing against her. But worst of all was the spark of interest he'd felt for her that had slowly made itself known as he'd noticed the sway of her hair, the tilt of her chin, the flash of her eyes.... Self-loathing ate at him. This was Amy's sister, not a woman who should interest him. Especially since he still didn't completely trust her. But all that didn't matter now. The only thing that mattered was that Sarah was living in a shelter.

His sister-in-law.

Mickie's aunt.

There was no way he was going to let her stay there.

"So—" Bill broke the silence "—are you ready to talk?"

Justin sighed. Bill was his friend. He trusted Bill more than anyone else. Maybe he needed to confide in a friend. "I guess at the time of Amy's death Sarah was a convenient person to blame. I was despondent, and according to Sarah, I unintentionally neglected Mickie because of my grief. Maybe Sarah had been acting in Mickie's best interest by taking me to court...or at least she thought she was. I can tell you it certainly woke me up to what was going on around me and that I had a daughter who needed me."

He wondered if Sarah had sensed that things weren't as good between Amy and him as they'd appeared. Had Amy told Sarah she wanted a divorce?

The night of Amy's death, she had admitted that her parents had encouraged the match, saying it was a way of showing the peace between their two families. Had Sarah known or suspected that? He'd been devastated when his wife had run from the house to go see the sister she hadn't talked to in months, because she was tired of trying to "work things out" as he'd insisted they do.

"Amy was angry that every time Sarah and I were near each other we fought. I knew this and tried to curb my tongue, but something got my dander up each time the woman came by. Sarah obviously felt the same way. Amy was caught in the middle and maybe that was why Sarah had fought back the way she did. She had been trying to protect Amy. I just don't know."

Justin ran a weary hand over his face. "She went too far when she tried to take Mickie."

Yes, it had jerked him out of his grief, but the strength he'd found was fueled by anger and hatred, not by God. Things had been disastrous at the trial, breaking the familial bonds between them forever. Or so he'd thought until today, when he'd found out that Sarah was living in a shelter and had tried in her own way to "bury the hatchet."

"You know you can't just go to her and force her to move home with you. If she thinks you're offering her charity she'll disappear. She's a very proud woman."

A very proud woman who was now out wandering the streets because the shelter's doors had closed while she'd been watching Mickie for him. What could he say to Bill? Why hadn't she told him? He had to do something.

An idea formed. Justin would bet that Sarah would be at the shelter tomorrow when the doors opened. She'd been staying there for a while, according to Bill. Yes, his plan just might work.

"Look, Bill, I'm desperate. I need a baby-sitter. I don't know how to get a hold of Sarah. Could you contact her for me tomorrow when the shelter opens for breakfast? Tell her I called looking for her and need her help."

Bill whistled on the other end. "She's gonna go crazy when she finds out you know about her living in a shelter."

"I understand. Maybe you can smooth that over, convince her I'm not handing out charity. My baby-sitter quit tonight and I'm stuck between a rock and a hard place. I need someone—immediately! If it'll help, tell her I'm desperate. You know her better than I do. Do what you have to and convince her to take the job. Call me first thing in the morning after you talk to her."

"Sure thing. And, Justin?"

"Yeah?"

"It's about time you faced this thing between you and Sarah." With those words Bill hung up.

Justin slowly replaced the receiver, trying not to read more into Bill's words than he'd intended. But the truth was, it was hard not to. Because, like a lightning bolt from the sky, he suddenly wondered if maybe that had not been part of the problem all along. Had he married Amy partly out of guilt? Oh, he'd been attracted to her, but what he'd done to her family's business had been part of the equation, too. Unfortunately, she'd married him only out of obligation to her family. He'd cared for Amy. At least on his part he had been willing to stay married forever. They had enjoyed a good comfortable relationship, and in his own way, he'd loved her.

But Bill's words unsettled him more than they should have. Was it not possible that he'd known, on some deeper level, that Amy hadn't loved him and he'd felt threatened by Sarah's anger and dislike?

The possibility was too awful to consider. He didn't want to think that he'd been so insecure back then that he had actually helped cause the wedge in his marriage.

With that thought, he slipped into bed and pulled the covers up to his waist. He would give Sarah a job, prove to her he held no grudges against her and prove to himself that there was really nothing between them at all. Then he'd have his peace again. He could close that part of his life and go forward to face whatever the future held, with no regrets or shadows from the past dogging his heels.

Chapter Three

The doorbell rang, but Justin didn't rush forward the way he wanted to. He didn't throw open the door and greet his sister-in-law with a blast of anger. Instead, he took two repetitive breaths, letting each one out slowly, readying himself for the battle he was sure to face. When he was certain he had control of his emotions, he calmly walked forward and pulled open the door.

She still wore the same jeans from yesterday. She'd changed her shirt, though, he noted. Instead of a white pullover, she wore a pink one.

"Well, are you done gawking at the charity case?"

He raised an eyebrow in silent query, but that only seemed to antagonize her.

"Don't you dare pull that patronizing look on me. It won't work. I've seen it before."

"I'm not trying to be patronizing, Sarah. I just wondered why you were in such a sour mood already this morning. It's not even ten a.m."

She dropped her arms from where she'd crossed them and let them hang at her sides. However, she looked anything but relaxed; she looked ready to pounce on him and take him apart limb by limb.

"You know exactly what's the matter. How could you get Bill involved in this?" she demanded. "He's a friend I trusted, until he hunted me down this morning and told me you had called him last night."

"Is that what's bothering you?"

"No, it's not," she fumed. "What's bothering me is he told you about…well…"

She trailed off and Justin understood it was her lack of a job and an apartment she referred to.

"You offered me work out of pity, and when I told Bill exactly what I thought of that, he told me you refused to take no for an answer and would come to the shelter yourself if I didn't show up here."

So, it had taken the threat of his tracking her down at the homeless shelter to convince her to come to his house this morning. Justin wasn't sure how he felt about that. Insulted? No. A little angry? Maybe. Frustrated? Definitely. But he understood how debasing it must feel for someone she considered her enemy to be offering her a job. However, they were no longer enemies, and the sooner she accepted that, the better.

"Come in." He stepped back. "Mickie is next door playing. She'll be home in a little while."

"Sent her off so she wouldn't see the fireworks?" Sarah replied nastily.

"Yes."

That one word seemed to deflate Sarah. She let out a

long sigh, raked a hand through her hair, then finally walked in. Justin didn't wait for her but continued to the kitchen, where he had juice and coffee waiting. He poured her both before hooking a kitchen stool with his foot and pulling it out. Slipping onto it, he indicated the one across from him.

He watched Sarah glance around and wondered what she saw. Little had changed since Amy. The kitchen was still a cozy little place for family meetings.

That's one reason Amy had liked it so much. Modern, with tiles, yellow paint and pale corn-silk flowers on the pastel printed wallpaper, it gave off a feeling of homeyness. A small table for four sat near a picture window that afforded a view of a large backyard and the forest beyond that. The appliances were new, with a small snack bar separating the breakfast area from the actual cooking area.

Did Sarah wonder if he and Amy had eaten their dinner in here or out in the more formal dining room? If they'd had intimate chats in the evening, staring out the window as the sun slowly sank beneath the trees? She was in for a surprise if she thought that.

One of the things Justin truly regretted was there had been none of that. He'd always been too busy to sit down and spend any time with his wife. The melancholy of that inconsideration tried to grab hold of him, but he shook it off. Better to get down to business with Sarah before she decided to get defensive again.

"I need help."

"I've never doubted that."

He smiled at her quick comeback. "My sitter quit. I

can't find anyone on such short notice and I have to go to the office today. I'm very picky about whom I leave Mickie with. As you might guess, losing a parent is very hard on a child so small. Even though it's been two years now, Mickie is still not over her mother's death. She needs stability, someone who can be here for her when I'm not.''

Justin fiddled with his coffee cup, staring into the depths of it before raising his gaze back to her.

''I know being a housekeeper-sitter is way beneath your training, but I have a proposition. I want you to work here—live here, too, as a matter of fact. That way, if any emergencies come up and I have to go out of town, someone will be here. The pay is good, but not as good as you would make as a legal assistant. However, while working here, you would be free to send out your résumés and seek a better paying position more in keeping with your experience. All I ask is that any interviews be set up at a time when I'm free to be here with Mickie, and that when you do quit, you give me at least a month's notice so I can find another housekeeper and let Mickie get used to her before you leave.''

Sarah stared at Justin, certain her mouth hung open. In one hand he offered her a job, but only until she could find something else. What did the other hand hold? The hatchet if she blundered? Did he realize how awful his offer sounded? Or had he only been trying to help her and had accidentally made it sound as though he didn't want her around?

Evidently, she'd voiced her opinions, because Justin responded.

"That's not the way I meant it. I simply meant you'd be doing me a great favor by helping me out. Look, Sarah, I know we never got along before, but you're family. Can we at least try—for Mickie's sake?"

Sarah swallowed. For Mickie's sake? Well, what did she expect? That Justin would say he had been wrong in the past, wrong because of all the pain he had caused her family? He'd come to them and told them he was sorry for what had happened, had even offered compensation and jobs...and married Amy, too. If that didn't show he felt remorseful, what did? But she'd never believed it. She'd thought he should pay for everything that had happened and have no happiness. She'd made it her crusade to make his life miserable, and she had succeeded. If rumor could be believed, he and Amy had been having problems. Amy had never said anything to her, but Sarah wondered now if it was because of all the grief she herself had caused him whenever she was around.

Guiltily, Sarah looked away from the deep brown eyes that stared at her with such intensity. She needed to let go of the past. Wasn't that just the reason she'd come yesterday? Justin was offering to let her look for a job while she worked for him. That was it. Very simple. A way to put the past where it belonged, while proving herself trustworthy.

It galled her, though, to feel that she was taking charity.

As if reading her mind, Justin said quietly, "I'm family, Sarah. Let me help you."

She swallowed her humiliation. She would take the

job, but she would make sure that she earned every
penny of her pay. "Very well."

He expelled a great breath. "Fantastic."

When he named her salary her eyes widened in shock.
"You can't be serious. That's too much." Her temper
rose again. She didn't think housekeepers made that in
a month and she didn't like that he thought she was an
idiot. After all, how hard could housekeeping and taking
care of a child be? She had kept her own house.

"I assure you, Sarah, for cooking, cleaning and taking
care of a child, that's the going rate. If you don't believe
me, you can call Bill."

Studying him, she decided he was telling the truth. In
any event it didn't matter. She was going to make sure
she earned her paycheck, with no room for questions.

"Is it a deal?"

"It's a deal."

"Okay. Uh, well, do we need to get clothes, car, anything like that?"

Sarah burned with embarrassment. "Most of my
clothes are in a suitcase at the shelter. I do have a few
boxes in a storage area that's paid up through next
month."

Sarah hated that she'd had to admit such a thing to
this man. But he hadn't said anything or given her the
slightest reason to think he pitied her. If he had, she
would have walked out, despite her desperation for needing the job.

"You can pick them up whenever you're ready." He
strode over to a door leading to the garage, where he
lifted a key off a hook on a piece of wood shaped like

a small house. He brought it back to her. "This is to the car. I'll drive the four-by-four to work—and don't object. We're low on groceries. If you have time today, you'll need to go shopping. Consider free use of my car part of the job." He opened his wallet and pulled out some money.

Sarah's eyes widened.

"This is your first month's salary plus household expenses. The other housekeeper just took the money and as we needed supplies or whatever she paid for them out of an account she'd set up in her own name. There was a box in the office, where she kept all her receipts and stuff. However, if you'd prefer not to have a separate household account, you can buy whatever you feel the house or Mickie needs, then I'll reimburse you."

"No, that's fine. I—I've never done this before. It'll take me a week or two to learn my way around."

"I would expect no less."

"Fine."

"Fine."

They stared at each other for what seemed like minutes before Sarah broke the stare. "Well, I—"

"Sarah," he said softly.

His hand came to rest on her shoulder to keep her from walking away.

"I hope this will be a time to heal for you, me...us. We need to let go of the past and go on."

Sarah couldn't turn around and face him right now. She could not talk about this because she knew her face would give away her feelings. She was attracted to this man. Had she been before her sister had died? She couldn't face that question and certainly couldn't face him as she wondered about it. So instead she simply nodded. "I agree."

When she still didn't turn around Justin dropped his hand.

"When will Mickie be home?"

"Any time. I need to go up and change. I have some important work that must be finished today. But let me show you around first."

Sarah followed but heard little of what Justin actually said. Her mind was on the agreement she'd just made. She would be here for at least one month and she already wondered if this might be a mistake. Would she be able to live in the same house her sister had lived in, with a man who had loved her sister but destroyed her family's business? The same man she found herself undeniably attracted to?

Well, the room definitely reminded Sarah of Amy's taste in decor. Amy had loved greens and yellows.

Sarah walked around the large suite that included a living room and bedroom. Decorated in her sister's favorite colors, it wasn't exactly her taste—she preferred earth tones—but she couldn't deny it was more than she'd had this morning. She could thank God she once again had a roof over her head, even if a man who still despised her had offered it.

Well, Father, she whispered, studying the nice-sized double bed covered in a forest green spread, *Show me what I must do to prove to this man I'm sorry for the past. Help me to restore his trust in me again. It's im-*

portant that I at least right that wrong so Mickie won't
suffer any pain.

Sarah wondered again if she was a fool coming here
like this. But when faced with the shocking news of her
infertility and the cruelties of André's family after he'd
left on a trip to sort everything out, she'd suddenly realized how much she regretted breaking off all contact
with Mickie.

True, Amy had married Justin at their parents' urging,
but it was possible she had come to love Justin, while
Sarah had still blamed him for everything that had happened to her family. She owed it to Amy and Mickie to
try to get to know him.

She remembered that time long ago when she'd first
seen him, how attractive she'd thought him when he'd
come to the office. Then she'd found out he wasn't one
of the underlings from the company that had just destroyed her parents' lives but the actual owner. He and
his partner had taken over the business. Her mother had
been too torn up to come in and her father too ill from
the shock of losing a business that had been in the family
for a hundred years. As the market had changed, so had
their family changed the goal of the business. It had been
her father's idea to turn the main part of the organization
toward producing computer software components.

When he'd lost the company, he'd suffered a mild
heart attack. Amy hadn't been keen on working in the
office so Sarah had gone in to handle the business until
whatever flunky the new owner would be sending
showed up and officially took over.

The man who arrived hadn't been the rude jerk who

had so cruelly laughed in her father's face when he'd demanded protection for the workers, but a much more handsome, kinder-looking man. But when she'd heard his name...

Sarah shook her head, wondering why she now remembered that she had been the first sister to find this man attractive.

And a few months later, he'd shown up at the door, apologizing for the way the takeover had been handled and offering reimbursement for those who had been let go with no warning.

Her family had been forgiving, willing to welcome him into their house. She hadn't been. They'd had no savings left because of her father's medical bills and because of the bonuses her family had given to help those very families Justin had mentioned. Then, when Justin had asked Amy out, her father had encouraged her to accept his invitations. Her father had formed a grudging but genuine respect for Justin. And perhaps he felt the business might stay in the family if Justin took a liking to Amy and married her, Sarah had often thought.

That had been the beginning of Sarah's separation from her family. She hadn't been able to handle her parents attitude or Amy's submissive acquiescence. She'd moved out almost immediately rather than face Justin and Amy together.

Looking back, Sarah realized part of moving out and breaking off her relations with her family had grown from her horror of the attraction she felt for the man who had, in her opinion, destroyed her family.

While she'd stubbornly hidden herself away, dear sweet Amy, who had always done exactly as her parents wished, had married Justin.

Now, though, Sarah had to wonder if perhaps Amy hadn't fallen in love with Justin.

Actually, she didn't want to think of that possibility at all. She didn't want to know. She corrected herself. Yes, she *did* want to know but didn't think she'd like the answer. She blushed, aware she shouldn't feel this way unless she was still attracted to the man!

Forcing her mind from those thoughts, she started toward the stairs to start lunch. Justin had said he'd be home by two and she wanted to make sure she couldn't be accused of easing off, even the first day of work.

"I'm home!"

The shout came from downstairs. Sarah smiled. "I'm up here, Mickie."

The little girl came clattering up the stairs. Sarah met her in the hall. Mickie halted abruptly and her expression turned shy. "Where's Daddy?"

"He's at work. Didn't he tell you?"

Mickie twisted her right foot from side to side. "I thought he might be back by now."

Sarah smiled at the little girl and started to reach out for her.

"You left last night without saying goodbye," the little girl admonished, stepping back so she could look Sarah in the eyes.

Sarah blinked, her smile leaving her face. Kneeling in front of Mickie, she took her hands. "That's right. I did. I didn't want to wake you. I'm sorry if it made you sad."

Mickie shrugged. "Mama did the same thing."

Sarah's heart twisted.

Mickie raised her questioning gaze to Sarah's. "Daddy said you're going to be living here. You're going to be the new housekeeper, and you'll make me peanut butter sandwiches with grape jelly. Is that what you were doing up here? Moving in?"

The innocence of children. Sarah nodded. "I'm going to be in the old housekeeper's room in case you ever need anything. And yes, I'll be taking care of you when you're home from school."

She stood and held out her hand. "But I have to wonder if your daddy said that part about grape jelly-and-peanut butter sandwiches."

Mickie wrinkled her freckled little nose. "Well, actually, Daddy said peanut butter sandwiches, but I like the grape jelly so I added that."

Her little hand warmly clasped Sarah's as they started down the stairs. "Well, what if I get you a snack of crackers with peanut butter and grape jelly then I'll make whatever you want for lunch. Your daddy will be back by then and we can have a big meal, then a smaller one tonight."

"You'll be here tonight?"

Sarah didn't pause, though she shuddered at the insecurities the young child must have felt since her mother's death. "I promise." Changing the subject, she asked, "What do you want me to make for dinner?"

In the kitchen she found the peanut butter and set it out with crackers while Mickie found the jelly.

"Fried chicken."

Sarah paused in scooping out the peanut butter into a small bowl. "Fried chicken?" She should have limited her offer to anything baked. She hated frying.

"And a chocolate coconut cake for dessert."

Sarah shook her head ruefully. She should have known. Amy had had a sweet tooth, too. "Well, I can do the fried chicken, but I'm not sure about the cake."

Mickie frowned. She studied the crackers before looking back up at Sarah. "Chocolate coconut cake is my daddy's favorite. The only time he gets it is if he makes it. But he doesn't ever have time. Mommy used to make fried chicken and chocolate coconut cake for dessert. I know Daddy would just love it." She slanted a look up at Sarah. "And so would I."

Sarah sighed. She handed the plate of snacks to Mickie, then poured her a glass of milk. "I'll see what I can do. So, you like coconut, do you?"

Mickie immediately denied it. "I don't. But Daddy does. I just pick it off the top."

So she really was thinking about her daddy. Sarah had thought the child was using a ploy. She still wasn't sure if she was or not. But she found that right now it didn't matter. After taking the chicken from the freezer, she set it in the microwave and punched the buttons to thaw it out. "What's so special about today that you want to fix your daddy's favorite meal."

Mickie shrugged. "He can't cook. I miss Mama's cooking. Can't you cook like her?"

Ah, Sarah thought. Emotions about her sister washed over her. Her sister, the quiet one, the domestic one, the one who had always been so perfect. "Not as well. But if your daddy is starving for good home-cooked meals—'' Sarah winked at Mickie to hide the pain she felt ''—then I suppose I can cook a few good meals for you both.''

Mickie smiled, satisfied.

Relieved, Sarah smiled back. The questions from a five-year-old who would very soon be six—in less than three months, in fact—had been harder than she'd anticipated. Still, it looked as though baby-sitting her was going to be easy. Sarah had survived her first test and had been accepted. How much harder could it be?

Chapter Four

"What in the world! Mickie, what have you gotten into?"

Sarah stared in horror at the living room and dining room. White powder dusted everything. Following the trail to the dining-room table, she found Mickie standing in a chair with toy cooking utensils, covered in white from head to toe.

"I was making a cake, since you were busy cooking chicken."

Mickie sneezed, then wiped a grimy hand across her face, smearing the white stuff again. She shook her head and a white cloud was released from her formerly brown hair.

"But I told you I'd try to get to it!" Sarah stared blankly at the mess. It was going to take her an hour to clean this up and there was no telling when Justin would be home.

Mickie's shoulders drooped. "I was only trying to help."

Realizing she had hurt Mickie's feelings released Sarah from her inability to react. She went forward and, with only a small reluctance at how dirty she was going to get, gathered Mickie in her arms. "It's okay. Let's go upstairs and run you some bathwater, then I'll clean up the mess."

"I just wanted Daddy to have a cake. He says I'm his little helper."

"It's okay. Really. But maybe next time," Sarah said, going upstairs, "we should do this together. Until you can prove to me you know how," she added, and filled the tub for Mickie.

"Mrs. Winters never would let me. She doesn't like messes."

"Well," Sarah said, stripping the little girl and helping her into the tub, "I don't mind a mess if we do it together. You see, that's the only way to learn. Now, if you promise not to try it by yourself again, maybe next week we can make some cookies together."

Mickie's eyes lit with excitement. "Really?"

"Really."

Sarah quickly washed Mickie's hair, then allowed Mickie to finish up. When she was done, she dried her off. "Can you pick out your clothes by yourself?"

Mickie gave her an exasperated look. "I'm not a baby," she said. "I'll be six January 10."

Sarah bit back a smile. "Of course. I'll be downstairs cleaning up the dining room. The chicken is done. I only have to finish vegetables and potatoes to finish. You can go get out three plates and the silverware while I clean up and finish fixing dinner.''

Evidently, Mickie thought she had the better of the two deals, because she didn't argue.

Sarah reentered the dining room and dismally surveyed the white mess. What to do first?

She sighed. Deciding just to wade in, she gathered the play dishes and the tin of flour, which Mickie had somehow sneaked out of the kitchen, and set them all back in their places. After returning to the dining room, she simply swept all the flour onto the floor. Then she wiped down the table and china cabinet and every other piece of furniture that looked to have received a dusting of flour.

Once she'd moved the chairs out of the way, she pulled out the vacuum cleaner and began to vacuum. Mickie came in to set the table. ''Place mats and napkins,'' Sarah said, nodding to where she'd set them out on the beautiful mahogany table.

Sarah had to stop twice to check the potatoes and vegetables she had boiling and then to mash the potatoes.

Then she had to change vacuum bags.

She was getting tired by the time she reached the living room. That was how she explained her accident. Why else would she trip over the vacuum cord, unless all the dusting and vacuuming was tiring her? That and the fact the vacuum cleaner Justin owned weighed almost a ton. He really should have one of those lightweight models, not the monster that made her huff with exertion when using it. Add that to the fact that she hadn't stopped running around since Mickie had entered the house three hours ago and an accident was obviously waiting to happen.

So, it was natural that, as she swept toward the entryway, her shoe tripped her up over the cord.

She squawked in surprise and went flying backward.

Windmilling, grabbing for purchase, Sarah teetered before succumbing to gravity. *I'll probably end up with a broken neck. Then Justin will gloat over just how unfit a parent I would make!*

With one last effort to catch herself before she ended up splitting her head on the floor, she twisted. Instead of ground, a hard dark object arrested her midflight.

The dark object grunted.

In her peripheral vision she saw a briefcase go flying. Strong arms wrapped around her. Her rescuer teetered before both she and her victim continued their fall to the floor.

Splat.

The cessation of noise proved even more telling than her screech when she'd started down.

In the moment it took her to orient herself, she registered several things. The body beside hers was warm and comforting—one arm was still wrapped around her shoulders—and he was in good shape.

She lifted her gaze from the white shirt and tie to Justin's sardonic expression.

She smiled weakly, wondering how to apologize.

He spoke first. ''Don't you think you're taking this housekeeping job just a little too seriously?''

''Daddy!''

Hearing Mickie's voice, Sarah immediately scrambled off Justin. "I'm so sorry. We had a little accident and I was sweeping. I wasn't paying attention to where I was going and got tangled up in the cord."

He stood, dusted off his suit, then scooped Mickie up in his arms. "Hiya, pumpkin," he said, bussing her cheek.

Sarah winced at how Mickie was dressed. Blue striped shorts with an orange checked top. Justin blinked, cast a glance at Sarah, then returned his attention to Mickie.

She squeezed his neck. "Sarah made your favorite meal but we didn't have time to bake a cake. I tried but made a mess, instead, and Aunt Sarah cleaned it up while I set the table."

Justin raised an eyebrow and scanned the room. He hugged Mickie again before setting her down. "My favorite meal, huh?" He made a big show of sniffing the air. "Fried chicken?"

Mickie laughed and nodded.

"That's great! Go upstairs and wash up. Let me get my briefcase and change. Then we'll eat."

Mickie immediately ran upstairs.

Justin gathered the contents of his briefcase and Sarah belatedly helped him. "So what's the special occasion?" he asked as he snapped the lid shut.

Sarah fidgeted. She hadn't expected to be questioned on what she had prepared. "I told Mickie I'd make her anything she wanted. And fried chicken with chocolate coconut cake was her choice."

An indefinable emotion crossed Justin's features before he sighed.

"Did I do something wrong?" Sarah asked, ill at ease with the unnamed emotion she'd seen.

"No." He shook his head.

"I know Mickie was young when Amy died, but she still remembers Amy in her own way. Certain things stand out in her mind, while others have faded. But one thing she remembers is one of the last big meals Amy, Mickie and I shared together as a family. It was fried chicken and a cake for dessert. Amy had made it for my birthday. It's not that it's my favorite, though I do love chicken. But in her mind..."

He trailed off.

Sarah understood. "Children remember things differently. I suppose remembering the special times is her way of holding on to Amy."

Justin nodded. "Mickie had a bad experience with the last housekeeper. The woman flat refused to fry food. She said it was bad for her. So the only time Mickie got fried chicken was when I fried it on the housekeeper's day off. I couldn't figure out for a long while why she wanted fried chicken until one day she told me it was my favorite. The story came out and I started seeing to it that we had it whenever Mickie requested it."

Justin went to the entry closet and placed his briefcase in there. "The only time she asks for it is when she's feeling insecure or sad."

Sarah looked down at her hands. "Do you think I triggered her sudden insecurity?"

Justin sighed. "It's possible. You knew Amy. Mickie has really been missing her mom lately. Maybe she just needs to be reassured that some things will stay the same.''

"You know, I think I need to mention I hurt her last night leaving without waking her up. She said her mom did the same thing."

A spasm of pain crossed his face. "Yeah. Amy and I had a fight. When she left, she flew out of the house. Mickie was asleep."

"She also asked if I could cook like Amy."

Justin dropped his head back and stared at the ceiling. Finally, he said, "I'm sorry, Sarah. Mickie doesn't understand other people's pain. She's only a child."

Sarah bristled. "I know that. I just thought maybe, well…to me, I guessed that she was missing her mom. I told her I'd try to make homemade meals like Amy, though I'm not as good a cook."

Justin nodded. "Thank you."

He turned and started up the stairs. Sarah stared after him, noting how wide his shoulders were. Wide enough to have carried the burden of losing his wife and being a single parent alone? Or had he depended on God to help him?

Sarah remembered his confessions of salvation and that was why he had changed his tune about so many things he'd always considered *woman* things. Her mother had insisted Justin had never been underhanded in business, but that after he'd been saved, Justin had felt the need to make restitution for things that had happened during the takeover, things Justin hadn't known about.

Justin disappeared from sight and she sighed. She really didn't want to remember how her parents had insisted Justin was a nice guy. She only wanted to be friends, make up for her past; not continue to feel guilty as more and more facets of his giving personality revealed themselves to show him as a truly caring man and loving father.

She went to the kitchen and brought out the food. Just as she carried in the glasses of iced tea, Justin and Mickie appeared. Mickie wore pink leggings and a sweatshirt with Daisy Duck on the front. Her outfit not only matched, but it suited the nippy weather outside.

Once seated, they offered thanks for the meal, then passed the food around the table. "So, Sarah, what are you doing for Thanksgiving?"

Sarah flushed and paused only a moment before passing the potatoes to Justin. When he took them from her, she reluctantly met his eyes. She saw in his gaze that he knew she had no family and he'd hurt her by asking. But what could she say? Her fiancé had planned for her to spend Thanksgiving at his house. But that was before he'd told her he was taking a couple of months off to think, before the letter from Watson and Watson had made it clear she was fired—because André hadn't had the guts to tell her himself. "I don't know. Maybe—"

"How about you spend it here," Justin interrupted, dishing some potatoes up for Mickie. "We don't have anyone else coming. Bill usually stops by. I don't know what he'll do now that he's married. But we'd love to have you."

Mickie, ever tuned in to any conversation around her, piped up, "Please, Aunt Sarah. And this year we could have a real turkey instead of the one Daddy buys at the store. It was too chewy,'' she added, making a face.

It was Justin's turn to flush. ''Hey, kiddo,'' he warned good-naturedly, ''it was either chewy turkey or going out to a restaurant. And I happen to like eating at home on a holiday, so we just might order chewy turkey again this year.''

''But you got cherry pie for dessert.''

Sarah chuckled. ''Well, maybe I could make up a pumpkin.''

Mickie wrinkled her nose in disgust.

''Or chocolate?''

Mickie grinned.

''Does that mean I've convinced you?'' Justin asked, smiling.

She grinned. ''Someone has convinced me…I think the part about picking up the meal held sway.''

Justin's smile deepened and Sarah suddenly felt awkward. Clearing her throat, she began to eat.

After a few minutes of silence, Justin asked, ''What are your plans for today?''

Sarah shrugged. ''I definitely need to go shopping. I thought I'd get some boxes from storage.'' She sipped her tea, then plunged ahead. ''You won't mind watching Mickie the rest of today, will you? I'll be back by dinner.''

Sarah wanted time away from the domestic scene so she could come to grips with all the changes since arriving at the house. It seemed that her whole life had been turned upside down in one short day.

Sarah looked up, expecting a frown. After all, Justin

had promised her Sunday to herself if she wanted it, not Saturday, and she wasn't even sure he was done with all his work. Instead, a knowing smile met her.

"I don't mind spending the day with Mickie for a minute. But if you think I'm going to let you work all day while we play..." He tsked. "I suggest we go with you so I can help load those boxes, then we'll all grab something for supper on the way home."

"No, really," she started to protest.

Justin stopped her by shaking his head. "I insist. Besides, it's Saturday. Saturday is supposed to be a fun day, isn't it, Mickie?"

Mickie squealed and immediately launched into what their Saturdays were usually like.

As Mickie rambled on, Justin smiled tenderly. Sarah, however, didn't hear what Mickie was saying.

Because when Justin turned that smile on her, she realized with a sinking heart that his smile was the true reason she wanted out of there for a while.

Chapter Five

"I have to say, this is the most interesting supper I've ever had."

Justin laughed and leaned his forearms on the picnic table at the local park where he'd taken Sarah and Mickie.

Sarah marveled at how comfortable he looked in his jeans and flax-colored blazer. She imagined he could wear a three-piece suit out here and still look just as relaxed as long as Mickie was around.

Glancing to the slide, she heard Mickie's squeal just as she came into view again. Ruefully, she shook her head. "I don't know how she can twist around in that thing right after eating and not get sick."

"She's always had that ability. I, on the other hand," Justin said, "feel queasy just watching her."

Sarah gathered up the plastic containers that had held their salads and sandwiches and took them over to the trash can.

When she was again seated by Justin, she noted his smile was pensive, possibly wistful. "There're not many warm days left for her to enjoy."

She was amazed, actually, that Justin had taken time to stop at a playground and allow Mickie to play. Of course, she shouldn't be surprised. He was so different from the man she remembered. "Has it been hard?" she asked, voicing her thoughts. As soon as she realized what she'd said she wanted to grab the words back, but it was too late. She swallowed. "I'm sorry, Justin. I have no right—"

"No, it's okay." He watched Mickie climb up the slide and come swirling down again before he answered. "Yeah, in many ways it has been, I suppose. It took some adjusting to being the only one for her to run to when she was hurt or excited or just wanted to talk. One of the most memorable adjustments was in buying her clothes and teaching her so many things."

He sighed, and Sarah could see how serious his eyes were as he looked into himself.

"I guess that has actually been the hardest—those things we traditionally think of as mother-daughter things. You know, the playing in the kitchen as she would have while watching her mom cook. Or even the special Mother Day's activities and school functions where the mothers are asked to attend. And the little everyday messes kids get into that moms handle."

"Like what?"

He smiled. "I can remember some of the messes my sister, Diode, got into. Though she's a missionary overseas now and I haven't seen her in four years I think about her a lot because of Mickie. I see Mickie and realize she'll never have the fun of playing dress-up in her mom's clothes the way Diode did or the forays into Mom's makeup or her perfumes. Then, of course, fixing Mom her Mother's Day breakfast.''

He had a wistful smile as he spoke of those times, Sarah noted, smiling herself.

Mickie squealed. Both Sarah and Justin glanced up to see if she was okay. When they were assured she was safe, Justin continued. ''I think the hardest is knowing she misses Amy. She'll be fine some days. Then there are times when I see her playing and I can tell she's thinking about her mommy.''

''Does she talk about Amy a lot?''

Justin shook his head. ''Only occasionally.''

He lapsed into silence. The sound of the oak trees echoed loudly in the silence, as did the rumble of an occasional car on the nearby highway. Several mothers with their children sat around at other picnic tables and a sporadic laugh could be heard. But since the three of them were on the other side of the park, an air of isolation permeated their table.

''I miss her,'' he finally said.

She felt Justin studying her but wouldn't meet his eyes. ''At first I was angry that she left, but now there's only sadness and good memories. I guess we just have to let go and get on with our lives.''

Coming to terms had been hard for Justin. She remembered the grief he'd experienced when she'd finally decided to take Mickie away from him.

''Where was she going that night?'' Sarah asked. It

was the first time they'd ever really talked about Amy's death. It felt so good, a cleansing of her soul, to at last be able to ask the questions she had wanted to ask for years.

Justin stiffened. His face turned dark. "I suppose you have a right to know. She was coming to see you. You see, she had decided to leave me."

"Divorce?" Amy almost fell off the bench. Her family hadn't believed in divorce. Amy had always been the perfect one, the one to follow all the rules set by her parents. "But why?"

He shrugged as though it didn't matter. But Sarah had a feeling it mattered very much if the way his features had gone so blank was any indication. "I'm sure you know your parents pushed the match."

Sarah glanced down, embarrassed. Oh, yes, she'd known that. "She came to love you."

"I don't think so. You see, the night she left me, she told me she was tired of living a sham her parents had forced her into. She couldn't handle the unreality of what we had and she was tired of not having a sister or experiencing any of the things she'd one day hoped to experience when she was out of her family's house. So she left, telling me we would talk about custody later."

Sarah was dizzy. Amy had said that? Her sister, Amy?

"Maybe it was just a remark in the heat of the moment," Sarah offered weakly.

Again, Justin shook his head. "I should have realized she was unhappy. It's just that I'd become settled in the relationship and loved her, and was certain her love would grow. I hoped she was just shy, then maybe undemonstrative. Finally, I decided she just didn't like to show emotion.''

He stretched as if he didn't have a care in the world, but Sarah knew different. Justin was still hurting over the pain her sister had inflicted the night before she'd run from him. How she knew that, she wasn't sure. But she knew Justin blamed himself for Amy's death as much as for marrying Amy when she hadn't really loved him. His next words confirmed her fears.

''You know, I sometimes wonder if there was something I could have done differently—''

''No, Justin. Don't ever second-guess the past.''

''Why not?'' he asked, bitterness in his voice.

Turning her face toward Mickie, she said, ''Because if we're going to second-guess, then we'll need to remember that I was her sister and I'm the one who acted like a spoiled child and broke off contact with the family. Had I been there for Amy to talk to, she might not have buried so many unresolved things inside her until she felt she had to leave to solve them.''

Though she said it, she wondered why her sister hadn't poured her heart out to God and allowed God to help her through her struggle. Of course, Amy had never liked confrontation of any sort. That was why she'd always done what her mother and father had told her to— unlike Sarah. ''If I hadn't been so filled with bitterness and anger...'' She shrugged.

Justin suddenly deflated. ''That's how I felt about my partner. He'd been like a brother to me. I couldn't believe it when I found out all the underhanded things he was into. It took God's infinite patience to teach me to forgive and let go of my bitterness. Actually, through that fiasco He taught me just how important forgiveness is.''

Yes, he'd asked Jesus into his heart just after that, Sarah mused. She wondered if he'd forgiven her as easily, or if he still harbored pain and bitterness.

But instead of asking, she offered, ''I learned that problems with work or other earthly matters seem unimportant compared with relationships like family. There are always going to be problems, but not always family. I just wish it hadn't taken so long for me to learn after I'd lost all my family.''

Justin finally turned to her and she saw compassion in his eyes.

''But you didn't, Sarah. You still have Mickie.''

Her heart flipped over at his words and the tenderness in his eyes. What could she say to that? Or to the very warm look he was giving her?

''Daddy, come push me!''

Relieved that she didn't have to reply, Sarah turned her attention to Mickie, who was climbing onto one of the swings near their table.

Justin stood, obviously as relieved to have the dark discussion over as she was. ''Okay, pumpkin, hang on tight,'' he warned, and strolled to where Mickie was already giggling and kicking her legs back and forth in excitement.

''High, Daddy, high!''

Justin grabbed the swing and pushed, sending her into a slow arc. ''Higher, higher!'' she cried, swinging her legs and laughing.

Sarah couldn't resist walking closer. Their laughter was infectious. She watched Justin, enthralled by how handsome he looked as he threw back his head and laughed.

Sarah wasn't prepared for when his gaze met hers, or for the gleam in his eye. "You know, Mickie, I think Aunt Sarah would enjoy being pushed, too. What do you think?"

"Oh, no, I don't think—"

"Yes! Oh, yes, Daddy. Push Sarah, too." Mickie looked from where she was still swinging. "He won't let you fall."

"Come on, Sarah," Justin entreated, smiling. He motioned to the swing. "Trust me."

With both of them encouraging her, how could she refuse? Wary, she approached the other swing. The sand shifted under her flats and she walked carefully, attempting to keep her balance on the shifting surface. "It's been years since I've been in a swing," she warned.

"Years?" Mickie asked in obvious horror.

"That's too long," Justin said.

Sarah felt him approaching. "Oh, I don't need to be pushed, too," she objected.

Then his hands closed over the chains on each side of her waist. His warm breath tickled her neck and his musky aftershave filled her senses. Sarah shivered in reaction and was appalled. She'd just been engaged. She could not be enjoying how close he stood to her. She wasn't even sure he had forgiven her!

She had no more time to think, as suddenly he pulled back her swing, then let loose. She gasped in dismay, then delight. She'd forgotten how free swinging felt, the weightless quality, the air rushing through her hair.

Then she was back, and Justin's strong hands pushed again, sending her even higher.

Sarah shrieked. His low laugh joined Mickie's as he alternated pushing them. "Stop that, Justin," she warned, when he again gave her swing a hard push. But there was no heat in her words. Indeed, laughter bubbled out.

"Stop what?" he asked innocently, and continued right along.

"You know very well what," she said, casting a glance at Mickie, who was high in the air, her eyes closed, her squeals pealing out over the area.

"Get off if you don't like it," he taunted, chuckling. The sound sent warm tingles over her nerves.

"I don't remember how to stop it!" she cried, but there was pleasure in her voice and she knew he heard it in the way his laugh rumbled again.

Sarah quickly relearned how to use her legs to propel herself forward. Justin climbed into another swing and swung, too, making outrageous faces at Mickie and Sarah as he passed them.

She thoroughly enjoyed herself. No man had ever teased or played with her the way Justin did. It was a new and delightful experience. It'd been years since she'd acted like a kid. But she found she loved it.

Was that something Justin had learned since Amy's death? How to enjoy his daughter and have fun? Or had he been like that before and she'd just never known?

She knew Justin certainly had a way of making a

woman feel feminine. Whether he realized it or not, the looks he'd given her today and the way he was so careful as he pushed her even when he was playing made her feel womanly, cherished and treated with regard. It was a nice feeling. One she really enjoyed. How long had it been since she'd enjoyed life? Since her fiancé? Or before?

"How do I stop this thing?" Sarah asked, deciding it was time to get off.

Justin jumped from his swing. "Right here," he said, and held out his arms.

"Oh, yeah, sure," she replied, and rolled her eyes.

He raised an eyebrow arrogantly. Turning toward Mickie, he held out his arms. "Let's show her, Mickie," he said, then broke eye contact and met his daughter's gleeful gaze.

"Here I come, Daddy!" She flew off the swing. Before Sarah could scream in fear, Mickie landed safely in his arms.

"Your turn," he said, and held out his arms.

"You're crazy," she replied, and kicked again, thinking to plant her feet in the sand and stop herself. So what if she would probably go face first into the dirt. She wasn't ready to jump into someone's arms.

"Chicken?" he taunted, his arms folded across his chest.

Her chin jutted out. Had he figured her out so quickly? Did he know that she wanted to trust him but feared it? She stared at him.

What would it hurt? It just might be fun, flying through the air and landing in Justin's embrace. With only a moment's hesitation, she decided. "Don't blame me if you break a few bones."

He held out his arms. She swung forward but all of a sudden found that her hands wouldn't release the chains. Justin was big, but was he big enough to hold her? She swung forward a second time. Was this really fun? She wondered as her hands began to sweat.

But it was Justin's smug look that goaded her into acting. She came forward again and pushed out of the swing. True, it was only a few feet, but it felt like miles before she thudded into Justin.

Strong arms wrapped around her, jarring her to a stop. Immediately, Justin pulled her closer toward his powerful, hard chest. His scent, as well as an extreme feeling of safety and security, enveloped her. She rested her cheek against his shoulder for an instant, surprised at her reaction, then pulled back.

In that moment, things changed. The world tilted just a bit—or maybe it was her. Because she suddenly realized just how attracted she was to Justin, more attracted than she'd been to her fiancé, or to any other man she'd ever dated. And there was nothing she could do about it, because Justin was the very man she'd tried to destroy two years ago.

Justin saw Sarah's eyes widen, then how she backed away. He was thankful she had put some distance between them, because he was afraid he might have just kissed her.

He hadn't thought about dating in ages. Oh, true, women approached him—pleasant, attractive women he met through business or at church—but he'd never been tempted in the least to pursue any of them. Earlier today, though, and now again...what was it about Sarah that was different from all the others? She brought out a surge of protectiveness and tenderness, true. He wanted to hold her and shield her. But why? Why her? His feelings were disconcerting, embarrassing.

Hearing Mickie's laughter, he wondered what his daughter would have thought if he'd kissed Sarah just now. He shook his head, feeling an emotion churning in his gut.

Loneliness.

He had to admit he was lonely. He loved his daughter, and Bill was a great guy. But Justin missed having someone closer around to share his experiences with. There was no one to talk to in the evening when he got home from work, no one to laugh together with over a joke or share those little secret smiles when Mickie did something really adorable. There was no one to hold when he felt overwhelmed or to love when he wanted to share that special experience.

But Sarah?

No.

He couldn't see himself with his sister-in-law, who probably still despised him despite what she said. Besides, he thought, going over to the picnic table where Mickie was slurping her cola, he would never risk entering into a marriage for convenience's sake, or for an attraction, either. He'd learned his lesson. Convenience could turn into inconvenience real quick, and passion could fade.

Odd though it sounded, he had vowed to marry only for love.

His lips twisted cynically. People always thought women were the romantic ones, yet here he was, insisting on a love-based marriage. And how many women in the past two years had hinted at so many other types of arrangements. Love based, with him? Not one woman who had shown an interest had wanted love. Sarah certainly wouldn't fall into that category, either...would she?

Hah.

He skeptically wondered if any women out there still believed in a marriage based on love.

Reaching his daughter's side, he realized Sarah was wiping up some cola Mickie had spilled on her top. His gaze settled on Sarah and against his will, he had to wonder why *love* and *Sarah* had come to him in the same thought.

Chapter Six

"I hope you decide to spend Thanksgiving with us."

"I'd enjoy it," Sarah replied.

It was dark. Mickie was asleep in the back seat and Sarah rested her head against the cushion of her seat in Justin's car.

But she was far from relaxed. Tumultuous emotions over the day spent at the park still filled her thoughts. After the swings, Justin had proceeded to push Mickie, and several other children, on a merry-go-round. Then he'd actually gone down one of the tamer slides with his daughter. They'd played until all three were exhausted and the sun had set.

Sarah couldn't remember enjoying a sunset more. Then they'd piled into the car to head home.

With the darkness surrounding them, and the peace and quiet, Sarah had had time to remember her reaction to Justin early that day. Tension built in the small enclosed space between the two of them until she could barely stand it.

When he spoke, it was a relief to have her mind on something else.

"I enjoyed today."

Of course he wouldn't keep the subject on something safe. "Do you play with Mickie like that often?"

"As much as I can. I love playing with Mickie. Sometimes I wish Amy and I had had more children." Sarah silently winced at his admission, but did her best to hide it.

"Did you have fun today, Sarah?"

"Yes, I did," she replied. "I just don't feel I'm earning my pay."

He chuckled. "Consider it part of your job to play with Mickie. After all, you're going to find Mickie is a very active child. And I can just about guarantee that you won't think you're not earning your pay after a week or two living here."

The headlights cut across the front of the house when they turned into the driveway, and Sarah realized they were home.

Justin stopped the car, then pushed open his door. Sarah blinked at the light, suddenly realizing she was tired.

"I'll unload the car later. Just grab the fruit and vegetables."

She reached in for the two bags, debating whether to get the boxed and canned goods or allow Justin to come back out for them. "I see now why you said no meats or dairy products."

He shrugged as he lifted his daughter into his arms. "Mickie doesn't get to go to the playground much. I wanted to spend time with her today."

"You're the boss," she murmured, and followed him to the house. She smiled over how wonderful he was with Mickie. Her sleepy little head lay against his left shoulder and her legs and arms surrounded him like a monkey holding on to its mom. Long curly hair covered her face and flowed over Justin's blazer. She could hear him murmuring something in the little girl's ear as he opened the door.

A small sigh escaped Mickie and she wiggled before letting out a half snore.

Tenderness welled in Sarah's heart as she watched Justin carry the child up the stairs. Sarah went to the kitchen and put away the vegetables. She marveled again at how beautiful the kitchen was. Amy had always had wonderful taste. The refrigerator was clean and it was easy to find where the fresh vegetables went. Perhaps tomorrow she'd make a salad with stuffed bell peppers for dinner. Maybe she ought to do up a menu and get Justin's approval each week first. After all, he might not eat some of the same things she did.

She made a mental note to ask him about that. Which made her realize she might not know as much about housekeeping as she thought.

Brass-and-black baskets hung over the counter near the refrigerator. One had potatoes and an onion in it. She put the other vegetables that didn't go in the refrigerator in that one, then unloaded the fruit in the other basket.

Bananas, tangelos, oranges, yellow apples—Mickie certainly liked fruit.

Two boxes of cereal went on top of the refrigerator. She looked at them and frowned over one. White sugar. If Mickie was active, as Justin had intimated, Sarah was sure she'd just found the culprit. When had Justin slipped that into the basket without her seeing?

Of course, Justin could have slipped anything into the basket and she would have missed it. She'd been feeling so inept around him that she hadn't paid attention to everything he had grabbed. And Mickie had been talking, too. She certainly could talk. Though Sarah didn't consider that a bad habit. It was wonderful listening to everything from her perspective.

Just as she finished putting away the eggs and bread, alarm swept through Sarah. She hadn't said good-night to Mickie. She folded the paper bags and placed them under the sink. Whether they were kept there or not, she wasn't sure. But it was where she'd always stored her bags. Then she hurried up the stairs and quickly headed to Mickie's room.

And almost ran Justin down.

She flushed and took a step back.

"What's the rush?" he asked, smiling down at her.

Sarah saw Justin had a frilly little nightie in his hand. She found the idea of him dressing Mickie funny. In her mind, dressing a child for bed had always been a mother's role. But, she thought, sobering, of course he would do it. Mickie no longer had a mother. "I forgot to tell Mickie good-night."

He looked confused only for a moment, then what she

thought was tenderness—but couldn't be sure—touched his eyes. How unusual. He was so big. Tall with broad shoulders. Towering over her. She'd always assumed he was gruff and belligerent, the way she'd always perceived him when in his company. To think that Justin could feel tenderness was just so out of keeping with the way she'd always imagined him. But she was almost certain that was what she'd seen in his eyes earlier today and again just now.

Feeling even more uncomfortable from that innocent revelation, she hurriedly said, "I promised Mickie I'd always make sure to tell her good-night so she'd know I hadn't left."

He stared at her a moment more and those feelings from earlier today resurfaced: need, wanting, longing.

Justin cleared his throat, the feelings in his gaze suddenly banked. He stepped back. "I was getting ready to put her in her p.j.'s. She can bathe tomorrow, since she's already asleep." He held out an arm, indicating an area just inside the door off to the side. "Come in."

He stepped back and Sarah stepped in. She liked Mickie's room. It had a nice feeling. The walls were a light blue. Colored balloons and painted pieces of cardboard cut in the shape of stars covered the surfaces. There were also pictures of different cartoon characters on the walls, cut out of magazines, as well as many copies of Sunday-school literature taped up on the wall with pictures of Jesus and other biblical figures in them.

Like most little girls her age, Mickie liked clutter. And she had varying taste, if the pictures were any indication.

Stepping over the dolls and the teddy bears, Sarah made her way to the side of the bed.

"Today is usually the day she cleans her room—every Saturday, unless we do something special," Justin explained.

"I was messy as a child," Sarah admitted. She was very conscious of Justin as he followed her over to where Mickie lay.

She sat down on the edge of the bed and stared at the sleeping child. "She sure is still," Sarah murmured.

A chuckle sounded behind her. "The only time she's still is when she's asleep," Justin replied.

Smoothing a strand of hair from Mickie's face, she leaned down and kissed the soft, pale cheek. "Good night, sweet princess," she teased, thinking Mickie already had her wrapped around her little finger.

She stood, nodded to Justin and attempted to make a quick escape.

But she wasn't fast enough.

"Sarah?" Justin called just as she got to the doorway.

She paused, then turned. "Yes?"

"Thanks for coming back into our lives."

Awkwardly, she nodded.

What could she say? Once she was in her room, she grabbed some clothes and went to the bathroom to shower. His words continued to echo in her head. *Thanks for coming back into our lives.* How could he say that? Especially after what she'd done? She remembered the shock and anger when she'd told him she wanted Mickie, that he wasn't a fit father. Then she remembered the steely determination when he'd faced her in court that day. Gone had been the thin, gaunt-cheeked man who had seemed so listless, so remote. In his place was a man wearing a designer suit, a man armed with a lawyer who had glanced at her across the courtroom with a pitying look. Of course she hadn't known then what Justin's lawyer was about to present to the court. Justin had definitely gone all out and found the best lawyer for the job.

Her lawyer had scrambled and tried to help her. But of course grief had been accepted as Justin's excuse, and expert witnesses testified that he had gotten through the worst of his mourning and on and on and on. She had been furious, believing Mickie belonged with her, that Justin was neglecting his daughter.

But her fury had been minor compared with Justin's when he'd told her never to come near his daughter again. She had actually felt chilled at his threats.

That seemed like aeons ago. And Justin acted as if he'd forgiven her.

She rinsed her hair, stepped out of the shower and dried off. Perhaps he just needed a sitter. But why would he be glad she was back in his life unless he had forgiven her?

She smoothed cream on her skin, then powdered herself before applying a spritz of perfume. She'd always loved to pamper herself after her bath. All three containers were almost empty, leftovers from her other life, as she thought of her life before her job and engagement ended. But she'd have some money now to indulge her one luxury.

Still, as she gathered up her toiletries, she thought of the person providing her with the paycheck.

How could he forgive her? Why? Why? Why? And why had he let her into his house?

Back in her room, she put her things away, turned out the lights, opened the curtains, then climbed up onto the big four-poster bed. *Father, Justin's so wonderful as a dad,* she began. *I never realized it. I was so wrong in my judgment of him. There's no way he can forget what I did. Is there? I doubt I'll ever forget it.*

Sarah sighed and pulled the white lacy pillow into her lap, then clung to it. *How can I,* she whispered finally, admitting to the enormity of what she'd done, *when it was Amy I wronged as well as Justin? And then there's Mickie.*

Sarah slipped under the covers and scooted back against the headboard. The darkness surrounded her; the only light in her room the moonlight that shone through the windows. A small smile curved her mouth and she relaxed as she thought of Mickie.

Thank you, Father, for the opportunity to get to know Mickie. Had You not interceded, I don't know if I'd ever have gotten up the nerve to come visit her. She's wonderful. She's so sweet and kind and fun. She's so fresh and innocent. Sarah felt old and weary next to Mickie's innocence, but she didn't say that. *I missed Amy's companionship and didn't know how much I was missing out on getting to know her daughter. Thank you, Father, for Your love and for Your gentleness and kindness. Help me to be what Mickie and Justin need.*

Sighing, she slid down in bed. *Despite the pain of*

*losing my fiancé, I'm happy now. I realize I had drifted
from You and hadn't cleared up my past. Give me courage to make up to Justin for the wrongs I paid him. And,
Father, I just know this is going to work out great with
Mickie! Despite what Justin says, Mickie seems like the
perfect little girl. I really don't think I'm going to have
problems there. Just, maybe, the housekeeping part. So
give Justin patience as I learn exactly when he likes to
eat and things like that. Amen.*

Feeling better after praying, she smiled as she closed
her eyes. She would be a good housekeeper and a caring
companion for Mickie. Things weren't going to be so
bad after all.

Chapter Seven

"It's a Sarah Connelly on the line, Mr. Warner."

Justin pushed back from the paperwork he'd been working on. Brushing a hand through his hair, he leaned forward and snagged the phone.

"Sarah?" he questioned. She'd been baby-sitting for him for over a week now and had never called him at the office. He couldn't imagine what in the world she'd phone him for, unless it was an emergency.

"I can't find her!"

The panicked voice sent a chill down his spine. "Find her? Find who, Sarah? Mickie?"

"Yes. School got out early today. You know that. But she had a tutoring session and I was trying to make that cake she wanted and time got away from me."

The chill turned to full-blown alarm. "Go on," he said, despite the fact he was certain he heard her sniffle. "Tell me."

"I was only ten minutes late. I rushed up to the

school. A few children were still around, so it wasn't as though I was *that* late. But she wasn't there.''

Terror gripped his heart, but he forced it down. Sarah was hysterical enough for both of them. "What did the principal say?"

"I didn't ask her. The teacher outside said she had just seen Mickie in the line but didn't notice her leave the school yard. I started tracing the route home, thinking she might have walked, but couldn't find her. I went back up to the school. I've even been home. She's nowhere. I thought about calling the police—"

"Mr. Warner?"

He waved at his secretary, motioning her out, but she came forward. "Mr. Warner, Stephanie Williams is on the phone. It's about Mickie."

His gaze snapped up at those words. Relief and a sudden suspicion filled his mind. "Sarah, hold on a minute. I may have found Mickie."

He punched the other line, feeling the tension increase. "Ms. Williams?"

A trilling laugh floated over the phone line. "I've told you a dozen times to call me Stephanie, Mr. Warner."

"My secretary said it's about Mickie," he interrupted, feeling his already frayed temper slipping even further from his control.

"Why, yes, it is. Why, the poor little dear. You know I volunteer up there three days a week. I stayed after to help test some of the slower children today during tutoring. You know, they had tutoring today. Anyway…"

Justin wished he could rip the words out of her, but Stephanie had her own way of telling a story and a talent for drawing the attention to herself. Already, though, his body was relaxing. Mickie was with Stephanie. Somehow he just knew it.

"Yes?" he questioned when she didn't continue.

"I was getting ready to bring my own child home and Mickie was still there. I had a feeling she was thinking about walking home the way she kept looking around for her ride. The poor little dear. I know you've been having trouble with baby-sitters, so I asked her if anyone was coming to pick her up. She said her aunt Sarah had forgotten her. I didn't know you had a sister. I insisted she ride home with me and we'd call as soon as we arrived, but we forgot, having our cookies and milk, so I'm calling you now."

Justin closed his eyes and counted to ten. Stephanie wanted him as her next husband. She'd done just about everything to get the message across except send him a telegram. She loved his house, his money and the social position she would have. Oh, he knew her kind. But this was too much. Mickie really liked Stephanie's daughter, but the woman was lonely and needy, imagining him as the answer to her problems. He didn't want to tell Stephanie exactly what he thought of her stunt or whom she had terrified, nor did he want to let her off scot-free. *Father, give me patience,* he thought. "I'll let Sarah know what happened and she'll come over and pick her up."

"Oh, that's not necessary. The girls are having a wonderful time. Why don't I just keep her until suppertime. You can stop by on your way home from work and have dinner with us…"

"Thank you, Stephanie," he said, "but I don't think that's possible. Sarah is the new housekeeper and she'll already have started supper. Besides, Mickie knows she's suppose to wait or call."

"Oh, I hope you're not going to chastise Mickie for the sitter's being late," Stephanie said in a pouty voice.

"No. No, not for that at all," he said, though he would have a talk with his daughter again about getting in a car with anyone other than the person supposed to pick her up. And walking home. He shuddered at the thought. "Look, I have to go. My housekeeper is on the other line. Thanks for calling." He hung up before she could get another word in.

"Sarah," he said into the other line, "she's two blocks over at Stephanie Williams's house."

Oh, thank you, Father, she whispered.

Justin was certain he could hear tears. "You might remember that next time you plan to pick Mickie up," he growled. He heard a swiftly indrawn breath but didn't care. He was still shaking himself. He tersely gave her directions to Stephanie Williams's house and hung up the phone.

"So, what has you looking so grim? Did you find a virus in our latest software package?" Bill quipped as he entered the office.

"Stephanie Williams just took my daughter home from school. It seems Mickie thought Sarah forgot to pick her up."

"And?"

"And?" Justin asked, staring incredulously at Bill.

"Well, for starters, I'm absolutely furious with Sarah. What are you shaking your head about?"

"I'd say you're feeling the aftereffects of terror."

Justin frowned. Bill was right. But he didn't have to like it. "Sarah has been here over a week. She should have been watching the time."

Bill raised an eyebrow.

"Mickie was about to walk home!" Justin exclaimed.

Bill chuckled. "I remember you telling me that Mickie once tried to walk to work to visit you."

Just like that, his fear and anger melted away. And with that, guilt swept in. He felt like a total heel for the way he'd treated Sarah on the phone a few minutes ago. Why hadn't he remembered this wasn't the first time his daughter had thought someone had forgotten to pick her up, after she'd waited only a few minutes? He knew it all came from the way Amy had left in the middle of the night, without saying goodbye to Mickie. The slightest incident triggered Mickie's feelings of abandonment, of being forgotten. Why had he been so angry at Sarah?

Yeah, Mickie had tried walking to his office, which was a forty-five-minute drive from his house. He shook his head and curved his lips as he remembered how Mrs. Winters had called him, hysterical that she couldn't find Mickie at school. He'd been terrified, too, until the school cross guard came walking back to the building with Mickie. Luckily, Mickie had asked the cross guard for directions downtown, explaining she had wanted to see her daddy. He shuddered recalling the long talk he'd had with his daughter about waiting where she was told to wait and trying to solve problems herself.

That had been just after Amy died.

"Is Sarah safe or should I go rescue her?"

Justin glanced up at Bill. "What do you mean?"

"Well, that look is off your face, which means Mickie is safe and sound and so is Sarah, so I guess she'll still be safe when you get home," Bill said, ignoring Justin's question.

He slouched in the chair in front of Justin. "So how's it going on the home front?"

Justin leaned back in his chair and crossed his hands over his stomach. "Fine. Why?"

Bill grinned. "I know both of you and how you're usually at each other's throats. I just wondered."

Justin shrugged. "Sarah's different." He thought about how she'd had dinner ready each night, and went to extra lengths every day to have everything done. She was working herself harder than any other housekeeper he'd ever had. He'd never thought of her as the domestic type. He'd also noticed circles under her eyes. He didn't think she was resting well, though she always smiled and had a kind word for him or a sweet smile and a hug for Mickie.

"She's eaten up with guilt."

"What?" Justin regarded Bill, almost having forgotten he was there.

"Guilt. You know what that is. She doesn't think she's good enough for anything."

This was new to Justin. He sat up straighter. "What

do you mean? She certainly hasn't acted like a cowed individual.''

Bill sighed. ''Guilt manifests itself in different ways, Justin. Just because she's not walking around with the 'woe is me' look Amy wore whenever she felt sorry for herself doesn't mean—''

''Let's leave Amy out of this.''

Bill nodded. ''I'm sorry, Justin. What I mean is, well—'' he shrugged, averting his eyes to the window and staring out ''—Sarah feels guilty about her boyfriend dumping her, I think. Add that to the way she keeps messing up every relationship she's involved in—''

''She hasn't messed up any relationships that I know of,'' Justin said, defending her.

''What would you call what happened between the two of you?''

Justin paused. ''Well, one mistake, then. She shouldn't have tried to take my daughter from me. But that's water under the bridge. Why does she blame herself for the breakup with her fiancé? What happened?''

Bill shrugged. ''All I can say is, it wasn't Sarah's fault.''

Justin accepted Bill's vague answer and respected Bill's ability to keep a confidence. Maybe that was why so many of Bill's friends confided in him. Yet why did he bring it up if he wasn't going to tell him? Justin wondered, frustrated.

''Look, just be careful about hurting her. Like when you go home today to discuss that she forgot your daughter. She's already blaming herself for everything that has gone wrong in the past decade, as far as I can tell. Don't add to the load.''

Justin was shocked. He'd never pictured Sarah as the sensitive type who would carry around extra baggage like that. He'd always thought of her as a "full steam ahead" type who did what she wanted and didn't really care about what she left in her wake. He remembered his curt words to her the first couple of days and wondered now if she really had been feeling guilty over everything between them these past years. Was that why she'd come to him?

"So, have you decided to date her?"

"Date?" Justin sputtered.

Bill grinned. "Yeah, as in 'let's go out and see a movie'?"

Justin shot Bill a frown. "Of course not. She's my sister-in-law.''

"Hey, I just wondered. You look so different."

Did he look different? He'd enjoyed having Sarah in his house this last week. She was sweet, kind and fun to talk with. But he wasn't in the market for a wife. Especially if what Bill said was true. For he wasn't going to marry someone else who came to him out of guilt.

Deciding to change the subject, he looked Bill up and down. "So, how's life been treating you? Looks like you've gained a little weight since you married."

Bill's grin spread across his face and he locked his hands behind his head. "Ah, yes, the little woman keeps me well-fed."

Justin stood, straightened his coat and came around the desk. "I'd like to hear what your wife would say about being called 'little woman.' Come on. If we're going to lunch, we'd better get out of here. I have a meeting at two-thirty.''

Bill chuckled and crossed the office with Justin.

He watched Bill's smile, the ease in his walk, how relaxed he was. Bill had certainly mellowed since marrying. A deep part in Justin yearned for that same thing that Bill had.

Would he ever find it?

Sarah paced the living room.

Mickie was on the swing in the backyard. Dinner was ready. But Justin wasn't home.

She had blown it today.

She'd thought being a baby-sitter would be a piece of cake.

And then she'd blown it.

How could she have forgotten Mickie? Justin's words came back to her. *You might remember that next time you plan to pick Mickie up.* It wasn't so much the words as the tone. He blamed her, as he should. But it had hurt just the same. She cared for Mickie, too. She hadn't meant to forget Mickie.

It was just that she was tired. So very tired. She'd been trying so hard to be a good housekeeper and everything that Mickie needed. Justin didn't know it, but she'd been up nights studying books on parenting and child development, as well as some of the latest housekeeping and cooking tips she found in women's magazines.

She was beginning to wonder how women had time

for anything else but housekeeping. She'd stripped the floors and rewaxed them. She'd shampooed the carpets. And the curtains...well, they'd said in one magazine that they should be taken down once a month to be cleaned to keep any problems with allergies out of the house. Then there were the meals.

Sarah was used to buying canned or frozen convenience foods, not fresh meats and vegetables. Her eating habits weren't very healthy. But she couldn't expect Mickie or Justin to eat like that. So she'd been doing her best to fix new innovative meals each night. And the meals she was fixing took anywhere from two to three hours each. Some she had to start right after Justin went to work because meats had to be marinated or set out to thaw.

Today she'd been trying to get all the ingredients mixed for the chocolate coconut cake Mickie wanted, before she had to leave to pick up the child from school. She'd just happened to glance up at the clock and see she should have been at school that very minute.

Had she been thinking, she would have called the school and asked them to tell Mickie she was on her way and for them to keep an eye on her.

But she hadn't been thinking. She'd simply run out the door in her haste to reach her niece.

"I'm home."

Sarah whirled toward the door to see Justin just entering. He looked handsome.

He always looked handsome. The tweed coat and jeans with cowboy boots were so Texan on him. Odd to think he was the head of such a large corporation yet he dressed like this. He was always full of surprises. "Mickie is out back."

"I see." Justin put his briefcase in the hall closet after taking out a few papers first. He started toward the library.

"May I talk to you?"

He looked over his shoulder, surprised. "Sure. I wanted to talk to you anyway."

Dread filled her. If she only got fired she'd be lucky. She wondered if he could bring her up on charges for abandonment or something.

Justin went to his desk and placed the papers there, then turned and leaned against the surface. "You look nice today."

She was shocked. But glad. She'd put on a new peach-colored top with her jeans knowing the shade complemented her coloring. Her hair was swept back into a French braid, clasped with a peach ribbon. While dressing this morning, she'd hoped taking more care with her appearance would lift her spirits, make her feel more feminine.

That was stupid, because she knew, deep down inside, that she would never be feminine enough. After all, she couldn't have children.... "I wanted to talk about this afternoon," she said, blocking the painful thought from her mind.

"I figured you did," Justin replied, his features relaxed.

"Look, Justin, no matter what you think of me, I wanted to tell you I'm really, really sorry for what happened. I got carried away with cooking and just let the hours slip by.''

"It's all right, Sarah. It's not entirely your fault. It's partly Amy's,'' he added quietly.

Sarah stared, confused. What did this have to do with Amy?

"I don't understand.''

How could Justin be so forgiving about this? She'd imagined he'd been waiting all along for an excuse to fire her and she'd just provided him one.

"Sit down.'' He motioned to a chair.

Sarah reluctantly eased onto the edge.

"The night Amy left, Mickie was asleep. Of course, Amy didn't wake her up to say good-bye. How could she have known Mickie would never see her again?''
He hesitated, then went on. ''Anyway, Mickie has never really gotten over the feelings of abandonment caused by the way Amy left us. If someone is supposed to pick her up and they're even a few minutes late, she can't handle it.'' He explained. ''I've been late to pick her up myself, due to traffic or whatever only to find she's gone off with a friend.''

Justin shook his head. ''So far, no harm has been done. We've had long talks about her actions and she always promises not to go off again unless it was a real emergency.''

"A real emergency?''

"I explained that if it was a real emergency—and her ride didn't come for say, an hour—she could go to her teacher, or find a policeman. Or even walk by herself to her friend's house who lives across from the school.''

"Ah…" Sarah said. "That explains it I guess, but it still doesn't excuse me for forgetting to pick her up."

Justin shook his head. "How about if I just say I think Mickie takes after her aunt?"

Sarah thought about that. Her heartbeat increased as she wondered exactly what he could mean. He loved his daughter. Did that mean he saw something good in her, Sarah? "I'm not exactly sure how to take that."

"Take it easy, Sarah. What I'm trying to say is I don't eat baby-sitters for lunch over minor mistakes."

"This wasn't minor."

"Yes, it was. Stephanie picked up Mickie from school, probably with some persuasion from Mickie," he added darkly. "I'll have a talk with Mickie again about waiting and taking rides from strangers. I'm sure you'll never forget her again, but if you are a little late, call the school."

She nodded. And trust God to keep Mickie safe. Boy, had she prayed while searching for Mickie and God had once again answered prayers by keeping her safe. "I'll finish dinner and get it on the table," she said, backing toward the door. "Thanks."

Justin nodded.

She couldn't understand why Justin had been so calm. She'd just known he was going to fire her and she'd once again lose the chance at the only family she would ever have. Longingly, she touched her stomach. For a moment a deep regret at what she couldn't have touched her soul. But then she was able to thank God. Because of that minor affliction she had woken up to what she already possessed and had neglected over the past two years. She had a wonderful niece and, she was beginning to see, an equally wonderful brother-in-law.

It would be enough. She had family, though she would never have her own family. She could surely forget that detail and go on with life, couldn't she?

Chapter Eight

Justin opened his eyes.

It was dark, the curtains pulled. Glancing at the bedside clock he saw it was two-thirty in the morning.

What had wakened him? Mickie hadn't crawled into bed with him. He listened but heard no noise in his room to account for the reason he'd awakened.

A whisper of noise reached him.

He sat up in bed, the crisp cotton sheet sliding down his chest. Listening again, he couldn't tell what it was he'd heard.

It hadn't come from downstairs. The alarm was on for the night and hadn't been triggered.

What could it have been? Maybe Mickie was having her nightmares again. She'd had nightmares right after Amy had died. But it had been at least six months since the last one.

He swung his long legs out of bed. After grabbing a

sweatshirt and jeans from the end of the bed, he slipped them on.

He padded barefoot to the door, running a tired hand through his disheveled hair, then made his way down the hallway. He paused outside Mickie's door, then pushed it wide and peeked in to where he could see her silhouette form in bed. She lay still, curled up in a ball, one hand tucked under her chin, the other under the side of her face. She looked peaceful.

Frowning, he went over and tucked the sheet more securely about her. Had she gone back to sleep so quickly? he wondered.

He left Mickie's room. Just as he started down the hall, thinking he must have heard something downstairs such as the heating system, the sound came again. A whimpering moan, barely audible, sounding so forlorn that the hairs on the back of his neck stood up. Had he believed in ghosts, he would have thought the place haunted. But he didn't.

The sound emanated from somewhere he could now easily identify as he stood this close to Mickie's door in the hallway.

It was from Sarah's room.

He walked slowly over to her door. He listened and heard something—he wasn't sure what—then it was quiet. He tapped on the door.

''No, no, no!''

Her broken cries chilled him. No one could be in there. They would have run when he'd knocked. She had to be having a nightmare. ''Sarah?'' he called out.

She didn't answer.

He cracked open the door, just to check. Maybe her nightmare was over and he could sneak back to his room. But he knew that wasn't true the minute he saw his sister-in-law. She thrashed about in bed, heart-wrenching whimpers escaping her throat. What chilled him the most was the way she tried to hold them back, only allowing them to escape when she gasped for air.

"Sarah?" he said, louder, then glanced toward Mickie's room. He didn't want to wake the little girl. No telling how she would react if she saw Sarah like this.

He stepped into the room, pushed the door closed, then hurried to the edge of the bed. She was asleep on top of the covers, fully clothed. A book about child care lay open on the floor. It looked as if she'd fallen asleep reading tonight. "Sarah, honey, come on, wake up. It's okay."

She stilled for a moment, then thrashed again. "No, oh, no, please," she pleaded in a whisper.

He edged onto the side of the bed and raised a hand to her shoulder. Touching it, he shook her. "Come on, honey, wake up. It's okay."

The torment he saw on her face tore at his heart. Her eyes opened, but he wasn't sure if she was seeing him or not. Pain, excruciating and unbearable, filled her gaze.

"There're no babies. They're all just out of my reach."

Alarmed, he cupped her cheek. "Look at me, Sarah. You're dreaming." She stared at him and blinked. He could tell she'd finally woken up. "It's okay," he soothed her. "You were just dreaming. Something about the babies."

Her eyes slowly lost their unfocused quality and she gazed at him. "Babies?" she asked, then blinked again. She glanced around wildly before shuttering her gaze. "I don't know what you're talking about."

She was lying. He could see a bleakness, even a shame, in her eyes. What was going on here?

She shuddered from the aftereffects of the dream, he was sure, then she focused her vulnerable gaze on him again.

Maybe it was the abject look of need that made him notice her as a woman, but in that instant he did. He inhaled the perfumed scent of her soap and shampoo. Her skin was velvety soft where he cupped her cheek, her hair like silk. Had he ever noticed that before? Or had he noticed how the slope of her cheekbone and curve of her jaw made her look so feminine? And those eyes. Beautifully blue and so expressive. And staring at him just as intensely as he stared at her.

He cleared his throat, shocked at his attraction to her. Standing, he backed up. "I'm sorry for entering your room at night, Sarah. I promised you privacy. But you were having a bad dream. You had me worried."

He tried to smile but failed miserably.

She slid up in bed, pulling an afghan up to her armpits he noticed, even though she was fully dressed underneath. Great, she probably thought who knew what, waking up to find a man sitting on the edge of her bed. A dull flush crept up his cheeks. He was thankful for the darkness. He'd been married, had dated for years before that, and yet he'd never found himself in this situation.

"Sometimes, when I'm stressed out, my dreams can take an odd turn."

She still wasn't telling him the truth. He could tell by the look in her lovely eyes. But right now, he thought accepting her words was the better part of valor. He didn't want to stay, knew it wasn't safe to stay because of his sudden urge to brush the stray strands of hair from her cheek, his impulse to comfort her, to persuade her to trust him.

"If you ever want to talk, I'd be happy to listen. I don't want you feeling *stressed out* over this job, Sarah. You're family."

Family. He had to remember that.

"Thank you, Justin, but I'm fine now."

"Well then." He retreated a couple of steps. "I'll just leave.

He backed into the wall, hooked the door with a finger and was gone before Sarah could say anything else.

Sarah watched him leave, the remnant of the dream fading and leaving her with only the longing she'd felt when she'd looked into Justin's eyes. Was she falling in love with him?

She couldn't feel that way about him. She just couldn't.

But she did.

She sighed and leaned back against the headboard. And when he'd seen the look in her eye, his distress had been obvious. It was apparent that he didn't share the same feelings she did. But it had simply been so easy to care for him. He was a good father, a good man from all she could tell. And yes, she admitted, he'd probably been a good man when she'd first met him, too. He had been trying to right what his partner had done.

But what was there to love about her? She had tried to take his child; she had most probably assisted in the problems in his marriage because she hadn't come to visit her sister. And now she had lost his child today. Not to mention that she had her own dark secret.

She remembered Stephanie Williams's scrutiny when she'd gone to get Mickie, the way the woman had studied her, then lifted a haughty eyebrow, as if she found Sarah wanting. It had angered Sarah just a bit, but also made her nervous. Stephanie evidently knew Justin well enough to feel free to pick up his child. Sarah had wondered if Stephanie might just have a right to be angry that Sarah had forgotten Mickie. Was Justin interested in Stephanie?

Still, she refused to rise to the bait and argue it with anyone but Justin. She might be wrong, but it was Justin's place to reprimand her, not some strange woman's.

Stiffening, she had gathered Mickie and her things and had come home.

She'd expected to be fired.

But she had received forgiveness, instead.

Something she had deserved termination for was not going to endear her to a man she'd already hurt. Still, he had forgiven.

She shook her head in disbelief at where her thoughts were leading. Justin could never have feelings for her. He had loved Amy. He couldn't be interested in her. He certainly wouldn't be interested in her if he found out her secret, the secret she'd been dreaming about.

Tears filled her eyes. No, Justin was too good a father not to want more children one day. He'd even told her so, that day they'd played with Mickie. So no matter how she felt, she knew those feelings would never be returned.

Sarah was just finishing up breakfast when Justin came in from running. She jumped when the back door opened.

He stopped short when he saw her. He looked great. Wearing gray jogging pants and a T-shirt that was now soaked with sweat, his hair in disarray from the wind, he still was handsome enough to make any woman take second notice. She hadn't been surprised when she'd first found out Justin ran. She'd guessed he exercised regularly to stay in such good shape.

"Sorry," he muttered. "I didn't mean to startle you."

"I just thought I was the first one up," she replied, pouring him a glass of juice. "I didn't realize you'd gone out already."

He nodded his thanks. "Mickie should be down soon." Nervously, he glanced at the wall clock. "I think she'll have something to say to you."

Sarah pushed at a stray piece of hair, feeling a smudge of flour on her face. She'd gotten out the cookbook, intent on making pancakes this morning for Justin and Mickie to try to make amends for the disaster yesterday. At his words, she paused in her actions. "Oh, Justin, you didn't yell at her over what happened, did you? I told you it was my fault.''

Justin finished his juice, then placed the empty glass in the sink. ''Let's just say I explained to Mickie that friend or not, she should never, ever get into someone else's car. I explained how it had scared both of us.''

Sarah relaxed. ''Oh.'' She turned her back on him and stirred the batter. ''That's fine. I just didn't want her to be in trouble for my mistake.''

She heard the squeak of his running shoes as he slowly crossed the floor. Tension crawled up her spine when she realized he was right behind her.

''I think we need to have a talk about this 'forgive and forget' thing.''

His words sent a shiver racing along her spine. She sensed his closeness, felt his concern for her, and his sensitivity to her feelings as well as Mickie's. She realized how much she would love to go on experiencing that every day.

''What do you mean?'' she asked, breathless. Her cheeks pinkened over her thoughts. She wanted to keep her back to him, afraid he might read the need of companionship in her eyes.

He wouldn't let her. He gently clasped her left shoulder and turned her until she faced him.

Her gaze rested on his chest. She couldn't look above that, until he put a hand under her chin and lifted it. When her eyes met his, she saw tenderness and understanding.

''You don't have to earn forgiveness, Sarah. Not for

what happened yesterday or for what happened last night. Or even before that.''

"Nothing happened last night," she argued.

He smiled, a small tilting of the corners of his mouth that said he thought different. "Stop trying to earn forgiveness and just accept your place here as family.''

"I'm the housekeeper," she whispered.

He smiled that smile again. "You take care of the house, but you're more than just the housekeeper," he said, his brown eyes tenderly perusing her reaction to his words.

She tried not to show him any emotion, but with him holding her chin, it was impossible for him not to glean some hint of what she felt. She swallowed then nodded. "Fine.''

His index finger stroked under her chin, then he released her and stepped back. "Good.''

She thought she was off the hook when he headed for the living room. But he stopped just short of the room and spun back around. "If you're not doing anything after breakfast, would you like to go to church with Mickie and me?''

Sarah stilled. He'd noticed she hadn't attended last week? She hadn't told him, or mentioned her reason. It was just so hard to go to the church that André's father went to and see him sitting there, looking through her as if she never existed.

She missed church dreadfully.

Maybe this was the opening of another door she should go through. She had intended to pull out a telephone book and start searching the directory after breakfast. But this would be so much better. She'd be going to a church where she knew at least two people. Granted, only one would be with her during the service, the very one who made her heart race every time he looked at her.

But wouldn't that be better than going into a church alone? And if she liked the church, then possibly her search for a new place would be over.

What would it hurt?

Coming to a decision, she turned to Justin and smiled at him. "I'd love to."

His eyes flared briefly. "Great. We leave here at nine-thirty to get there on time. I'll make sure Mickie is up and see you when breakfast is ready."

She nodded.

"Oh, and Sarah?"

She turned back. "Yes?"

"Just to give you a little extra time this morning, Mickie and I will load the dishwasher while you change."

"Oh, you don't—"

"Don't argue," he admonished. "We'll be down in a bit."

And he was gone, just like that, leaving Sarah standing alone in the kitchen. But the loneliness no longer bothered her. Sarah suddenly felt better than she had in months. She realized it was because she was looking forward to going to church with no worries over what she wore or how she looked. What an eye-opening revelation, she thought, stunned. She'd always felt pressured to dress for André's father. But Justin wouldn't care if her dress was simple or elegant, if she wore her hair in a French braid instead of a French twist. She had a feeling Justin was the type who enjoyed going to church simply to worship. And she was looking forward to that, indeed.

With a sense of freedom, she whispered another small prayer. *Thank You, Father, that You led me here. I have a feeling I was in a bigger slump than I realized. Realizing how much I had dreaded going to church only goes to show me how out of line my priorities had gotten. Thank You for the joy You've restored and the forgiveness I saw in Justin's eyes. And most especially, Father, thank You that I'm once again going to be back in church with someone who evidently shares the excitement of going.*

She smiled and, with renewed energy, whipped the batter for her pancakes, thinking she'd better hurry or she'd end up making them all late.

Chapter Nine

She'd been right.

Justin took one glance at her simple drop-waist, floral dress and smiled. "You look great," he murmured, and held the door open for her as she climbed into the sleek Mercedes he'd been allowing her to drive.

He slid into the driver's seat. "Fasten your seat belt," he said to Mickie, glancing in the rearview mirror.

Sarah fastened her own, watching as Justin stretched to reach his belt and clasp it. In his charcoal gray suit, he, too, looked great. She had to grin over his tie, though.

"What has you smiling?"

She met his amused gaze. "Cartoon characters?" she asked, motioning to the brightly colored tie.

"I got to pick it out," Mickie said from the back seat. "I gave it to him for his birthday last year."

She tried not to laugh. "I see."

He lifted it and waved the end at Sarah, daring her to

say anything. "I think it's great," he said, grinning, his eyes twinkling. "Mickie has wonderful taste, don't you think?"

"Uh-huh. A great artistic eye."

She relaxed in the seat as Justin drove them to the service. When they got out of the car, Mickie ran ahead of them. Sarah started to call her back, but Justin forestalled her.

"Don't worry. This is a small church. Everyone knows everyone else. And the kids run in a gang until church starts."

Sure enough, two little boys and three other young girls met Mickie at the door, then in unison they turned and headed inside the church.

"The congregation of the church I went to numbered almost one thousand."

"I like the smaller church better. More intimate."

"Well, hello, Justin."

Sarah knew that voice—unfortunately. Turning, she saw she was right. Stephanie Williams, dressed in a fashionable, expensive-looking suit came forward. Her hair was perfectly styled in a sleek, chin-length cut and she brushed a stray lock aside with a flick of one manicured finger. Sarah looked down at her housework-chafed hands and felt positively dowdy.

She noticed Justin had a smile pasted on his face. But it was different from the smile she'd witnessed at home. It was what she thought of as his practiced business smile.

"Hello, Stephanie. You've met Sarah, haven't you?"

Stephanie ran her gaze over Sarah's dress and hairdo,

then turned back to Justin, dismissing her. "Why, yes, I have. Tell me, has Mickie gotten over her little trauma? The poor dear was inconsolable when I found her."

Sarah flushed but didn't comment.

"She's just fine," Justin replied.

"That's good," Stephanie cooed. "You'll have to come over someday soon for dinner, Justin. Bring Mickie. She always has so much fun with my daughter. I'm sure your housekeeper wouldn't mind a day off."

"My sister-in-law knows she can have a day off whenever she wants," Justin said.

Well, Sarah was thankful for that. She'd felt Stephanie's animosity and didn't understand it. But that line about coming over for dinner had made the woman's intentions perfectly clear. Stephanie had her eyes set on Justin.

"Oh, my, of course. I had forgotten she was your sister-in-law. Anyway, think about it. Maybe next Saturday or Sunday."

"We'll see," he said noncommittally. Then, dismissing Stephanie by turning to Sarah, he said, "We need to find a seat before the service starts. Have a nice day, Stephanie."

Taking Sarah's elbow, he led her off, leaving Stephanie standing in the foyer. Sarah raised an eyebrow. "Using me as a convenient excuse?"

"The woman is, ah, interested in getting better acquainted," he said.

"I hadn't noticed," Sarah remarked dryly.

"Go ahead, laugh. She's just about relentless. Won't take no for an answer. Mickie said she insisted she get in the car and discouraged her from calling, saying she could phone when they got to her house.''

Sarah frowned. ''That's awful.''

''Yeah, well, I told Mickie if that ever happened again to find the nearest teacher and hug her legs until she got her attention. She's not to go anywhere with anyone, no matter how insistent the person is. I told her the teacher would understand if she got out of line to tell her what was happening.''

''How can you still talk to Stephanie after that?''

Justin shrugged. ''I'm polite only because if I really said what I was feeling, I'd be at the altar praying for the next week or two. When I calm down enough to discuss it without saying anything in anger, I'll tell Stephanie not to try that again. I've already spoken to the principal. She assured me there would be no repeat performance. That's the important thing.''

Sarah seated herself on the pew and watched as family after family came in, greeting others, laughing, talking, sharing what had happened during the week, before finally finding their seats. Several people stopped by and Justin introduced them to her. All were friendly, open and so kind. Justin was right. A small church was much nicer. Sarah had never attended a really small church of a hundred or so, which was what she estimated this group to be.

The music started and she stood. The songs were a lot like her old church's: upbeat, fast. Then the tempo slowed and became more worshipful, the songs talking about simple things—loving the Lord, praising Him for what He had done.

Peace flooded Sarah's soul as the congregation sang and offered a special prayer for the sick and needy. They mentioned a family who needed help with their house. A recent storm had torn up one corner of the roof and the pastor called for volunteers to help rebuild it.

Then the pastor opened his Bible. "'Therefore, there is no condemnation for those who are in Christ Jesus because through Christ Jesus the law of the spirit of life set me free from the law of sin and death.' Romans 8:1." The pastor closed his Bible. "We're going to discuss two things today in this sermon—sin, which is the breaking of God's law and is forgiven simply by asking God to forgive you for your transgression, and guilt, which is after God has forgiven you, the inability to forget it, as God does, but instead, hold on to it in the form of guilt as your penance for the wrong you've committed."

Sarah sat up, her eyes widening. Oh, no, she thought. This was a sermon she didn't want to hear, one that was already convicting her.

"People don't often realize that conviction and guilt are two different things. Whereas conviction brings you to your knees to tell God you messed up and want to start over again, guilt has you dropping your head and hiding in shame over and over and over again. Yet once it's forgiven it's forgotten.

"Self-condemnation brings it up again, not the spirit of God. Jesus paid the price, and all we are required to do is go to Him and confess our sins and He is faithful and just to forgive us our sins. And forget them.

"When it includes others we've wronged, we should go to that person and apologize and ask for forgiveness.

After that, though, it's off our shoulders. God doesn't require us to carry around unforgiveness against us, but simply to ask Him for forgiveness and any person we have wronged.''

The preacher continued, but Sarah didn't hear. Her heart was too busy reacting to what the preacher had said. In all the time she'd been with Justin she realized she had been trying to earn his forgiveness because she hadn't let go of her guilt for what she'd done. Each time Justin had done something nice, said something sweet, she'd forced herself to work harder to prove how wrong she'd been. It had been like an arrow through her heart whenever he had smiled at her. The smiles, the attraction she felt, had only heaped guilt upon that condemnation. And now the pastor was explaining that once forgiven it should be forgotten.

Of course she realized that.

But she hadn't realized just what she'd been carrying around until the pastor had stated it so bluntly. She didn't know how long she sat there, stunned by how heavy a load lay on her shoulders, until Justin was standing next to her.

They had prayer and the pastor asked for those under a heavy burden to come down.

She went. When she bowed her head to pray, she was surprised to find Justin standing next to her and to feel his hand on her shoulder. Then she felt others around her who had come down for prayer, too.

Sarah prayed, admitting to God that she had been carrying around burdens that He had died for and would willingly take from her. She promised God she'd try harder not to hold on to the guilt and the past and to look to the future, instead.

When she was done, she felt lighter, freer than she had in a long time. They went back to their seats, gathered their Bibles and her purse and they left.

Many stopped her to say hi and welcome, then Mickie was there and they were in the car, ready to go. On the way home, Justin finally spoke.

"You look more relaxed than I've seen you since you came to work, Sarah."

She smiled. "I guess I am. You know, it's hard sometimes to forget the past and let go."

Justin laughed. "Don't I know. There are many things I regret about…" he said, glancing in the mirror at Mickie.

Sarah understood he was talking about Amy but didn't want to mention her name and alert his daughter. "But I finally received peace over those problems and had to just put them to rest. A few old ghosts are still hanging around, but you just have to put the past in the past and let it go."

This morning Sarah had done that with most of the things that had bothered her. But there was one thing she couldn't come to grips with, and that was her infertility. She'd lost André over it. There was nothing she could do about her condition, but she still felt guilty that she'd hurt André, no matter how rotten he'd treated her. But more than condemnation or guilt, she felt fear. She wondered how she would deal with telling anyone about her problem. "So let's say you had information that was going to hurt someone, should you feel guilty keeping that information secret?''

Justin chuckled. ''That's a hard one. Some people say to be honest no matter what. Others say a white lie is acceptable to spare feelings.'' His smile left as he thought about it. ''I suppose my feelings on the subject are that there should never be any secrets between a husband and a wife. Secrets break down the marriage, whereas the truth might hurt, but you can work through the hurt if you know there's a problem. As for others, what's not their business is just that, none of their business. If you don't like someone's dress you don't have to say, 'I love your dress' if you can say, instead, 'I love your hair.'''

She was relieved he felt that way. Because despite the wonderful service and the guilt she'd released over Amy's death and her treatment of this wonderful man, she still felt guilty for not telling him about what had truly prompted her to come to him in the first place: her infertility.

She knew it was because of her inability to have children that she'd suddenly started to consider family. Thinking of how much she was going to miss by never giving birth to children of her own had led her to pray. During that time with God, she realized she had wronged Justin and wanted to apologize. She'd hoped that if she apologized, then maybe he'd allow her to get to know her niece. She'd have a second chance at being a part of a family.

Justin's words—that some matters weren't anyone's business but a spouse's—encouraged her. She didn't feel as guilty over not telling him now and could relax. After all, they weren't married. They certainly weren't involved. Why, he'd never asked her out on a date or anything.

So, what did she have to feel guilty about? Yes, life was indeed much better without the guilt and fears.

Chapter Ten

"You're asking me out on a date?"

Justin actually flushed. Then he got defensive. Oh, he didn't really show it, except the way his gaze turned colder and his body stiffened. Smiling that *business* smile of his, he said, "I need a dinner companion for a work-related meeting. I thought you would enjoy the night out, and since you haven't taken a day off since I hired you, I thought it my duty to drag you to a movie after. Of course, if you don't want to go to a movie, I certainly won't force you."

He wasn't fooling her. Justin never did anything without a reason. But he had to have some other reason to take her to a movie besides just wanting to be with her. She couldn't let herself believe he actually cared about her in that way. "What about Mickie?" she asked weakly, still in shock over his earlier query.

"My secretary has volunteered to watch Mickie. I gave her some money to rent some children's movies, plus pizza and popcorn. She'll bring her granddaughter, too, so Mickie will have someone to play with.''

The shock wore off, to be replaced with delight. It had been aeons since she'd gone to a movie. She couldn't even remember the last time. André had preferred supper theater or the country club. Realizing her thoughts, she forced down her excitement. She was actually trembling inside. There was no reason at all she should be so jittery. He needed her. It was that simple. And to pay her back for going with him to dinner, he was taking her to a movie.

Yes, that had to be it.

Still, the idea of a night out appealed to her. ''That sounds fine,'' she said, hoping her voice was normal. ''What time do you want me to be ready?''

''Five-thirty? I'll be home early to pick you up.''

She nodded. He went out the door. Mickie was off school today because of teachers' meetings, so she was upstairs playing with a friend. Sarah set about straightening up. She felt so much more at ease with Justin since the Sunday service. She'd even thrown away all the magazines that had articles on keeping a perfect house.

Surveying the room, she noted the kitchen floor needed mopping and the living room needed to be picked up and vacuumed. She had two loads of laundry—mostly Mickie's—that needed washing.

Which meant she had plenty of time to bake Mickie her special chocolate coconut cake for tonight. The last time she'd tried, she'd been interrupted and then so upset by Mickie's disappearance that she'd never finished making it.

The day passed quickly as Sarah mopped the floor, fixed lunch, helped Mickie with her homework later that afternoon and got the laundry done before she felt ready to tackle the cake.

"Whatcha doing?"

Sarah glanced up from where she was pulling ingredients out of a cabinet. "I'm getting ready to make you a special treat for tonight." She gathered the flour, sugar and eggs. "I thought you were doing your math homework?"

Mickie smiled, twirling her hair with a finger. "I finished it." Suddenly, she stopped twirling her hair and looked up sweetly at Sarah. "I want to be a boo-tish-un," she said, frowning hard over the word.

Sarah grinned. "Beautician?" she asked.

"Yeah, boo-tish-un." She curled her fingers in her hair. "Do you have lipstick and stuff like that?"

Sarah poured the dry ingredients into a bowl. "I certainly do. Haven't you ever seen me sitting at the vanity when I put it on?"

Mickie shook her head. Frowning, she curled one of her long curls around her finger and held it above her eyes. "You have bangs and so does my friend, Katie. How come I don't have bangs?"

Sarah stopped stirring the cake mix. "Well, I suppose it's because your daddy never took you to get your hair cut."

"Could I have bangs?"

Sarah reached over and patted Mickie's head. "I imagine you can do whatever you want to your hair. Your daddy only wants you happy."

"Would your boo-tish-un give me bangs?" Mickie asked.

Sarah chuckled. "I'm afraid I cut my own bangs, Mickie. But we can talk to your daddy later, if you want, about getting your bangs cut."

She'd sloshed some cake batter over the side and she turned to clean it up. When she turned back, Mickie was pushing a chair over to watch her. Deciding to broach the subject of tonight, she asked Mickie. "You know your daddy's secretary is going to watch you this evening. She'll be bringing her granddaughter."

Mickie cut her eyes toward Sarah as she nonchalantly stuck her finger in the bowl and gathered up a lick of batter. "Miss Christine is nice, but I really like Shelley. She plays dolls, too."

"Well, I have it on good authority that Miss Christine is going to rent a movie and bring over pizza."

Mickie sucked her finger a moment longer before wiping it on her shirt. She grinned. "Pizza is almost my favorite food. Next to peanut butter and jelly. That's so cool."

Sarah grinned at how grown up Mickie tried to sound saying that.

Mickie turned around and sat down in the chair. She kicked her feet as she began to wind her hair around her finger. "Do you think Daddy would mind if I had bangs?"

Sarah wondered where the preoccupation with bangs had come from. "Not at all," she reassured her, and vowed to talk to Justin tonight about his daughter's desire. "Why don't you go find a board game to play. I'll finish up this cake, then meet you in your bedroom to play.''

Mickie nodded, slipped off the chair and walked out the door, never looking back, her fingers still curling and uncurling her hair.

As Sarah finished the cake, she wondered what she was going to wear tonight. She'd unpacked a few things from storage. The only nice outfit she had was still in a box. It was black and had a scooped neck and capped sleeves. Formfitting, it stopped just above the knees. She'd worn it whenever she'd gone to the theater with André. It was worth a try. Of course, she had a blue two-piece outfit that was nice, but she thought that maybe the black would be more formal.

She decided to go ahead and wear the blue outfit. It had a short straight skirt, white knit top and a blue sweater-style jacket. She wore it for business sometimes, but with the jacket off, it would look casual at the movie. No reason to break out the black thing when she'd always hated that dress.

She slipped the cake in the oven, happy she was finally getting to bake it for Mickie. Then she hurried out to the garage to find the blue outfit. She had some great handmade silver jewelry that would be fun to wear with it. She'd worn the earrings and bracelets when she'd started working at Watson and Watson but had stopped when André's father had frowned at her appearance. The jewelry didn't look businesslike, he'd said.

Quickly, she hunted the jewelry out, then carried it to her room with her outfit. But when she unpacked the outfit, it looked totally wrinkled. ''I need to iron something real quick, Mickie, then we'll have that game,'' she called, heading back downstairs with her clothes.

She couldn't believe Mickie had allowed her this much time without interrupting. Usually, Mickie came down every five minutes or so to ask her a question.

Sarah looked at her watch. She had enough time to iron, go upstairs, play a game with Mickie until the cake was done, then shower and dress and be ready before Justin got home.

She pulled out the iron, then ran it lightly over her skirt and top. As she ironed, she wondered why Mickie hadn't impatiently come to find her.

After quickly finishing, she put the iron away, then went upstairs. ''Mickie?'' she called, uneasy at how quiet it was.

She checked in each room. ''Mickie?'' she called again, her unease growing to panic. Had Mickie run away? Surely after the talk her dad had given her, she wouldn't go anywhere again on her own. ''Mickie?'' she said, louder, checking under her bed and out the window.

Then she heard it.

A muffled sound coming from the closet.

Concern replaced fear and she hurried over to the door. ''Mickie, honey,'' she called, opening the door.

The little girl was at the back of the closet, amid the shoes and boxes. Her head was bowed over her arms, which were propped on her knees. And her shoulders shook. Sarah knelt in front of her, totally mystified. ''Mickie, honey, what is it?''

''Um, I, uh, was playing boo-tish-un,'' she mumbled.

Sarah reached out, but hesitated to touch her. Mickie might really want to be alone right now. "Can you say that again, Mickie?" she asked, thinking that if she could understand her, then maybe she'd know how to handle the situation.

"Daddy's gonna be mad."

What did Justin have to do with this? Then it dawned on Sarah. Justin was the law of the house in his little girl's eyes. Sarah had done something wrong. "Oh, Sarah, honey, if you've done something wrong, your daddy's not going to get mad, unless you endangered your life. Tell me what happened."

Still the little girl wouldn't look up. "I wanted to be beautiful like you. I don't remember how Mama looked. But I bet she had bangs, too. She doesn't have any hair in my picture."

Sarah knew the only picture of Amy that Mickie had was in Mickie's room. Amy had her hair slicked back in a tight professional-looking bun in the photo. No, Amy had never had bangs.

A feeling of dread suddenly coiled in the pit of Sarah's stomach. "Mickie, look up at me, dear. Did you cut your hair?"

The little girl started sobbing again. "It's awful. I'll never be a boo-tish-un."

"Look at me, Mickie."

Sarah waited. Finally, Mickie lifted her head. *Oh, Father, Justin is going to be mad over this. Help me to handle the situation.*

Mickie's hair was cut in a slash across the front of her head. One eye was completely covered, and in a couple of spots her hair stuck out awkwardly on top, which told Sarah bangs weren't the only thing that had suffered Mickie's attempts.

"Where'd you find the makeup?" Sarah asked gently. Mauve lipstick—if Sarah wasn't mistaken it was her lipstick—covered the girl's mouth and blush was on her cheeks. Brown eye shadow was under both eyes and even spotted her forehead. Looking at Mickie's hands, Sarah saw smears and realized the little girl had been wiping away tears. "Don't answer that. I take it you found my makeup, in the location I volunteered earlier."

She reached for Mickie's hand and pulled her out of the closet. "Come on, sweetie, let's go get you cleaned up, then we'll put some makeup on you and fix your hair nicely for your daddy."

"It can't be fixed," the little girl cried.

"Of course it can," Sarah soothed. "And next week I promise to take you to a beautician if you still want to go, and let her explain about cutting hair."

She escorted the little girl into the bathroom. "We'll use my special cleaner to get all this off. It's creamy and cool and won't hurt the way scrubbing with a washcloth does," she teased.

And she proceeded to remove every speck of makeup from Mickie's face.

"Now for the hair. Stick your head under the faucet." Mickie did.

Sarah ran her hands through the mounds and mounds of curly hair. "Has your daddy ever cut it?"

"No," Mickie sniffled, though she sounded much better than she had only minutes before. "He said Mama never would cut it."

Oh, boy, she thought. When she was done wetting Mickie's hair, Sarah ran a towel over it, then combed it. Well, she decided, looking at the mess, she'd started this, she might as well go ahead and finish it. "Do you want it medium length like mine or do you want to keep it long like your mommy's?" she questioned, thinking Mickie would, of course, pick the latter.

"Like yours," Mickie immediately replied.

Of course. She should have known. "Let's tackle those bangs first," she said, then with a deep breath she combed the hair over the child's face.

Finding the shortest piece, which was, luckily, not too awfully short, she began snipping. "Why, look at that," Sarah exclaimed, "you're losing all your curl!"

The curly ends disappeared and only a small wave remained. She quickly feathered the hair around the child's face, then worked painstakingly to layer it where the little girl had left it awkward.

Mickie's eyes widened. "Why don't I have no more curl?"

"You know, your mommy's hair did the same thing when she was a little girl. I'd forgotten that. She kept just a bit of wave, but all the curl disappeared. Maybe that's why your mom never wanted to cut your hair."

Sarah lifted and snipped and combed and snipped some more, until she had a towelful of leftovers. "I think you have more hair down there than you do up here," she said, tapping Mickie's head on the last word.

"I'm beautiful," Mickie said, her eyes shining.

"Oh, honey," Sarah said, turning her around and hugging her, "you've always been beautiful. But there's something more than outward beauty and that's what's in your heart. As long as you are good in there, that's all that matters." She kissed her. "Come on. Let's put a little makeup on to complete the rest."

Mickie frowned.

"Hey, trust me." She led Mickie from her bathroom to her vanity. After she sat her down, she took out a compact of powder. "Now, little girls have to wear only certain types of makeup. You'll find that as you get older you have to keep changing the type of makeup you wear. This is the best type. It's young girls' makeup. As a matter of fact, even though I'm getting old, I can still wear this."

She took the pad and rubbed it over the powder. "Let's dust your face with this. See how you bring it down your nose and over your cheeks and on your forehead? We only want a bit. We don't want to look fake."

"Like Miss Stephanie?"

Although Mickie had asked the question innocently, Sarah couldn't resist smiling. "Well, some women like to wear more makeup. But I myself think makeup should cover only the freckles on my nose and stuff like that." She put down the compact and met Mickie's eyes in the mirror.

"As for lipstick, the color you had on was way too dark. However, I just happen to have something I wear on my lips when I'm outside."

She pulled out a cherry-flavored conditioner for

chapped lips. "It's almost like lipstick and even tastes good. Pucker up."

Mickie did, wrinkling her nose. "Daddy says this is my face when I eat a lemon."

Sarah laughed and applied the lipstick. "Oh, that's perfect!"

Mickie looked around and grinned. "I like it. But Daddy will tell me I shouldn't wear makeup."

"I bet he doesn't mind this." In actuality, Sarah couldn't see Mickie's powder, and it looked as though she'd licked her lips.

Mickie grinned. "I can't wait to show Daddy when he gets home."

When he gets home? Oh, dear! Sarah glanced at her watch. She'd been up here an hour and a half.

Mickie sniffed. "What's that?"

Sarah smelled it at the same time. "The cake!"

She'd completely forgotten about the cake. "It's burning!"

Sarah turned to run downstairs. As if sensing her anxiety, the fire alarms chose that moment to go off. Shrieks filled the air as the smoke began to drift up the stairs. "Mickie, run outside! I'll go check and make sure nothing is really on fire."

She took off down the hall, Mickie's hand in hers. She had really messed things up this time. Justin was due home any minute and his house was likely on fire. Justin would surely dismiss her this time.

Chapter Eleven

Justin had just reached for his briefcase, when he heard the smoke alarms. He jerked his head toward the house and his heart exploded in his chest. Forgetting the briefcase, he took off across the garage and burst in through the kitchen door, right into swirling smoke.

He immediately realized it was coming from the oven. "Sarah!" he called, dashing over and jerking the stove door open, only to fall back coughing as black smoke came pouring out.

After grabbing the oven mittens, he reached in and pulled out a pan. He heard the swinging door that led to the kitchen slam against the wall; heard a gasp and realized Sarah had arrived. "Where's Mickie?" he demanded, dropping the black thing in the round cake pan into the sink.

"She's outside. I told her to wait out there until I knew what was going on."

The blaring alarm was so strident he could hardly hear

her. She was squinting, holding her hands over her ears, coughing each time she tried to take a breath, tears streaming down her face.

He turned on the water, and a loud hissing issued from the lump.

''I'm sorry,'' she said.

''What?'' he asked, then shook his head and pushed past her. He grabbed a kitchen chair, dragged it over beside the wall and stood on it. Once he'd pulled the smoke alarm off the wall, he jerked out the battery.

The cessation of noise was so absolute the silence was almost as painful as the earlier din. Justin returned to the sink and simply stared at her, still gripping the hot pads in his hands.

She couldn't tell by his face if he was mad or not. ''I was making a cake.''

''You burned it.'' He said it simply, no inflection in his voice to hint at how angry he might be.

''I can explain,'' she began.

He turned from her and shut off the water. Staring at the hard black lump in the pan, he finally said, ''That was a cake?''

''Chocolate coconut,'' she confirmed.

He pushed open the window over the sink. The garage door was still open and the fan overhead was running.

''Do you want to hear my explanation now?''

''Daddy's home!'' Mickie came running into the house through the garage door.

Before she could say a word, Justin turned to greet his daughter—and froze. ''Mickie?'' His voice rose on the last syllable.

Mickie threw herself at her daddy's legs. "Don't I look beautiful?" she said, and gave him a hug.

He frowned at Sarah. "Yes, sweetheart, you look absolutely fabulous. You're my special little darling. Now, what are you doing in the house when the fire alarm is going off?"

"You're home and the alarm stopped." Mickie smiled up innocently at her daddy. "I wanted to see if Aunt Sarah had messed up the cake again."

"Thanks a lot, kiddo," Sarah muttered.

"It looks that way," Justin added.

Mickie sighed. "I guess after pizza I can have peanut butter and jelly for dessert."

Justin chuckled. "Sounds fine. You wanna run out back and play on the swing? I'd like to talk to your aunt Sarah while we clean this up. Besides, it's still sorta smelly in here, isn't it?" He wrinkled his nose as if smelling something really disgusting.

Mickie giggled. "You're silly, Daddy."

She skipped out the door and Sarah watched as she unlatched the gate and went into the backyard.

When she was gone, Justin turned back to Sarah. His smile was gone and his eyes were serious. "Care to explain what happened?"

She grimaced. "I did offer."

He tossed down the hot mitts and motioned her into the living room. After divesting himself of his suit jacket, he tossed it over the back of the couch and sank down. "Go on."

"Mickie decided that she wants to be a beautician."

"And?" he questioned when she hesitated.

"Well, I was making a cake—"

"I gathered that," he remarked dryly.

"And," she said, shooting him a dark look, "well, I didn't realize that Mickie might take it into her head to start practicing her salon skills immediately."

She settled on a chair, the adrenaline rush leaving her suddenly shaky. "I straightened it up as best I could, but that meant a lot of cutting. I'm sorry if it doesn't look good. I'm really sorry about the cake, too. I just got so involved with her..." She trailed off and shrugged.

"At least my house is still standing," he replied.

Sarah sighed and stood. "I have to clean the bathroom upstairs, then I guess I'll retire to my room for the night. I'm really sorry about all the trouble."

Justin sat up, alarm in his eyes as his gaze connected with hers. "Retire? Have you forgotten your promise to go out with me tonight?"

Sarah paused, but she kept her gaze steady as she replied, "After the mess I've made and the mess I'll have to leave the house in if I attend, you still want me to go?"

He shrugged, then leaned back in the chair looking nonchalant, as if she hadn't just caused a major disaster. "Accidents happen. And the housework will be here in the morning. Besides, Mickie is excited about the pizza. She doesn't need the cake tonight."

Sarah couldn't believe he still wanted her to go out with him. She smiled with relief. "Give me a few minutes to get ready."

Justin watched her rush up the stairs and chuckled

over her sudden energy. His heart was still beating a staccato over the fire alarm. All he could picture when he'd heard the blaring noise was Mickie and Sarah burning in the house before he could get to them. It had shaken him and awoken him to just how he felt about Sarah. In the past few weeks she'd become a part of his life, for better and worse.

Despite her forgetting to pick up Mickie and the other minor mishaps, things were working out well. At least, they had been until that fire alarm today. Talk about an eye-opening experience. He realized how much he'd come to enjoy having Sarah around. She was wonderful, fun, not at all the way she had been when he'd known her before Amy's death. She was also tender and caring, as Mickie's haircut attested.

Justin had been uncomfortable about taking Mickie to a salon for a haircut. Amy had always talked about letting Mickie's hair grow until she was old enough to decide for herself how she wanted it styled. She had insisted the child would want curly hair when she was older. Evidently, he hadn't realized Mickie had wanted to experience what her other friends had—a simple haircut. Or maybe she'd just wanted it to be short like Sarah's. Who knows? But one thing was certain—when Mickie had messed up her hair, Sarah had taken time with her to fix it in a very pretty style and had somehow made Mickie feel beautiful all at once.

She was good for Mickie. And Mickie was falling under her spell. Several nights he'd heard Sarah reading to Mickie before he got up there to tuck Mickie in. And they'd shared secret smiles occasionally—girl smiles, he called them.

And here he was taking Sarah out on a date tonight.

How had his feelings become involved? He had promised himself not to fall for a woman who couldn't love him back. He had insisted his odd feelings for Sarah were crazy and nothing could come of it. But now he discovered he already cared deeply for Sarah. He wasn't sure if it was love or not, but knew it could easily develop into that. His feelings today were a dead giveaway. When he'd heard the alarm, his first thought after Mickie was what would he do without Sarah?

He sighed. *Is it possible, Father, that she could actually come to love me one day? Could she forget it was her sister I married and her sister I made so unhappy that she ended up dying on a rainy highway? After all, she did come to apologize for trying to take Mickie away and says she shares the blame for the problems with Amy.*

Could she eventually come to love him?

There was only one way to find out. Things were going in a much different direction than he'd planned. So he would let things develop, ask Sarah out when he could, let her get to know him and spend time getting to know her. If it was God's will that she be his soul mate for the rest of his life, God would work things out between them. *I put it in your hands, Heavenly Father.*

He glanced at his watch and realized he needed to change if he was going to be downstairs and presentable when Christine got here with her granddaughter and he and Sarah were going to make it to the dinner engagement on time.

Hurrying up the stairs, he wondered just what their dinner was going to be like.

"Your meeting is at Jon Bilovi's?" Sarah asked, staring in surprise at the really nice restaurant. "I'd have worn something else if I'd known we were coming here."

Justin smiled, his gaze taking in her outfit. "Oh, no, Sarah. How could you say that? You're a knockout in that."

Sarah's hand went to the soft bun on her head—a nervous gesture to cover Justin's comment. What had he meant by that? Did he really like it? Was he just flirting with her? No, he wouldn't flirt. Of course not. It was just what a man said to a woman, though the look in his eyes made her nervous. He didn't find her attractive, did he?

He came around and opened her door. "Relax, sweetheart. Not meaning to hurt you," he said, shutting the door behind her and slipping his hand to the small of her back, "but you were engaged not too long ago. Surely you know how to take a compliment."

"Of course I do," she muttered. But André had never looked at her quite the way Justin had. That was what bothered her. Justin hadn't looked at her like *that* before, either. What was going on here?

"Who are we meeting?" she asked as they walked into the darkened restaurant and Justin escorted her to one of the back rooms.

"Phillip, my assistant, and his fiancée, Julie. He's tall, blond and has a megawatt smile. You'll like him. He's easy to get along with—as long as he's not involved in a business deal. And one of the lawyers we've just taken on to help with different things that need doing will be there. He'll also act as an adviser about certain laws in this state. His name is Drydan Watson and his wife, Barbara, should be with him."

Sarah stiffened, but Justin didn't notice, as he had removed his hand from her back and was stretching it out toward the very man who had caused Sarah's reaction.

Drydan Watson, her ex-boss and father of her ex-fiancé, sat at the table in the private dining room they'd just entered.

Sarah felt nauseous, thought about running away, then firmed her spine. *Father, please help me get through this,* she prayed. Pasting a smile on her face, she continued forward.

She noted the welcoming smiles on Phillip's and Julie's faces. Not so Drydan or his wife, Barbara, who turned her head to study a picture.

"And this is Sarah Connelly," Justin was saying as he pulled out the chair directly across from Drydan, "my sister-in-law."

Julie smiled and Phillip stood and shook her hand. Turning her smile upon Drydan, she said, "We've met," and seated herself.

An odd look flashed in Justin's eyes, then was gone as he took his seat at the head of the table.

"So, Drydan," Justin said, leaning forward and picking up his menu, "tell me what you think of the latest merger prospect of East Texas Software."

Drydan launched into his opinion and Sarah relaxed. As long as Justin kept him speaking, she could handle the situation. Barbara refused to look at her and Julie was making small talk.

Feeling a gaze on her, she glanced up to find Drydan staring right at her as Phillip snagged Justin's attention. She was shocked at the anger in his eyes.

Sarah realized Drydan was doing his best to make her uncomfortable.

And he was succeeding. Should she get up and leave? But that would hurt Justin. Perhaps just a short trip to the bathroom. But then Drydan might think her a coward.

With a sigh of resignation, she realized she would just have to put up with him. She didn't want to be here, though. After all, he was the one who had always thought her beneath his family. He and Barbara, that is, she added as she saw the way Barbara had drawn Julie's attention away from her.

The food came shortly, with conversation flowing easily around her. Justin had engaged her a few times in conversation, but after her monosyllabic answers, he stopped trying. She did make an effort to smile at him and reassure him she wasn't angry. She could feel the tension coming off him in waves. What could she say to Justin in front of these people?

She choked down every bite of food into a stomach that felt as though it was tied up in knots, and barely finished a third of her meal.

When Justin pushed back his chair, she knew she couldn't say polite goodbyes to these people. Her pain was too fresh. Besides, if she uttered one word to Drydan, she was certain he would reply something to embarrass her. He hadn't stopped shooting her looks all night.

"Excuse me, Justin," she said as he pulled her chair out. "I'll meet you out front."

Again he gave her that odd, piercing stare, then he nodded.

She escaped to the bathroom. As soon as the door was closed, she let her shoulders drop. André's parents. What had they thought of her being there with Justin tonight? Why would Justin associate with someone like them?

Of course, Drydan was a pretty good lawyer; he even went to church. But he certainly didn't practice what was preached. She'd always thought him a little intimidating. His wife was condescending while acting helpful. But André hadn't been like them. At least, she'd thought that. It was awful to find out she and Drydan were both working for the same man.

A shudder rippled through her.

At least she wouldn't have to see much of him, unless Justin invited him over for dinner.

After washing her hands, she quickly dried them, checked her hair and lipstick, then finally headed out the door. Justin would be waiting, and surely Drydan and his wife would be gone by now.

Drydan stood by the phones, talking into one, but the minute he saw her, he hung up.

"It sure didn't take you long, did it?"

Sarah braced herself. "I'm sorry you're bitter about my breakup with your son, but I have nothing to say, Mr. Watson," she said, trying to get around him. His large frame blocked her exit.

"I told André I had you pegged from the beginning. Jumping from one man to another, just as I said—another fortune hunter."

The blood drained from her face at his harsh and untrue words.

But Drydan wasn't done. "Does Justin know your little secret? Would he be so interested then, I wonder, if he found out?"

Infertile. He would tell Justin she was infertile just out of spite. The world spun and she thought she would have to rush right back into the bathroom and be sick. Then she realized something. "You won't tell him. It'd be too embarrassing for him to find out André had actually broken our engagement because he found out I was flawed."

She saw she'd scored a point.

Squaring her shoulders, she advanced. "And it wouldn't matter if you did, Mr. Watson. Justin is my brother-in-law and a good Christian man. I'm his housekeeper and sitter. There's no romantic relationship between us, so that wouldn't matter."

She strode past him through the space that had opened up when he'd stepped back in anger.

"Mark my words, missy. He won't have you. No man will when he finds out your secret."

She tuned out his voice and continued to the lobby.

She was heading toward the door, when a touch on her arm stopped her. She jumped and whirled around.

"Sarah, are you okay?" Justin stood there, looking, for all the world, like a concerned date.

No man will have you. She swallowed and tried to smile. "I'm fine. I thought you'd be outside."

"I didn't want you going to the car alone. Besides, I have a couple of questions to ask you."

They walked out of the restaurant together. "Oh?" she said, trying to sound carefree and failing miserably.

"The first is, do you still want to go to the movie?"

"Of course," she immediately replied.

"And the second…" he paused as he got to the car. Unlocking the door, he opened it and stepped back to allow her to enter.

She waited, but he didn't go on. Nor did he close the door. Finally, she looked up at him. That was what he'd been waiting for.

"What's going on between you and Drydan?"

She knew she was going to be sick.

Chapter Twelve

"Please just drive."

Justin watched Sarah as she visibly shook while trying to remove her purse strap from her shoulder. Such a simple task had become a major chore. He closed her door and went around to his side of the car. After sliding in, he started the car and drove off. He was halfway to the movie before she finally asked, "Why is Watson working for you?"

He shrugged. "Just one of the lawyers we hired to help with the overflow. He has a very sound head on his shoulders, has done wonders for other companies and is known as a very good attorney with contracts and such."

"Oh, he is. He's very good at what he does. Probably at the very top."

"How would you know that, Sarah?" But he had a feeling he knew. He'd never really heard the last name of her fiancé. Could it be—

"My ex-boss. I was engaged to his son."

Bingo.

"You see, he never liked me. Once André and I were serious, Drydan did everything in his power to get me to quit. He's the one who delivered the news that I was fired. And he enjoyed telling me a minute ago that I'd proven him true by chasing after you, hoping to cash in on your fortune."

"He said what!" The car swerved, but Justin immediately jerked the wheel, steering the vehicle back into his lane.

Sarah's eyes widened in shock as she stared at Justin. Her misery vanished as she realized Justin was absolutely furious. "I'm sorry, Justin. That's just Drydan. He doesn't like me and wanted to make sure he scored a few points. I didn't mean to cause any problems when I saw him by the phones. Maybe I should have just pleaded illness and left—"

"Not another word."

She snapped her mouth shut, taken aback by the savage sound of his voice.

"Don't apologize for things that aren't your fault. That's one pet peeve I have developed about you that's going to drive me crazy, Sarah. You take *too* much blame."

"You don't have to be mad at me!" she cried.

Justin shook his head, his anger cooling some. "I'm not mad at you. I'm angry at what I allowed to go on when I was only a few feet away. Why didn't you tell me, Sarah, that you were uncomfortable? I never would've stayed."

She shrugged. "It was a business meeting—"

"It could have taken place later."

"I didn't know that!" she argued, irritably.

"Point made," he said.

And she thought he actually grumbled the words. Turning, she saw he was frowning out the windshield. "Please, don't be angry," she said softly, sorry she had repeated what Drydan had told her.

Finally, he sighed. "I'll try. After all, I don't want you to think I'm *always* like this."

He actually gave her a small grin.

"I think I know that," she replied, smiling.

"Do you?" he asked quietly, intensely.

She didn't answer. She didn't have to because Justin returned his gaze to the street as they arrived at the movie theater.

After he parked, he came around and opened her door again. This time he reached in and took her hand. Shaking his head, he smacked his lips. "I think between the movie and you, that you, darlin', are going to be the better to watch."

She laughed. "What do you mean by that?"

"I'm taking you to one of those sappy romantic movies. I figured that's what all women would want to see." He gave her a long-suffering look.

"Actually," she replied, blithely lying, "I'm a horror person myself."

His eyes widened, then gleamed with amusement. "*Revenge of the Swamp Monster* is showing, if you prefer. I hear aliens came to Earth and repaired the creature so that he lives once again."

She burst out laughing and started across the parking lot with him. "I give in. Sappy, syrupy romance is fine."

While Sarah waited, Justin paid for two tickets. "It's been aeons since I've been to a movie theater," she confided as they went inside.

"Then I think you should enjoy first class," he replied, leading her over to the concessions.

"Oh, please, don't buy those. The prices at these counters are outrageous."

"You didn't eat any dinner. I don't want to sit through the entire show listening to your stomach growl."

She flushed.

He chuckled. "A 'monster buster popcorn,'" he said, reading from the menu, "and two medium drinks."

"You don't expect to eat all that popcorn, do you?" Sarah asked, aghast at the size of the popcorn he'd ordered.

"If we don't I can guarantee you that Mickie will finish off the leftovers. She eats about half of one of these whenever we come to the movies. She loves popcorn."

"As much as peanut butter and jelly?"

"I don't think so." He grinned. "Of course, you have to understand, in six months or so she'll have another all-time-favorite food."

They found seats just in time—the lights were already dimming. Sarah had never realized how close the seats were before. Justin's arm brushed hers as he jerked on his jacket before finally getting it off. His light musky cologne wafted over to her and she inhaled it, enjoying the scent and the warmth of his presence next to her.

How could she have guessed he would have stood up for her against Drydan? Even André hadn't done that. André had only shrugged and said his father and mother were worried about him. He'd never been outraged or offended by the way his parents had insulted her. But Justin had. And he'd felt upset he hadn't been there to defend her. It gave her a very warm, special feeling to know he wasn't angry with her.

She turned her attention to the screen and began to eat popcorn. Occasionally, their hands would bump and she and Justin would each offer an "Excuse me." The tension—tension she was still surprised to find between them—built.

She was so nervous she missed the entire movie. All she caught was that it was about two people who fell in love, but the disclosure of some deep dark secret broke them apart. In the end, love overcame the obstacle.

The story line did nothing for her stretched nerves. There was no love between her and Justin. She felt only an attraction. He'd invited her out and let her feel like an adult for a night. However, the plot, along with Drydan's words, made her wonder how Justin would feel if he suddenly found out what had originally motivated her to pray and finally come see him.

Would he be hurt? Angry? Bitter?

It wasn't that she didn't care for him, that she hadn't wanted to see Mickie before she'd found out she was infertile. It was just that…what?

That her priorities hadn't been right? That she'd had so many things going in her life that she'd relegated Justin and Mickie to the far corners of her mind?

They were all awful reasons, but all true. How self-centered she could be? The occasional brush of his leg or arm was driving her crazy! she thought, distracted once again by the warm, intimate brush of his trousers against her nylon-covered leg.

"You ready?"

She blinked, glanced at Justin and realized the credits were just coming up on the screen. She nodded. "A good movie," she said.

"I should have chosen action." He chuckled, then winked. "I would've gotten more of a reaction from you."

She laughed, not sure what he meant. His warm hand slipped to her back and again she recognized how much of a gentleman Justin was.

He escorted her to the car and closed the door behind her before slipping in on his own side. The ride was quiet, not filled with chatter, as they drove along the highway.

"Did you really enjoy the movie?" he asked as they approached his house.

"Very much," Sarah murmured. "Or, at least, going out. I hadn't realized just how much my world had started revolving around Mickie and housework."

He chuckled again, a husky sound that sent shivers down her arms.

"I force myself to take off at least once a month and go to a museum during lunch or just for a walk. It not only gets me away from the office but gives me time to relax and think about what I have, how lucky I am. Just to enjoy being a person instead of a dad or a president of his own company.''

"Well, I can say it was nice. I think I'd forgotten what quiet is. Or just sitting still."

He pulled into the driveway, right into the garage, and turned off the engine. The garage light automatically came on, illuminating the way to the kitchen door.

She pushed open her own door and slipped out of the car before he could come around.

"Shame on you," he chided, standing in front of the vehicle.

She shrugged. "You're tired."

He smiled, an odd smile. "Now, why would you say that?"

"You've been so quiet."

"I was just thinking," he replied, escorting her to the door.

His hand was at her back again, the light touch thoroughly distracting her.

Reaching into his pocket, he pulled out his keys—and promptly dropped them.

Sarah, nervous for some unknown reason, tried to get them at the same time he did. She chuckled self-consciously and stood back up, only to find she was inches from Justin. Her gaze snapped up to his.

Justin's eyes darkened as he looked at her face, her eyes and, finally, her mouth.

Frozen, Sarah watched as his head bent. Slowly, his mouth closed the distance to her lips.

Her breathing increased.

What in the world is happening? her mind screamed

at her. *This is Justin!* But it didn't matter. She felt warm, strong hands on her arms, and then she was being pulled against Justin's hard frame. She relaxed in his embrace as she told herself no. Then she lifted her lips to his.

Warm, soft, tender. Those were the words to describe how it felt to be kissed by Justin Warner. His arms slid behind her and held her to him; his lips touched hers and caressed her tenderly, then with more urgency. She kissed him back, a tumult of warm, sweet emotions swirling within her.

Then Justin eased back. When she opened her eyes, he was staring at her in shock.

Her own breathing was unsteady. But she flushed at the surprised look on his face. "What? Have I grown two heads?" she quipped, but her voice came out like a croak, definitely not normal.

Justin didn't get the chance to answer, she was thankful, for Christine showed up at the door and pulled it open.

"I thought I heard you get home. Did you forget your key?"

Justin stepped back. Sarah immediately slipped around Christine. "Good night. Thanks," she called, and strode quickly toward the stairs.

Have I grown two heads? Great line, Connelly, she admonished herself. She went into Mickie's room and kissed the little girl good-night, then hurried into her room before Justin could catch her, if he even intended to.

She didn't bother with a shower, and instead changed

right into her nightie. No way was she going to risk going out there and running into Justin again.

She flipped out the light and in a few minutes heard his tread up the stairs. It sounded as if he hesitated outside her door but then went on. She wasn't sure. She was thankful he hadn't knocked if he had indeed passed by.

Oh, how she was thankful. She'd had no business kissing Justin like that. She was his employee, nothing more. No wonder he looked shocked.

True, he had initiated the kiss. Was it possible he'd felt responsible for what had happened at the restaurant and had thought to apologize, then reacted to the yearning for him he'd seen in her eyes? Or maybe it had just been one of those fluke things. After all, there was a full moon tonight, and full moons made people go crazy, didn't they?

She pulled the covers over her head. She didn't want to think about it. She couldn't think about it. She had just come out of a bad relationship with André, a man she'd *thought* she'd loved, though she realized now she had just enjoyed his company.

André was sweet, but there had never been a real spark between them. He certainly hadn't caused the reaction in her that Justin had just caused.

No, she would not compare them. Justin was…Justin. Her brother-in-law and her employer. That was all. And he would stay that. She would make sure to forget what had happened, then he wouldn't have to look so shocked again.

Yes, that's what she'd do. She couldn't afford to get

close to someone else a second time. She knew he'd forgiven her for the past, but he wouldn't forgive her if he found out she was infertile. He would believe that was the only reason she'd come back in the first place. And he'd be basically right. She wouldn't be able to argue, and he'd throw her out and probably refuse to allow her to see Mickie again. There would be hurt all around.

Dear Father, what have I done? Please, please, please help me to ignore my feelings and just do the job I came here to do.

She admitted she'd wanted to get to know Mickie and Justin, too—but not that way. Only hurt could come of it. She touched her lips, recalling their kiss, then gasped when she realized what she was doing.

Burrowing her head under her pillow, she vowed that tomorrow she would force herself to forget what had happened tonight. Yes, as the old saying went, tomorrow was another day. She'd start fresh, avoid Justin if necessary. But she would, in no way, let him think she was interested in more than a working relationship…no matter what her heart and lips were telling her.

Chapter Thirteen

"**I**'m a singing angel!"

Sarah swung around from the counter, where she was putting the finishing touch on a bowl of potato salad. Mickie bounced into the kitchen from the garage door, Justin right behind her.

Looking as handsome as ever. Almost two weeks after that kiss and she couldn't seem to stop noticing how good he looked. He wore a pair of well-worn jeans, boots and a soft tan shirt with a darker pullover sweater. His hair was tousled from the crisp, cool November wind and his cheeks had just a hint of color.

"My little angel. Of course she sings," Justin teased.

"No, Daddy," Mickie said, exasperation in her voice. "Daddy took me by the school today to see the posted list—after we got the cranberries for the meal—and my name was under the singing angels! Aunt Sarah, can you make my costume?"

Sarah, who was smiling happily at her niece, suddenly winced. "Um, honey…" She trailed off.

Justin, evidently seeing her dilemma, scooped up his daughter and gave her whisker brushes against her cheeks, earning a squeal. "If Auntie Sarah can't, we'll find someone who can, pumpkin."

Sarah felt she'd let Mickie down—and Justin, if he felt he had to distract his daughter—so, she piped up, "I can certainly go to school and see what the other parents are doing and if I don't think I can, then I'll find you someone, sweetie. Is that a deal?"

Mickie squirmed from her daddy's grasp, then ran over and wrapped her arms around Sarah's legs, almost overturning her. "Deal," she said.

The doorbell rang.

"I'll get it," Mickie yelled, heading for the door at a dead run.

For the first time in over a week, Sarah was alone with Justin. His scrutiny made her nervous. To cover her unease, she turned back to the counter and stirred the potato salad. Justin had picked up the rest of the food from a local restaurant. All she had to make was potato salad, then serve what Bill and his wife brought.

Justin started forward and she stiffened. There had been an uncomfortable truce since the night she'd run off and hidden in her room. She wasn't looking forward to discussing it. She'd thought maybe Justin had regretted it as much as she did. After all, he had suddenly had all these extra hours he'd had to put in. It was only last night when she'd called Justin for something that Christine had mentioned he always doubled his hours just before Thanksgiving and Christmas. She said it was to catch up so he could have free time.

Now, with the look on his face and the way he was approaching, she was afraid he was going to broach the subject of their embrace. A subject she'd prefer to leave undiscussed.

The sound of the door whooshing open was a relief. No longer alone, she felt safe to relax. Arms snaked around her and she jumped, before she realized it wasn't Justin. "Hi there, sweetheart, gotta hug for me?"

"Bill!" Sarah turned in his arms and gave him an enthusiastic hug.

He chuckled. "Gonna have my wife scalping me if you don't watch it."

"And where is she?" Sarah demanded, stepping back. "I haven't seen her in at least three months."

"I've been keeping her busy taking care of me since we got married." He nodded and shook Justin's hand. "She's playing with Mickie. Here are some deviled eggs," he said, handing Sarah a platter covered with foil. "I'll be right back with the ham."

He paused at the door and winked. "I just might have an announcement later that you'll be interested in. Come on, Justin, say hi to Marcy while I get the ham."

Justin followed him out. Sarah was relieved. She put the platter on the counter next to the potato salad and went to the sink to wash her hands. The door whooshed back open. "Just place the ham on the counter, Bill, and I'll let Justin cut it up."

"Unfortunately, I'm not Bill."

Sarah whirled, slinging water over the countertop. She

grabbed a towel to wipe her hands and mop up the mess, remembering to turn off the water as she did. Only a moment of silence lingered before Justin sauntered over and leaned against the counter near her.

"Why do I have a feeling you'd be more comfortable if I *were* Bill?"

"That's not true," she said, but didn't lift her eyes.

"You've been avoiding me," he said softly.

"No!" she denied quickly.

"Yes," he countered quietly.

She shrugged, not liking the look in his eyes. Oh, why had she avoided him and let the unknown build between them? She didn't like confrontations anymore. Not with him. Justin always won.

"Does this have to do with the other night?"

"No," she denied again, lifting her chin and meeting his eyes.

A gleam appeared in his eyes at her challenging stance. "Yes," he whispered.

"If you have all the answers, why ask?" she demanded, disagreeably.

"I have a feeling this has to do with that guilt thing again," he said, stepping closer.

He was right. How did he know she was feeling guilty for practically attacking him on his own doorstep? She refused to answer, mutely staring at him.

"Tic tac toe?" he said, turning to where his hip was leaning against the counter. He dropped his arms, allowing his right elbow to rest on the counter. "Three no's in a row?"

With his left hand, he reached out and snagged her

elbow to keep her from backing any farther away. "You've nothing to feel guilty about unless you were only kissing me out of obligation."

Sarah saw the sudden watchful gaze in his eyes and realized he really didn't know how she felt. Though she wouldn't enlighten him on the latter, she would put his mind at ease on the former. "No," she whispered, aching at the thought of ever intentionally hurting this man's feelings again.

"Good," he said, and satisfaction shone in his eyes. Before she knew what he was doing, he grabbed both her arms and pulled her forward. "Because I've wanted to do this again since that night."

He lowered his head and pressed his lips to hers.

He felt so good. His arms slid around her and his head turned, slanting gently across her mouth as he expertly showed her exactly how much he enjoyed sharing this kiss.

Sarah trembled even as she held on to handfuls of his sweater and returned the kiss. This felt so good, so right. He was gentle, tender, demanding, patient. He was perfect.

"Ahem."

Sarah pushed back and dazedly glanced toward the source of the noise. She immediately flushed when she saw Bill standing there, nonchalantly leaning against the counter near the door. "Excuse me," she said. She grabbed the potato salad and headed into the other room.

The door swished shut behind her. The silence was thick for a moment before Bill finally asked, "Did I see what I thought I saw?"

"You saw a kiss," Justin replied.

"Oh, yeah, Justin. I saw a kiss...and much more. The look on your face is more than just a kiss."

Justin stiffened, but Bill held up a hand. "Hey, I think it's great. But she *is* living here."

Justin sighed and ran a weary hand through his hair. "I agree this isn't the best situation. I know it's important to avoid all appearance of impropriety. However, I've given this over two weeks of thought, Bill.

"Mrs. Winters will be home in another week or two. I talked with her last night. She's more than willing to come back here on a part-time basis until I can find a new sitter. I have a couple of openings coming up at work, jobs that Sarah is qualified for that will give her enough money to afford a place of her own."

"Wow," Bill said, low. "That serious, huh?"

Justin nodded. "I think so."

"So, what about until then?" he asked.

Justin turned toward the window and stared out. "We're both adults. We're both Christian, with moral values. We know how to behave, even though we're attracted to each other."

"Said Adam to God just before Eve showed up."

"Very funny," Justin said when Bill chuckled.

"I'm sorry," Bill replied. "Look, I love you both. You're like a brother and Sarah is like a sister. I'd hate for anything to happen between you that you'd regret later."

"We have a sitter. Mickie, if you've forgotten."

"Who has an earlier bedtime," Bill reminded him. "Anyway, if things get too intense, please twist Sarah's arm to take that garage apartment that's empty at my house. I've told her she's always welcome. Hey, I'll admit she wouldn't take it before, but I just bet she'd let me help her out now.''

Justin turned back to his friend. "Thanks, Bill. I will."

The door swung open and Sarah warily walked back into the kitchen. "So, do I get to watch the football game here?" Bill asked Justin.

Justin groaned. "As long as it's Dallas we watch."

"You know that's not my team."

Sarah hurried past, grabbed some other dishes, shot a glance at both men, then gave Bill a dark look. "You wanna eat, help me set the table." She went back out.

Bill grinned, grabbed some of the dishes and said, "She knows I was reading you the riot act."

Justin picked up the platter of eggs. "She knows and she doesn't like anyone interfering in her life."

"So sue me," he said, and followed Sarah out the door.

Sarah decided the meal went fine. Thanksgiving was a joyous occasion, she thought, smiling wistfully, especially when it was shared with family and friends. André's family had been so formal, exchanging only polite talk. Here, there was joking and any subject was open for debate.

And joke telling was the most popular, especially when she and Mickie got into a contest to see who could come up with the corniest jokes.

"Hey, Aunt Sarah, April showers bring May flowers. What do *Mayflowers* bring?"

Sarah looked stumped.

Everyone else at the table said in unison, "Pilgrims!"

Sarah chuckled. "Please no more, dear. You beat me hands down on the jokes."

Mickie giggled.

Bill interrupted the gaiety with a big smile. "Well, I can't think of a better time to tell our news than now, when we're with our spiritual family, can you, Marcy?"

Sarah was smiling, but at the sudden glow in Marcy's eyes, Sarah's smile froze. Bill and Marcy had been married only three months. Surely their news couldn't be...

"Well, come on," Justin said. "Don't keep us in suspense."

Bill grabbed Marcy's hand. "Marcy is due the last part of June. We're gonna have a baby."

"Congratulations!" Justin exclaimed, jumping up and slapping Bill on the back.

"Congratulations," Sarah echoed, smiling at Marcy, even though the edge of her vision was turning black.

She hadn't realized someone else's news would hurt so much. Of course, it was the first time she'd been confronted with this since her own news.

"Why do you have to wait till June?" Mickie demanded.

Marcy smiled. "Well, it takes that long for the baby in my tummy to get big enough to be born."

Mickie immediately jumped up and ran around the table. Looking at her stomach, she studied it a long moment. Finally, she asked, "How'd it get in there?"

Bill laughed.

Marcy turned pink.

"We'll discuss that later, sweetheart," Justin said.

"Maybe when I get a brother or sister of my own?" she asked.

It was Justin's turn to blush.

Sarah felt like throwing up. With as good a smile as she could manage, she stood. "I'll be right back."

She headed toward the back of the house for the guest bathroom. But that wasn't where she was going. She wanted to be alone. After slipping into the darkened study, she softly closed the door behind her.

As soon as she was sure she wouldn't be overheard, she broke down. *Why, God? Why? I don't begrudge Marcy her child. I'm happy for her and Bill. But I'm jealous too, envious, even hurt. Why won't I ever have children of my own?*

Deep racking sobs shook her body and she cried out all her pain and rage. *It doesn't seem fair. I love children. I've always wanted children. Why?*

She ranted and raved within as she reached out to heaven in beseeching appeal. Finally, a peace settled into her heart and she knew that no matter what, she would serve God. Sometimes, she wouldn't know the reasons here on Earth, but one day, in heaven, she'd know, and understand why the doctor had this diagnosis.

She found the box of tissues, blew her nose and tried to repair her makeup. She knew she'd been gone too long but hoped she'd have time to sneak upstairs and cover her blotchy red face before anyone found her.

However, even that small peace was denied her as the door opened behind her. She could only hope it was Mickie.

"Sarah?"

It just *had* to be Justin.

"Um-hmm?" she answered, afraid her voice would give away her crying jag.

The door shut behind him. "What's the matter? I could tell something troubled you at the table."

She kept her head down as Justin approached. When he placed his hand under her chin and urged her to look up, she resisted. But she could tell he wasn't going to take no for an answer.

Slowly, she allowed him to lift her face to his scrutiny. "Oh, Sarah," he said, concern etching his voice. "What happened to cause this?"

She shrugged, his compassion nearly releasing a fresh flood of tears.

"When Marcy announced—"

He got no further. She stiffened.

"What?" he asked determinedly, though he said it with a gentle insistence.

"Nothing."

"Is it Marcy or maybe Bill?" His eyes widened. "Surely you're not jealous that Bill is married and having a baby."

"No!" she denied, but could tell he was still suspicious that he'd found the answer. "Honestly," she said, because now it was true. She had been jealous and envious for a moment. But now she was just sad, aching for something she would never have.

He wasn't going to believe her unless she told him the truth. She could already see him mentally pulling away. She should let him. It would be best for both of them. No, it would be best for her. It would hurt him unnecessarily. "I just want kids and don't have any," she finally admitted, feeling fresh tears in her eyes.

"Oh, Sarah," he murmured, and pulled her into his arms.

This time she couldn't control the tears that wet the front of his shirt as he stroked her back and her hair over and over, murmuring and praying as she cried her heart out anew.

Slowly, her tears subsided. Justin continued to hold her. Lifting her tear-drenched face, she whispered rawly, "I'm so sorry you saw me this way."

Tenderly, he shook his head. "Never, ever apologize for your pain, Sarah. We all have pain and it hurts us to hold it in, especially as painful as yours seems to be. God put us on this Earth and told us to bear one another's burdens. I'm here for you. Bill is, too. And Marcy. As is my pastor, who happens to adore you, you know. Never, ever think you have to hold such a load by yourself."

He stroked her cheek and she was so thankful for the man she'd come to work for. He was more than just a brother-in-law, much more than she'd thought he was back when she'd first met him. He was the man she loved.

Her heart flip-flopped at the realization.

She loved him.

And she was infertile.

That could have easily brought on a new round of crying if he hadn't chosen that moment to lower his head and kiss her. He feathered his mouth over hers, then over her eyes, her cheeks and finally her mouth again.

What he gave her in his kiss felt like life-giving nectar for a starving soul.

"Bill told me I could come check on you."

Mickie's small voice at the door caused them both to break apart. Once again Sarah was mortified, until she heard Justin's dark reply, "Thank you, Bill."

A giggle escaped her. Justin sighed and abruptly sat down on the couch. His reaction pulled another, then another, giggle out of her.

Soon Justin's strained chuckle joined her voice and the tension was relieved.

But Sarah knew, deep down, the problems had just begun.

Chapter Fourteen

At the sound of the doorbell, Sarah came jogging down the stairs. "That's probably the lady with the pattern for your outfit, Mickie," Sarah said as Mickie dashed from the kitchen. "The president of the PTA promised to have someone bring it to me today, even if it is the day after Thanksgiving."

"I'll get it!" Mickie cried, grabbing the door even as Justin came out of the kitchen, where he and Mickie had been making cookies.

Sarah slowed her sprint to a sedate walk, not wanting to be caught running down the stairs.

Justin grinned and smiled giving her a "I know that bad habit from Mickie and you can't trick me" look.

She reached the front door just as Mickie swung it open. And Sarah wished she'd stayed upstairs and let Justin handle it.

"Come on in, Miss Stephanie."

Stephanie smiled her saccharine-sweet smile and maneuvered her way inside. "Why, hello, Sarah. I bet you didn't expect it to be me who brought this by, but I told Mary Ann that I just lived right around the corner practically and knew you wouldn't want to get out—well, hi, Justin," she said, feigning shock. "What are you doing home today?"

Sarah sighed and took the pattern Stephanie thrust in her hands as she walked past.

"It is the day after Thanksgiving, Mrs.—Stephanie," he said.

As if the woman hadn't known he'd be here, Sarah thought, disgusted.

"Well, Mary Ann told me Sarah had called with concerns about the outfit for Mickie and I just had to come over to make sure Mickie was going to get what she needed. It's such a shame she doesn't have someone who can sew and do all those little things for her. Isn't that right, sweetheart?" Stephanie cooed to Mickie, who had come over to get the pattern and look at it.

Sarah wanted to hug Mickie when she said, "Oh, Aunt Sarah will take care of everything," and then beamed up at her.

Stephanie only looked disconcerted for a moment before turning back to Justin. "I hope you had a nice Thanksgiving. Though my husband is dead, I make sure to cook a fresh turkey every year with all the trimmings. I feel it's important for the children to experience traditions, not the store-bought things so many people are serving up these days."

Did the woman have a spy watching their every move? Sarah wondered with displeasure. Stephanie could make her feel a failure faster than any other woman she knew. And Justin just stood there and smiled politely. It was really nauseating.

"We had friends over," Justin said.

"You had friends over? I'm sure they appreciated your housekeeper's cooking, then."

Justin, thankfully, didn't rise to the bait. He smiled. "We had an enjoyable time."

"I must say, the house has stood up tolerably well, considering poor little Mickie has only had a string of sitters. You've done an admirable job. You should also be very proud of the part she got in the play. Not all the little girls are getting to be a front-row angel."

Sarah rolled her eyes. This cooing over Justin was going to go on forever. And she refused to stand here and listen to it while being purposely ignored by the woman. With a smile, she said, "Excuse me. I have some chores to take care of."

Justin narrowed his eyes slightly, but Stephanie looked smug. Sarah merely smiled sweetly, patted Mickie as she walked past where she clung to her daddy's leg and headed up the stairs.

Sarah did have work to do. Maybe it was wrong to leave the way she had, but she didn't like standing there watching another woman coo over Justin.

Mickie said it was tradition to get down the Christmas ornaments the day after Thanksgiving and she'd looked so wistful that Sarah hadn't been able to resist. Since Justin had offered to make cutout cookies with Mickie—something Sarah had never done before—Sarah had decided to explore the attic and surprise Mickie with the ornaments. She had just pulled down the ladder to the attic that was located at the end of the hallway near Justin's room, when the doorbell had rung.

She'd rather be searching for ornaments than listening to Stephanie.

She climbed up the attic and moved boxes around until she found one labeled "Christmas." With a sigh she pulled it out. Just as she was about to open it, she found a smaller one, farther back, covered in dust and spider webs. She supposed as housekeeper, cleaning the attic would fall to her, too. It certainly needed it. This one said "X-mas" on it. But this one, unlike the other one, was labeled in Amy's handwriting.

Sarah pulled it out and opened it.

Well, she'd found the ornaments. Fond memories assailed her as she pulled them out. Each girl had her own collection of ornaments as they'd grown up. Their mother had said it was a tradition they should keep and that when they married, their first tree would have memories on it.

Amy had been much more creative than Sarah. She had made her own ornaments each year, in addition to the one her parents would buy her. One by one Sarah pulled them out and touched them, remembering how they had been lovingly crafted.

"Those were Amy's."

Sarah looked up to see Justin's head and shoulders poking through the entrance. "Mickie's playing Nintendo. I was looking for you and saw the ladder down."

"Running from Stephanie?" A soft smile curved her lips.

"Thank you for leaving me there with her," he muttered darkly, and came up the stairs. "She's gone, too. I told her I had to find my housekeeper and explain the rules of decorum."

"You didn't!" Sarah gasped.

He chuckled. "Consider yourself properly chastised."

She chuckled. "I promised Mickie I'd get these down for her. She said you always brought them out of the attic the day after Thanksgiving."

"Not those," he said.

Sarah's hands stilled. "I don't understand."

Justin pulled over a small trunk and sat down next to her. He took the small tan cloth ornament with a Christmas tree cross-stitched on it. "I haven't used these since Amy died."

"I'm so sorry." Sarah realized her blunder. "I saw this box." She indicated the nearer one. "And then this one. I just thought you must have kept your ornaments separate."

He rubbed his thumb over the material. "She was so proud of these. They were so filled with memories for her. The year she died, well, it was only a week after Thanksgiving and I just couldn't bring myself to use her ornaments. We went out and bought all new ones."

"Oh, Justin," she whispered, her heart breaking. She started to reach for the ornament he had, but he stopped her.

Taking the box from her lap, he began to go through it. "This one she said she made when she was sixteen." He held up two hearts entwined.

Sarah chuckled. "She was certain she was in love and

was going to stitch the names in there when the boy declared himself.''

Rummaging through the box, he found another one. "She made this one when Mickie was born.''

A cradle with the year on it in blues and greens graced the front of the small stuffed pillow-shaped ornament. "It's beautiful.''

She fingered one and tears touched her eyes. "This was one of my favorites.'' She held up one with a cross that had a cradle in front of it. "She made this one the year she asked Jesus into her heart.''

Justin sighed, put the other ornaments back into the box, then dropped his head. "You know, Sarah, I really loved Amy. It was a comfortable, caring relationship, one I went into because I thought she loved me.''

"I know,'' Sarah replied. And though it sounded funny for her to be saying that to Justin, she realized it was the truth. No matter what she'd thought in the past, she knew Justin wasn't the type to marry Amy out of a sense of obligation or guilt. She silently asked why her parents had encouraged Amy to marry him. It had only ended up hurting everyone involved. Amy just didn't know how to say no. The only time she had tried, she'd died out on a lonely road, alone. "I miss her.''

Justin slipped an arm around her and gave Sarah a small squeeze. "I do, too. It was really hard when she first died. There was so much guilt over her death and I had a small child and I didn't know what I was going to do. I blamed Amy for leaving me. But slowly, day after day, I began to function again, and now, when I think about Amy, it's like another lifetime, bittersweet.

I loved her, but we were both young, inexperienced. I was so different. I know she's happy where she is now and the only thing I still grieve over is that Mickie won't know her.''

''She remembers bits and snatches.''

''I wonder if she does or if it's that I remind her.''

He slipped his arm from around her and put the lid on the ornaments. ''Whichever,'' he said, tucking the box under his arm, ''I think it's time to bring these back out and start some new memories of our own.''

''Our own?'' she asked, shocked at what he'd said.

''Mickie and me,'' he said, and looked at her strangely.

Oh, of course. Now, why had she thought he was referring to her? ''I agree. It'll be nice for Mickie to have the ornaments for herself. Our mom said we could do whatever we wanted with our ornaments. And I'm sure Amy would want her daughter to have hers.''

''You have some, too?''

Sarah flushed. ''Yes. Both Amy and I did.''

''Would you like to add them to the tree?''

Sarah immediately shook her head. ''No. They'd get mixed up when it was time to take the tree down, and well, they're in storage and everything.''

She would've sworn Justin looked disappointed. ''Well, if you'd like to see them,'' she offered shyly.

''That'd be great!'' He stood. ''Let me push the other box over to the entrance, then I'll stand below to catch it.''

''You sure you don't have Stephanie down there to watch your macho show of strength,'' she teased.

"Maybe you've considered remarriage and think you have to impress her."

He paused by the stairs and turned back to her. There was no teasing glint in his eyes. No, he looked very serious when he said, "Stephanie is mainly attracted to my bank account. I can guarantee you, I'll only be marrying someone who can love me in the truest sense of the word."

The look in his eyes sent a shiver of awareness through her. She nervously licked her lips and wiped her hands on her jeans. Oh, she could love him in the truest sense of the word, and easily, but she wondered if he could love her when he found out her secret.

The sound of Mickie thudding up the stairs, and her voice, broke the spell, "Telephone, Aunt Sarah!"

She smiled, albeit shakily. "Saved by the bell."

He smiled back. "Only a reprieve, Sarah. We'll have to discuss these emotions bouncing around between us sooner or later."

She climbed down the stairs, then ran to the library so she could have some privacy. She couldn't think of who had the phone number here, or even who would be calling her.

"I want to know what you told your boss that caused him to take his business away from my firm." The nasty voice of Drydan Watson reverberated through the phone.

"I don't know what you're talking about."

"Oh, don't play dumb with me, missy. I know you're wrapping Justin around your little finger. That's the only reason he'd trade a reputable firm such as mine for a smaller, no-name outfit. I purposely didn't call his work today but instead called you to warn you that if you don't do something to get Watson and Watson back in his good graces, your little secret is going to be out.''

Sarah, who had been stunned by hearing his voice, now got angry. ''Go ahead and tell him, Drydan. It doesn't matter to me.''

''When you lose your power over him it will. After all, who's paying your bills, letting you live in his house, eat his food and who knows what else under his roof? It'll matter plenty if you don't do something. I'll give you until the first of January. After all, with the holidays, he won't have much time to get anything done. But come January 1, if you haven't convinced Justin that everything you've said about my family is lies, he's going to know your guilty little secret.''

The phone slammed in her ear.

Slowly, she replaced her receiver. So Justin had let Drydan Watson go. Was it because of what she'd told him? Justin had certainly been furious.

For some reason, that brought a bit of joy to her heart. Justin had actually defended her by dropping Drydan and hiring someone else. A silly grin spread across her face. If she hadn't loved him before, she certainly did now.

Why would he do such a thing over Drydan's stupid tantrums? She knew Drydan Watson would get over his anger and things would go on. He only stepped on those smaller than him or those who threatened him in some way. She'd been a threat to his son, so he'd made sure to stomp out that threat. But now she was a threat to him through Justin's business.

Her smile left her face. That meant Drydan just might reveal her secret to Justin in order to get even.

"Hey, I forgot to ask you what I'd wanted to when I hunted you down earlier."

Sarah whirled, finding Justin at the door.

"Are you okay? Bad news?" He indicated the telephone by cutting his eyes to the instrument, then back to her.

"No. No, you just startled me."

His smile returned. "Well, I remember what it was that I forgot when I saw the ornaments."

He came into the room, brushing at his light blue sweater, then wiping his hands on his jeans. "The decorations are only part of the tradition. I'm a firm believer in traditions and I've decided Mickie is old enough to appreciate a live Christmas tree."

He pulled his wallet out of the desk and stuffed it in his back pocket. "So this year I've decided it's time to take Mickie to a Christmas-tree farm. I thought she would really enjoy it. What do you think?"

Sarah nodded. "She'd love it. We always begged our parents for a real tree, but they hated the pine needles."

Justin smiled. "I have a housekeeper. I don't have to worry about cleaning up pine needles."

"Thanks a lot," she said, laughing.

"Good. Grab your jacket or sweater. It's cool out today. I'll get Mickie's pullover and we can go. We should get there just about sunset."

"You want me to go with you?" Sarah asked, surprised.

Justin had the audacity to look affronted. "Of course

I do. Who else will I be able to pawn Mickie off on if she gets too excited over this new event?''

"Again, thank you," Sarah said, though she wasn't upset. She was actually very excited to be included.

Justin smiled his smug smile. "Anytime. Now go! I'll get the four-by-four warmed up."

Chapter Fifteen

❧

"A real-live Christmas tree?" Mickie exclaimed as Justin drove the truck into the tree lot.

"That's right. Any one you decide on," Justin said.

Sarah shot him a warning look. "But I bet you'd sure like your daddy's opinion."

Mickie nodded. "I know exactly what I want. It's got to be big, and just right."

The vehicle stopped and she jumped out. Sarah was slower pushing open her front door, but she was just as excited. Justin chuckled and slid out his side of the truck. "You both look awed."

"I've never been here. I didn't know they grew trees in rows," she said, regarding the lines and lines of trees. "I thought this was just a piece of property and you had to go out and hunt in the forest."

"You've been neglected." He tsked, took a handsaw from the person at the gate, then caught up to where his daughter impatiently waited for them. "They have a hay ride and a gift shop and a place where you can order special trees, and even some trees, that have been shipped from up north—trees you normally wouldn't see down here. Come on.''

The person told them where everything was located and they started down the paths. ''Oh, here's one, Daddy,'' Mickie immediately exclaimed, stopping in front of a tree not quite four feet high. ''Except that it's not as tall as you and it's got a big hole in the daddy branches.''

''Daddy branches?'' Justin asked.

''Yeah, you know, daddy branches.'' She pointed at another one. ''The mama branches have a hole in that one.''

''Honey, I don't know what you mean, either,'' Sarah said as she hurried behind the young girl, trying to keep step with Justin.

''You know, daddy, mama and children branches. That's how my teacher explained it.''

When Sarah shrugged Mickie explained. ''Daddy branches hold up the mama branches and mama branches hold up the children branches, then the baby branch goes on top for the star.''

Sarah was still confused, but Justin had evidently caught on. Mickie grabbed his hand and stood him next to a tree to compare the height, then shook her head and walked on.

''You wanna translate, Justin?'' Sarah asked, trailing along beside them.

''She's got quite an interesting teacher. They have an artificial tree at school and I imagine she means the

A-shape of the tree, the larger branches on the bottom being the daddy branches and so on.''

Light dawned in Sarah's eyes, then she lifted an eyebrow in disbelief. ''That's what they're teaching kids in school?''

Justin shrugged. ''I guess it's a way to explain the family unit or something. As I said, this teacher is very inventive. Had Mickie not been in her class all year, I would've been stumped, too. But this explanation of a tree is mild compared with some of the things Mickie has told me.''

Mickie stopped him several more times but found fault with each tree. It was finally Sarah who noted it was almost completely dark out, that gently suggested a tree to Mickie. ''Oh, yes, Aunt Sarah. This one is perfect. My own mama couldn't have picked out a more perfect tree. See how much taller it is than Daddy. It reaches way up and will almost touch the sky.''

''And our ceiling,'' Justin murmured.

''You can cut it if it's too big,'' Sarah said, afraid they'd end up on another trek if Mickie changed her mind.

''Right there, Daddy. Cut it.''

Justin crawled underneath the tree and began to saw. ''Wait a minute, it's tipping,'' Sarah warned, reaching out for it. ''Get back, Mickie, so it won't fall on you.''

Sarah leaned over the large branches and grabbed near the top to try to steady the tree. She realized too late how far off balance this put her. ''Watch out, Justin!''

She jerked back, but too late. The weight of the falling tree propelled her forward. She let out a squeak and landed right on top of the tree, which had fallen directly on top of Justin.

A grunt was all she heard. She tried to scramble off the tree as gingerly as possible.

"Watch it, will you?"

"Oh," he groaned as she scooted backward.

She shoved at the tree until it was out of the way. Justin lay on the soft needle-covered ground, thankfully in one piece. "I'm sorry?" She said it more as a question than a statement.

"I suppose you are, since I'm holding the car keys and you'd be stuck here if you did me under. Here, help me up," he said, extending his hand.

Mickie laughed. "You look funny, Daddy. You've got pine needles in your hair."

"Thanks, kid," he said, smiling.

He swiped at his hair but missed most of the needles, so Sarah moved forward and brushed at them. His hands stilled and his eyes met hers.

"Come on, Daddy. Let's take the tree home!"

Justin's gaze left Sarah's. "How about we let them tie this to the top of the car, then we go on a hay ride."

"Oh, cool!" Mickie clapped her hands, jumping up and down. "The church hay ride's in October, but I didn't get to go because I was too little. I'm not too little, am I, Daddy?"

He shook his head. "I saw a baby on one when we drove in and you're certainly not a baby anymore."

Mickie was almost dancing in excitement. Sarah smiled and followed Justin and the little girl to the front part of the building. "Can we look in the store while you get the tree taken care of?" she asked Justin.

"Sure. Meet me out here." He looked indulgently at his daughter before heading off toward the car.

Sarah and Mickie went into the small shop and walked up and down the aisles.

"Oh, look, Aunt Sarah." Mickie touched a necklace with a red heart and green bells. "Isn't it just so pretty?"

"I'll tell you what. You need something to remind you of your trip here. What if I buy you that and you can wear it outside and show your daddy."

"I like that." Mickie picked it up and turned it back and forth to admire every angle.

"I think I'll buy myself a bell necklace, too. Want to take these over to the counter, then go watch for your daddy so he won't miss seeing us?"

Mickie immediately obeyed. When she was gone, Sarah bought two other things that had caught her attention. One was a small round glass ornament painted with two hearts and green confetti in the background—Mickie would love that as a surprise under the tree—and the other was a cup with a picture of a man toting a Christmas tree on his back. It was dated with the current year.

She went to the counter, paid for the things and dropped the surprises in her purse. "Here, Mickie," she called, and draped the necklace around the little girl's neck. Dropping the long satin string of the other necklace over her own neck, she giggled at Mickie's incredulous expression.

"It almost touches your jeans," Mickie noted.

"That it does. But I like odd-looking jewelry. Let's go find your daddy."

He was at the car, assisting the men in tying the tree down. Sarah dropped her purse in the car, then locked the door.

"My," Justin drawled, staring down at his daughter, "what have we here?"

"Isn't it just the most beautiful necklace you've ever seen, Daddy?"

She held it up, turning it back and forth so Justin could get a good look. "You know what I think? The most beautiful girl I've ever seen is wearing it, so that makes it beautiful."

Mickie giggled and rolled her eyes before skipping toward where a few couples were just climbing onto the flatbed truck filled with hay.

"I like your necklace, too," Justin said and reached out and lifted it away from Sarah's neck. It was getting dark. He wasn't close enough for her to see his expression.

"We'd better catch Mickie before they leave us," she said to cover her nervousness.

He dropped the necklace. "I doubt she'd miss us."

"But I'd miss the ride."

He chuckled. "You're as bad as she is."

"And you're not having fun?" she asked, hurrying over to the truck.

Justin lifted his daughter in. "I just love having a tree squish me," he said dryly.

She stepped up and felt his hands on her waist, steadying her. Her heart rate accelerated. She didn't comment but went to where Mickie sat right at the back of the cab of the truck.

Justin seated himself next to her and willingly accepted Mickie's squeezing in between them. A helpless smile filled his eyes, which were only inches away from her. His look said *I tried.*

Sarah felt flattered. There was no doubt after today that Justin was acting more than just brotherly toward her. She had a feeling he had actually begun to like her. He might even be interested in her, if she wasn't mistaken.

She was surprised she didn't think of André and miss him when Justin smiled at her. No, instead she thought only of how perfect Justin was for her and how wonderful it was to be out from under the constant strain of André being so passive and compliant whenever his parents had criticized her.

She still hadn't forgotten that Justin had let Drydan Watson go, after what she had told him. She felt a little guilty. After all, what had happened to her had nothing to do with the business end of Justin's life; it had been strictly personal. And she would mention it to Justin—soon, because she didn't want Drydan revealing anything if Justin truly was developing feelings for her. Yes, that was her task to do. Still, it was nice to know he had believed her and taken her side, even though she hadn't asked him to.

The stars twinkled brightly in the sky and the moon was almost full again. It was hard to believe she'd been at Justin's over a month now.

Speakers softly played Christmas music. Couples settled down in the hay, snuggling against the cool crisp wind. Funny that Mickie was the only child on the ride. Maybe because it was after dark and most families had already left the farm.

Mickie wiggled between them. "This hay is poking me."

Justin reached to lift her onto his lap just as the ride started up. Mickie surprised them both by evading her daddy and crawling into Sarah's lap.

"I want Aunt Sarah to hold me."

Sarah's heart expanded as the little girl nestled in her arms, resting her head against Sarah's shoulder. She stretched her legs across Sarah's lap, then frowned at her daddy.

"She's softer."

Justin chuckled. "I imagine she is." But there was a tenderness reflected in his eyes from the small electrical lanterns overhead.

Mickie found a strand of hair that was hanging over Sarah's shoulder and stroked it with her tiny fingers.

"She's tired," Justin murmured, though he sounded just a little choked up over his daughter's need to be held by Sarah.

"Am not!" Mickie piped up, then nestled closer.

Sarah smiled and nodded slightly. She saw the gleaming moisture in Justin's eyes and realized how much it affected him that Mickie didn't have a mother. Sometimes a girl just needed a mom. She wondered how those many motherless children survived without the nurturing care of a mother. She thanked God she'd never had to find out, though she still missed her mom some now, then said a quick prayer that Mickie wouldn't suffer from missing Amy.

As the music of one of her favorite Christmas songs started, she began to hum along with it. The ride rocked them and in less than five minutes Mickie was slumped against her.

"She's asleep," she said softly to Justin, who had been strangely quiet.

"You have a beautiful voice," he murmured.

Sarah blushed and was glad it was dark. "Thank you."

"Please, go ahead, sing some more."

"Oh, I couldn't," she protested.

"For me? You don't have to sing loud enough for anyone else, Sarah. But please, do it for me."

How could she resist?

The song "Away in the Manger" came on and she began to sing. "'Away in the manger no crib for a bed, the little Lord Jesus lay down his swe—'"

They hit a bump and she broke off, tightening her hold on Mickie. Justin moved his daughter's feet and inched closer, then his arm encircled around her. He pulled her snugly against his side. His other hand came around and rested on Mickie's leg.

She continued singing softly, just so he could hear. On the second verse, Justin joined his voice with hers. He loved the feel of her against him, the protectiveness she brought out, the feelings of attraction. But most of all, he just enjoyed her presence. He couldn't imagine his life without her.

When the song was over, Justin turned toward Sarah.

He wanted to ask her about coming to work for him, had thought to do it tonight. He knew he was enjoying her too much in his arms and that could lead to dangerous temptations at his house. After all, God had made man and woman to feel attracted to each other. But there were rules. And it was extremely difficult to follow those rules when the woman looked so longingly at him.

So instead of discussing her future, he leaned forward and kissed her, tenderly, gently, a simple sharing. She'd been so tense the past week or so, but tonight Sarah was relaxed, not hiding anything from him. He liked that and wondered if she could read what was in his eyes.

Seeing Mickie sleeping so contentedly in her arms, he remembered her outburst when Bill had shared the news about Marcy. He wondered how she *really* felt about André.

Yes, that concerned him, because sitting here, looking at her like this, he realized he could give his heart to her—if she could simply love him back.

Oh, he realized he was afraid to love again, but he didn't know how to let go of that fear. Or if he should. Should he simply declare his feelings and not worry that she might feel obligated to accept anything from him because he had provided so much for her?

No. He couldn't do it. He needed to know that she had some sort of feelings for him other than gratitude.

"Look, a meteorite!"

He glanced up and saw a streak across the sky. It was gone almost immediately.

"Do you suppose that's what led the Wise Men to Jesus? That or a comet?"

Justin shook his head. "I doubt it. After all, Jesus was almost two by the time they located him. Maybe it was a supernova."

"I guess the miracle wasn't in what led them there, but that the Scriptures foretold it."

"Yeah, that and the miracle that Jesus was born into the world."

"And lived and died," Sarah added, snuggling closer in his arms.

He smiled warmly, thinking how wonderful it was to know true joy. "And that He rose again."

"And is always here for us. What love that is," Sarah murmured.

"How true. What love He had to provide such a plan of redemption." *Which reminds me,* Justin thought, *that even if Sarah never loves me I have a Heavenly Father who does. He knows my needs and desires and will fulfill them in the way He knows they should be fulfilled.*

The truck slowed and they were back at the beginning point. Justin smiled at Sarah, lifted Mickie from her arms, then assisted Sarah in standing.

"Thank you for the evening," Sarah whispered as they walked toward the car.

"Thank you, Sarah, for sharing it with us. I think Mickie really enjoyed not only the shopping and the tree but your company, as well."

"I enjoyed her, too." She paused by the car door. "And being with you."

Potent words. He could easily picture the two of them together. He forced the thought away. "It was a very nice evening."

He walked around, strapped Mickie into her seat belt—Mickie simply sighed and continued to sleep—then slipped into his own seat.

He turned on a music station that was playing Christmas music, then backed out of the parking place.

"Why don't you rest. It'll take us at least forty-five minutes to get back."

"I'll try," she murmured, sounding sleepy.

He shook himself, trying to get rid of the romantic thoughts going around in his head. They both needed time to let this relationship develop. And he'd make sure they had it. Control. He would just have to control his impulses until he was certain Sarah knew what she wanted.

Whatever happened between them, he knew one thing: he wanted God's will. That was the most important thing. He had to let God show him the answers.

Chapter Sixteen

"Are you sure you want me going to the holiday open house?" Sarah asked Justin, pulling on her coat as she came down the stairs.

Justin smiled. "I'd like you there as...protection."

"And just why do you need protection?"

He gave her a look of mock outrage. "People like Stephanie," he said. "There are three different ladies who have marked me single and seek me out any time I'm within two blocks of the school."

Sarah chuckled, and Justin smiled at the sound. He enjoyed listening to Sarah when she was happy. Her eyes sparkled and her whole demeanor radiated energy when she was in a good mood.

"Daddy, I can't go. I've got a tummy ache."

Justin turned at the sound of his daughter's voice. Mickie, dressed in her red-and-green holiday outfit, had a hand on her tummy and stood near the hallway to his library.

"When did this happen?" Justin asked, concerned, going to her and dropping onto one knee. He felt her head. It was cool. He checked her color, which was normal. Then he looked into her eyes. That was when he knew something else was going on.

"A while ago," Mickie mumbled.

Sarah walked up and stroked Mickie's head, going down on one knee by Justin. "I can stay home with her if you think this is serious."

Mickie's eyes brightened.

Justin's suspicions deepened. Sometimes when Mickie didn't want to go to school she said she had a tummy ache. But he'd thought they were through that stage.

He wondered if maybe the teacher had sent home a note that he'd never gotten. He hesitated a minute, then made his decision. "Oh, I think Mickie's well enough to go, aren't you, sweetie? If you get sick then we'll just stop by the doctor's and see what he can do to help."

Mickie lowered her gaze. "Yes, sir," she said, her mouth drooping.

He stood and saw Sarah's distress. Silently, he shook his head, indicating she shouldn't say anything else.

"Come on, pumpkin, let me carry you to the car. You've been running ahead of me lately and I still like to carry my little girl once in a while."

Mickie smiled, though she was still subdued. Walking toward the car, he placed a smacking kiss on her cheek. "Did I tell you today how much I love you?"

"Maybe," she replied, her eyes dropping.

"No matter what, you're the most important girl in

my life. Nothing could ever change that.'' He let her down and she climbed into the car.

Sarah gave him a questioning look, but he didn't explain. She decided to change the subject. ''It sure is cold out tonight. Do you think it might snow?''

Mickie brightened considerably. ''Do you think we could make a snowman? Have you ever made a snowman, Aunt Sarah?''

''Oh, my, yes. It's been so many years, though, since we've had real snow around Christmas. You know what I wish? I wish we have a snowy Christmas so we can build a huge snowman.''

''Well, we've got a couple of more weeks until Christmas, so you can keep wishing.''

''So, Mickie, what do you want for Christmas?''

Mickie suddenly quieted.

''What? No wishes?''

''Wishes don't come true if you tell them, do they?''

Justin saw Sarah smile, as if remembering her childhood. ''Well, I know you're not supposed to tell them, but sometimes it doesn't matter. Besides, how are you going to get what you want if you don't ask?''

''I wrote a letter to Santa. He'll know.''

Sarah glanced at Justin. Justin shrugged slightly. He hadn't known Mickie could write well enough to write an entire letter. He'd have to find it and see what he could do about fulfilling the list. He had to wonder if the Fashion Kathy Super House he'd bought might be on it.

''Well, I know what I want,'' Sarah announced.

Justin smiled when Mickie asked, ''What?'' as if

Sarah were getting ready to reveal some deep dark secret.

"Actually, I bought it the other day. I wanted perfumed soaps."

"But, Aunt Sarah, you aren't supposed to buy your own presents."

Sarah chuckled. "When you live on your own, you buy your own gifts."

"But you live with us."

Sarah blinked. "Um, well, actually, I *work* for you, sweetie. It's a little different."

Justin was irritated by her explanation. He was also irritated that she obviously had lived alone so long that she'd forgotten what it was like to receive gifts. Or maybe she was just still so upset about André that she didn't think anyone else would care to get her something special.

"We're here," he said, glad to end the subject before they could ask him what he wanted. He was afraid he would end up saying what he wanted more and more since Sarah had moved in. He wanted a wife. And not just any wife. But he refused to face just who it was he wanted. He wouldn't give up that last bit of fight and succumb to the emotions within him. Because if he did and he found out that Sarah couldn't love him back, he wasn't sure they would ever overcome the breach that would make in their relationship.

Mickie was quiet again. When he stopped the car, she jumped out. "Come on, Aunt Sarah, I want you to see the playground first."

Yep, she was definitely in trouble, Justin thought.

"Go on, Sarah. Meet me in the class in about five minutes."

She smiled. "Okay, Mickie, show me the playground."

He walked into the school and headed down the hall toward Mickie's class. The first incident happened only twenty feet beyond the door.

"Hey, great news. I'm happy to hear it."

The assistant coach slapped him on the back as he passed.

Justin started to ask him what he meant, but the man was already talking with someone else.

Great news?

He continued down the hall. Two more people smiled and called out congratulations. Others whispered when he walked past.

Had news of the merger and the additional two hundred jobs it would create for the local community leaked out already? He hadn't wanted it out until everything was finalized, but maybe Phillip had let the cat out of the bag. What odd looks he was getting, he thought as he continued along the hall.

The crowning incident came when the truth was finally revealed. A couple of parents with their children were just leaving Mickie's class as he entered. There were other families around the different displays, but the teacher, Mrs. Bell, focused on him. Her long gray-and-black hair hung down her back, pinned off her face with two combs. Her skin was wrinkled, but her blue eyes twinkled with the joy that only a teacher who had spent thirty years teaching kindergarten and survived could possess. Her flowing floral skirt and long-sleeved white top perfectly fit the graceful, warm image she projected.

"Well, congratulations, Mr. Warner. I was so happy when Mickie shared her news and...ah, well, this must be Mrs. Warner," she said.

Justin turned in surprise. Sarah was standing behind him, trying to cover her bafflement with a small smile. He glanced from Mrs. Bell to Mickie, who was studying the floor. A huge knot formed in the pit of his stomach. Not of anger, but of pain for what his little girl had done.

He knew, he just *knew* what she had told everyone.

"Did I say something wrong?" Mrs. Bell asked.

But he ignored her, intent on his hurting child. Why hadn't he realized she had been so affected by losing her mom?

Kneeling, he tipped his daughter's chin up until she met his gaze. Her eyes were already awash with tears. "Mickie, honey, have you been telling everyone that you have a new mommy?"

He heard Sarah's gasp, heard the teacher's murmured, "Oh, dear," but didn't take his gaze off his daughter.

"She makes me peanut butter-and-jelly sandwiches and fixes me cookies and comes to meet me after school."

"But there's more than that to being a mommy, honey."

"And she hugs me and reads to me. And she smells good," the little girl said, her chin wobbling. "And now she's gonna hate me, isn't she?"

Suddenly, as if it were too much for her, Mickie

turned and ran off down the hall. Justin stood and started after her.

"Let me," Sarah said. "Give me a couple of minutes."

Then she was gone.

"I'm so sorry, Mr. Warner. I had no idea. Mickie came to school one day and said that she had a new mommy, that her aunt Sarah was now her mommy. I just assumed that was Aunt Sarah and that you married her."

"That was Aunt Sarah," Justin said, "but I haven't married her. I'll check with you later about Mickie's progress. Right now I need to go find her."

He pulled his coat around him and headed down the hall without a single word to anyone. His heart was breaking over the pain he'd seen in Mickie's eyes. He wondered if Sarah was succeeding at removing that look.

Mickie sat at the bottom of the slide, her face buried against her knees, when Sarah caught up with her. Sarah slowed to a walk. "Mickie, honey, may I sit down?"

Mickie shrugged.

Sarah took that as a yes. She picked up the girl and settled her on her lap, sitting on the swing instead of the slide. Mickie burst into fresh sobs. Slowly, Sarah pushed the swing back and forth, a gentle rocking motion as she let Mickie cry. She saw Justin in the shadows near the building but didn't acknowledge his presence. He was staying put and allowing her to handle this, so he'd just have to wait. She was in no hurry.

Finally, Mickie's cries subsided. "I missed my

mommy when she died,'' Sarah finally said. ''It made me very sad not to have someone around.''

Mickie sniffled. ''Daddy's lonely.''

''Ah, is that so?''

Mickie nodded. ''So am I.''

''So am I sometimes. I miss your mommy, too, and wish she'd come back. She could make me laugh and make me mad. We had such fun.''

''Did I have fun with her?''

Sarah felt tears well. ''Oh, yes, dear. She use to blow bubbles on your tummy and hug you and love you, just as your daddy does now.''

''Other kids have mommies.'' Her little arms squeezed Sarah tighter.

''That's true. And other people don't have mommies, too.''

Mickie finally looked up at Sarah. ''You mean I'm not the only one who doesn't have a mommy?''

''No, you're not. And I'll tell you something else. It's okay to want another mommy...but the time has to be right. You have to wait until just the right time when your daddy finally asks someone to marry him and be his wife. Then that woman will be your mommy.''

''Daddy has to marry her?'' She sounded surprised.

''Yes, he does. And then that woman will be your mommy. But she has to be real special and your daddy has to really love her. And it has to be the right time.''

''The right day?'' Mickie asked, sounding excited.

''The exactly right day,'' Sarah said, not sure why Mickie had suddenly brightened at her words. ''You know, your daddy doesn't run up and ask. It has to be special and he has to propose—ask her to marry him.''

"He has to love her, ask her on the right day, then marry her, for me to have a mommy,'' Mickie repeated softly, then nodded as if she'd come to some great discovery.

Mickie sat there in Sarah's lap as Sarah continued to push the swing back and forth. Finally, in barely a whisper, Mickie asked, "Are you mad at me?''

Sarah chuckled. "Not at all. I'm very proud that you wanted me to be your mommy. But I really like being your aunt. So what do you say if I just be your aunt and we can do the snuggling and cookie making and all the fun stuff until your daddy finds a wife.''

Mickie thought about it a minute. "I guess so.''

"And how about you go give your daddy hugs. I think he's feeling a little left out.''

Justin stepped out of the shadows so Mickie could see him. He bent down and held out his arms.

Mickie ran to him and hugged him hard around the neck. "I'm sorry, Daddy. I'm so sorry. I love you.''

Justin rubbed her up and down the back, his deep voice rumbling, but Sarah was unable to make out any words.

"I promise,'' Mickie said, and hugged her daddy again.

He crooked his head toward the car and started walking, all the while murmuring in his daughter's ear. Sarah silently followed.

In the car, Mickie almost immediately fell asleep.

The radio played lowly in the background, soothing both Sarah's and Justin's frazzled nerves. Neither spoke.

In minutes Justin was home and he lifted Mickie out of the car. Sarah gathered her purse and Mickie's doll, which she'd left in the back seat, and followed more slowly.

She went in and changed, then went to Mickie's room, placed her doll by her side and gave her a soft kiss goodnight.

Then she went downstairs, intending to get a glass of milk before going to bed. Justin was in the kitchen. At the sound of the swinging door being pushed open, he turned.

Pouring her a glass of milk, he said, ''Well, what a mess we're in.''

Chapter Seventeen

Sarah laughed, a little nervously. "Well, I'm glad I'm not the one who has to face the school tomorrow."

Justin shook his head. "I'm not sure how to handle it. I never realized Amy's death…" He trailed off.

Sarah stepped forward and placed her hand on his arm. He'd taken off his sweater and she could feel his muscles under the long-sleeved shirt bunch. "It's her age. She's meeting other children and their parents and she has recognized the differences. She doesn't really remember Amy. All she knows is she's different. It's normal, Justin. There's no reason to blame yourself."

Justin sighed, moved over to the small kitchen table and looked out into the yard, which was brightened by a security light. "I'm sorry you got caught in the middle of this, Sarah."

Sarah sat down at the table. "No problem. That's what family is for. Besides, she could have told people Stephanie was her new mommy."

Justin groaned. "That's true." He glanced at her and must have seen something in her eyes, for he suddenly asked, "You aren't feeling guilty, are you?"

She smiled. "It's true I do battle guilt, isn't it? Actually, I'm wondering if Stephanie was right when she inquired the other day if your other housekeepers had lived in."

Justin growled. "That woman—"

"At least she's consistent," Sarah said. "I do have an idea, if you don't mind."

All serious now, Justin said, "Shoot."

"Mickie actually thought she was the only child who had ever been without a mom. I'm sure someone at church is in the same situation, but I know Bill was without his mom. If I contact Bill and we go over to see Marcy, since Mickie is so in love with her, it might help for her to let them share with her. And then there's a book, written on a child's level, about death and pain and going on with life. It's a real good book that subtly addresses those issues, if you wouldn't mind my picking it up for her."

Justin smiled, relieved. "Both ideas sound wonderful. I'll try to spend a little more time with her in the evening to fill in that loss she's experiencing."

"I don't know if it'll do any good. Mickie may just want a mommy, and it's something she's going to have to work through. Kids can be very stubborn sometimes."

"You're telling me."

"Hey, I've learned since I've been here." Sarah stood. "Don't worry about it. Pray, let God work it out.

Who knows, maybe He wants Mickie to have a mommy and that was your wake-up call.'' She winked and left.

Justin sat at the table, dumbstruck at Sarah's words, until he heard her door click closed upstairs, then he stood and went up to bed, his mind still on the bombshell Sarah had dropped before leaving. Justin wondered if Sarah had any idea that he had been thinking along the same lines as Mickie these past two weeks.

He wondered what she'd do if she knew.

But since he wasn't going to tell her, it was a moot point.

''I'm surprised you're picking up Mickie today,'' the all-too-familiar voice said.

Lord, why me? Why is this woman becoming my thorn in the flesh?

''Why wouldn't I, Stephanie?'' Sarah asked mildly as she watched the last moments of the rehearsal. Other mothers were standing around waiting. She saw two fathers and a teenager, too.

''Well, after what happened at open house... Of course, we don't blame Mickie. I imagine it's all so confusing for her, having no mom and a woman living in the house like that.''

She made it sound so tawdry, Sarah thought, disgusted. ''Mickie has had other housekeepers,'' Sarah said, though she did admit that with her feelings for Justin she had been thinking more and more lately of moving out. Not only because the attraction was mutual, but because she was afraid she was going to end up hurting him. She had gone back and forth in her mind about the infertility issue. The fact was, she was absolutely terrified to mention it to him.

However, she knew she was going to have to do something, and Stephanie's words only reminded her of that.

"Well, I'm not one to gossip—"

Yeah, right, Sarah thought.

"But there were a couple of women at church the other day who were asking just who you were and why you always came to church with Justin. I tried to explain you were only the housekeeper, but I don't think they believed me."

Sarah smiled. "That's a shame. Sunday in church, why don't you introduce me. I'd like to meet them."

She walked off. Stephanie's simple jealousy was going to give Justin a bad name at church. She didn't know what to do. Since they were going to see Bill today, maybe she'd ask him if he had any ideas.

"I'm ready!" Mickie said, running up. "Are we still going to go see Bill today?"

Sarah smiled. "And Marcy."

"Great!" She jumped up and down, then took off toward the exit. She waited for Sarah at the door, then walked across the parking lot. As soon as she hit the grass, she ran to where the car was parked on the other side of the field.

Mickie rattled on about school and practice until they pulled into the driveway to Bill's place. Bill lived in a nice family house, one passed down through his father. She knew Bill had money but that he had never given up his job, insisting he was needed where he was.

Sarah wondered if he didn't sometimes resent his father's money and that was why he worked—to prove to everyone he could make it on his own. Still, Bill was a wonderful guy and had married a wonderful woman. She liked being around them both. He'd been her friend forever.

"Well, hello, pumpkin," Bill said, grinning and opening his arms to Mickie. She ran right into his hug.

"We got to come visit today because Aunt Sarah said so," Mickie announced, then squirmed out of his arms and raced toward Marcy.

Marcy knelt and hugged the little girl, then took her to the kitchen, where she cut up an apple and gave her a glass of milk. "Aunt Sarah says you don't have a mama, either," Mickie said to Bill as she munched the apple.

Bill chuckled. "Thank goodness we have such a forthright child. Why don't you and Marcy go look at that centerpiece you were going to borrow for Christmas dinner."

He sat down next to Mickie and smiled. "I guess that's just one more thing we have in common, isn't it, Mickie mine?"

Mickie, who had been swallowing a gulp of milk, set down the glass. Looking up, interested, she asked, "What else do we have in common?" She didn't comment on the nickname, just giggled.

"Well, we both had good daddies," he said, nodding at her with a grin.

Mickie smiled back. "Oh, yeah, my daddy's real good. He took me to the park the other day and tucks me in at night. Do you know, Nicole's dad never tucks her in? But my daddy does. Of course—'' Mickie frowned ''—her mama tucks her in.''

She finished her snack and slid off the stool to play with the cat at her feet.

Bill knew Sarah had brought Mickie over for a reason. He had prayed about what to say. Watching Mickie now, he realized this was the first time he'd ever heard her talk about her mommy. ''You miss her, don't you?'' he said softly, picking up a box of treats and tossing one of the little cubes at the cat. The cat rolled over, holding it between its paws before biting down.

''Can I do that?'' Mickie asked.

Bill tossed her a treat and she held it above the cat. She giggled when it sat up on its hind legs just like a dog, the way Bill had trained it to.

''Having a mommy must be the best thing in the world,'' Mickie finally said.

Bill shrugged. ''My mom died when I was five. I missed her a lot. But I had my daddy.''

''Jimmy told me I was the only one in the world without a mommy.''

Bill shook his head. ''Well, that's just not true. Many, many people don't have mommies. But tell me, what can a mommy do that a daddy can't?''

Mickie paused in stroking the cat, which was now curled contentedly in Mickie's lap, sniffing the box of treats as Mickie stroked her. ''Make chocolate coconut cakes?''

Bill frowned, hard. ''I dunno. Seems to me your daddy has made that cake once or twice for us.''

Mickie nodded slowly. "Buy me dresses?"

Bill shook his head again. "I was with your daddy last year when he bought your Christmas present."

She fell silent for a long time. "Mommies can make daddies happy when daddies are alone," she finally said.

Bill was stunned. "Well, there you got me. But, honey," Bill said carefully, not wanting to hurt this little girl, "do you think your daddy is lonely?"

"Oh, no. He has me. That's just what Mrs. Winters said to a friend of hers. I just wish, sometimes, I had a mommy so she could go with me to plays and stuff, like the other kids."

Bill sighed. "Yeah, so did I. But my dad loved me. I was much luckier than others. At least I had a daddy."

Mickie looked confused. "If you didn't have a mommy, then you had to have a daddy, didn't you?"

Marcy and Sarah were coming into the room and Marcy was lugging a photo album. Bill was happy when Marcy spoke up.

"Oh, no, sweetheart. I didn't have a mommy or a daddy. I had several. My mommy and daddy both died when I was six years old. I had three different sets of parents raise me."

Mickie was intrigued. "What do you mean?"

Marcy sat down and for the next hour she and Mickie laughed over pictures of Marcy when she was a little girl. She told Mickie how she'd bought a camera with some money her first set of parents had given her. Then, when she moved from foster home to foster home, she took pictures. She did admit there was one foster home she didn't like, but that the third set of parents kept her until she moved out after she was grown.

Mickie was astonished, then happy when she realized other people besides her didn't have a mommy or a daddy. She was especially happy when Marcy mentioned someone at church who didn't have a mommy, a young girl she knew. Mickie told Marcy very solemnly that she would talk to Missy next week and explain that not everyone had mommies.

Sarah was satisfied with the day's events. But she wasn't surprised, when, after looking at the pictures, having another snack and finally preparing to leave, Mickie said, "But I still want a mommy."

What did surprise Sarah was when Mickie started her next sentence.

"I can't wait until Christmas because—" The little girl suddenly clamped a hand over her mouth.

Sarah stared quizzically at the child. "What Mickie?"

"Oh, no, Santa won't bring me what I ask for if I tell."

She stroked the cat again, then said, "I do wish I had a cat, though. Do you think Daddy might get me a cat?"

Sarah stared at Mickie. Was that what she had wished for? Oh, dear. She'd have to tell Justin because she was certain that wasn't on his Christmas list.

They started toward the door. Bill and Marcy escorted them out. But as Sarah started to get in the car, Bill stopped her. "Though you brought Mickie here today to talk, something is bothering you. Marcy mentioned you wanted to speak to me but said it could wait."

Now she knew what they'd been whispering about on

the porch as she'd helped Mickie into the car. She shrugged. "I do have a problem and thought maybe to ask you about it."

Bill nodded. "I'm glad you came to me. Can you meet me for lunch tomorrow at the little restaurant near where Justin and I work?"

She knew which one he was talking about. He ate there all the time. Or he used to. She doubted he did much eating away from home since he'd married.

"Sure. It's nothing really serious," she said, her smile leaving her face as she thought about just what she'd wanted to discuss with Bill. "But if you're busy maybe I should—"

Bill took her shoulders. "You're like my sister, Sarah. When I didn't have anyone, you were there. I'm never too busy for you. If you'd only stop letting your pride get in the way when I offer help."

"But Marcy might not like—" she began, only to be cut off.

"Marcy knows you're nothing more than a friend to me. She loves you for what you did during our teenage years."

Sarah shrugged, feeling uncomfortable with the praise. "I didn't realize you'd ever told her how close we were. And I love Marcy dearly but was afraid she'd feel threatened by an unknown."

Bill chuckled. "We love each other too much for there to be any mistrust between us."

Sarah shook her head. "You're one of the lucky few, then. Okay. I'll meet you around noon tomorrow."

He gave her a peck on the cheek, then waved to

Mickie. Marcy was just coming down the steps after having gone back into the house to answer the phone. She hugged Sarah, too, and gave her a peck. "Take care, Mickie. And next time you see Jimmy, don't forget to tell him about the woman you met who had three mommies!"

Mickie giggled and waved bye.

Sarah got in the car and left. She could sigh in relief that she had accomplished two missions today.

First, Mickie knew she wasn't the only one in the world without a mommy. Sarah wasn't sure how much it would help. Maybe it would only open the door for Mickie to ask more questions, or maybe she would be satisfied completely. Still, it was a step forward.

And second, she had taken a step forward facing her fears about her infertility. She would talk to Bill and share with him the secret that she'd shared with no one except André. She would tell Bill what had really caused her breakup with André, tell him her fears and see how he reacted, then maybe she could figure out just how to tell Justin about her inability to have children.

She would decide if a relationship with him truly was a lost cause and she should just drift away, leaving him to find someone else to fill the empty space in his heart.

And she knew it was there. She'd glimpsed it in the short time they'd become closer. Oh, yes, Justin was just as lonely as she was. And if she wasn't wrong, she thought he might be seriously considering asking her to live happily ever after with him.

But *could* he be happy after her secret was discovered?

Chapter Eighteen

Sarah glanced around nervously, straightening the collar of her top, then smoothing her skirt.

"Relax, I'm sure Mickie's teacher has explained everything."

Sarah watched all the people mingling in the school auditorium, moving back and forth, finding seats, laughing, shaking hands, rushing children toward the back of the closed curtains on the dais. "Why did I come?" she asked, more to herself than anyone around her.

"Besides the fact that you're like me and obviously love to be embarrassed," Justin joked, then grinned, "you have a niece who would have been very upset if you hadn't shown up."

Sarah glanced up at Justin, who was in a pair of jeans and a pullover sweater, looking as if he hadn't a care in the world. "I'm sorry," she said in a low voice. "I didn't realize you'd be embarrassed, too."

Justin shrugged. "Not exactly embarrassed, just expecting some less-than-sensitive person to make a joke about what Mickie said.''

He urged her forward toward the fourth row, then motioned her toward the middle. ''I'm worried about someone making a nasty comment,'' she replied, murmuring it for his ears only.

''No one will,'' he said, so certain.

''How can you be so sure?'' She seated herself, noting a small crowd not too far away pointing, their heads together. Her cheeks turned pink.

''I'm intimidating, if nothing else,'' he replied, and took his seat beside her.

That caught her attention. ''You *know* that?''

He chuckled and turned his warm gaze on her. ''I've perfected it for business. One look can send troublemakers running.''

She rolled her eyes and fell back against her seat. ''I don't believe you. All this time I thought you didn't realize how you make people quake in their boots.''

''They quake in their boots, do they?'' he asked arrogantly.

She couldn't help but giggle. ''You're incorrigible!''

''Maybe, but you're smiling now.''

Seeing the glint in his eyes, she said, ''You did that on purpose.''

He shrugged.

Deciding it was wise to change the subject, she said, ''So, is Mickie excited?''

Justin nodded. ''She was dancing circles around the teacher when I dropped her off. She certainly has enough energy for the entire class tonight.''

Sarah smiled softly. "I know. She made me try the costume on her each time I put another seam together. She had to watch its creation, step by step."

"That's Mickie. Do you know, at three years of age she asked me how the earth was made and how come, if the sun was a star, the other stars didn't have earths, too?"

Seeing the proud smile on his face, she realized he wasn't complaining at all. "She's something special."

"She sure is. I love her. My only regret is that she doesn't have a brother or sister."

Just like that, Sarah's smile collapsed. But she was saved from Justin's noting it by the dimming house-lights. Kids. Did that mean he wanted another one or that he *had,* at some time, wanted one when Mickie was younger? Maybe he thought he was too old now to have another baby. At least, she tried to tell herself that.

She felt his warm hand close over her smaller one and couldn't resist the touch. Justin was not only causing her current conflict, he was also the very one who soothed it whenever she got too uptight.

Though he didn't know what was the matter, he always seemed to sense when something bothered her and found ways to put her at ease.

His hand felt good, warm, secure. She liked the feel of it. She didn't fight him but leaned closer, resting her arm against his and absorbing the heat from him, as if she could absorb his peace.

To a point it worked. The play started and she was able to relax as the children came out and sang an open-ing song. The play was about the shoemaker and the elves who came to help him make his shoes. Of course, it didn't follow the fairy tale exactly. Everyone had a lot of fun as the different shoes sang their songs of what Christmas was about. One pair, ballerina slippers, sang about the dancing at Christmas. Another pair, children's shoes, sang about favorite baby dolls that children liked. Then a pair of tennis shoes that belonged to a little boy sang about how bad he'd been and how he wouldn't get anything this Christmas. Through it all the adults laughed at the proper moments and cheered the different children. Only two small children forgot their lines.

Then it was Mickie's turn. The shopkeeper was at his lowest and angels appeared, singing the joys of Christmas.

"Doesn't she look great?" Justin whispered proudly as Mickie and the other children sang.

"Perfect," Sarah answered, just as quietly.

Then the elves were out fixing the shoes. Before long, the angels were singing again, then the shopkeeper gave the shoes to the owners and was able to save his shop after all.

The angels came back out for the final scene, and Sarah watched Justin's surprise and delight as Mickie sang a short solo. Her voice was loud and clear, and though she seemed scared when she first started, once she turned to her teacher and started singing, it went fine.

Justin looked as if he could pop buttons on his top he was so proud.

"Why didn't she tell me?" he asked.

Sarah grinned. "She wanted to surprise you."

"I didn't know she could keep a secret," he murmured, standing as the song finished and clapping along with everyone else.

Mickie came running out to where Justin and Sarah stood. "Are you proud, Daddy? Did I sing good?"

Justin swooped her up in his arms. "I'm very proud and you could make the angels sit up and take notice," he said, bussing her cheek. "How about I take you out for a chocolate sundae to show you how proud I am?"

"Oh, cool! And I can stay up late since there's no more school until after Christmas, can't I?"

"I suppose so," Justin said. "As long as you don't get cranky."

"Ice cream when it's cold outside?" Sarah asked.

Justin chuckled. "That's the best time."

They stopped at an ice-cream shop on the way home and Mickie enjoyed a sundae with Justin, while Sarah insisted she didn't want anything. She enjoyed watching the two decide on just what ice cream and toppings they wanted, arguing good-naturedly over what was the best, before they finally settled down at a table.

"I still can't believe you wouldn't have anything at all," Justin said, taking a bite of his sundae.

"Doesn't Aunt Sarah like ice cream?" Mickie whispered loudly to her daddy.

Justin turned to her, an eyebrow raised. "Is that the case? You don't like ice cream?"

She smiled. "I'd be cold for hours if I put that in me," she replied. "I do like it. But only in the summer."

"But, Aunt Sarah," Mickie said, "you just have to put more blankets on your bed when you get home and you won't be cold."

Sarah rolled her eyes. "Why didn't I think of that?" she teased.

"In that case, you have to have one small taste," Justin said, dipping his spoon in his sundae and holding it out to her.

Sarah looked at the spoon, then at Justin's mouth, and flushed. Somehow, eating after him seemed so personal. And he knew it, if the innocent look he was giving her was any indication. She was never one to back down from a dare but there was always a first time. "I think…I'll pass this time, thanks," Sarah said quietly.

Justin hesitated a moment, then set the spoon back in his container. "Maybe that's wiser after all," Justin murmured, holding her gaze.

Then Mickie was done with her ice cream and ready to go. She noticed Justin had lost interest in his. The container was still almost full. He took it and dumped it in the garbage can.

They hurried through the biting wind to the car and in seconds were on their way home.

When they arrived, Sarah wasn't surprised to find Mickie had drifted off. "She's had a full day," she said softly, opening the door for Justin.

He motioned her inside. Closing the door behind him, he said, "But as you know, she's an early riser."

He headed upstairs and Sarah trailed along. Going to her drawers, she dug out Mickie's warm p.j.'s and handed them to Justin, who had already stripped off her shoes and socks. He lifted her and slipped the costume over her head, then pulled her top on.

Sarah folded back the sheets and added another blanket. "It's getting colder earlier this year," she whispered as Justin covered up Mickie.

He said a quick prayer over her, then kissed her and stood. Sarah added a kiss to Mickie's cheek, then left the room. Justin pulled the door closed behind him.

Then they both stood there staring at each other. Sarah had enjoyed the companionship tonight, the feel of another human next to her, the joy of sharing a joke. She hated for it to end.

Evidently, so did Justin. "You want some cocoa before you go to bed?"

Sarah's eyes widened. She opened her mouth to say yes, but he must have thought otherwise, for he added, "You did say you'd have trouble warming up."

She chuckled, her mouth spreading into a smile. "I'd love some. But why don't you let me make it."

He nodded. They walked down the stairs together and she went into the kitchen, where she quickly made up some cocoa. Coming back out, she found Justin, his hands in his jean pockets, standing before the blinking Christmas tree, staring thoughtfully at it.

The whole room looked like Christmas with the tree blinking, the silver icicles waving gently from the air blowing out of the overhead ducts. Greenery with gold and red was draped across everything. Stockings were suspended from the mantel. And mistletoe hung from the fan in the middle of the living room.

The room had a very homey feeling, one she was proud of, since she'd done most of the decorating.

"This is the best the house has looked since before Amy died," Justin said, turning from the tree and coming over to take his cocoa. He seated himself by Sarah on the couch.

Sarah took a sip of her cocoa, continuing to stare at the tree despite Justin's presence next to her on the right or the fireplace on the left. She kicked off her shoes and folded one foot under her, then slipped the other one up on the coffee table. "Everything was in the attic, Justin. All you had to do was pull it down and put it up."

Justin shrugged. "When Amy died, some of the magic died, too, I suppose. I had no desire or wish to celebrate an all-out humdinger of a Christmas again." He took a sip of his cocoa, then said, "But I'd forgotten what I was missing. What *Mickie* was missing."

Sarah wrapped her hands around her mug. "No wishes?" she asked, thinking of all the wishes she'd had that Christmas.

"No happy ones," he said, echoing her feelings. "They were all tainted with my dark thoughts over all the grief Mickie and I were experiencing."

He shifted his body, which brought him closer, though she doubted he realized it, staring as intently as he was at the blinking lights. "But that's what I was doing just now—thinking about Christmas wishes. Christmas has always been considered a time for kids, but I've always made my own Christmas wishes, too. After all, wasn't that when we received the greatest gift? It reminds us that there is such a thing as happiness and goodness and the chance for things to turn out right in the end."

Sarah nodded. "I agree. It should be a time of hope and joy, and a time to remember that Amy's in a better place."

Justin sank back into the cushions of the couch. "That was the conclusion I came to last year. I guess that's why this year it has been easier during the holidays and we've done so much better."

He took another sip of his cocoa, then turned toward Sarah. "So tell me, what is your Christmas wish this year?"

The crackling of the flames from the fire Justin had started while she was in the kitchen was the only sound in the room. She looked into Justin's deep brown eyes and wanted to tell him, *You. I want you for Christmas.* But since that wasn't appropriate—she could just imagine her mother rolling over in her grave if she said that— she said, instead, "I don't know. Maybe a family."

She saw him set his cup down and she felt the air around them change.

"But you have us, Sarah."

She nodded, Oh, dear. Her and her big mouth. She couldn't explain that she wanted a baby to hold, couldn't tell him about the pain inside her heart. But the pain wasn't as bad if she thought of Mickie as partly hers. No, she couldn't say that, so instead she asked him, "And you? What do you want for Christmas? What are your wishes?"

Justin turned his gaze back to the tree, which relieved Sarah. He was too perceptive and she'd just known he was going to see something she hadn't wanted him to. She studied his masculine jaw, the hint of shadow his gold whiskers caused. Short light lashes didn't move as he stared hard at the tree.

"Earlier in the year I might have said the only wish

I had was for my favorite little girl to be happy." A ghost of a smile touched his lips. "Mickie is already a very happy girl, though. Still, I'd like to erase the loneliness in her eyes sometimes. Of course, I could've also wished business were better, but it's going really good." The smiled widened and he turned, his eyes touching hers. "I could also wish for a normal tie that didn't have some sort of cartoon or fish or even flower on it."

Sarah laughed, but the laughter was strained because the look on his face had just turned serious.

"But things have changed," he said. "If I had to ask Santa now, it'd be for a warm, loving woman who could love me in return."

Her mouth fell open. Her breath lodged in her chest. She couldn't comment for anything in the world.

And she didn't have to. Justin, taking her quiet as a signal for him to continue, pulled her gently into his arms and lowered his lips to hers.

I could love you, she thought fleetingly as his warm, tender lips, expertly wrung a response from her. *I do love you.*

She had been wanting, for more than an hour, for him to kiss her. The kiss was brief and achingly tender. Her heart was racing and her fingers tingling when he pulled back. She opened heavy eyelids to see Justin gazing down at her.

"You know any women like that?" he asked huskily.

Sarah stared at him a moment, trying to figure out what he was talking about. When she realized he was asking her if she loved him in return, her gaze slid away. "It's not that easy," she said, trying to hide the pain.

Did he really mean he loved her and was serious about her? Her heart thudded in her chest.

"Yes, Sarah, it is. It's that easy. All you have to say is yes."

Oh, no! No! No! No! It wasn't that easy at all. Her chest felt as if it were going to explode with the pain of what she needed to tell him. *Why didn't you tell him before this?* Because she hadn't known this was coming. What could she say? She knew what she wanted to say. But fairy tales were just that. Fairy tales. Make-believe. They didn't come true. "Can you give me some time?" she asked hesitantly, not wanting to see the hurt in his eyes.

But she felt it. He stiffened and pulled back. "Of course I can, Sarah. I'd never pressure any woman for an answer like that."

She'd ruined the night. That sweet sharing spirit was gone, replaced by one of formality. As if to prove her point, Justin changed the subject.

"I wanted to let you know there are two openings at my business that I think you're qualified for."

She turned shocked eyes on him. Surely he wasn't that upset.

"It's not what you're thinking. I said I'd give you time to think, and I will. But just because I'm giving you time doesn't mean I won't stop wanting a relationship with you."

This time Sarah's eyes widened with comprehension. He really did care for her, really did have serious feelings for her....

"However, I think it's time that we changed the living and working arrangements. I don't want you to feel pressured or feel uncomfortable. We both know that despite our feelings nothing improper has gone on here. But people like Stephanie Williams may start gossip. I want to protect you from that sort of thing," he added.

She nodded. "Fine. Okay." She stood.

Justin turned his gaze back toward the Christmas tree, and though she knew he was amused at her reaction, she could still see the sadness in his eyes. "If you'll excuse me, I'll clean up the cups tomorrow. I think I should just go to bed."

Justin nodded. "Good idea, Sarah mine. Go to sleep and dream of tonight. Let me know when you're ready to talk again."

Knees knocking, she almost ran up the stairs. She wondered what he thought her reasons were for not answering. Surely he realized she was just as attracted to him, that she had fallen head over heels in love with the kind, generous, loving person he was. She could easily live happily ever after with him.

But of course he wouldn't know that, nor would he know it was he who would be having second thoughts when she finally told him the reason she had avoided answering him: she had to give him a chance to turn her down after he heard about her problem.

And she would make sure to go talk to Bill tomorrow. Maybe he would have a suggestion on how to tell Justin about her affliction without his being hurt or feeling used.

Please, Father, help me, she whispered, going into her room. *Please help me find a way to keep from hurting him. I've waited too long already and all I can now see is pain in the future.*

Chapter Nineteen

"Over here."

Sarah glanced across the lunch crowd to where Bill was seated. She waved and crossed to him. "Boy, I'd forgotten how busy this place is. It's been an eternity since I've been here."

Bill pulled out her chair and she rolled her eyes.

"So, what'll you have?" he asked as the waitress walked up.

Sarah thought about not ordering anything. She'd been a nervous wreck since talking with Justin the night before. But she knew Bill wouldn't let her get away without eating. "Soup, salad and sandwich of the day," she said to the waitress. "And ice water."

Bill ordered the same, and in no time at all the waitress was back with their salad. Bill devoured half of his before pushing it away and starting his quiz. "So, you wanna tell me what was eating at you when you were over at the house?"

Sarah swallowed a bite of salad, feeling that it was a lump of coal instead of a tasty ranch-dressing-coated piece of lettuce. "I enjoy my job," she started, wondering now if she should really discuss this with Bill. She loved Justin. It was him she should be telling, not Bill.

But Bill couldn't hurt her the way Justin could, she realized.

"I'm not blind. Your job isn't the only thing you enjoy there, either," he said bluntly. "Tell me, what's bothering you."

"You're always so impatient," she grouched. She nodded toward her salad when the waitress came back, indicating she was done, then accepted the soup. "I was furious, humiliated, upset and a whole other list of things when André left."

"I know. I remember your shock over his actions. I still can't believe he just walked away and mailed you a letter."

"It wasn't exactly like that," Sarah said, remembering she hadn't told Bill everything.

Bill paused in taking a sip of soup. He raised an eyebrow. "And just how was it?" he asked pointedly.

"Don't get that look with me, Bill. You may be like a brother to me, but that doesn't mean I have to tell you everything. You were engaged at the time, remember?"

He nodded, a wary expression on his face. "And?"

"Well, remember the surgery I had a few months ago?"

"For the tumor on your ovaries? Yes?"

"I didn't tell you everything the doctor said. Unfortunately, I didn't think it would be a problem, until I met André.''

Sarah laid down her spoon. The helplessness and rage boiled up again. Why, oh, why, had she lost almost all of her ovaries. ''The doctor said that with only a quarter of one ovary left I'd likely never have babies.''

Only silence met that statement. She couldn't look up at Bill and see the same disgust or even pity that might be on his face. But when he reached over and touched her hand, she couldn't help but cast a glance at him. Only pain registered in his eyes. Surprised, she kept her gaze on his.

''And that's why André left?'' he asked.

Sarah felt tears brim in her eyes. ''Yes. He said he needed time and took a vacation, but then he had his father get rid of me. I can't explain the pain. I felt so inadequate as a woman, so angry at myself because I was useless.''

''Sarah, no. You aren't useless.''

''Oh, yeah, I know that here.'' She touched her head. ''But not here.'' She touched her heart. ''Or here.'' She touched her abdomen. ''I'd always wanted kids. I thought André would adopt. I mean, true, I was devastated. I didn't realize how important it was to him or his family that their line be carried on. I guess I should have. Every man wants a boy to carry on the family name.''

''Adoption would carry on the name.''

''But not the bloodline.''

Bill's hands fisted and he said something under his breath. Sarah didn't want to know. ''Don't be angry,

Bill. It's over and done with. And don't pity me. I've accepted it, sort of.''

The waitress brought their sandwiches and they began to eat. Bill had gotten through half of his before he'd calmed down enough to resume the conversation. ''What did you want to see me for, then?''

''It's about Justin.''

''Has he done the same thing?'' Bill demanded, his face beginning to turn red with outrage.

''No!'' Sarah said, dropping her sandwich. She toyed with it for a moment before looking up at Bill. ''He doesn't know.''

''You're serious about him,'' he said, satisfied. Then he frowned. ''Just how serious?''

''Very serious.''

Bill whistled. ''And you haven't told him?''

Sarah shook her head. ''I kept putting it off because I was so embarrassed. After all, there was nothing really going on between us, so there was no need for him to know.''

Bill nodded. ''I can understand your reasoning. Then it got serious and you couldn't just blurt it out.''

''That's right,'' she said, relieved he wasn't going to condemn her.

''He asked me last night if I could love him. Oh, Bill, I want to say yes, but I know he'll think I was hiding this from him. I don't want to hurt him. He's so good with kids. You know, he told me he regretted not giving Mickie a brother.''

Bill reached out and took her hand. ''But if you love

him, Sarah, you have to tell him and leave the decision up to him.''

She nodded, blinking back her tears. ''I know that. I just don't know how. How do you say, 'oh, by the way, I'm infertile and I know you want more kids, but you're gonna have to pick between the two'?''

Bill frowned, then asked, ''How'd you tell André?''

She laughed bitterly. ''That was easy. One night he asked me if I wanted kids. Thinking he didn't really want them, I said I was infertile so it didn't matter.''

Bill winced.

''Exactly. Imagine my surprise when he asked me what had given me the idea he didn't want kids. Then he said it was expected that the family bloodline be carried on through him. And all the time I'd thought he was different from his parents.''

''Justin isn't like that.''

''But I just can't ask him to pick,'' she whispered.

''That's his right, Sarah. Unless you can read his mind, you don't know what he wants.''

''Just like André, huh,'' she said, resigned.

''Yeah. Give Justin a chance.''

''But how?'' she asked. ''I've gone over this a million times. How do I go about telling him? What if he has questions? How can I stand there in front of him and give him all these answers without my emotions taking over?''

Bill now toyed with his sandwich instead of eating it. Bill never toyed with his food. That just went to show how touchy this subject was to a man.

Finally, Bill's face brightened. "Do you have a copy of your doctor's reports?"

"No. I never thought I could get them."

"Of course you can. Here's what you do. Use my phone," he said, digging out his cell phone. "Call your doctor. Tell him you're on your way over for copies of his reports. Get the copies, then highlight any pertinent information. Outline your speech, just as lawyers do when they're working up a case, then present the argument to Justin. You can hand him the report copies and tell him he can read them over if he has any questions."

Sarah brightened, too, feeling a burden lift from her shoulders. "You know, that just might work. If I have everything in front of me to show him, it might actually give me the courage to go through with this. At least then, when he backs off, I'll know it wasn't my fault because I bungled the telling, as with André."

She dialed her doctor's number.

"André isn't like Justin," Bill said. "Besides, I doubt you'll get through the speech before Justin sweeps you into his arms and tells you it doesn't matter."

Sarah spoke into the receiver to the nurse who'd answered the phone, before responding to Bill. "I only wish it wouldn't matter. But think how you'd feel if this were Marcy," she said.

"I am," he said softly just as Sarah turned her attention back to the phone and set up a time to pick up the records.

"I can go right over," she said, handing Bill the phone back. She looked at him and her distress must have shown, because he reached out and took her hand.

"Sarah, he might be upset, but it'll be for your benefit, not his. If he loves you, that's all that'll matter."

"But it didn't to André."

"He didn't love you," Bill replied. "Besides, he's weak. Justin isn't. Would a weak man go back to a family who had been wronged by his partner and offer recompense for his wrongs?"

Fresh tears filled her eyes. "You're right. What a fool I've been." She stood and hugged Bill. "I've got to go." She took out some money and tossed it on the table. "Don't argue," she warned when he opened his mouth. "You can treat me next time. And don't mention this conversation to anyone until I get back and tell you the outcome."

She headed toward the door, excitement making her steps bounce.

"Was that Sarah?"

Bill turned to see Justin walking up. "Yeah. We had lunch today. What brings you here?"

Justin seated himself across from Bill. "I called your office and they told me you were here."

Bill was thankful Justin hadn't shown up any earlier. Sarah would have found her plans to confide in Bill destroyed. She might not have had the ability to tell Justin everything as calmly and logically as she would now with her confidence restored. Bill didn't say that; instead, he merely nodded. "So, what's up?"

Justin ordered coffee, then turned to Bill. "Sarah is."

Bill raised his eyebrows. "What do you mean by that?"

"I hesitate to tell you just after finding you here with Sarah."

Bill chuckled. "I don't break confidences. But if you don't want to talk about her, then let me tell you about Marcy."

"I asked Sarah if she loves me."

Oh, well, so much for his not wanting to confide in Bill. Bill didn't think Justin had even heard his comment about Marcy.

Justin sipped his coffee and played with the sugar holder. "Well, I didn't exactly phrase it that way. I never would have thought I'd say that to anyone again. But Sarah has a way of getting under your skin. I mean, I did hire her simply because I needed a sitter and wanted to prove to her I bore her no ill will. But I didn't expect this."

Oh, yeah, his buddy had it bad. And he couldn't be more thrilled. Unlike Sarah, Bill didn't think it would make a huge difference to Justin that Sarah probably couldn't have children. No, Justin just wanted to find someone who would love him and love his little girl. No one could fill that bill better than Sarah. "So, what did you expect?" Bill asked, amused at the way his friend was fighting his feelings. He did feel just a little sorry for him, but he'd have tons of teasing material after Justin and Sarah were married.

"I don't know. I didn't know from the first day she showed up on my doorstep what to expect. It's like I've been sucked into a tornado. My common sense went on vacation and I've been operating solely on emotions ever since."

Bill chuckled. "Is that so bad?"

Justin grinned, but it was a self-deprecating grin. "I never dreamed I'd want home and hearth with a woman again, want to go shopping with her, see her carrying my child, watch her when she's cooking or outside pruning the roses."

Bill frowned at Justin's words. "Well, what if she can't cook or hates roses or doesn't want kids?"

Justin shrugged. "Sarah can cook, likes roses *and* kids."

"There's a difference between liking kids and wanting kids."

Again Justin shrugged. "That can be worked through. I just want her love." He frowned then. "But she wants time. I know I'm being crazy, but I'm wondering if maybe she doesn't feel obligated or something and that's why she wants time, to work herself up into accepting my proposal."

"Sarah's not like that," Bill said. "I'd bet she loves you, too." It was as close as he could come without breaking his word to Sarah—something he wouldn't do, no matter how much he wanted to at the moment.

Justin still didn't look convinced, so Bill added, "Give her time. She'll open up. Why else would she be marrying, if not for love?"

"So, how'd you get so wise?" Justin asked, joking.

Bill spread his arms. "Marcy fell into my arms with no problems, so I must be wise."

Justin only laughed.

And though Bill laughed with him, he felt the first inkling of unease. Could Sarah have been right to worry about Justin's reactions? Sarah had seemed so sure that Justin would be upset. And it was only now that Bill was finally realizing that Justin might actually not trust another female after the way Amy had hurt him.

He said a quick prayer that God would work everything out according to His will.

Chapter Twenty

"Daddy, do you love Aunt Sarah?"

Justin almost ran off the road.

"Wh-what did you ask, honey?" he sputtered. Kids always saw everything, he supposed, chastising himself for not hiding his feelings better.

"I love Aunt Sarah. She's really nice. I just wondered if you love her, too."

"Well, it's sorta hard to explain," he said, then glanced over and saw his daughter's guileless look. "Yes, honey, I love Aunt Sarah. She's very nice. But you have to remember, adult love is different. I mean, there's more than just love to consider—"

He broke off and shook his head. Mickie wouldn't understand what he was trying to say, when he himself didn't understand what it was. Besides, she was grinning and looking at something she saw out the window. She didn't need to hear his fears. He'd admitted to Mickie he cared for Sarah. What would Mickie understand besides that?

A lot, he thought warily, looking again to see if she was going to bring up the subject. When she didn't, he realized a weight had lifted off him. He'd been wondering how to break his feelings to Mickie and just when to tell her. She acted as though it didn't matter at all. Maybe that meant it wouldn't matter if he and Sarah decided to marry. After all, Mickie had told everyone at school Aunt Sarah was her mom. Of course, lying about it and actually allowing someone else into his life were two different things.

Getting remarried was just too much for any one person to handle. He wondered how people managed the stress. Which made him wonder again why Sarah had been so hesitant to return his love. Oh, she enjoyed his kisses and embraces. They had a wonderful time together. And he saw something in her eyes that he'd never seen in his wife's. Or was it his imagination? Did he really see a tenderness and yearning in Sarah, a desire to be with him always?

Suddenly aware of how much he wanted to see something special in Sarah's eyes made him realize he'd made the right decision to bring home those applications. She was becoming too much of a temptation and he wouldn't dare do anything that would hurt his daughter or Sarah's reputation—or his soul.

"Look! Mrs. Winters is home!"

Justin had just pulled into his driveway, and he saw Mrs. Winters unloading her car. Relieved, he realized he could get Sarah out of the house quickly now. Maybe that was the problem. She was afraid to admit to him she cared for him because she was still living in the house. It would be much harder on them both if she admitted it while still living there. The temptation would be too great.

Getting out of the car, he allowed Mickie to go over and say hi to one of her favorite neighbors.

"Well, hi there, Mickie. How have you been doing?"

"Great! Did you know my aunt Sarah is living with us now?"

Mrs. Winters chuckled. "Is that so? You like her as your baby-sitter, do you?"

"Yeah, but she can't cook as good as you. But that's okay. Sometimes she cooks really, *really* good."

Mrs. Winters chuckled again and turned to Justin. "I was going to come over later to let you know I was home. Whenever you needed me to baby-sit, I'll be here."

Mickie frowned and turned to her daddy. "We won't need her if Aunt Sarah is here, will we, Daddy?"

Justin laughed. "Well, pumpkin, Aunt Sarah may be getting another job and leaving temporarily."

Seeing the fear in her eyes, he added, "But she'll be visiting you just about every day."

"But you love her," Mickie said.

Justin flushed under Mrs. Winters's knowing look. Maybe he shouldn't have told his daughter that, he thought wryly. He simply shrugged at Mrs. Winters. "Sometimes, pumpkin, that's why you have to move out. It's better since we aren't married yet."

Realizing that he'd accidentally added "yet," he

flushed in earnest. He wasn't one to let something slip like that and he didn't like that he'd done it in front of someone other than Sarah. "You'll move out one day, honey," Justin said, trying to cover his mistake, hoping Mickie wouldn't realize what he'd said.

"Never, Daddy. I'll always live with you."

When she didn't say anything else, he breathed a small sigh of relief. Things were just too good right now. He was lucky Mickie hadn't caught his mistake and advertised it to the entire neighborhood. Turning back to Mrs. Winters, he said, "You'll have to come over and meet Sarah before she leaves. Maybe for supper one night. Let me speak to her first."

"Of course," Mrs. Winters replied, and headed toward her door. "Take care of that daddy of yours, Mickie."

"I will," she said, and crossed the street holding her daddy's hand.

"Well now, if you're gonna take care of me, then don't you tell Sarah about the gifts we shopped for. Just go find her and tell her I'm home for lunch."

"Okay!" Mickie said, and started up the stairs.

Sarah stared down at the pile of papers on the small writing desk. On top of them lay a clean sheet of computer paper with the words *To Do:*
Underneath she wrote:

1. Tell Justin I'm infertile.
2. Tumors discovered during annual Pap. Only one-quarter of an ovary left.
3. Why André dumped me...

No! she thought, and drew a line through the phrase.

3. Doesn't deserve half a wife.
4. But I love him.
5. Give him doctor's reports and tell him he can have time to read them.

Loud steps sounded on the stairs and Sarah realized Mickie and her daddy were home. Quickly, she shoved all the papers in the top drawer. Mickie was a dear, but she would question her to death if she caught her writing.

"Guess what?" Mickie said, running in. "Mrs. Winters is back and we bought Christmas presents and Daddy says you'll move out, probably until you marry him, and he's only going to be home for lunch today and you need to come fix it for him—can I go to the next-door neighbors' since I've already eaten?"

Sarah blinked. Then she nodded. "But, Mickie," she said as Mickie turned to run out the door, "don't be telling anyone else what you told me, okay?"

Mickie shrugged and was out the door. Sarah realized she hadn't made a bit of sense, but how could she have when she'd suddenly found out Justin was talking to his daughter about her and Justin getting married. And she hadn't even had her talk with him yet!

Going down the stairs, she caught Justin just as he was coming into the living room. Swallowing her fear, she said, "I need to speak with you."

When she realized she'd left her notes upstairs she started to turn. Justin's smile stopped her.

"I want to talk to you, too." He caught her hand. "Come in here."

The phone rang, stopping him, for which she was thankful. She turned once again to go get her notes. That was when she saw Justin's face darken.

Looking up at her, he said, "Can you hold this until I go into the other room?"

She nodded and went over to where Justin stood. Lifting the phone to her ear, she planned to wait until she heard the click of the extension. She was distracted when Mickie came barreling down the stairs with her doll. Sarah covered the receiver and asked Mickie to close the door.

When she lifted the receiver back to her ear, she got the shock of her life.

"Okay, Drydan, what do you want?"

Drydan Watson was on the line. Her stomach dropped to her toes and she felt ill. *Put the phone down. You're invading his privacy,* her mind screamed, but her heart kept the phone to her ear.

"I want bygones to be bygones. My son is back in town and I finally found out what was going on between those two."

"This really isn't any of my business, Drydan."

"But it is when she's tried to ruin my reputation. You see, my son found out she was infertile and trying to marry him for his money...."

The sound of a car door penetrated Sarah's hypnotic haze and she lowered the phone. She stood staring at the receiver, dizzy with pain. She had wanted to tell Justin. Drydan would make her sound guilty. She knew how manipulative he was.

She had to tell Justin her side of the story.

Panic gripped her heart and she forced herself to take first one step, then another, toward the library. She would go in there, explain that Drydan was a liar, tell Justin everything: that she was infertile—or at least, they were ninety-nine percent certain. No, she would be honest. There was no way she could have kids. The chances were less than a million to one, as far as her doctor was concerned. She would tell Justin that and explain that she was just afraid.

Her heart beat loudly in her ears, sounding like someone pounding on wood.

Sarah's head whipped around. No, someone *was* knocking. She hadn't been able to distinguish the sound over her own thudding heart.

Who in the world could it be? Now, right when everything was caving in on her, who could be knocking at her door?

She hesitated, thought not to answer it, but then, feeling her courage drain in the face of what Drydan had had time to tell Justin, she turned and ran to the door as if she'd been tossed a lifeline. Maybe it was Bill. Maybe it was Marcy or maybe...

"Oh, no... It can't be!" she whispered when she opened the door. She grabbed the wooden structure for support and gripped it as her knees gave out.

"Sarah? We need to talk."

André stood there, his hair ruffled from the breeze, a look of seriousness in his eyes that boded ill will.

Chapter Twenty-One

"May I come in?"

Sarah swallowed hard. "Yes."

When she just stood there, André took her elbow and escorted her to the couch. Sarah's mind was numb. All she could think was that Justin was in one room talking to Drydan and her whole present was about to fall apart, while André had just shown up at her door to rehash the past.

"Sarah. Did you hear me?"

"Huh?" she focused on André. Dear, gorgeous André, who had his whole life ahead of him now that he'd gotten rid of his little problem. Namely her.

"I said, I can't believe what my father did. I meant what I said when I told you I was taking some time off to think. My father had no authority to have you fired. You were my legal assistant. He took too much upon himself."

Forcing herself to concentrate on André, she was surprised by his words. "Look, André, you were dumping me. What did it matter?" All she wanted was to get to Justin and explain.

"Dumping you?" André shook his head, shock evident on his face. "Sarah, I told you I needed time to think. That's what I did. My father is the one who was behind the rest."

Sarah didn't understand, but he certainly had her attention. "What are you trying to say, André?"

"I love you. I still want to marry you. Look, I know my parents put you through the ringer, and I've had a long talk with them. They won't interfere again. I was especially furious when my father told me you were working as a housekeeper! A housekeeper, with your experience."

"Well, it wasn't as if I could get a reference from your father," she said sarcastically, her pain and anger coming out against this man.

"No. And for that I'm sorry. Why didn't you call me? I left my number with…"

His voice trailed off and she couldn't resist asking, "Your father?"

He sighed and rubbed a hand down his face. "Yes, my father." He growled. "I've been an idiot. I thought I needed time alone and found all I could think of was you. Only you."

He stood and began to pace, pushing his coat back so he could slide his hands into his pockets. "It doesn't matter if we have children or not. I've let my father dictate my life too long. It's you I want. I understand you were hurt and didn't have anywhere to go and your ex-brother-in-law took you in. I just hope he hasn't taken advantage of the situation.''

"André!" Sarah said, shocked.

André turned back to her. "I didn't mean that. I'm still upset over the fight I just had with my dad. Can't you understand? I love you. I want you back. Are you planning to work here the rest of your life?"

Sarah thought of the applications Justin was supposed to bring her. "No, André," she said wearily. "I don't plan on staying a housekeeper."

"Good. I'm setting up my own practice. I want you to work for me. You won't have to worry about my father again. What do you say?"

"That sounds like a good idea, Sarah. Maybe you ought to consider it."

"Justin?" She whirled around to find him standing near the foot of the stairs at the entrance to the side hallway.

He sauntered into the room. His features were masked, but there was something roiling in his gaze. Anger? Disillusionment? Hurt? Pain? "I said André has offered you everything back. Sounds too good to pass up. You ought to consider it."

Just like that her hope died. Justin had talked to Drydan and Drydan had carried through on his threat. He had told Justin about her infertility, plus who knew what else. And Justin saw this as the perfect way to get rid of her. She wouldn't have believed it of him.

Of course, she didn't have any right to be upset. She'd told herself she'd give him the right to choose. And he chose a better life for his daughter than her being an only child.

She was glad for the numbness right now. It would help her deal with everything. But later—oh, yes, later—she would grieve what she was losing. Because she realized she didn't love André at all. No, it was Justin she loved—deeply. And she doubted she would ever love anyone again as much as she loved Justin.

Forcing herself to swallow, she nodded. "Thank you, Justin. If you don't mind, I'll leave now."

"You don't have anywhere to live," Justin reminded her.

"I'll see she has a place," André said, not unkindly. "You can't expect me to allow her to continue to work as a housekeeper here, though."

"No, I don't suppose I'd like it, either," Justin said.

Sarah noted the way the two men talked over her. Normally, she would be spitting mad, but she still didn't feel anything.

"I'll send someone for my things," she said, and without looking back walked to the door. "Tell Mickie—" the pain in her heart broke through the numbness and she gasped "—tell her goodbye."

"Sarah…" Justin said.

But she didn't stop. She felt André's hand on her, escorting her to his car. She was grateful.

"I'll take you to my house and—"

"Take me to Bill's."

"Now, Sarah," he began.

"Take me there or I'll walk."

"As you wish," André said reluctantly.

Sarah laid back her head and closed her eyes. Only then did she finally allow the pain to engulf her, and the tears to silently flow down her face.

"What a fool," Justin berated himself, going back into his office and sinking into his chair. "Why did you let her go like that?"

But Justin knew. Oh, it wasn't because of what Drydan had said.

He knew that Drydan had not told him the truth. Sarah wasn't a manipulative person who tried to marry André for his money.

No, Sarah had loved André. And for some reason, André had left her. Probably because he'd found out she was infertile.

Justin wondered if Sarah had planned to tell him. He was still reeling over that. Why hadn't she told him? Was she worried he'd be angry? Or maybe she was worried he'd kick her out? After all, he'd taken her in off the streets.

But he wouldn't have done anything like that, because he loved her.

He'd gone out to confront her, and had heard André saying his father had been behind everything.

It was then that he realized why Sarah hadn't been able to voice her love for him. She was still in love with André. And knowing Sarah as he now did, he understood that she wouldn't have told him, would feel guilty for leading him on.

It had broken his heart to know she was coming to him just as Amy had.

But he wouldn't let her do it. Not just for him and Mickie, but for her, too. That's why he'd told her she might want to try going back to André.

And she hadn't even put up a fuss; she'd jumped at the idea.

He'd thought he hurt when Amy died, but he knew he was hurting again—a wound he wasn't sure he would get over this time.

He scrubbed at his eyes, trying to erase the images his mind conjured up of Sarah. But it was no use. She was there, would be there—

"Daddy, where did Aunt Sarah go?"

Justin's head shot up.

Mickie was standing in the doorway, holding her doll, staring at him uncertainly.

What could he tell Mickie? How could he tell her?

"She moved out, honey," he said.

"Moved out? But she didn't tell me goodbye. She promised she'd always tell me goodbye."

Justin didn't know what to say. Angry at Sarah and himself for putting his daughter through this, he vowed never again to get involved with a woman. He held out his arms. "I'm sorry, pumpkin."

In a flash she was across the floor and climbing into his arms. Little sobs shook her body, and he rocked her, his own tears silently falling down his face. Why, oh, why, had he allowed the woman such a place in his heart?

He didn't realize his daughter had stopped crying or that it had gotten dark out. He did feel the touch of her small hand on his cheek and hear her whispered words.

"It's all right, Daddy. She'll come back. Don't you worry."

Looking down at the small child who was trying to comfort him, he hugged her close. Kissing the top of her head, he said, "What say we go make a chocolate coconut cake with extra coconut?"

"That sounds good," she said. But though she replied positively, her little eyes were far too serious.

Justin realized then that he'd have to push Sarah from his mind and concentrate, instead, on the life he had right in front of him. In time, he and Mickie would heal. Someday they'd be happy again.

Wouldn't they?

Chapter Twenty-Two

"Sarah, it's Bill."

Sarah glanced toward the front door of the garage apartment Bill had leased to her. Bill had pushed open the door and was peeking inside. Seeing him, his head covered with snowflakes, she motioned to him. "Come in," she said. "I was just finishing up my résumé for the job I'm applying for Monday."

"Marcy sent me over. It's Christmas Eve. She wanted to know if you'd come over and share dinner with us."

Christmas Eve? Already. An entire week had passed and she hadn't realized it. In another way, it seemed that an entire lifetime had passed since she'd walked out of Justin's life. "I don't know, Bill. I have so much to do—"

"May I ask you a question?" Bill sat down on the couch across the room from where Sarah sat at the table.

Sarah avoided his gaze and went back to typing.

"Sure. Shoot. After all, you rented me this place without any questions. I'm sure you're entitled to a few."

She knew that was a low blow, but she really didn't want him asking questions.

"Good try, Sarah," he said. "But I don't run when you get nasty."

"I'm sorry, Bill," she said, and looked up at him, only to see his compassionate gaze. "Don't," she warned.

"You're gonna drive yourself into a grave. Every time I glance over here I see the light on. You've done more this past week than anyone should do in a month. You need to slow down."

"I'm just trying to find a job."

"If that's so, why didn't you take the one Justin offered?"

She stiffened.

"I see," he said at last when she didn't comment. "What happened, Sarah? I don't understand why you're here. Justin loves you."

"Yeah, sure," she finally said, bitterness slipping into her voice.

Bill looked surprised but said, "So it is Justin. I'd wondered."

"Bill, don't bring it up. Please."

He ignored her. After going over to where she sat, he forced her around and took her hands. "I don't know what happened, Sarah. But I do know one thing. Justin loves you. Whatever's the matter can be worked out. You've got to try." When she didn't comment, he asked,

"Does this have to do with what you told him—that you were infertile?"

Sarah tried to run away, but he wouldn't let her. "Does it? Are you telling me he went crazy over that? Well?"

She struggled against his hold, then stopped fighting. Her voice a broken whisper, she finally admitted, "I never got the chance to tell him."

Bill stared at her for only a minute, then : : go of her hands and took a seat next to her. "Then what is all this about?"

Tears brimming her eyes, Sarah said, "I didn't get a chance to tell him because Drydan did."

He shook his head. "Wait a minute. You want to run that by me again? You said nothing about Drydan going over there that day."

Sarah sighed and dropped her head to her chest, her shoulders feeling heavy with the truth of that day. Finally, she said, "You remember your advice about notes? Well, I did it. I'd decided to confess everything. I went downstairs, planning on just that. But when I got down there, the phone rang. Drydan was on the line. He told Justin all kinds of things. Enough that when Justin came out he sent me home with André."

"Why didn't you try to tell him that what Drydan said was wrong?"

Sarah looked up helplessly. "I don't know. André was telling me he still loved me. Justin was telling me it'd be best if I went with André. And I was still in shock from what had happened. Honestly, I didn't think of anything until I was in the car. Then I had enough sense to demand that André bring me here.''

"Which explains what Marcy was saying about a strange man driving you here and her hearing an argument before you came into the house.''

"Yeah,'' Sarah replied. "André didn't want to leave me. I didn't mean to hurt him, but he had to understand I didn't love him and wasn't taking the job he offered. I think maybe he realized that I had become his courage to face his father. It was a step he needed to take to finally grow up. But it wasn't love. When it came out that Drydan had just called Justin, I don't think he believed me.'' She shrugged.

"Oh, Sarah, honey.'' He reached out and touched her shoulder, then drew back his hand. "Go to Justin. Explain. I know he loves you.''

"How? How do you know?''

Bill looked her straight in the eye. "He told me. I don't think he'd honestly care about your infertility. If nothing else, think what you're doing to Mickie in all this.''

Sarah knew she looked stricken, but that was one of the reasons she hadn't been able to sleep. "I didn't even get to say goodbye to her.''

"Oh, Sarah.'' Bill sighed. Then he stood and grabbed her by the hand. "Come on. Whether you want to or not, we're going over there.''

"I can't. Bill, you don't understand. I don't think he wants me over there.''

Bill wouldn't take no for an answer. He pulled her toward the door until she reluctantly followed. "I'll make you a deal. If he gives you any problems, I beat him to a pulp for you.''

Sarah laughed, though not out of amusement but excess nervous energy. "I just don't know...." She hesitated. "I don't want to make things worse."

"Bill! Bill!"

Marcy's frantic voice reached them. Bill threw open the door and Sarah saw Marcy running up the stairs, which were now covered with snow.

Bill immediately released Sarah and ran to Marcy. "What is it, sweetheart? The baby?" His hand went to her abdomen.

"No. Justin called. It's Mickie. She's missing."

Justin paced his house, frantic for any word. Where was she? Where had Mickie gone? She'd been away three hours now.

He'd tucked her in, then come downstairs to work. At one point he'd gone out back to stand in the fresh snow, thinking of all that had happened since Sarah had left, remembering her wish for snow on Christmas so she and Mickie could build a snowman.

He and Mickie were both miserable. They both wanted her back. He'd been praying, trying to decide if her returning would be the best course.

Then he'd gone in and taken a hot shower to warm up. Before getting into bed, he'd gone to check on Mickie. It wasn't until he found her coat and backpack missing that he realized she'd run away.

The pounding on the front door had him racing to it. Bill, Marcy and Sarah stood there.

"Have they found her yet?" Marcy asked, going to him and giving him a hug.

Justin's disappointment was acute. He shook his head. "The police have been out an hour. I've looked all over and haven't been able to spot her. They asked me to stay here in case she calls."

He heard the police officer behind him go back to the phone. They'd left one man behind. He didn't know why. Maybe to keep him there when he finally went crazy and wanted to go back out on the streets and search for his daughter.

"What happened?"

He turned to Bill. "I don't know. I was outside, then I showered. When I went to check on Mickie, she was just gone."

"Any clues?" Bill asked.

Justin finally looked at the last person in the group. He replied to Sarah instead of Bill. "She was miserable this past week. She didn't understand why you'd left."

Sarah appeared tired, as tired as he felt. Deep purple smudges circled her eyes. Guilt etched her face.

"I'm so sorry," she whispered.

He could hear the truth in her voice.

"We should have talked. I should have said goodbye. I should have told you I didn't love André and asked for visitation rights. I don't know what I should have done—"

"Stop it," Justin suddenly whispered, his heart aching. "Come here," he said, and opened his arms.

She ran to him and threw herself at him. He wrapped

his arms around her small body and felt her shake with sobs.

"She's so alone, right now," she cried. "Why would she do it?"

"I don't know," he murmured, rocking her. "I just don't know."

He continued to rock her, thinking how right she felt against him. He loved her more than life itself. Why had he ever let her go? Why hadn't he explained that he didn't blame her, that he thought she loved....

"You don't love André?" he questioned, pushing her back. "I don't understand. I thought that's why you left."

Sarah reluctantly released Justin. She looked up and met his gaze. "I left because you told me you thought it was best. Drydan had called you and told... I was going to tell you, Justin. I had the doctor's reports, and even notes to answer questions. They're probably still upstairs on the desk."

"You think I care that you're infertile?" he asked astounded.

She dropped her gaze. "You want more children."

Suddenly angry, he growled, "I *want* you. I *love* you. We can adopt children. My lands, Sarah, didn't you know how much I love you?" Sarah looked up at him and he could see the hope and despair mixed in her eyes.

"No," she whispered. "I didn't."

He jerked her back against him and held on tight, his whole body shaking at the revelation. "Sarah, I asked you if you could love me. What did you think I meant? I want you in my life forever.

"Infertility doesn't matter. If you were blind or crippled it wouldn't matter. Don't you understand, it's you I love.

"Only you.

"Your brightness, your tender spirit, your kindness, thoughtfulness. Just you. All I wanted was your love. Anything else can be overcome. But when I thought you were only considering me because I had given you a job—"

"What?" she asked, shocked. "You thought...how could you?" she asked.

He saw the spark of anger in her eyes and his anger melted.

"I love you for who you are. But you wanted kids. You'd mentioned it and I didn't know if you could accept me after Amy—"

"Whoa, right there," he warned. "The past is the past. Amy was put to rest. I won't ever compare you with her. As I said I want only you."

"You're all I want, too," she said, and went back into his arms. "But, Mickie..."

"Yeah," he said, when she trailed off. "I should have called you and asked you to come over. But I was too proud. I didn't want you to see me like that. I was hurting too much...." He sighed, a defeated sound in a room that should have had only merriment.

Then Sarah's hand cautiously stroked his back, tentatively, as she tried to relieve the hurt and pain he was experiencing.

"Don't blame yourself. We were both wrong. Now all we can do is pray that Mickie is found quickly."

Bill heard that and came forward. Taking their hands, he and Marcy began to pray, asking God to protect her and guide the police to her.

When the door opened, Sarah was the first to see the bundle in the police officer's arms. She cried out, covering her mouth in joy.

Justin looked up, saw the brown head sticking up out of a blanket and dropped Sarah's and Bill's hands. "Mickie?" he asked, scared to find out if she was hurt. Then it didn't matter. He shot across the room and was reaching out for his daughter. "Mickie, honey?"

Her head popped out of the blanket. Tears covered her face. "I'm sorry, Daddy, but I had to get her."

"Who, honey?" he asked, rubbing her legs and arms, chafing warmth into her. "Where'd you find her?"

"About two miles from here, Mr. Warner," the officer said.

"I had to find Aunt Sarah."

Justin stared at his daughter. His knees were knocking in relief. "You were going to walk to Bill's?"

Mickie shrugged.

"I told you never, ever to try that, honey. You scared us all to death."

The tears started again and Justin immediately felt awful for chastising her. He gathered her close and turned toward Sarah, his only purpose to get her to the woman she had been seeking. Mickie's next words stopped him.

"You don't understand. You said you loved her. And you told me if it was a real emergency I didn't have to wait for a grown-up. I could walk someplace myself."

He started to explain he'd meant to find a teacher or policeman to help her, but she wasn't done.

"I asked Santa for a mommy. I prayed and told Jesus to send just the right one. Well, Aunt Sarah was just right. You did say you loved her, Daddy. But you see, it's Christmas Eve, and I couldn't find my letter to put on the tree and I was afraid Santa would forget to bring her. I just had to find her."

Justin couldn't help it; he started crying. He wasn't sure if it was relief or joy.

"Don't cry, Daddy," she whispered. "There's a police officer here and he'll see you."

That caused him to chuckle as tears streamed down his face. Justin continued across the room to where Sarah was crying, too. Halfway there, Mickie saw Sarah.

"You're here!" she cried out, and wiggled from her daddy's grasp. "He found my letter!" She ran over to Sarah and threw her arms around her. "Did Santa find you?" she asked.

"Not exactly," Sarah said, bending down and pulling the small child into her embrace. Mickie locked her arms around her neck, then she pushed back. "But how'd you know to come?" she asked, puzzled.

Sarah looked up at Justin. "Your daddy called me."

Mickie looked up at her daddy. "Does this mean you married her now? I know you said she had to move out until you could get married, but I want her back for good."

Justin turned to Sarah. His heart ached with the love he felt for these two. The officer standing near the door, Bill and Marcy near the stairs—their stares didn't matter.

All that mattered was the two people he loved most on the face of this Earth, who stood before him. He smiled at his daughter.

''Well, pumpkin,'' he drawled, ''I don't know. You see, Aunt Sarah has to agree to that. Now, if she will, I know a judge or two who might be romantically inclined and might marry us tonight so Sarah will never have to leave this house again. What do you think about that?''

Mickie jumped up and down and turned hopeful eyes on her aunt Sarah. ''Oh, please, Aunt Sarah. Will you marry us? I promise to be real good and not ask for chocolate coconut cake again.''

''She can't bake that, sweetheart,'' Justin said, enjoying the look on Sarah's face.

''I won't even ask for too many peanut butter-and-jelly sandwiches,'' Mickie said, though reluctantly. Then, turning wide eyes on Sarah, she said, ''We love you, Aunt Sarah, and want you here.'' She fidgeted, as if she were afraid of Sarah's answer.

Fresh tears streaked down Sarah's face and she leaned down and hugged Mickie. ''And I love you, too. I'll be glad to marry you—and your daddy. Do you think I should tell him?''

Justin's heart tripped over. ''I think he heard you,'' he said, and walked forward. ''How about giving me a kiss to seal that?''

Sarah looked up from Mickie, her cheeks suddenly flushing. Her eyes sparkled with love. Slowly, Sarah stood and walked forward. Shyly, she held out her hand. Justin took it, then pulled her into his arms, but he hesitated as he stared at her beautiful face.

"Come on!" Bill called out. Marcy laughed and urged him on, as well.

"An audience," he murmured. Then, not letting that stop him, he shifted her and bent her back over his arm. "Your acceptance kiss," he said softly before taking her lips.

The kiss left Sarah weak and breathless, supported only by his arms. When she opened her eyes, Mickie was clapping.

"Do it again, Daddy. Do it again."

Justin was short of breath, but looking very smug, Sarah noticed. He smiled and shook his head. "I think I'll save the next one for after we say 'I do.'"

Sarah blushed, then she said tenderly, stroking his face. "I love you, Justin. You're the best Christmas present I've ever received."

Justin pushed her hair behind her ear and nodded. "Let's go find the judge."

Mickie ran up and grabbed her daddy around the legs. He picked her up and started toward the door.

"You know what, Daddy?" she asked.

"What's that, pumpkin?" he said.

"This is gonna be the best Christmas ever."

Looking over at Sarah, he said, "I couldn't agree more."

*   *   *   *   *

Dear Reader,

I love kids. And I'm very blessed to have two wonderful, loving children, as well as a loving husband. However, not everyone is that lucky. Some people have children but have lost their spouse. Others are married but are unable to have children. This story is about two such people: a woman who comes face-to-face with the possibility of never having children, and a man who has found himself alone, doing his best to raise his daughter.

But with God, all things are possible. In my story, God brings two hurting people together to allow their healing and love to blossom. I'm an eternal optimist and believe there is no situation that God can't turn around for good. With His love leading us, He can give us joy and the true desires of our hearts if we only stop and listen to His voice. I hope you have enjoyed Sarah and Justin's story, as together they discovered God's plan for their lives—along with a little help from Justin's rambunctious daughter, Mickie. I'd love to hear from you, too. Write to me at P.O. Box 106, Faxon, OK 73540.

Cheryl Wolverton

A MOTHER'S LOVE

He shall call upon me, and I will answer him:
I will be with him in trouble; I will deliver him,
and honor him.
—*Psalms* 91:15

To Marcia Bender, who was the first to ever tell me how much she loved my books. This one's for you. Thank you to Donna Blacklock and Denise Gray, who have supported each and every book I've written with book-signings and encouragement and who were both enthusiastic when I told them about this one. You'll never know how much that means. And to my sister, Deborah. I love you, hon. I hope this one touches your heart, too.

Prologue

Maggie looked at the suitcase sitting by the front door. It didn't contain much, just her most treasured possessions. Funny how everything she really cared about could fit into one suitcase.

Looking back at the house and the lavish staircase, she realized what a pampered life she'd led.

Fear clutched her heart, emerging from her numbness. So much had happened in the past seven weeks, things that had totally changed her outlook on life. No more was this house a haven for her; no more was it a place she could run to when she was hurt or afraid.

She saw a maid peek around the corner, heard the muffled sniffles of another when she picked up her suitcase. Maggie hadn't realized how much the staff cared for her. Of course they wouldn't say anything about her leaving. Their jobs wouldn't permit it.

Had her whole life been so marked by privilege? She'd been so innocent, working at a job that had been provided for her, going to the church where she'd been raised, doing everything she'd always been told.

Until now.

But she just couldn't do what her parents had asked of her.

She couldn't.

At twenty-six, she was old enough to make her own decisions. It was time to stop listening to everyone else. *Past time.*

So, when the ultimatum had been given, she had shocked everyone by accepting it.

She went to the door, then looked back one last time. Black dots danced before her eyes, and she swayed before fighting off the dizziness. She'd never been on her own before. She was scared, more scared than she could ever remember being. She took a deep breath.

Pushing the desolation from her thoughts, she reached for the brass doorknob and pulled the door open. She wished once again there was an easy way out of the mess she was in.

But there wasn't. That was why she was leaving.

For better or worse, she had made her bed; now she had to lie in it.

Squaring her shoulders, she headed toward the cab, refusing to look back, promising herself to only look ahead. She would rely only on herself from this day forward to get herself through the next six months.

Chapter One

~

"Shirley quit?" Jake Mathison swerved to avoid a huge puddle in the middle of the road, the beat-up truck bouncing as he hit a pothole instead. He moved the cell phone from his ear, then brought it back. "But she was assisting with those plans we've been working on as well as keeping my notes. And," he suddenly added, "she helps with the children's programs."

Doom loomed before him as he realized all that would be left hanging with Shirley gone. He almost missed Jennifer's next words, but instead nodded with exasperation. "I know, Jennifer. I'm not blaming her. If Charlie finally asked her to get married, I can see why she jumped at it. She's been head over heels in love with him forever. I even counseled her when he left. That's why she took that vacation out there." Jake now wished in a small way that he'd had her wait just a bit longer.

No, that wasn't true. He was happy for her.

He listened as Jennifer quickly suggested a solution.

"Yeah, okay. You do that. Maybe if you put it in the church bulletin, someone will be interested in temporarily assisting me."

Though it was the middle of the afternoon, Jake squinted through the deepening gloom that had settled over the small streets of Centerton, Louisiana. It was the time of year for hurricanes. And whether they had hurricanes or not, the summer months always brought rain. So what if today was like a monsoon? Yesterday had been, also.

"Yeah, Jennifer. No, I won't be back today," he replied to her question. "Go on home to Gage."

He squinted again as he went down the country road. "You, too. Bye." He hung up.

Jennifer was a wonder. He adored her, had been delighted when she'd come to work for him as the daycare manager at his small church. Jake had even performed her marriage ceremony six months ago. He depended on her help.

Just as he had Shirley's.

So, what was he going to do without his assistant? Not only had she kept his files in order, helped him when he went on his children crusades into the inner city, but she'd also been working closely with him on his latest project: getting the cities around Baton Rouge to pitch in and work together to build an inner-city recreation center where the kids would have a place to go, to get off the streets and away from drugs.

And now Shirley was gone.

Maybe it was the rain or his telephone call that kept

him from seeing the woman until he was right beside her.

He caught only a flash of someone with long limp hair, huddled in an oversize yellow raincoat, before his truck splashed her and she cringed.

He hit the brakes, pulling off the road immediately. In his rearview mirror he saw the person stumble and fall from trying to avoid his splash.

"Oh, great! Good going, Jake," he berated himself. He grabbed his umbrella and ran back to where the young girl was struggling up. Concerned, he held the umbrella out over her, trying to protect her from the rain.

Reaching down, he extended his hand. "Are you okay?"

The girl placed her pale-white hand in his. He felt calluses on the pads of her fingers, saw short clipped nails that were clean of nail polish. She struggled up.

When she lifted her head, green, the brightest he'd ever seen, met his gaze and he was transfixed. This girl—*no,* he corrected himself, *this woman,* had the most exquisite eyes he'd ever seen. They were beautiful. Large and innocent, they were framed by dark lashes. Perfectly arched eyebrows, a darker shade than her eyelashes, crested over her eyes. A few small freckles dotted the bridge of her nose, the same color as her dripping red hair.

Then her expression changed, became guarded, world-weary. "Are you okay?" he repeated, wondering what had caused the change.

"Fine."

He waited, but she didn't say anything else.

"Can I give you a ride somewhere?"

She started to shake her head, but he stopped her. "It's pouring rain. Come on. I can't leave you out here like this."

She lifted her chin, then sighed, her shoulders drooping.

What could make this beautiful woman look so beaten down? His heart went out to her. "It's okay," he reassured her. "I won't hurt you. Besides, it's the least I can do, since I wasn't paying attention and splashed you."

She raised her wary gaze to his again, then nodded once, curtly. "Thank you."

He walked beside her to the car. "I'm Jake Mathison."

"I'm Margaret..." She hesitated.

"Margaret? You look more like a Maggie," he joked, trying to put her at ease as he opened his truck door.

She lifted astonished eyes to him.

"You *are* a Maggie." Jake laughed, knowing he'd guessed right, and her gaze softened for just a minute.

"I'm sometimes called that," she finally replied. She turned her back on him and climbed into the cab.

He wished he'd brought his car, but he'd had to do some errands for the church. Though his congregation ran just over one hundred now, it didn't seem as if he ever had enough help.

Going around, he hopped in the driver's seat. "Well, Maggie, where can I take you?"

"My car is about two more miles down the road. I need to stop and see if I can figure out what's wrong. If you'll just drop me off there..."

He looked at the hat—the one with the familiar logo—she was wearing on top of her sodden curls as he pulled back onto the highway. "You work at the fast-food restaurant about five miles back?" he asked.

"Umm-hmm," she said, staring out the window, not meeting his eyes.

So, she didn't want to talk. But Jake couldn't let it go. He was concerned. She shouldn't be out walking the streets, especially in a rainstorm. "You on your way to work?"

Another sigh escaped her, and then he saw it. One lone tear slipped from her eye and trailed down her cheek, mingling with the wetness already there.

Uh-oh, he thought. *Help me, Father.*

Very softly he said, "You want to talk about it?"

She shrugged.

He didn't push her but waited.

Finally, she said, "I was at work, but they let me go."

He drove along the bumpy road, doing his best to avoid potholes. Jake wondered if she saw the green trees lining the highway or if she was simply looking inside herself at something he couldn't see. He was almost certain it was the latter.

"You were late because of your car?" he prompted.

She shrugged. "That was only an excuse. It doesn't matter," she added, suddenly sounding stronger. "I don't need anyone. I'll find another job."

They arrived at a broken-down, rusted-out yellow compact. She started to get out. Jake touched her arm to stop her but wasn't prepared for her reaction.

She jumped and jerked her head around. Fear flashed through her eyes, before warning replaced it.

He immediately pulled back, giving her space.

"I'm an old hand at working on cars. Let me have a look at it."

"It's not necessary—"

"Think of me as a knight in shining armor," he teased, smiling at her. "My mama would come back from her grave and tan my hide if I left a lovely woman like you stranded with a broken-down car."

The first smile he'd seen cracked her lips. It transformed her face, made her eyes look even greener.

Oh, boy, he thought, stunned by her effect on him.

He quickly exited the car. Going over to the compact, he popped the hood and looked under it. "Uh-huh, here's your problem," he said, fingering a belt. "I have a friend who owes me a favor. What say you let me have your car towed to your house, and I can fix this for you?"

She stiffened. "I don't think so. I'll take care of it myself."

Puzzled by the sudden anger in her eyes, he wondered what he'd said. "I've got a cell phone in the truck. Just hang on...."

"I can't pay for the repair," she finally confided, lifting her chin haughtily.

Realizing she was embarrassed, he smiled. "There's no charge. Like I said, he's a friend and I'll put the belt on for you. The belt is only a couple of dollars."

"I can't ask you—"

He strode back over to her, touching her shoulders. Her arms felt small through the slicker.

When she stiffened again, he immediately let go. "You aren't asking me for anything. But there's no way on this earth I'm leaving you out here in this downpour to get soaked."

He turned, swiped a hand at the rain pouring down his face, then went back to his truck to make a call. By the time he was done, the rain had almost quit.

And Maggie was again looking nervous. When he walked up she surprised him. Instead of trying to talk him out of helping again, she offered a tentative smile. "Thank you."

"You're welcome."

"Your friend doesn't mind getting out in this?" she asked, looking up at the sky.

He smiled. "Nah. He's a good guy."

She had the front of his truck between them, and he allowed it. After all, he was a stranger. It was only right that she be cautious. He wanted to reassure her but wasn't sure how to put her at ease. The road was deserted, lonely. She had a right to be wary.

"Am I keeping you from something?"

He smiled, trying to help lessen the tension. "No, ma'am. As a matter of fact, I was just on my way home."

"Do you need to call your wife or something?"

His grin widened. "No wife or something. No relatives at all."

She ducked her head.

Interesting.

He sidled over to front of the truck. "Have you lived here long?"

She shrugged. "Two months."

"I bet you live in the trailer park about two more miles up the road."

She looked up, surprised.

He answered her unspoken question. "It's the only thing up the road besides the church and a couple of subdivisions."

"How do you know I don't live in one of those subdivisions?" she asked.

"I don't. But the hat you're wearing wouldn't pay the rent on those houses. Unless you're independently wealthy and just work at the fast-food restaurant for fun."

She opened her mouth to comment, when suddenly her stomach growled.

Red crawled up her face to her hairline.

He grinned. "My stomach's telling me the same thing."

Her lips formed a small smile again. "I get hungry a lot."

The sound of a truck caught their attention, and they turned. Jake was relieved. He'd never had such a stilted conversation in his life. He was down-to-earth, always putting everyone at ease. This woman had a wall thicker than the Great Wall of China built around her. "That's Tyler. Go ahead and get in the truck. We'll hook your car up and then you can give us directions to your house."

He started to walk off, but the woman called his name.

"Yes?" he asked, turning.

"When we get to my house, I'll be glad to feed you dinner for your help."

He could tell that offer cost her a lot. Still, he was glad for the invitation. He nodded. "That's very nice of you, Maggie. Go on, now. Get in the truck. I'll be right there."

"She sure is a pretty little thing," Tyler said as Jake walked up. He and Jake worked on getting the car hooked up to his truck.

Jake glanced back to see the woman sitting alone in the dilapidated old truck. "Yeah, I suppose she is." He remembered the haunted look in her eyes.

"So she's caught your eye, has she?" Tyler joked.

Jake turned back around and chuckled. "How could she not? She's beautiful." It was the honest truth. He saw no reason not to admit that to Tyler. But he didn't mention there was something more than beauty that had snared his attention. He couldn't quite put his finger on it. Maybe it was the simple fact that she needed someone, and Jake was the giving type.

Tyler laughed. "I'm surprised you even noticed."

Jake raised an eyebrow, then chuckled. "I've dated, Tyler. You know that. I just have too much to do and no time to go looking."

"I know other preachers who've gotten married," Tyler replied, going around to the other side of the car.

"I have, too. Some of them are my friends. But the right woman has just never come along."

He finished adjusting the chains, then nodded. "Follow us. Maggie said she'd give me directions."

"Sure thing, Jake," Tyler said, and headed toward the truck.

Jake went back to his truck. *Marriage.* Now, where had that come from? He supposed many in his congregation wondered why he'd never married. He was finally realizing a lifelong goal in his inner-city ministry program. He honestly didn't believe he had time for marriage with all that going on. Or he, at least, had no time to look.

"It shouldn't take too long," he said, turning his attention to Maggie when he got in the truck. He was pleased when she smiled....

He started the truck. "Which way?"

She pointed one long slender finger. "You were right about the trailer park. If you turn in the second entrance, I'm the first trailer on the right under the big oak tree with the long patio porch."

"So," he said, pulling back out onto the highway, watching as Tyler slowly followed, "do you have any new job prospects?"

If she thought his question too personal, she didn't show it. She only shrugged. "I'll find a job."

"What type of work do you do?"

If he hadn't chosen that moment to glance at her, he was certain he would have missed the flash of bitterness in her eyes. As it was, she covered it quickly. "I do a bit of everything. I've done inventories, was an executive secretary, a cook, fast-food."

Surprised, he asked, "Why aren't you in Baton Rouge looking for a job? Executive secretaries make much more than a fast-food restaurant worker would."

"There are no openings where I applied. Besides, I have no references."

An idea formed. He had to tread carefully, though, because he didn't want to push Maggie the wrong way. "Have you ever worked construction or anything like that?"

She didn't answer.

Oh well, it had only been a hope. He'd been lucky that Shirley had experience in that area. Still, maybe if this woman could just keep good notes...

"I worked in a building company," Maggie said, breaking into his thoughts. "I did everything from dealing with the people who ordered lumber to talking with people who were building their own houses. I loved that. I thought, at one time, building would be my future."

She had a distant look. He wondered what experience from her memories of that job had to do with the lingering pain in her eyes. He couldn't help but ask, "Why aren't you still there?"

Maggie snapped back to the present, the wary look returning. "No reason. Why are you asking me all these questions?"

He smiled. "I just might know of a job."

He turned in to the trailer park. "But why don't we talk about that after I get your car fixed, okay?"

"Sure," she said.

He didn't hear much hope in her voice, though.

"It pays better than a fast-food restaurant, and I think you'll be perfect," he added, and was glad he did when he saw a small spark of hope in her eyes.

"I'll go fix dinner," she said. "If you'll excuse me…"

Jake turned off the engine and slipped out. After going around to her side of the vehicle, he opened her door to assist her down. "I appreciate the meal. Watch your step here," he warned, realizing he'd parked in a huge puddle.

Jake reached up to help her at the same time her foot slipped on the running board. She fell forward against him.

He caught her small body against his, feeling her arms snake around his neck for support. The soft smell of strawberries wafted up from somewhere. He gazed into her deep-green eyes and saw her hint of dismay.

Then it registered what else he was feeling.

His eyes widened, and he glanced down. Sure enough. Though they were touching in the middle, the rest of her body came nowhere near to touching him.

He thought of the pictures of starving kids in Africa but of course knew that wasn't her problem.

Totally surprised, he looked back into her eyes and said, "You're pregnant."

"Gee," she replied, roughly, her eyes brimming with sudden defiance and a cynical smile slowly twisting her lips, "what was your first clue?"

Chapter Two

"I'm so sorry. I didn't mean that the way it sounded."

Maggie shrugged. "No big deal," she said. And it wasn't. She had no business thinking of this man the way she had been thinking of him.

"Go on and fix the car. I have to prepare dinner."

She walked off, leaving him standing there gaping. No wonder he'd been so nice to her, she thought dispiritedly. He hadn't realized she was pregnant. How could he have missed it?

After unlocking the dead bolt, she went inside before pushing the metal door closed behind her.

Wearily Maggie took off her raincoat and her shoes. She was soaked. She went to the bathroom, grabbed a towel to dry her hair, then combed the long curly red strands before clipping it back out of her face with a large clasp. Gazing at herself in the mirror, she realized she looked tired. Purple circles shadowed her eyes.

She'd get some sleep tonight, she vowed. No more nightmares.

She changed into a blue summer dress with flowers. She'd found it at a secondhand store. "Beggars couldn't be choosers," the saying went. And it was true. She'd learned a lot about shopping and buying things she wouldn't necessarily have ever considered before. However, the dress looked okay on her. She would have preferred green or black, but blue it was.

Maggie pulled on a pair of fuzzy slippers. With a long sigh she pushed herself up and then padded back into the kitchen to see what she had to fix.

She wondered if Jake was still out there, or if had he run as soon as she was out of sight. He'd been shocked enough to want nothing more to do with her.

Pulling back the flowered curtain, she peeked out the kitchen window. Nope, he and his friend were still there, working on her car, talking—probably about her. Slightly curly, dark-brown hair was slicked down against Jake's head. His wide shoulders blocked out most of the engine as he pointed to something and motioned at Tyler.

When he'd first stopped she'd been frightened. Of course, that was a leftover from the past, from things she tried to forget. Since she knew what an acquaintance could do to a woman, a stranger automatically made her nervous. People didn't really help other people. She didn't believe it.

But Jake had been willing to help her.

She still couldn't get over how friendly he had been, or how willing to help. She knew nothing about him. He didn't know her, yet he'd pulled more information out of her than anyone else had over the past six months.

He was easy to talk to. Too easy.

And she'd been glad to have him there. That had made her automatically nervous. She didn't need anyone. She'd learned that, and she wasn't about to risk it now. But if she decided to take a chance, she thought, glancing out the window again, she'd definitely want it to be with him.

He certainly was gorgeous, she acknowledged as she watched him stand up straight. Tall, a good six inches taller than her, and strong. He'd held her above the ground a minute ago while staring into her eyes as her condition dawned on him. He hadn't acted as though she weighed anything. But where strength had scared her before, it was strangely reassuring when coming from the man with the gentle eyes. While her heart had been tripping over a surprising attraction, his had been recoiling at his discovery.

Her cheeks burned with embarrassment. It had to be her hormones that had made her react to the man.

Maggie opened her cabinets, trying to figure out what to fix. It'd been a while since she'd cooked. She was very careful and rationed her food to make it last. Two bags of egg noodles, one larger bag of spaghetti noodles, four cans of tomato sauce, various spices, six macaroni-and-cheese dinners.

Spaghetti it was. She couldn't offer him any of the other supplies.

She went to her freezer and looked in. One small container of hamburger meat and a whole chicken sat there.

She'd splurge and add meat to the spaghetti sauce. She pulled the meat out and put it in the frying pan to thaw, wishing again for a microwave.

But she couldn't afford a microwave without a job. Nor would she be able to afford more groceries. That's why her car was so important. Next week's paycheck was supposed to go for groceries.

This week's had to go for rent. She rented on a month-to-month basis, with the understanding that if she dropped over fifteen days behind she'd be evicted. She had three days to go.

Her jobs just weren't bringing in enough money to support her, and she didn't know what she was going to do.

When she'd walked in today and seen her manager's face, she'd realized her parents had found out where she was.

Maggie had asked the manager point-blank if her parents were behind her dismissal. He'd avoided her eyes when he said no.

She had her answer.

She'd fought her parents on the decision about her unborn child, and they were determined that she leave the area.... Her chest tightened on that thought.

She would not think about the confrontation that had forced her from the only home she'd ever known, forced her into working the way she was. Through her trials, though, she'd come to appreciate money. All her life she'd had everything. It was good for her to find out what it was like to have nothing.

Or at least she kept telling herself that.

Deep down inside, though, she felt lonely. God seemed so far away, as if he didn't care. She couldn't understand why He'd let everything happen to her that had.

Seeing that the meat was thawed, she opened a can of tomato sauce and then, thinking that both Tyler and Jake were big men, decided to open two. She'd find a way to buy more groceries.

She'd find a job.

At the thought of a job, she wondered what job Jake had in mind for her. Without references, no one would look at her résumé. If the job was in Baton Rouge, well, she might as well forget about it right now. Her parents controlled a huge business in Baton Rouge and were very well known in the business world. That was why she didn't work there now. They'd put the word out that she was being a problem and rebelling. So of course no one wanted her. And if she did get hired, her parents would hear about it and make sure she didn't keep the job.

She was too much of an embarrassment to them.

Maggie turned abruptly away from the sauce and went to the cabinets, where she pulled out a pan. After filling it with water, she dropped the noodles in to cook.

Looking around, she wondered what Jake would think of where she lived. The trailer had come furnished. A small, checked, broken-down couch sat against one wall; a chair across from it, with a coffee table in between.

She hurried across the room and snatched up her nightgown, which was lying on the couch. The shag carpet was clean. Though she didn't have a vacuum, she'd used a broom yesterday to sweep it out.

The linoleum in the kitchen was cracked in places but had been mopped.

A small table sat in the corner with two chairs. On it was one place mat and a napkin holder—and a dead bug.

Yuck!

She hated the bugs. She'd never had bugs at her old house. Maggie went over and used a paper towel to sweep it into the garbage. One spray, maybe two more, and the place would be devoid of vermin.

A knock on the door sounded just as an engine started up. Maggie hurried over to answer it.

Jake stood there.

"Where's your friend going?" she asked, seeing the other man driving away.

"He said to tell you thank-you, but he had to get home."

"Oh." She shifted uncomfortably; then, realizing she was keeping him outside, forced down her fears and stepped back. "Come on in."

He nodded, a gentle smile on his face. "Thank you."

He sniffed, and his mouth shifted into a wide grin. "That smells good."

Maggie actually blushed. She was glad she'd gone to the trouble to add meat. "Thank you. It's not much. But I hope you like it."

Jake smiled at her. "I'm sure it will be delicious."

She returned his smile. She couldn't help it. Despite her wariness around men, she liked Jake. He had a warmth about him that she hadn't seen in other men before.

Old bitterness reared its ugly head. After everything that had happened, she had at least expected her church and her family to support her. Yet they hadn't. Not one person had had the guts to stand up with her. Nor had a single person comforted her. Every single one had blamed her for what had happened, believed her a liar, a Jezebel, a Mary Magdalene....

"I'm sorry. Come on in. I have juice, milk and water to drink. I was just about to make up some tea, though."

He smiled. "Tea sounds fine."

"It's herbal," she warned, a hint of defiance creeping into her voice.

He frowned and walked forward. She stiffened, not sure what he was going to say. He floored her when he took her hand and stroked it.

"I'm really sorry about my surprise out there. My only excuse is that I was so captivated by your face I never looked lower."

She burst out laughing. "Now, there's a line I've never heard."

His smile returned, his eyes sparkled. "Be that as it may, I can only beg your forgiveness."

Ruefully Maggie shook her head. "I'll forgive you if you set the table."

She pulled out two plates and silverware and handed them to him.

Jake easily arranged the table, noting the layout with a discerning eye. This woman was low on funds. He'd been in enough houses before to tell. The cabinets were

bare, with nothing hanging on the wall to hint at per-
manence. And her clothes were probably secondhand
since they didn't fit her very well.

He felt guilty eating a meal she had prepared. He wondered if she had enough food. But he wouldn't ask her.
Jake didn't know her well enough and wouldn't stick his
nose in unless he felt directed by God.

Besides, he still had the idea for a job that might work.
But first, he had to put her at ease. He didn't know why
she was so worried, unless pastors just made her nervous.

"Have you lived here long?" he asked, taking the hot
pot of noodles from her hands and setting it on the table.

"Thank you," she said, and turned back to the stove
to finish the sauce. "No. I moved in here two months
ago when I came to this area."

He nodded. "Here, let me help you," he said, lifting
the pan with the sauce in it from her.

"I'm pregnant, not helpless," she muttered.

He grinned. "Consider it chivalrous. As long as
there's someone here to lift for you, why do it yourself?"

"I don't want to turn into a lazy housewife," she
returned, sitting down.

He smiled, but his eyes were serious as he said, "I
doubt that'd ever happen."

She put her napkin in her lap.

"Do you mind if we pray?" he queried.

Surprised, she lifted her eyes. "Not at all."

He watched her wariness finally fade, and she bowed
her head.

After a quick prayer, they served up their plates.

"So, what about this job?" she asked.

Jake felt guilty for keeping her in suspense when he saw how interested she was, though she tried to hide it. "It's here in town."

"Not in Baton Rouge?"

He shook his head. "No. My secretary just quit...."

"Your secretary?"

Jake saw he'd surprised her again. "I guess I didn't explain enough earlier. That's why I inadvertently splashed you. I was talking on the phone and had just found out Shirley quit. I have no replacement and no idea who to hire. I need someone who has good book-keeping skills, as well as secretarial skills. The person would also need to know about lumber and building and things of that nature, if possible. You see, we're under-taking a major building project for the inner-city youth and I'm the one who is spearheading the project."

"What project?" she asked.

"A large recreational center, a place where kids can go and be safe."

She nodded. He could see the cautious hope in her eyes. "I think I could handle the job. But what about references?"

Holding up his fork that had spaghetti on it, he said, "This is reference enough."

"I'm serious," Maggie said, frowning. "I don't have any references. I can't get any. Why would you consider hiring me without them?"

He wondered if Maggie realized how negative she sounded. Patiently he explained, "Any woman who is trusting enough to fix a stranger a meal simply because he helped her out is reference enough with me. In my opinion it tells me you aren't totally self-absorbed and that you care.''

She stiffened. ''You've drawn a lot of conclusions from one simple act of kindness.''

''Maybe God is prompting me, too,'' he quipped.

She didn't return his smile. He cleared his throat. ''The hours would be full-time. Of course, with your condition, we could certainly allow time for rests and doctors appointments. And the last person who helped me also ran the children's programs and assisted me on Saturdays with the kids.''

Puzzled, she asked, ''Just what type of job is this? Lumber, kids, children's programs? Do you treat your entire staff this way?''

Jake stilled. He'd told her what his job was, hadn't he? Surely he wouldn't have forgotten something so important that would put the woman at ease immediately and stop her from worrying about him being some rapist. ''Didn't I tell you what I do for a living?'' he asked.

Caution immediately returned, dominating her small round face, and she set her fork down. ''No, you didn't.''

He widened his eyes in dismay. ''I'm so sorry, Maggie. I'd thought I mentioned it when I introduced myself. I'm the local pastor at the church down the road.''

Chapter Three

She paled.

He'd seen it before. People oftentimes reacted negatively to his position. He just hadn't pegged Maggie as that type. Then she glanced down at her stomach, and he saw her problem. "Maggie," he said, pulling her look back to him by the soft yet authoritative tone in his voice. "I'm still the same person I was ten minutes ago. So are you. I still want you for the job."

She glanced everywhere before finally, reluctantly, turning her gaze back to him. "If you're willing to try me out on a trial basis, how can I refuse? What about my car?" she added, pushing her plate away. "Can you tell me if it's working so I can get there?"

"Didn't I mention the house?"

"What house?"

Jake ran a hand through his hair. "You've disrupted more than my dinner, Maggie." He was usually so efficient, keeping his mind on the problem at hand. Maggie had the ability to make him forget everything. "There's a small house next to the church. The rent is very cheap. It's only a two-bedroom, eight hundred square feet. But it's roomy enough for one person. My last secretary lived there."

He named a price that was lower than what she paid here.

Her eyes widened. "You're not misquoting the amount on purpose, are you?"

"No. Since the job doesn't pay much above minimum wage, the rent is cut way back. We make just enough to keep up repairs and pay the taxes each year. That way, the secretary, who ends up spending almost as much time as I do at church, will have a place to live that doesn't cost an arm and a leg."

"Where do you live?"

He could tell she hadn't meant to blurt that out. She actually blushed. He couldn't help but grin. "Well, I don't live there," he drawled, and her blush deepened. "The house is yours, if you want it. If not, we'll rent it out to someone else."

How could she pass it up? "I guess I agree," she replied. Staring at the man in front of her, she still found it hard to believe he was a pastor. He was so good-looking and so sweet. He hadn't condemned her for her condition or questioned her about it. Instead, compassion showed in his eyes as he smiled at her. Not pity. Never pity. She would have thrown him out if he'd given her the look of others. That look of condemnation. The look her parents had given her. No, he simply smiled at her as if she was an actual person, as if he might understand what she was going through.

Of course, that was impossible. Why would he have to worry about what everyone thought of him or be on guard constantly?

Then she realized that was it. As a pastor, she imagined many people had the opportunity to dissect him over lunch, just as her parents had done with their own pastor. Maybe he did know something of the humiliation and pain she'd been through because of the way everyone had treated her.

Still, working for a pastor. At a church. She wasn't sure. She loved God. But she hurt so much. It seemed that everything that could go wrong had gone wrong in the past seven months. And it all evolved around her family and church friends.

She'd blamed God for casting her out.

I will never leave you or forsake you.

That inner voice reminded her of God's promise. Then why? Why had all this happened to her? Why wasn't she allowed to have any happiness?

Jake was offering her a chance at peace, if not happiness. And she had just said she would take it. "I'll be glad to move in then," she said, and that settled that.

"Good!" He clapped his hands, finished off his spaghetti, then stood. "I need to get going. Listen, is two days from now too soon to move you? That would be Saturday, and I'm sure I can find some men to come over and pack up whatever you want to take. We could get you moved in and unpacked in one day."

"I don't have much. The furniture's not mine. All I have is one suitcase, maybe two."

He paused, his look probing her. She stiffened, certain the questions would come. Instead, he smiled. "Great. Then we'll have the house ready for you Saturday. I'll come by with a couple of the women so we can help you get the house cleaned up for inspection."

"I don't need any help."

Jake rolled his eyes. "Don't balk, Maggie. Of course you need help. You're pregnant."

"I haven't had any help yet," she blurted out, then gasped; Maggie clapped a hand over her mouth.

Silence fell, and Jake studied her a minute. He reached out and stroked her cheek with his finger. "You've had a tough time of it, haven't you, Maggie? And it's hard for you to trust."

Unexpected tears filled her eyes.

He dropped his hand and cleared his throat, stepping back instead of forward the way he wanted to. "Don't worry. You'll be welcome at church."

"But what will people say to you?" she asked, not believing him. "You're going to catch the very devil for hiring a single pregnant woman."

There, she'd said it. She was single and not married. She couldn't tell him the rest. But that was enough to condemn her in most people's eyes.

She waited. A slow smile curved his lips, lighting up his face. "'Be joyful in hope, patient in affliction, faithful in prayer,'" he quoted from Romans.

"And what do you mean by that?" she asked, not understanding.

He grinned. "Well," he drawled, "we can *hope* no one says anything. But if someone does, then we can be patient and pray and allow God to handle the problem."

She shook her head. "An optimist."

"God gave us hope when He sent His son, Maggie. Why let someone's possible actions rob us of that?"

Maggie raised weary eyes to Jake's. "I've learned already that the world isn't a place of optimism."

"Look inside yourself. Ask God to restore your joy. Don't let them," he said, waving his hand toward the outside, "rob you of it. There are always going to be negative people around who can't stand to see you succeed or be happy. And there are always going to be people to kick you while you're down. But if I think you're a good secretary, as I know you're a good person, then no one is going to tell me who to hire and who to fire."

"But you don't know if I'm a good secretary," she argued, frustrated.

He grinned. "Then don't disappoint me."

He went to the door. Pausing on the bottom step, he turned back toward her. "See you Saturday, Maggie-May," he singsonged.

She couldn't help the reluctant smile that came to her lips.

She'd never met anyone like Jake.

Not even her ex-fiancé.

Her ex-fiancé. Boy, had that been a mistake. She'd thought he loved her. She'd thought she loved him. But then she'd changed her mind.

She didn't want to think about the trouble, think about

the nightmares it gave her. Instead, she wanted to think about the laughing eyes of the gorgeous man who had just given her a ride home and rescued her from certain poverty.

But she knew better than to think it was only Jake who had rescued her. "Thank you, God, for providing a way when I couldn't see one. I'm glad about this job. But—" she walked over to the couch and sank onto it "—I don't know if I can believe in happily ever after again. Every time I think I've finally found a job, or a place to live, or something great, it seems the rug is jerked out from under me. Is this going to be any different?"

She got up and went into the kitchen. She could save the spaghetti and have enough to last until Saturday. Then maybe she could make her groceries last until her next paycheck.

And maybe, just maybe, she'd pass Jake's approval and get to stay at this job longer than a month or two.

Chapter Four

"You didn't tell me you lived right behind me!"

Jake, who had just finished the inner-city work an hour earlier before swinging by to pick up Maggie, smiled, surprised. "Does it matter?"

Maggie frowned warily. "I can only imagine the talk there will be."

"You're my secretary, Maggie. My last secretary lived here. The entire church knows it. Don't worry about it."

Maggie still didn't appear convinced. Jake wondered what drove her to be so cautious but didn't ask. "As you can see," he said, going on into the house, "here is the living room. The carpet is old but clean. The couch actually folds out into an extra bed if you have company." Jake wondered if she minded an orange couch and chair. "Shirley had them re-upholstered in those colors. You might, uh, try throwing a small blanket across the back."

Jake heard a chuckle behind him and turned. "Yellow and orange are fine. And yes, I have a small blanket to cut the glare."

Relieved, Jake smiled. "I never asked her what color she wanted to redo the material in. At least the curtains aren't white."

Jake pointed at the light-blue curtains until he saw Maggie's wince.

"Let's just see the rest of the house, shall we?"

Jake nodded. Glancing around the room, he suddenly realized that Shirley must have had very poor taste in decorating. Blue curtains, tan rug, orange and yellow furniture.

"The kitchen has a small table for four in it. The stove is gas and there's a frost-free refrigerator."

Maggie thought it was much nicer than the trailer she'd been in. The living room might be a bit bright, but this room, she thought, with the light white-and-blue floor with soft blue-and-pink wallpaper, was homey.

"One of the women repapered the walls before you moved in."

"That explains the smell. I wondered what that smell was." The counters were clean, and there was even a toaster and a food processor on the counter.

"To the back are the two bedrooms and the bathroom."

Maggie strode there to look. The master bedroom was bigger than the trailer she'd been in, with a double bed and two chests and a small vanity. She turned to the bathroom. It was old but very neat. "I don't think I've ever seen a claw-foot tub before."

"That's next on our list of renovations. This house is more than fifty years old. We've been renovating one room at a time over the past year. The kitchen and the second bedroom are done."

Maggie went to the second bedroom and smiled. "Earthtones, yellows and greens. It's beautiful."

Maggie heard Jake's step approaching and turned, feeling trapped in the hall. Thankfully, Jake stopped near the entrance. "Of course we'll be glad to remove the bed and put in a crib for you. Tyler would have gotten that done earlier—"

"Oh, no, Mr.—uh, Reverend, Pastor..." Helplessly, she lifted her hands. She could feel the blush warming her cheeks.

"Just 'Jake.'"

His warm smile could melt chocolate on a winter day. It certainly melted her heart. She found herself smiling back. "Well then, just Jake," she said, "please don't bother with that until I know what I'm going to do. Or if you're certain you even want me here."

Jake's smile left his face. The shimmer in his dark eyes dimmed. "Maggie, I don't know why you're so worried, but I think you should know, we're a small church. If you can type and have any kind of head for business we can work the rest out. Unless you aren't happy here, then there might be a problem. So please, stop worrying."

Maggie nodded. "I'm sorry." She didn't say she'd had so many jobs in the past six months that she'd become cynical. Or that she was certain it was only a matter of time before her parents found out where she was.

They would exert some sort of nasty little influence to get her out of the area so she wouldn't be an embarrassment to them. Again.

Seeing Jake's concerned expression, she pasted the smile back on her face. "This is more than I could hope for. Why don't you show me where I am going to work."

Jake nodded, relieved, though still concerned that she was hiding more than she was telling. *Father, help her,* he silently asked. "Right this way. As I said, the church has only between 100 and 150 in attendance, according to what is going on. Our average crowd is just over 100. Of course, we have the day care, which has 185 children, grades kindergarten through third. I never dreamed it would grow so fast."

Jake led her across a small path lined with azaleas to the church. The smell emanating from the pink and purple blooms was sweet, teasing her nostrils and surrounding her in a soft gentle fragrance that relaxed her.

"I love azaleas," Maggie murmured.

Jake smiled. "Mrs. Titterson wanted to donate them to the church. She thought they'd be beautiful lining the path here as well as both yards." Jake motioned back at the houses. "They are beautiful in the spring. We have crepe myrtles in the front of the church and snowball bushes along the far side. You'll notice the bridal bushes around the parking lot."

"I never met a man who knew so much about shrubbery." Maggie glanced at him curiously.

Jake turned and grinned at her. "Didn't you realize a

pastor is a jack-of-all-trades? Who do you think helped plant all these bushes?''

Maggie chuckled. Jake liked the way it sounded, low, warm, husky. Realizing where his thoughts had drifted, he stopped, disconcerted. Shaking himself mentally, he stepped off the path and in front of the long rectangular concrete building.

''This was once a business. We bought it, then tore out the inside and rebuilt it. It was big enough for anything we might want to do later. I'm thankful now that we did that. Otherwise we wouldn't have been able to start up a school.''

Maggie nodded.

Jake decided she probably wasn't interested and held open the door. He saw her look down at the carpet. ''The blue doesn't show dirt as easily. It was a choice between that and red. If you'll just turn to the right, you'll find the offices. The left leads out to the sanctuary and the school, which I'll be glad to show you later.''

Jake reached out and took Maggie's elbow in his hand to guide her down the hall. He'd thought to do it as a gentlemanly gesture but found he liked the feel of her soft skin in his hand. He immediately released it. This woman was a walking problem. He had no doubt she would flee if she knew his thoughts ran toward the curious and I find you fascinating.

He didn't understand it. He hadn't known her long enough to be attracted to her. Besides, she was pregnant. There was a broken heart in there somewhere. And though he felt she was the right one for the job, saw a softness in her, that didn't tell him one iota about her relationship with God.

No, indeed, he had no right to be wondering if Maggie was married, divorced, single or carrying twins or quadruplets for that matter.

Besides, he'd learned long ago that women didn't fall for men who owned nothing. Jake had a salary, and a roof over his head, but there wasn't much left over. He had been saving what he could. Soon he would be able to buy a new car since the other one had over 100,000 miles. Janie had made it clear that if he wouldn't go to a bigger church where he could make better money, she didn't want him.

He remembered that breakup just before he'd moved to this church. Jake had never completely recovered. Janie couldn't understand why he didn't want a better job. When he'd tried to explain that this church was where God wanted him, that his heart was in building a place for the inner-city youth, she'd broken off their engagement.

Jake had decided then and there to concentrate fully on his ministry. God called him to do a job, and he would do that job. If love came one day, fine. But he wasn't going to search for it.

"Here we are," he said to Maggie.

Glancing around the office, he tried to imagine what she saw. "It's rather messy right now. I've been trying to do the filing, and Jennifer Dalton has been coming in to help."

"Jennifer?" Maggie asked, still studying the office.

Jake nodded. He moved over to the desk, gathered

four file folders and straightened them. "She's the head of our day-care center now. A wonderful woman. You'll love her."

He put the folders in the box on her desk and then smiled. "This will be your desk. The copier is here." He pointed to the corner. "And we have the latest in word processing on the computer. My office is through the door behind me. Since I do a lot of counseling, I need privacy, so you'll have to screen my calls and run interference. Most everyone here is really understanding. There are a few, though..." He trailed off and shrugged. "You know how that goes. Life isn't perfect."

Maggie nodded. She looked around again and then toward the door.

Jake took her out and showed her the day care and the rest of the church.

"Jennifer!"

Maggie noted how Jake's face suddenly lit up with a bright smile for the young girl coming their way. She was petite, the girl-next-door type, with long blond hair falling out of a French braid that was pinned up on the back of her head. She wore a purple and gold LSU shirt and baggy jeans. As she approached, Maggie realized there was paint all over her clothes and on her hands.

"This must be Maggie," the young woman said, coming forward, beaming.

On closer inspection, Maggie realized Jennifer was older than she looked. Small smile lines around her eyes gave that away. Maggie smiled and nodded. "And you're the famed Jennifer I've heard so much about."

She actually blushed. "Jake has been telling tales

again? Don't you listen to a one of them." Turning on Jake, the young woman gave him a reproving look. "You didn't tell her about the snake, did you? Or the rappelling accident?"

Jake lifted his hands in surrender. "I haven't told her anything except what an excellent job you do here."

Maggie liked the way the light jacket stretched on Jake's shoulders, outlining them, showing their width. She'd never seen a pastor who wore jeans with a jacket. But it suited him.

"Oh," Jennifer said.

Maggie glanced at Jennifer and saw she was pink again. Then what she had said registered. "Rappelling accident?"

Jennifer turned even brighter red. "Don't ask. Maybe one day we'll have time to sit down, and I can tell you all about it. Unfortunately, I was just about to go wash up. Gage is coming by and picking me up for lunch, and I got carried away with the kids and didn't realize it was so late."

Jake shook his head. "I'm just showing Maggie around. Go on."

"Nice meeting you," Jennifer said.

Maggie murmured her agreement. "Rappelling accident?" she asked when Jennifer was gone.

Jake chuckled and led her back toward the front entrance of the church. "It's a long story. But it ends well. Jennifer got a pet snake out of it, and a husband."

"You're kidding."

Jake shook his head. "Gage is quite a man. Come on,

let's go out this door and get your stuff unpacked from the car. Then I'll let you rest.''

Jake pushed open the door for her and Maggie went out. She had thought Jake unusual in how friendly and outgoing he was. She had never met a pastor quite like him.

He'd been enthusiastic, fun loving, excited, when he had picked her up and then rattled on and on about the kids and the puppet show. While showing her the house, he had actually been nervous about whether she was going to like it. But the house was a deal she couldn't pass up. Who cared about the yellow-and-orange furniture or the yellow-and-orange coat rack in the corner?

Maggie had heard the pride as he had talked about helping plant the bushes, and the joy behind his words as he'd talked about the people at the church.

There had been no formality or reserve in his voice or his stance. His fluid movements as he'd taken her around proved to her how at ease he was with this.

''Meeeooowwr.''

Maggie didn't even see the pitiful sight until she was almost upon it. ''Oh, my heavens!''

Maggie stared in horror at the bloody mess that was a peach-colored cat. At least she thought it was peach. It was hard to tell with all the blood. ''Jake!''

Jake moved up by Maggie and put a hand on her shoulder. ''Let me handle it, Maggie.''

Jake started forward, and the cat hissed. He paused. ''Maybe we'd better call animal control. The poor thing looks to be in bad shape.''

The cat lay there on its side, breathing hard, fur ripped

away in tufts. She thought it had been in a cat fight since part of an ear was missing, except that she'd never seen a cat break another cat's tail. And that had to be one of the problems with this cat, since its tail lay at such an odd angle. One leg was twisted, too. Tears came to Maggie's eyes. "We can't just leave it here."

"I know, I know. Let me go call city hall and see if they can send someone out. I'll be right back."

Jake hurried in to call for help. Maggie continued to stare at the cat. Silent tears fell as she watched it labor for breath. She could see the terror and pain in its eyes and felt it reach out to her and wrap itself around her heart. It hadn't been too many months ago she'd felt pain and terror.

Please don't let it die, God. Please, please, please, she prayed, and inched forward.

The cat hissed again, and she whimpered. "Please don't let it bite me. Please, please, please."

It hissed once more and then made an awful, plaintive sound. "Father, help it. Help me. I'm not letting it be die just because it's in pain and scared."

The cat eyed every inch she moved.

Maggie got close enough to kneel down. She put her hand out, and the cat swiped at it with one of its uninjured paws. Maggie jumped but didn't back away. "I'm not going to hurt you. Please let me help you, sweetie. Just let me help you. No one helped me, but I can help you," she whispered.

Carefully she moved her hand closer.

This time the cat only eyed her hand.

She slipped it under the cat's head, then its body. The cat growled.

Maggie made sympathetic noises, crying right along with the cat as she slipped her other hand under it and then picked it up.

Its tail hung sideways. "Oh dear—oh dear," she cried, over and over until she had gathered the cat to her bosom. "We'll get you help immediately. I promise you. I won't let you down."

Maggie heard the church door open. "The animal shelter…Maggie!" Alarm in his voice tensed her spine.

Jake hurried forward when he saw the bloody mess in her arms. "You're pregnant. What if it has rabies? What if it had bitten you?"

Maggie's face turned as hard as stone. "Will you drive me to a vet?"

Jake hesitated then nodded. "Just let me take—"

The cat hissed and swiped at Jake. His eyes widened and he lifted his hands in surrender, backing up.

"Okay. Okay. You hold it. But I'll be praying the thing doesn't take its pain out on you before we get to the vet."

"It won't," Maggie said, looking back down at the cat.

Jake paused in pulling his keys from his jeans pocket. He eyed her his features probing, searching before he nodded, "You know, Maggie-May, I think you just might be right."

He slipped a hand to her lower back, then guided her toward the truck. "There's a clinic less than two blocks away."

Chapter Five

She wouldn't let them cut its tail off.

Jake was still shaking his head over that. Jake sneezed again as he turned into the driveway next to the church.

"Are you sure you're not allergic to cats?" Maggie asked worriedly.

Jake shook his head. "I'm not allergic to anything." He rubbed at his watering eyes. "Just dust or something, I'm sure."

He pulled to a stop and hopped out, then went around the hood to open her door. Once again the cat hissed at him.

He sneezed.

"Be careful," she warned when he reached out to ease her out of the truck's seat. "I don't want you to scare her."

Scare her? Jake looked at the way the cat rolled its eyes at him and didn't think the animal was in any way scared. "Careful, now. We don't want you falling."

"I'm fine," Maggie said, holding the cat close. "I still can't believe she only had a cut on her side, was missing part of her ear and had a broken tail and broken foot."

"Well, if the doc was right and it climbed up in someone's car, I'd say it was real lucky."

Maggie nodded, sighing when both feet found solid ground. "The cat is a she, not an it."

"Oh." Jake nodded. He went ahead of her and opened the door to her house. As she approached he sneezed again. "You sure you'll be okay with her here? Doc offered to keep her for you until the owner was found."

Maggie shook her head. "I'll look after her. We don't even know if she had an owner. There were no records. That's why the vet went ahead and gave her shots."

Jake sighed. He watched Maggie cooing to the cat the entire time the cat growled back at her. The hair on the back of his neck stood up at how mean that cat sounded, but Maggie sat there and made faces at the animal.

"If you need anything…"

Maggie looked up, opened her mouth, then shook her head.

"What?"

"Nothing. I can get it later."

Jake studied her as she went over and sat down on the couch. His gaze drifted to the cat. Suddenly it dawned on him. "Cat food."

Maggie glanced up, surprised. "Yes. I do need cat food. But I am paying for this."

She narrowed her eyes to let him know she was serious.

Jake shrugged. "I didn't mind paying for the vet. You saved the cat when the shelter would have put her down. It was the least I could do."

Maggie laid the cat carefully on her jacket, which was on the couch, and stood. She crossed the room to her purse and opened it. Jake watched her discreetly count out her money, then hand him some. "I would appreciate it. I'm just afraid to leave her right now."

Jake smiled. "No problem. I'll run up to the store and be right back."

Maggie's face softened. "Thank you."

Her smile could easily knock a man off his feet. He couldn't remember anyone with a smile like that. He found himself grinning like an idiot. "Uh, yeah." Jake cleared his throat. "Okay. I'll just...go."

Maggie nodded, turning back to the cat when she growled again.

Jake shook his head and left, sneezing three times before he got out the door. He tried to remember if he'd ever been around cats and couldn't recall a single incident except when he was a child. "No. I do not have allergies," he reassured himself.

Jake turned and headed across the driveway to his truck. He saw Jennifer and her husband locking up the day care for the evening and paused.

Jennifer and Gage came over. Gage stuck out his hand and Jake automatically shook it. "How's the new secretary? She getting settled in?"

Jake nodded, blinking at the itchy sensation. "She's fine. I'm sorry, Jennifer, that I was gone so long. It took the doc longer to patch up that cat than we realized."

"No problem." Jennifer peered at him. "Cat allergies?" she asked sympathetically.

"No." Jake shook his head. "I just...the truck needs to be cleaned out bad."

Gage raised an eyebrow in disbelief.

Jennifer looked confused. "If you say so. Do you need anything before I leave?"

Again Jake shook his head. "I'm on my way to the store. No one called, did they?"

"Yes. Mrs. Rawley. She wanted to make sure this was her Sunday to work in the nursery. Gloria called and rescheduled her appointment from Monday to Tuesday to talk with you. She said she just couldn't make it."

Jake sighed. Gloria was putting off their talk and that worried him. She had come to him about the problems going on in her marriage and their one talk was enough to make him really concerned.

"And Sister Hollings called. She wanted to talk to you about the music again. She says it's way too loud on Sunday morning. If it wasn't turned down, then she said she was going to turn it down herself."

Jake smiled. "I know...that guitar..."

"Just drives me crazy," Jennifer said with him, and they both chuckled.

"Gotta love her," he said. "You left the messages on my desk?"

"Yeah. They're all there except Gloria's. I slipped that in your top desk drawer on top of the phone book."

"Thank you, Jennifer. I'll see you tomorrow."

"You get some sleep tonight," Gage said, slipping his arm around his wife but keeping his gaze on Jake.

"Those plans for the inner-city program can wait until later."

Jake groaned. "I completely forgot."

Jennifer elbowed her husband. "Thanks, Gage."

Gage shrugged. "Sorry."

"Seriously, Jake. I've looked over them and talked with the committee. They've agreed to give you another week."

Wearily Jake nodded. "Fine. Fine. Good night."

They waved and left.

Jake climbed in his truck and ran up to the local dollar store.

Once there, Jake went through the aisles, trying to decide what the cat would need and if he could pay for it with the money Maggie had given him.

He shook his head.

Impossible.

With God, all things are possible, he acknowledged silently. "So, how are we going to work this out so as not to embarrass her?" he muttered.

Jake thought.

They could afford cat food. That was a must. Cat litter, too. But that left only three dollars for a litter box and bowls.

Remembering being on the streets when he was a kid, he smiled. Other people had had pets, but they certainly hadn't been able to afford all the fancy stuff advertised on these aisles as musts for cat owners. No, a simple bowl out of the kitchen and a plastic-lined box had suited them fine.

He took the two items up the cash register and paid

for them, feeling guilty. Of course, what Maggie didn't know was that he'd had the cabinets filled from their food pantry as a welcome gift from the church. So maybe this money wouldn't be missed so much when she realized she had food.

After paying for the items, he took them out to the truck and hurried back to Maggie's.

He knocked.

"Come in, Jake."

He opened the door and went inside, carrying the items. "You really should have that locked."

He stopped, unable to believe what he was seeing. Maggie had taken the extra pillow, put her raincoat over it, then a sheet and finally the cat on top of it.

The cat saw him and growled.

He sneezed.

Maggie looked up, noticed the bag and smiled. "Thank you."

Jake handed her the food. "I'll carry the litter. It's too heavy."

"Okay." Maggie nodded and went into the kitchen. She rummaged around until she found two old bowls, then filled one with water and one with food.

"About the door..." he began.

"I would have had it locked, but I went out to get my suitcases. I had just gotten back in before you arrived."

"I told you I'd get those for you," Jake said, somehow feeling he'd failed to help her.

Maggie glanced over her shoulder at him. Jake noted the way her hair had come out of the ponytail and several strands fell loosely against her cheek. "That wasn't necessary, Jake."

Jake stared at her smile, thinking how soft it made her look. When she tipped her head quizzically he cleared his throat. "Oh, um…well, carrying those can't be good for you as far along as you are."

Maggie chuckled, finished pouring the food and brought both bowls back over to the cat. "There you go, my darlin'," she crooned, obviously not hearing the growl when she rubbed the cat on the head.

"I'm just over seven months pregnant, Jake. I have eight weeks to go. Actually, tomorrow I'll be seven months. Anyway, I'm big but not helpless. The doctor at the clinic told me I'd get a lot bigger the last two months."

Jake nodded. "Elizabeth was as big as a barrel before her twins were born."

Maggie laughed. "I hope I don't look like a barrel."

Jake flushed. "I didn't mean that."

Maggie looked up impishly. "You're a pastor. I thought all pastors had a talent to wax eloquent."

Her attitude surprised a laugh out of him. "I don't know where my talent for words has gone. I have never been able to wax eloquent, Maggie-May. I'm just a country boy at heart and I'm afraid that comes out in my sermons."

Maggie didn't answer but slowly pushed herself to her feet.

Jake couldn't resist the urge to reach out to her. He caught her elbow to steady her, wondering how she kept her balance.

She must have known anyway what he thought because of the knowing smile she gave him. "Thank you, Jake, for helping me today."

Jake nodded, taking that as his cue to leave. He started toward the door.

"And thank you for the food in the cabinets."

So, she knew about that. "That was a welcoming gift from the church. We have a food pantry, and it's well stocked right now."

Maggie had an unfathomable look on her face. Jake hoped he hadn't gone too far. He waited as she studied him. Finally, she nodded. "It means a lot."

Relieved, Jake smiled. "Good. You're part of our family now, Maggie. You shouldn't go in need of food or help. If you have a need, please tell someone."

"I haven't even attended your church yet, Jake. How can I be part of your family?"

Jake saw the yearning in her eyes and wondered at it. Was it loneliness? A desire to belong somewhere? He didn't know, but he wanted to reassure her. "Whether you attended our church or another, we're all family. As a Christian, that's what God expects. But I've met you, you're working for me, I know you as part of God's family. So, we're here for you."

Maggie slowly shook her head, the light dimming in her eyes. "I've heard that preached, Jake, but I have yet to see that truly practiced."

Jake wanted to retort that she'd been going to the wrong churches. But he didn't. He couldn't judge what he didn't know, where he hadn't been. And he was glad it wasn't his job. Instead, he said, "Give us a try. I'm not saying we're perfect. I don't think there's a church that is, but God won't fail you when we do.''

Maggie thought about what he said and nodded. God hadn't failed her. She didn't understand how this had happened to her, why she'd ended up pregnant, but she did know that every time she had lost a job, something had turned up almost immediately. She had never run out of food, though she had come close. And when she had been at her lowest, this man had appeared, offering her hope again—or at least it looked that way. She'd have to reserve judgment on that until later.

''No, God never fails us, does He?'' she repeated softly, her heart echoing loudly in her own ears. ''Thank you, Jake.''

Jake nodded. ''Well, let me get out of here so you can get some sleep. Church starts at ten in the morning. I hope to see you there.''

Maggie nodded again. ''Good night.''

''Good night.''

Jake went out the door but paused. ''Lock it before I leave the porch.''

Maggie held back a chuckle. She walked across the floor and locked the door.

She heard his feet echo on the steps and then peeked out the window. He walked—no, it reminded her more of a stroll—to his car as if he had all the time in the world, as if there weren't any problems pressing down on his shoulders, as if he were happy and carefree. ''Oh, Father, why can't I feel like that? Where has my joy gone? Have I been down in the pit so long that I can't see out?''

Maggie turned and headed back over to the cat, which was trying to lap up the water. "You poor thing," she whispered, and bent down to help her.

The cat let out a whimper, then allowed her to help. "You don't fool me. As much as you're hurting and you act like you don't want the help, deep down you do. Maybe you don't realize it yet, but I'm not going to let you sit here and die of thirst when I can help you."

A line of a song came to her: "He's my rock, He's my fortress, He's my deliverer...."

"Father, You've been my rock, or I would have never made it this far. My fortress. I don't know that I've allowed You to be that, hiding myself away. And my deliverer..."

Maggie sighed. "Please, Father, be my deliverer. Deliver me from the fear of the night, the fear of being alone...and the fear of sleeping. Jake was right. You never fail. If we would only turn to You immediately, instead of hiding away, we'd be so much better off."

Maggie felt a peace. She noted the cat had stopped drinking, having gained her fill. Maggie moved the bowl back and stood, then went to fix a box for the litter. She hadn't thought of litter; she was glad Jake had.

"Thank You, Father for sending this man my way. Help me to learn to trust him. And keep any disasters from befalling him because of our relationship."

She finished the box, set it next to the cat and vowed to keep an ear open in case the cat had any problems in the night.

Maggie went to her room, changed into her orange nightgown and crawled into bed. For the first time in a long time, she felt, if not total peace, then a safety knowing there was someone nearby if she needed help.

The dancing brown eyes of Jake Mathison stayed before her face as she drifted off to sleep, thinking maybe things might not be so bad after all.

Chapter Six

Maggie had heard the old saying "Don't count your chickens before they are hatched." And after all she'd been through the past six months, she should have learned that lesson.

Jake was a nice man. He seemed like a jewel after what she'd experienced. But just because he said everything would be okay didn't mean that it would.

Oh, Maggie thought it had gone fine this morning when she'd gotten up and dressed in her nicest pants and top that fit over her tummy.

She'd walked over to church and immediately met Gage and Jennifer, who had then introduced her to Max and Kaitland, who had a newborn in her arms and two twins hanging on her legs. Kaitland—or "Katie" as Max had called her—then took her and introduced her to her brother-in-law, Rand, and his wife Elizabeth, who had a small child in her arms.

And on and on it went, until the names had blurred

together. She had been pulled into the midst of these people she had read so much about in the paper.

Maggie had reveled in it. She enjoyed the warmth and joking among them before church and the worship service. This wasn't like her old church. They were freer in the way they worshipped, had all kinds of instruments and really seemed to enjoy church, unlike her parents, who saw it as an imposition.

And then Jake had stood up to preach. He looked wonderful in his nice pair of slacks and casual blazer.

And his preaching was different from what she had heard before. It was…powerful. Not condemning, not filled with dire predictions, but filled with love and hope and promise. Oh, he did touch on the negative issues, but those issues always ended with hope. That hope was Jesus Christ.

She liked Jake's message. It touched her heart unlike any message she had heard in a long time. And she found tears running down her face as she listened. He said that no matter what your circumstances, Jesus was the answer. He had all the answers. He loved and cared and provided, maybe not in the way people expected but in His own way.

Her heart filled with joy at Jake's words as she realized that God would take care of the problems.

At the end, they had an altar call and then church was over.

When people turned to one another and began discussing dinner plans and meetings, Maggie decided to ease her way out.

She needed to check on her cat—Kathryn, as she had

named her. Maggie was also starving. For some reason, going for more than two hours without food almost killed her. She would get the shakes and feel that she was actually getting ill.

She saw Jake looking her way and waved slightly, then turned toward the door.

"You're the new secretary?"

Maggie turned, wanting to see who had said that.

Her heart fell to her shoes when she saw the woman. She reminded Maggie of her mother. Proud, haughty and looking down her nose while smiling oh, so sweetly.

"Yes, I am."

"Oh, well. I thought the new secretary was single."

Maggie felt a dull flush rising on her cheeks. Her stomach churned and her hands shook. "I am single. My name is Maggie." Maggie stuck out her hand, just trying to get through this.

The woman took her hand politely. She didn't once glance at Maggie's abdomen, which made it even worse. Maggie knew what the woman was thinking.

"I'm sorry, are you widowed, then, or divorced? I know how hard it can be on a woman in that position. I'm widowed."

The woman said the words, but Maggie could tell she had already been tried and condemned. The woman's eyes were filled with condemnation, even though she smiled.

"No, Mrs., er…"

"Robertson."

"No, Mrs. Robertson, I'm not widowed or divorced, just plain single."

Maggie refused to say another word. If the woman wanted to know how she could be single *and* pregnant, she'd be more than glad to give her an earful. She knew better though.

This woman would spread rumors and innuendo, instead of attacking her, and Jake would be hurt and embarrassed, and then he'd have to ask her to leave....

"I see you've met Mrs. Robertson."

The vibrations of Jake's deep voice ran down her spine, soothing her. His hand touching her back lightly reassured her as nothing else could. "Yes, I have. And so many others I can't even begin to put names and faces to them."

"I hate to interrupt, Mrs. Robertson, but Rand and Max asked me to drag her back over there. They wanted to invite her over for lunch. Excuse us, please."

Mrs. Robertson nodded.

Jake guided Maggie away before Mrs. Robertson could utter a word. She could feel Jake's stare but refused to meet his gaze.

"Remember how I said no church was perfect, Maggie?"

She heard his whisper and nodded, lips tight with worry.

"The woman can be a dear, but she also has a small problem about being judgmental, too. We're praying about it. Ignore her and leave her to me."

"She'll cause problems. She wanted to know about the baby. She found every way she could to ask if the baby was illegitimate, narrowing the options down one by one until there were no others."

"Maggie, that's between you and God. Don't answer anyone's questions if you don't want to. And like I said, leave Mrs. Robertson to me. I spiked her guns when I told her Max and Rand wanted to invite you to dinner. She really likes to be invited over there with the other church members and would never say anything if it would risk her chances of getting an invitation."

"Oh, Jake, that's awful," Maggie said, horrified and just a little proud of his ingenious way of handling it. Tension quickly drained out of her, and she realized her past hurts were coloring her perceptions again.

"Hey, I'm not lying. They do want you to come over for dinner. And they did ask me to come over and grab you. They've seen Mrs. Robertson eat others alive, and wanted you rescued, by the way. I don't know, Maggie. It looks like some of our members have taken a shining to you."

Maggie blushed at Jake's words. Still, she couldn't help but add, "We'll see what happens when everyone figures out I'm not married."

Jake shrugged. "Stop being so hard on yourself. Mrs. Robertson will get over it as she comes to know you. She really is a softy at heart—eventually."

Maggie chuckled. "I'll bet."

"And so are Elizabeth and Kaitland and their husbands. Now, let's go over and—"

"Oh, no, Jake. I can't."

Jake paused and looked down at her. "Are you sure? We've both been invited. I thought you'd love to come, get to meet some of the people from here, maybe make some new friends."

How could she tell him that crowds bothered her, that she preferred to be alone. "I have to check on Kathryn, the cat. I named her," she said at his quizzical look. "'Captain Kat,'" she said, grinning to hide her nervousness. "Anyway, I need to check on her and I'm tired. I'm going to rest after that."

Jake studied her seriously. "Okay, Maggie-May. But let me tell you something, hiding out isn't going to help the pain go away."

"Pain?" Maggie's heart tripped as she thought that he might have some idea what she was going through.

"It's in your eyes when you don't realize anyone is looking. I'm not asking what it is. If you decide you want to tell me, I'm here. Both as a pastor and, I hope, as a friend. It's your choice. But, Maggie, just know there are people here who will care, who will be here if you reach out, okay?"

Maggie nodded, feeling an odd sting in her eyes and nose, and knew she was about to cry. "Please, make my excuses."

Jake nodded. "Okay. I'll see you tonight?"

"Yes," she whispered, and hurried toward the back door.

"What happened?"

Jake heard Elizabeth's voice and turned, smiling. "She's tired and wanted to go home and rest."

Elizabeth frowned. "I think she needs a friend."

Jake sighed. "Maybe. Give it time, though."

And he vowed to give Maggie until exactly six o'clock tonight to get over it before he put his nose in where it probably didn't belong.

* * *

"And a trip to the park with ice cream is in my job description?" Maggie smiled, amused, staring at the double scoop of chunky-choco chocolate ice cream that Jake had ordered her. She reached out and took it.

"Yes, it is. The mall closes in an hour, but I wanted you to see something here."

"You keep saying that," Maggie complained good-naturedly, wondering what in the world could be at the park this late at night.

"Like I explained earlier tonight at church, it has to do with the Saturday ministry. You'll be involved in it, so you should have some idea how it works."

"And I'll find out all about that here? At the park? I'll admit this is a place I haven't been to in months, but I don't remember any churches or anything stashed away in some corner somewhere."

Jake shook his head, motioned to her ice cream, then took a lick of his own.

Maggie sighed and tasted hers, and was surprised at how delicious it was. "Oh, my, I'd forgotten how rich their ice cream is here," she murmured, closing her eyes and taking another taste.

She smiled, allowing the ice cream to melt in her mouth before swallowing. When she opened her eyes, Jake was staring at her oddly. "What?" she asked.

"How long has it been since you've had ice cream?"

Maggie flushed and started walking. "I don't get out much."

"I try to come here at least once a month. If I don't

I'm sure I'm having withdrawal. Sometimes I even buy a quart and bring it home.''

Maggie looked over at Jake, relieved to see him eating his cone and no longer staring as he walked beside her.

She took another bite of her own dessert, relaxing. "So, what brings us here?''

Maggie lifted her cone to lick at it and paused. "Oh, look, a clown." A man dressed in a bright polka-dot clown suit with purple-and-orange hair and a big red nose, sat in the middle of the children's area that this park had for kids to watch special shows.

He was performing tricks and talking to the kids the entire time. What was so amazing to Maggie was that the kids didn't move. Not one twitched.

"This is like your heart," the clown was saying, and held up a dirty handkerchief. "Sometimes we lie, or maybe do something else bad like steal...."

She watched him tucking the hankie in a small rectangular box.

"But Jesus tells us he'll clean our heart, take away the bad and give us a new heart. Just as that hankie was dirty, our hearts get dirty."

He held up the box, showing the kids as they asked how they got new hearts and on and on.

Finally, when they quieted, he held up the box again and smiled. "Oh, it's real simple. You just tell Jesus you're sorry and you want him to help you and your heart will be made all clean. Remember the hankie? Well, we don't have to do the washing or the scrubbing—God does that." He opened the box back up and pulled out the hankie, and to Maggie's amazement, it was white, no dirt stains on it.

"How'd he do that?" she asked Jake, amazed.

Jake smiled.

The kids oohed and aahed. "It's that easy, kids. "This is a trick, but Jesus doesn't have to use tricks like that. You ask Him, and Jesus will help you do the right things. Now, who wants a piece of candy?"

The clown stood up and walked over to pick up a big bag and pass out candy. Parents and kids stood. Maggie took that to mean the show was over.

"He's talented," Maggie said, impressed. "Did you see how those kids were listening to him? I didn't know they had anything like this here. Is that what you do on Saturdays?"

Jake chuckled. "Actually, you guessed it. Our clown here comes out once a month to talk to the kids. But you've already met him."

As if just noticing them, the clown looked up, smiled and waved.

"I have?" Maggie asked.

Jake nodded. "You have. That's my friend who towed your car. Tyler Jenson. He's from Texas but has lived here almost ten years now."

Maggie's eyes widened. "I had no idea. His makeup is really good."

"If you have him, why do you need my help?"

"I need help with the puppets and passing out candy and a myriad of other things, including someone to sit by the kids or listen when they have to whisper something to someone, or hold them if they fall asleep. The list is endless. That's what Shirley did.''

Maggie watched the kids take the candy, hug Tyler, chatter back and forth with their parents, and suddenly didn't know if she could do it.

She felt like such a fraud. Her relationship with her parents wasn't like this. Those mothers responded so loving and gentle. She was going to be a parent, too, unless she put her child up for adoption. With the way she'd been raised, would she be a good parent?

If she couldn't, what made her think she could she give these little kids what they needed?

"We'll take it one step at a time."

Jake's soft voice snapped her back to the present. She glanced at him, wondering how he knew what she'd been thinking. "I don't know if I can, Jake. I have nothing left in me except bitterness."

Maggie wondered why in the world she would confess something like that to this near stranger with the compassionate eyes.

That was it. It was his eyes. She'd never seen eyes like that before.

"You do have more, Maggie-May," Jake said gently. "It's just going to take you time to realize that."

"You don't understand. It seems that everything I touch turns bad." Maggie struggled, trying to believe, but she was scared.

Thankfully, Tyler Jenson interrupted.

"I see you brought your new helper by."

Jake stared at her a moment longer, his eyes probing, before he turned to Tyler and shook his hand. "I wanted you to meet her—again. Or rather, I suppose I should say I wanted her to meet the real you.''

Tyler chuckled. ''Nice to meet you again, Maggie.''

Maggie remembered. ''You helped me with my car.''

''That I did.'' Tyler smiled, then turned to Jake. ''I'll see you Saturday, then?''

Jake nodded.

''Bye,'' Maggie said.

Tyler waved as he walked off.

''That's why you brought me down here?''

Jake shook his head. ''I wanted to see your reaction to a bunch of kids in an open area.'' Jake pointed to the six or seven benches with the huge animals to climb on and nothing else to keep the kids in one area.

''And?'' she asked, certain he was disappointed in her.

He smiled. ''You did wonderfully.''

Maggie dumped the last bit of her cone in the trash. ''How can you say that? When I saw all those kids I realized I probably can't handle it at all.''

''Exactly.''

Jake looked longingly at his cone, then tossed it, too.

''You didn't have to do that,'' she said, even as he turned and started walking back toward the car.

''We should get you home for the night. Your job starts later than most, but you should get extra rest.''

''I—''

''If you had been overconfident or blasé about the entire thing, Maggie, then I would have worried. But the concern mirrored on your face told me you care about kids and the position you'll be in when you're helping me with them. That's the most important thing. Everything else can be learned. True caring and compassion can't.''

''But I can't do what Tyler did. The kids aren't going to listen to me.''

''Maggie, Maggie,'' Jake said, taking her hand and guiding her toward the car. ''I didn't ask you to be Tyler. God didn't ask you to be Tyler. Just be yourself. They'll listen to you. I guarantee it.''

He smiled confidently.

Maggie remembered what she'd seen and returned the smile weakly, hoping he was right.

Chapter Seven

He was dead wrong.

These kids were nothing like those sweet little angels in the park. In a short time Maggie had seen one lob a rock at someone, then run off, another bite the finger of the child next to her and yet another tie a little girl's hair in knots.

And these kids didn't sit still. Oh, for Tyler they had eagerly followed him. But now they jumped and shouted during his story.

It didn't seem to faze him, or Jake, who calmly walked over and picked up a child who was trying to poke the kid next to him in the ear with a stick. He set the child down on his lap and continued to listen as if this were a regular occurrence. He encircled the other one with an arm and acted as if the child hadn't just tried to make the other one deaf.

He looked handsome in his jeans and blue shirt. Maggie had noticed that first thing. Perfectly at home, somehow.

"Hey, lady," a small child who had stationed herself by her side when she arrived said, interrupting Maggie's thoughts.

"Yes, Tonika?" she asked.

The little girl was rubbing Maggie's tummy—again. "How come your stomach keeps moving around like that? It looks all crooked now. See that?"

Maggie glanced down to where Tonika was poking and saw the bulge of an elbow or knee.

"That's 'cause she's pregnant, you idiot."

Ah, the heckler. She'd been watching the young boy move around the crowd for the past fifteen minutes, interrupting, scolding the other kids, being a general nuisance. "That's not nice to say, Eddie," she said. She had a feeling he was just wanting attention.

"Why not? You're pregnant. My big sister is, too. I know what it looks like. That's the baby kid kicking."

Eddie had short, curly black hair and deep-brown eyes that twinkled mischievously when he was being loud. Right now they looked way too old for those of a ten-year-old child.

"I meant 'idiot,' Eddie. That's not nice. Apologize."

Maggie hated that word and didn't like the way Tonika's face had fallen when Eddie had called her that. She had been patient with the young boy, but she wouldn't tolerate his calling Tonika names.

He shrugged. "Hey, it's no skin off my nose. Sorry, Tonika. You just ain't been around this none, I suppose."

Tonika sniffled, but when Maggie's stomach suddenly moved again, Tonika forgot her hurt feelings and went back to feeling Maggie's rounded bulge again.

Maggie had no idea how the seven-year-old girl had ended up in her lap, but she continued to sit there, rubbing the protruding mound with abject fascination, doing her best to get the baby to move.

Jake glanced over and smiled, giving her a thumbs-up just before he stood and nonchalantly went back to work the puppets.

Eddie snickered and pointed, having seen Jake's move. Maggie shot him a dark look. "Don't do it," she warned when he started to shout out what he'd seen.

Eddie eyed her and then finally shrugged, turning away. What a little turkey, she thought. Immediately guilt assailed her. Maggie had never been down to this part of town. Earlier, when they'd been going door-to-door to the houses Jake seemed to know so well, Maggie had been appalled at how poor some of these people were.

Eddie had come from one such house. The sister he spoke of couldn't even be fifteen and had sneered at them. The mother had been on the couch asleep. Eddie had been cooking lunch.

The puppet show started with Tyler talking and Jake playing the part of a talking cow. Jake had told her he'd do the puppets first, just to show her how they interacted and what they usually did. He assured her there was no set pattern. The puppets taught a memory verse, joked around with the kids and made a point of backing up the story. That was it.

Toward the end, when they brought out the second puppet to make another point of the story and tie the memory verse back in, she was to sneak back there and work it. Really easy, he'd told her.

Yeah, she thought, right. If you had a quick wit and vivid imagination.

Maggie shifted as the baby made itself known in a most uncomfortable way, and she suddenly realized she was going to have a problem being out on the streets like this as her pregnancy advanced.

"Hey, lady, what's the matter?"

Maggie blinked and looked down at Tonika, then blushed when she saw the girl staring at her so knowingly. "Nothing, dear."

"You gotta go, don'tcha?" the girl persisted.

Maggie saw other kids glance at her, then back at what was going on up front. Figuring there was no reason to lie, she nodded. "I sure do."

If she thought that would end it, she was wrong. "I gotta go, too."

Patiently Maggie smiled and shushed the girl. "Let's not disturb Pastor Jake or his helpers."

"You can go to my house with me."

Maggie sighed, nodded and stood, thinking it'd be good to get the young girl away, since the crowd had finally quieted and was listening to what was being said. "Okay, that sounds great."

She was surprised when the young girl grabbed her hand and led her along to her house as though she were a long-lost friend. Tonika pulled out a key and opened the door.

The house was poor. Maggie noted that immediately. It reminded her of her own house currently. However, despite the lack of money, the house was also neat and spotless, and obviously filled with love; Maggie saw tiny little personalized things from Tonika hanging about everywhere, as well as small comforts for the little girl. "Tonika, where is your mom?"

Tonika shrugged. "She had to go to work today. I'm not allowed to leave except for Pastor Jake's show. Since you're with the group, my mama won't mind me bringing you in."

"You don't stay here alone, do you?"

Again Tonika shrugged. "Miss Emmaline next door keeps a watch on me. If I get bored, she lets me come over there."

Maggie gaped, unsure what to say. She was horrified, but understood the need of the parent to bring in money. Absently Maggie lay a hand on top of her own child, thinking how she might be in that very position one day.

If she kept the child.

Pain pierced her heart, not only from memories of the conception of the child but at the thought of any child living like this, too.

"It's in here," the little girl said, pointing. Then she followed the words with action by running into the bathroom and slamming the door.

She was back in a short time. "You can use it, too, but don't forget to wash your hands."

Maggie chuckled at the admonishment. "Thank you, Tonika, I won't."

Maggie slipped into the bathroom. When she finished

washing her hands and went back out, Tonika was finishing up a glass of milk. "I'm ready!"

With renewed energy, the little girl ran to the door.

Maggie followed. She watched, impressed, as Tonika closed the door and made sure it was locked. Then she changed from grown-up to kid and took off skipping down the street, carefree again.

Thoughts swirled in Maggie's head about her own unborn child, thoughts she'd never faced before. Since finding out she was pregnant she had functioned on autopilot, not certain what to do, just surviving as the child developed within her. She had never really acknowledged that there was a child, other than realizing her own body was changing to accommodate it.

Now for the first time, seeing this child who was raised by a mother who was obviously single, Maggie faced the truth that she was in the same situation. She was pregnant, alone and was going to have a baby.

She would very likely end up working like this mother and have to leave her child. Could she do that if she decided to keep the baby?

Too many questions and too many emotions were opened up thinking about that. She didn't want to deal with the pain those questions brought. Didn't want to deal with the decisions she had to make.

So, instead, she concentrated on what was going on at that moment.

Back in the park, Jake held up a picture of a chicken with several chicks around it and patiently explained how the mother was trying to protect the chicks from a fire that would consume them if they didn't run to her.

One chick was being stubborn, though, he went on.

Maggie realized it was nearing the time she was supposed to move behind the little stage to work the puppets.

Tyler gave her a cue from the audience, nodding toward the back of the stage.

Nervously she nodded.

Maggie went back behind the small wooden stage and looked around. A box of puppets set beneath the curtained window. On the back of the wood was taped a script of what was scheduled and when her puppet was supposed to appear.

As Maggie listened to Jake talking about how the mama chicken gave her life saving those chicks, her heart rate accelerated.

What was she doing here?

How could she do this?

She'd never worked with children before. Not like this. Nor had she ever been in this part of town. You couldn't fool streetwise kids like this. They were going to know she was a fake. They were going to know she had no idea what she was doing.

Sweat slicked her palms as she reached for the little girl puppet and slipped it on her arm.

Experimentally, Maggie moved the mouth of the puppet, feeling awkward as she did. Kneeling down, she put it by the edge of the curtain, waiting and listening. "Help me, Father. I have no idea what to do," she said.

"You're gonna chicken out, aren't you?"

Maggie jumped, turning her head in surprise. "Eddie!

What are you doing here?'' She whispered the question, very aware of the kids on the other side of the curtain.

Eddie's hand was on the stage. One push and she'd be exposed. She paled. Maggie didn't want this ruined for the other kids or Jake.

"I thought so. You don't look like no inner-city worker that's been here before. Brother Jake's friend Shirley was better. You don't even know how to use no puppet."

Maggie stared at Eddie, then sighed. "You're right, Eddie. I don't."

What could she do? Lie to the kid? He saw too much as it was.

With a disgusted look, Eddie strode over, dropped down next to her, grabbed a puppet and then stuck his arm up out of the curtain.

Only then did she realize Jake had knocked twice on the stage, trying to get someone to answer the door.

Eddie screwed his face up and made his voice crackle as he said, "Yeah, who is it? Who is it?"

Maggie realized he had on a grandma puppet.

Dumbfounded, she stared.

Eddie, the troublemaker, actually helping?

She shook her head.

"Well, hello, Grandma," Jake said from the other side of the curtain. "I was just telling these kids about how a chicken gave up her life to save her babies."

"Oh, babies? Babies? I know all about them. Let me tell you, ain't that the truth, them good for nothing babies needing saving."

Maggie gulped; not sure where Eddie was going, she stuck her own puppet up.

"Just like this one," Grandma said, while Eddie grinned at her nastily from behind the scenes.

Maggie glared back. "I don't need saving," she said with the puppet.

Of course Eddie couldn't pass that up, and went into a long speech about how this young'un had almost broken her neck on roller blades and a car. Maggie was dumbfounded at the story Eddie spun.

Then Jake led the puppet show back to the memory verse. "You know, Grandma, your story reminds me of a verse about God sending His son. Do you or maybe your granddaughter know that one?"

Maggie opened her mouth to reply, but again Eddie beat her to it.

"Of course I do. God so loved the world that He gave His only begotten son that whoever believed in Him would have eternal life."

Maggie grinned, thinking that was close but not an actual quote. And Jake had planned to use only the first half of the verse. But still, that Eddie knew it impressed and humbled her.

"That's right, Grandma. God so loved the world..."

Jake turned back to the kids and had them repeat the phrase, then mentioned finding it in *John* 3:16.

Before Maggie could decide if Eddie had saved the show or not, Jake turned back and spoke to the granddaughter. "You should remember that, too, Nelly. And that He'll save you and protect you, just as He did today when He kept you from getting run over by that car when you were roller blading.''

Maggie replied, though she wasn't sure what, and then they pulled their hands back from the curtain.

She removed the puppet and dropped it into the box, staring at Eddie.

Eddie wouldn't meet her eyes. Instead, he pulled off the puppet, his little chin going up in the air as he stuffed his hands in his pockets.

Something gave in Maggie's heart as she realized this was all a mask, a wall of protection Eddie had built up around himself.

''Thank you,'' Maggie said softly, her heart opening up to the young boy.

Eddie shrugged. ''I didn't do nothing except show Tonika how stupid you was not to know how to do puppets.''

Eddie nonchalantly gave her a hug, totally surprising her, then resumed the tough look on his face and sauntered off.

Maggie shook her head, not offended by Eddie's words but perhaps understanding that he was protecting himself.

Maggie sat there watching as Eddie took up his place near the back of the audience.

Then it was over, and Eddie took off at a run to go play.

Tonika got up and hurried home. Several of the other children all ran up and hugged Jake and the clown and got a few more candy treats before they left.

Then Jake came to where she stood, while Tyler broke down the stage and loaded it into the truck.

"You did great!"

Surprised, Maggie looked at Jake. "Please don't lie, Jake. I did miserably."

Genuinely surprised, Jake replied, "Maggie, you did not. Whatever gave you that idea?"

Maggie motioned toward the stage that Tyler was loading into the truck. "I froze and had no idea what to do."

Jake actually laughed. "Is that what it felt like to you? You did fine on this side. And what's more important, Eddie helped you."

Confused, Maggie asked, "Why is that so important?"

Jake smiled softly. "Eddie is one tough nut to crack. He doesn't take to others too much. If he came back there and helped, regardless of what he said, that means he's taken to you."

"I find that hard to believe," Maggie said, shaking her head.

"Believe it." Jake slipped a hand to the small of Maggie's back and guided her toward the truck. "Eddie has grown up in a rough area. He doesn't have role models. Eddie is the one basically taking care of the family. It's a very sad situation. He doesn't have a lot of respect for adults because of that. However, for some reason, all day he's been eyeing you strangely."

Jake opened the door and gently lifted her up into the truck. He smiled at her before he got in next to her. "To be honest, as I watched today, I think the reason he was so curious about you is simply that you cared enough to talk to him like an adult and correct him when he was teasing the other kids.''

''I don't remember liking discipline,'' Maggie said, ''I didn't like the way he picked at Tonika, either.''

Jake chuckled. ''That Tonika. She is a pill. She and Eddie go at it like they were really siblings. Sometimes Eddie does get carried away though and hurts her feelings.''

''Well, he did today.''

Jake nodded. ''You made him apologize?''

Maggie nodded firmly.

''Good. I'm glad to hear that. He needs to learn it's okay to make a mistake and apologize. Just like Tonika needs to hear him say he's sorry.''

Jake started the truck and headed back toward the church. ''I remember, though, one incident where Tonika had him by the ears and he was hollering his head off. When I broke them apart and asked what she was doing, she informed me he'd said something to her and she was pinning his ears back for it. Evidently, that's one of her mother's favorite sayings when Tonika misbehaves.''

Jake laughed.

Maggie watched him as he chuckled, thinking how carefree he looked when he laughed like that.

''I'm surprised.''

Still smiling, Jake turned inquisitive eyes on her. ''What?''

Maggie hadn't meant to say that out loud. ''I, well,

you seem so happy and free. With all the responsibilities I've seen you handle so far, how do you do it?''

Jake shook his head, his smile fading a bit. ''I wish, Maggie-May, that I could say I was carefree and had no problems or didn't worry. But this center we're building—it means everything to me.''

Maggie watched the rest of his smile fade as he scanned the traffic while he drove.

''I didn't mean to force the smile from your face.''

He glanced at her, giving her a quirky grin. ''You didn't. It's hard to explain what the center means to me.''

His eyes went back to the traffic as he circled around onto the interstate. ''I suppose it's because I grew up on the streets just like Eddie and Tonika and all the others. I want this center built. I want a place where kids can go to get off the streets, a place that's an alternative to the gangs and drugs, a place where the kids can get the Word of God and have a safe place to play.''

Maggie noted the way he gripped the steering wheel, the determined glint in his eye, and realized she'd found his goal in life.

''It means a lot to you?'' she questioned softly.

''Yes,'' he replied.

Maggie leaned back against the seat, gazing at the traffic, thinking woe to anyone who came between this man and his goal to see the center built.

There was a lot more to Jake than met the eye. The light-hearted man had been replaced with one full of steely determination.

"Why is it so important?" Maggie probably shouldn't ask, but she couldn't curb her curiosity.

Jake didn't glance at her, and she didn't need to see his face to interpret what he was feeling when he replied, in a flat voice.

"So other kids won't end up like my kid brother. You see, while I was a teenager strung out on drugs, my kid brother was shot to death playing kick ball in the street."

Chapter Eight

"Oh, Jake!" Maggie reeled from Jake's words. "I'm so sorry."

"It was a long time ago. I'm over it now," he said, shrugging. He exited the highway and started the last short journey toward home.

He wasn't over it, though. Maggie could see plainly the truth written all over his demeanor whether he admitted it or not. "It wasn't your fault," she said gently.

Jake laughed, but the laugh was one of buried grief. "We'll never know if he would still be alive had I not been so out of it. Kids playing on the streets in neighborhoods like that." Jake shook his head. "I want to give others a chance, since my brother didn't have one."

"It's a wonderful goal," she murmured, touching her stomach as she did. Her being pregnant certainly wasn't going to endear him to the people at his church. What if they decided not to give any more money to help him get this center built? She knew things like pregnancy and her working for him would cast a bad light on a pastor, whether the child was his or not.

"You're worried about your pregnancy?"

Jake's soft query sounded like the snap of a whip in the truck. How had he known that?

Surprised, Maggie stared.

He nodded toward her stomach. Only then did she realize she was rubbing it.

Flushing, she shrugged. "A bit, I suppose."

Jake studied her until the light changed, then he turned his attention forward again. "Are you worried about the baby in general or how it's going to affect my job?"

The man was very astute. Maggie decided it must be that he worked with people on a regular basis and had to interpret what they didn't say as much as what they did—that, or God was giving him some extra help.

"Both."

Silence fell.

Maggie shifted.

They turned onto the country road that led to the church at the edge of town before Jake broke the silence. "There is no reason for you to worry about my job, Maggie. As for the other, I'm more than willing to listen if you want to talk."

Dark memories swirled in Maggie's mind of the conception of the child and all the indecision and fear since. How she would love to confide in someone, but she had learned what that meant—and just how people responded.

No, she couldn't, wouldn't, confide. "I'm fine on that, too. I don't need anyone to talk to."

She stared out the window.

Jake glanced over at her, his brow furrowed. He wondered if she realized how her voice lifted slightly when she lied.

He'd watched her all day. She was good with the kids, a little awkward at having never worked around them, but there was a tenderness she projected when the children approached her. It was no wonder the kids swarmed to her.

He couldn't believe she didn't realize it. But she didn't.

His little secretary had no idea how maternal she was—to every kid except the one she carried.

When he had pointed out the way she rubbed her stomach she stopped.

Curiosity ate at him—and not entirely on a professional level.

Maggie was very attractive. Her gentle spirit had distracted him more than once today. The husky laugh when one of the kids had said something amusing made his mind go blank more than once.

Jake shook his head, certain he had gone off the deep end. What was the matter with him? His mind had been wandering all day to Maggie and her voice, her smile, her life.

He felt just a bit guilty for hoping Maggie would confide in him a moment ago. Yes, he would listen professionally and offer prayer and advice, but he admitted it was the man in him who wanted to know.

Whose child did she carry? Was she in love with the man still? She wore no ring, though it looked like one might have been worn there before. Was Maggie divorced, then? And if she was, why?

He didn't like that curiosity ate at him this way, nor that, despite how standoffish Maggie acted, he still found himself attracted to her.

He'd been so distracted by Maggie that he'd actually told her about his kid brother and the problem he'd had with drugs. How many people did he discuss his past with? Yet, with Maggie, it'd seemed natural to be honest with her.

Wearily he shook his head again. It was none of his business, and he shouldn't push her.

He glanced over again and saw her pleating the bottom of her top with two fingers and decided Maggie had no idea she was doing it. Maggie wasn't the type to show emotion. She hurt. It shone in her eyes. When he'd asked about the child, her eyes went blank and she smiled. The look she gave everyone, including him when he tried to get close, drove him crazy.

"Do you have a doctor?"

Maggie blinked, then turned to him, smiling, that same blank expression in her eyes. "I've been going to the clinic when I could. Unfortunately, I've had some trouble driving standard, so I can't make the appointments."

Jake frowned. "That's not good. You shouldn't have to miss seeing the doctor."

"It's only driving long lengths. My legs get tired and cramp up. I'm worried about wrecks in heavy traffic. Short legs and a big stomach don't mix."

Jake turned into the driveway and stopped at his

house. He hopped out and came around to her door and opened it, then reached up to help her down. Despite her shape, she was light, which concerned him. "Tell you what, Maggie-May. You make that appointment, and I'll see you get to it on time."

He smiled at the surprise in her eyes, glad to see an honest reaction.

"Oh, no, I couldn't trouble anyone…I mean, babies are babies and they grow and don't really require all the fuss doctors say they do."

Jake took Maggie's elbow and walked her over to her house, his concern growing again. At the porch he stopped and looked down at her. Corkscrew curls danced around her face where they'd fallen from the clip at the base of her neck. Wide green eyes stared up at him so solemnly. "Why are you scared to face the existence of the child, Maggie?"

She paled, her lips parting slightly. "I—I—I'm not."

Jake studied her, felt the tremor in her. He shouldn't have asked her. The reality of the child brought pain to her for some reason. It wasn't his business. Yet seeing that pain, the helplessness in her eyes as she stood there refusing to respond to his query, twisted his heart.

"You don't have to tell me. But I'm not taking no for an answer regarding the doctor's appointment. Call, then let me know when the appointment is."

He thought from the way the end of her nose turned pink that she was holding back tears but couldn't be sure. Leaning forward he brushed his lips across her forehead, a purely platonic action.

It disconcerted him, though, when the fruity smell of

shampoo drifted from her hair, catching his attention, and the warm vanilla scent of her perfume wrapped itself around him.

Confused, he pulled back. "I'll be in the office doing some work. If you can get the clinic on the line today, give me a call. Otherwise, I'll expect to hear something on this subject Monday."

Maggie's cheeks were pink, which made Jake feel even more the fool. Why in the world had he kissed her on the forehead?

Admit it, you fool, he thought, disgusted. You're attracted to her.

He stepped back and turned, before going down the steps. Jake told himself he couldn't be attracted to her. There were too many problems. He didn't know whose baby Maggie carried and if she was over that man. He didn't know if she was even interested in a relationship. And besides, he had so much work to do on the center he didn't have time for dating.

Father, I have got to be out of my mind. Please help me just redirect my thinking back to where it should be.

Jake found it didn't help to say that. His mind was still on the softly rounded figure of the woman he'd left on the front steps of her house.

Maggie went into her house dumbfounded and a little nervous by what had just happened.

"Don't read anything into it. The man was just showing you compassion."

But it'd been so long since anyone had touched her

in any way. She'd forgotten how nice it could feel to have someone take her elbow or help her out of a car.

Of course, with her bulk, she needed help now to get out of a truck. But still, it felt good. When Jake had touched her shoulders and placed that soft kiss on her forehead she had almost burst into tears.

He had no idea what she had gone through, or was going through, yet he'd offered her comfort. Although she had trouble believing he kissed all his flock on the forehead.

Maggie grinned thinking of him trying to kiss Tyler on the head, then sniffed as her eyes filled with tears.

"Meeewwoooorrrr."

The pitiful sound of Captain Kat broke through the bittersweet pain she was experiencing.

"Kathryn! I didn't forget about you," Maggie said, though she temporarily had.

She went over and carefully squatted down to slip her hands under the cat and lift her.

The cat hissed, then growled at her. "Now, you just stop that, Captain Kat. I won't put up with it. You're not going to get your way on this. I happen to know you need help, and you're going to get it whether you want it or not."

Maggie thought of Jake's attitude and reddened. "This is different," she said, and set the cat over in the litter box. "You have to do this," she told the cat before pushing herself up and going into the kitchen to get the cat fresh water and food. "I—"

Maggie poured the food and then the water. "I don't really need him. Besides, you know what'll happen.

Eventually, someone is going to see me, and my parents will try to cause problems. If they don't, well then, his church surely will because of the child and my single status.''

Maggie carried the food back into the room and lifted the cat out of the box, ignoring the growl.

She placed Captain Kat back on the pillow. "There you go. Here're some food and water. You just rest."

Maggie grabbed up the litter box and dumped the contents in the commode, then returned the box next to the cat.

Maggie got the antiseptic solution the doctor had given her and set to work carefully cleaning the wounds on the cat.

"Still," she said, musing softly as she cleaned the cat, "wouldn't it be wonderful if there really was such a thing as happily ever after on this earth?"

Maggie thought about the verse that said with God all things were possible. She believed that; she really did.

Then she looked down at her stomach, remembered what her parents and her former fiancé had said and sighed.

But in this case, Maggie didn't think there was much hope.

Chapter Nine

Maggie clasped her hands nervously, glancing sideways at Jake, who was slipping in and out of traffic.

"I'd never expect you to drive a midsize car."

Jake glanced at her and laughed.

She liked the tiny crinkles that appeared around his eyes, the way his dimples showed. "Thought because all I rode around in was a truck…"

She shook her head. "I just hadn't seen this."

Jake glanced back around, changing lanes. "This is a car that I saved a long time for. It's expensive, well okay, expensive for my income, but I know I'll have it ten years down the road."

Maggie considered how a year ago she wouldn't have been caught in a car like this. And would never have driven the same car for over a year. Of course, this car was much better than the small piece of barely running metal she owned now.

How attitudes change, she acknowledged, looking out to see how much farther they had to go.

"So tell me, Maggie. Who is this doctor of yours? How long has he been practicing?"

Maggie glanced back at Jake, surprised. Studying him, she couldn't see anything in his face to indicate why he had asked. She decided to tell him. "*She* is a very good doctor. She really does care for the people here, but she's overworked, just like all the other doctors who work the clinic." Maggie sighed. "I feel lucky to have been placed with her."

"You didn't get to choose your doctor."

Maggie recognized the statement was not meant as a question, but she answered anyway. "No. At a free clinic you don't have a choice."

Jake pulled into the parking lot and got out of the car, then walked around the dark-mauve hood to open her door.

Maggie appreciated it, appreciated the help when he reached in for her hand, appreciated the fact that he didn't laugh at her when she struggled out.

Flushing, she said, "I feel like an ox."

Jake smiled softly. "You look like an angel."

Maggie blinked, then laughed. "Oh, I think I'll keep you around just to hear things like that."

Though she had said it, she was suddenly very aware of Jake as more than just her employer or the pastor of the church she'd gone to Sunday. He was very much a person who had feelings and emotions.

Curiously, she had to wonder if he really meant his sweet words or was only flattering her. She hoped it was the latter, knowing how dangerous it would be for him to fall for someone like her.

Maggie quickly scooped her purse and slung it over her shoulder before turning to the clinic.

"I have to get my records and then go down to the last waiting room on the right."

Jake nodded.

"You've been here before?"

"With various people from the church, yes."

Well, there went her hope that he was treating her differently. Of course she was rather relieved, wasn't she? He threw her already roiling emotions right back into turmoil with his next words.

"I go everywhere, Maggie, when I'm called."

She wondered if he meant just with others or her included. Deciding she could beat herself to death over the subject, she determined to take it how it was probably meant. "That's your job. To help those of us who need it."

Jake frowned as Maggie started down the hall.

That was not what he'd meant at all. Actually, he was surprised with the conversation today. Jake always put his work first.

Time didn't permit him to disrupt his work now to flirt with a woman who was surely still hurting over the desertion of an ex-boyfriend or husband.

He'd do best to remember that. Of course, Jake wondered, when did he ever do what was considered *best?*

If he'd done what was best he wouldn't be seeing the dream of his heart fulfilled—a center for kids. Nor would he even be where he was today when everyone he'd known had told him he wasn't really called to preach, to find something else, something that someone who hadn't been all messed up could do.

Jake shrugged. Maggie was hurting. No matter what he felt, he wouldn't act on it until her heart had time to heal.

He walked into the lobby and took a seat next to where Maggie sat.

"It shouldn't be long," Maggie whispered.

She looked around. She hadn't missed the glances of some of the other women when Jake had walked in. Several raised appraising eyebrows. Maybe he didn't realize it, but she was certain those women thought Jake was the father. She wasn't sure which embarrassed her more—that she was single and pregnant, like many of the women here, or that they thought the pastor had fathered...

"You flush any brighter and we'll just switch these lights off, Maggie-May, and let your face light the room."

The softly spoken words from Jake had her warming all the way down her neck.

He chuckled sensually. "Let me guess. You're embarrassed because they probably think I'm the father. Or is it because I'm a pastor and they think I'm the father?"

Maggie couldn't help the involuntary reaction to his words.

He reached over and took her hand, patting it gently. "Pastors do have children, too, I'm told."

"Stop it," she said, her embarrassment obvious in her words.

"I'm sorry, Maggie. I'm simply a man. That's all they know, so don't worry about what they think."

"The Bible says avoid all appearance of evil," Maggie whispered.

Jake started coughing, covering his mouth.

"You're laughing," she lamented.

"I didn't realize this would bother you so much. I can't help it. You're quoting Scriptures to me."

He chuckled again, and she reached over and slapped his arm, mortified. "Will you cut it out?"

His grin was infectious, though. Before long she was grinning.

When they recovered, he smiled at her. "Maggie, sitting in a waiting room with a pregnant woman is not evil."

Maggie had to admit, when he said it in that tone, it sounded silly. "But what if they know you are a pastor and they see you with me and..."

"Maggie." Jake's eyes turned serious. "I live in a glass house it's true. But all I can do is live my life as I feel God would want me to. I can't live it the way others want me to. If I did, I would constantly have to change how I lived because someone would find something wrong with every single thing I did. Believe me, I have already been through most anything you could imagine at one time or another."

Maggie lifted a brow skeptically. "Even hiring a single pregnant woman as your secretary? Having her working with you at the children's ministry and then taking her to appointments?"

"Well, there you've got me. This is the first time for

that. Don't worry. If I hadn't felt a peace in my heart about it, you never would have gotten the job."

"You're saying you think God wanted you to give me the job?" Maggie couldn't believe he was saying this.

He smiled. "Yes, I do."

"Well, just don't get too comfortable. I probably won't be around too long."

Maggie's eyes widened when she realized what she'd said.

Jake frowned. "You're not thinking of running out on me, are you?"

Maggie was relieved he thought that. He couldn't know about her parents. "No, Jake. I'm not. I just imagine in a month or two you'll get tired of me and be ready to hire someone who doesn't have to miss work all the time for appointments and take breaks in the afternoon to prop up her feet."

"Dadadada…"

Maggie looked down at the small child who had toddled up to Jake.

Jake turned and grinned at the blond-haired, blue-eyed cherub slobbering all over his pants and patting them with the wet hand she'd been chewing on. "Well now, hello there, little one."

Jake glanced up to see who the baby might belong to and spotted one mother with a child similar in looks, changing the child's diaper.

"Dadadada…"

The child patted his leg again and then proceeded to crawl up onto his lap.

Jake chuckled. "Dadadadadadadada to you, too."

The child chortled, clapping her hands.

Jake bounced his knee, keeping a firm grip on her as he made soft silly noises, just long enough until the mother turned to check her other child and noted her gone.

Maggie was enchanted. She watched Jake hand the child back over and the child fuss, not wanting to leave. Jake tickled the child's belly.

The baby chortled again.

"Ms. Garderé?"

Maggie glanced over and saw the nurse. "Yes?"

She started to push herself up, but Jake was suddenly there, helping her.

"I'm not an invalid," she said, her cheeks turning pink.

Jake paused, studying her. "I know that. And I think you know that, too."

"Jake, I..."

"Right this way," the nurse interrupted.

Maggie turned and went in for the doctor's appointment, wishing she could have apologized for what she'd said.

Through her entire appointment, where they measured her, checked the baby, listened to the heartbeat and asked a million questions, her attitude toward Jake still weighed heavily on her mind.

When she went back out, she intended to apologize, but stopped at what she saw. Sitting over in the corner with a woman was Jake, holding the woman's hand as she cried softly.

He was simply a man. He'd said that.

But how many men did she know who would feel comfortable enough to sit and comfort a total stranger, especially a woman while she cried her heart out to him?

Jake suddenly looked right at her, startling her. It was as if he'd sensed the moment she walked in. He nodded at her and then turned back to the woman.

Maggie moved toward them, sitting far enough away so she wouldn't overhear what was said.

Jake continued to talk until another person came up. The woman, who looked to be older than the one Jake sat with, plopped down and started talking. She wore a tailored outfit, very nice, with her hair pulled back in clips.

In a bit Jake squeezed the woman's hand and got up, saying a few more words before leaving.

Maggie was curious but wasn't sure if she should ask what had gone on.

They walked in silence to the car. Jake opened the door and helped her in, then went around and climbed in his side. Instead of starting the car, he sat, leaning his head against the steering wheel.

"Are you okay?"

Jake sighed and finally lifted his head. "The woman is carrying twins. They just told her the likelihood of her carrying both to term is almost 100 percent unlikely. They wanted to take one baby now so the other could have a chance."

"Oh, no," Maggie said, her heart flip-flopping.

Jake nodded. "She doesn't want to lose the chances of a child but refuses to consider abortion, either."

Maggie nodded. "God's hands."

"Yeah. I prayed with her, talked with her, listened to her until J.J. got there. Then I turned her over to her."

"J.J.?"

Jake chuckled. "J.J. is the nickname she earned for telling everyone she meets it's 'Just Julie.' She is a pastor at one of the local churches. She's a dear, absolutely hilarious."

Maggie listened to the description of Just Julie and found herself mildly depressed, until his next words.

"She rules her three kids with an iron hand. And melts like butter on a grill when her husband smiles her way."

"The woman goes to her church?"

Jake nodded. "She had already called J.J. but needed someone to sit with her."

Maggie nodded. "Of course she did."

"Sorry to have kept you waiting."

Maggie studied Jake. "Why in the world would you apologize for comforting that woman?"

Jake glanced at her, then sighed. "Some people wouldn't appreciate it. Since I brought you here, it was rude of me to make you sit for an extra fifteen minutes when your appointment was over. It could have been an hour if J.J. had been unreachable for some reason."

"Jake. That's your job. That's just part of it."

Jake suddenly grinned. "It's nice to know you understand. It happens a lot."

Maggie smiled, remembering the tender look of understanding on Jake's face, and could see how it would. He cared. He really cared about people.

"How do you do it?"

Jake glanced over at Maggie. "Do what?"

"How do you care so deeply? Doesn't it ever get to you? The pain? The fears? The hurt?"

Jake sat still for a while, then finally started the car. "Yeah, it gets to me. But I have God, who knows what that feels like and takes that burden from me, wearing it Himself. I could let the pain and fear and stress consume me. Just like you could, Maggie. You could let your fears and pain over your problems consume you and you could hide away, stop coping. But God has promised His yoke is easy, His burden is light. All we have to do is go to Him."

Maggie nodded. She shifted around in the seat and put her seat belt on, thinking about what Jake said. God's yoke is easy, His burden is light, she thought. Even if it doesn't seem like it, He told us His grace was sufficient. She wondered when she'd forgotten that.

"Can I take you out to lunch?"

Jake's deep warm voice interrupted her thoughts and she looked over at him. She realized they were still sitting at the clinic. "Don't you have to get back to work?"

Jake chuckled. "I have to eat, too. I'm a growing boy. My stomach is telling me it's time to eat."

On cue, her stomach rumbled.

"Sounds like junior or juniorette is telling you something, also."

She laughed. "Don't be silly. That wasn't the baby. That was my stomach."

"Ah, then you're telling me you are hungry?"

Maggie smirked. "Oh, that was very funny. Get me to admit it's *my* stomach, then I can't argue."

He grinned. "It worked."

"Okay. That sounds good."

Maggie could enjoy the world of make-believe for a while. She could pretend everything was normal and she was out with a gorgeous hunk of a man on a lunch date.

Unfortunately, reality intruded with the huge lump that stuck out in front of her. Looking down at her stomach as Jake drove out of the parking lot, she touched her stomach softly.

Yes, she could pretend, but the truth wouldn't go away. She was a single, pregnant, alone.

"Do you still love him?"

"Who?" she asked, listening to the hum of the engine as the drove down the street.

"The father."

Memories of the last time she'd seen him, the time all her feelings had been shattered, played through her mind. "No," she whispered. "I don't love him."

"Good."

Surprised at Jake's reply, she met his gaze. "Why? Why good?"

Jake smiled before turning into a salad-and-soup shop.

"Because I find you different from any woman I've met. Because I can't imagine you wasting away hurting over some man who isn't here. Because you deserve better. Because there's so much out there for you. Choose one."

Because I care about you. That was what she would have chosen. But it wasn't one of the choices. Instead, she replied, "I'm carrying another man's child. I'm broke. The luck that follows me…"

She trailed off, unable to go on.

"You're carrying your child. You have a job, and God is all you need. Don't sell yourself short, Maggie. God made you special. He wants to heal your heart. Just let Him do it. Take it one step at a time."

He wants to heal your heart. Yes, she would suppose the pain in her heart did need healing. But what Jake didn't understand was with parents like hers, no matter how much he tried to help her, it was just going to fail in the end.

"I suppose so, Jake."

"I know so, Maggie. Now, I'm done lecturing. Let's go feed you and fatten you up."

Maggie jerked her gaze up to Jake's to see a soft look in his eyes that was at odds with his words.

"Fatten me up? What? Am I to be a sacrifice or something?"

Jake chuckled, sending shivers down her spine.

"Oh, Maggie. I love it when that sense of humor of yours breaks free. One day, one day—" he reached out and touched her cheek, his warm fingers bringing a feeling of safety to her "—yes, one day, I hope you can be much freer with that and not have to be prodded to let go."

Maggie stared into the deep dark eyes of the man in front of her and sighed, wishing the same thing, but as frozen up as she felt inside, she doubted that could ever happen.

To laugh and joke meant to trust. How could she trust or open up when she knew things could only end in disaster?

Chapter Ten

"Yoo-hoo?"

Maggie jumped, looking from where she was just finishing with the bandages on the cat.

"It's me, Jennifer. The day-care manager."

Maggie smiled and went to the door, not too surprised by the unexpected visit. "Hello, Jennifer. Come in."

Jennifer was dressed in a pair of jeans and a huge untucked man's shirt, her hair pulled up under a baseball cap. In her hands she carried a large plastic container with condensation on the outside.

"I was on my way to work. But you know, when I got there, I found I'd brought too many veggie snacks for the kids today. I knew you were pregnant and wondered if you would take these."

If that wasn't a lie, Maggie didn't know what was. But the way Jennifer smiled so sweetly kept Maggie from being embarrassed about the handout. "Thank you," she said softly. "I imagine this is like the orange juice two days ago?"

"No, we didn't have enough room then."

Maggie chuckled and shook her head. Jennifer had been by three times now since she'd been here. The woman was more like a child than a woman, in her opinion. She dressed so informally, got right down and played with the kids and was so...carefree.

Maggie wondered if she herself had ever been like that, tried to remember back a year ago and found it hard to fight past the pain. "Let me just put this up." Maggie walked into the kitchen.

"How's Kat?"

Maggie looked to where the cat lay growling, the whites of her eyes showing, and noted Jennifer didn't even blink at how the cat eyed her. She smiled. "Better."

"I thought so. Her growl is louder."

Maggie chuckled. "So, you noticed."

"I've heard all about this cat from Jake. He's certain one of these days you aren't going to show up for work and he's going to come over here and find you devoured by her."

Maggie switched the veggies—broccoli, squash, carrots, cauliflower—all to another dish and then rinsed out Jennifer's dish before drying it and returning it to her.

Maggie reached down and patted the cat. "So, Jake thinks Captain Kat is going to eat me, does he?"

Jennifer shoved the plastic container under her arm. "Yep. Of course, he was certain the gunrunners were going to get me on my way to San Gabriel. Jake worries, and is very protective of his own.''

Maggie felt her heart trip at those words. "His own?" She laughed uneasily as she went to get her keys. ''Well, I'm certainly not *his own*.''

''Just a saying. You're one of the church so you're one of *his own*.''

''Oh, yes. I—of course.'' Maggie blushed.

''He's always doing that, too,'' Jennifer said, going out the door.

''What's that?''

''Mistaking what I say. Why, just yesterday I said, 'Jake, you know I think you've developed a dependency on Maggie.'''

''You what?'' Maggie stopped on the porch and stared at Jennifer, dumbfounded. ''That's ridiculous. He doesn't even know me. He—''

Jennifer chuckled. ''Similar to what Jake said, until I mentioned the office and then he started singing your praises.''

Maggie flushed, then shook her head. ''I doubt that. I can't figure out Shirley's filing system. It's driving me crazy.''

Maggie went carefully down the stairs and turned on the path to the church.

''Yeah, well, that's what Jake had to say. He also said you were doing admirably with it. You see, Shirley had her own system. Purchases she put under 'Bought.'''

''All of them?''

''Yep. All of them. And what was it…oh! Yes. Sunday-school material was all placed under 'Teaching.'''

"Oh, dear."

Jennifer laughed, a soft sweet sound, which urged Maggie to join in. Maggie found herself automatically relaxing around Jennifer.

Over the past few days Maggie had found herself relaxing a lot. The people here were all nice. Only a couple had avoided her glance when she came in or when they came to speak to the pastor. Most engaged her easily in conversation, didn't treat her like a pariah and didn't ask questions.

But Jennifer—Jennifer topped the list of oddities. She treated Maggie like a long-lost sister. There were no questions, no strange looks. Not even a blink of the eye. Jennifer just laughed and then launched into a story.

Jennifer was an optimist, Maggie decided. She always smiled, never frowned, never said a bad word against anyone.

"How do you do it?" Maggie opened the back door of the church and went inside, sighing in relief as the cool air-conditioned air hit her humidity-soaked skin.

"Do what?" Jennifer asked, throwing her arms open and letting out a big "Ahhh" as the air hit her.

"Stay so...up? Haven't you ever been through anything to bring you down?" Maggie flushed. "I didn't mean to sound so bitter. I—I just..." Maggie trailed off, wishing the floor would open up and devour her.

"Don't be embarrassed." Jennifer reached out and slipped an arm around Maggie's shoulders and hugged her.

Maggie was surprised at the action but didn't push her away as she might have anyone else.

Jennifer released her and started toward the office. Jake wasn't there. Jake spent the first couple of hours each morning praying and then went on hospital visits and anything of that nature.

"You know, Maggie. The Bible says to let God fight our battles. God is our refuge, our rock, the person we run to when we're scared or afraid. It took me a long time to learn that. But I did."

Jennifer smiled and went into Maggie's office. "And I really had to learn that lesson when my mother died and left me with her day-care center—a center no one would leave their kids at because I wasn't anything more than a kid myself. I had to learn it when one of those children was killed by snake bites because the mother couldn't afford to leave the child anywhere else, and I'd had to shut the center down."

Jennifer dropped into a chair and smiled softly up at Maggie. "And still, sometimes, I have to relearn the lesson when I allow things in my heart to fester instead of releasing them and going on."

Maggie turned to the filing cabinets, feeling the blood drain out of her face. "It's so hard sometimes."

"Yes, it is. But to go on, to live again, fall in love, trust, sometimes we have to let go of those hurts."

Maggie wondered how in the world the woman knew what was going on, then remembered Jennifer hadn't actually named what was going on in her heart, just pinpointed some of the problems. "Even if I do, Jennifer, it'll all end up going wrong in the end."

Maggie opened the drawer and stared at the files. She didn't hear Jennifer cross the carpet, only felt her small hand touch her shoulder. "Just trust God, Maggie. And Jake. It'll all work out."

Maggie nodded.

She didn't move until she heard the woman talking to someone out in the lobby, then she folded into her chair, her heart beating staccato.

"Good morning!"

Maggie jumped, grabbing at her chest. "Jake, you scared me to death!"

Jake slowed his tread, smiling at Maggie. "I might have to try that more often if it'll put color in your cheeks like that."

She flushed and his grin widened.

"Oh, you!" She yanked a tissue out of the box and tossed it at him.

He made a dodging grab for it just as she did. He ended up with her hand. To avoid pulling her arm out, he tried to compensate and ended up sprawled across her desk, his head in her chest.

Maggie gasped.

Jake jerked back, raking everything off the desk as he went.

When Maggie saw he was actually red, she laughed.

"I was getting ready to apologize. However, if it makes you laugh I'll attempt something else."

Maggie, who could tell her own cheeks were pink, just shook her head. "What put you in such a good mood, and why are you in early today?

Jake sighed and put on a mock frown as he scooped up the miscellaneous things he'd knocked off her desk. "Sounding like Shirley already. What is it? Does it have something to do with that chair? You sit in it and become bossy? Wait a minute—let me try it.''

He started around the desk and Maggie held out a hand in protest. ''Not one more step! If this chair is bossy, I'm going to keep it.''

Jake stopped. ''It was worth a try.''

Leaning back against the edge of her desk, he smiled.

Maggie liked his smile. He wore a pair of khaki pants with a navy pullover.

All in all, the man looked great.

Realizing she was studying him, she forced her gaze up—and met his knowing grin.

Deciding to ignore it, she tried to bluff her way through. ''I just wondered why you were, uh, so dressed up? Something special?''

Jake slowly nodded, his gaze traveling slowly over her. Maggie knew what he'd see. She was wearing a balloon dress, as she liked to call it. Powder blue with a bouquet of flowers right over the big protrusion in front of her. It had cute little cap sleeves and a scoop neck, then just ballooned out the rest of the way down.

She'd clipped her hair up with a pretty floral clip, but still it didn't help. She felt round and short.

She appeared like a pregnant woman who was about to drop her baby.

''You look beautiful today.''

The softly spoken sentence astonished her, and she glanced at him with surprise.

It evidently shocked Jake, too, for he seemed disconcerted. Slowly, though, the odd expression left his face, to be replaced by a smile. Finally, he answered her question, not commenting again on how she looked. "Yes, I'm going somewhere today. I got a call. It's definite. We've been approved to build the project on the land we bought. These plans were accepted. I have to run out later and sign some paperwork. I'll want you to type special informational sheets for me, and letters. And I'd like you to go with me if you have a chance. It'll be after lunch."

Maggie nodded. "Of course."

Jake studied Maggie again. "You know, you really do look wonderful today. Your face looks fresh, relaxed. Strain lines that were there when you first started working here are gone."

"Gee, thanks." Maggie didn't mean to sound sarcastic, but that wasn't what a woman with swollen ankles wanted to hear.

Jake chuckled, reached out and chucked her under the chin. "Would you like to hear the rest of what I was thinking? I think the green of your eyes reminds me of the same color on hyacinth leaves and that the shade of lipstick you're wearing is like azaleas fresh in bloom and that when you smile like you were you could light up a whole room."

Maggie gulped, staring at Jake, feeling the warmth of his hand imprinted on her chin. Though he continued to smile, she could see the seriousness in his eyes. "You're just being nice," she whispered.

Slowly he shook his head. "I don't lie, Maggie-May. It bothers me that you don't see your own beauty."

"But—but—but I'm pregnant!" She pointed at her stomach, flustered, stuttering over his words.

Jake smiled. "Are you now, sweetheart?" He looked down and his eyes widened as though he had just realized that. "Oh, my, when did that happen?" Putting a hand to his forehead, he shook his head. "And pregnant women are just so lovely...."

"Yeah, swollen ankles and all," she said, trying to joke and stop him before he ruined his nice words with a description of just how she really looked.

Jake paused, tilting his head slightly. "I wasn't teasing about that, Maggie. Watch most pregnant women you know. Most have a glow about them, a secret look as if they hold the future within them—which they do. I think God gave women a special blessing when He allowed them to be the bearer of life."

Maggie didn't know what to say. She touched her stomach, stunned by the beauty of Jake's words.

Jake eyed her stomach. "It's a special gift you carry, Maggie. Life. Don't ever let anyone belittle you about it. Mistakes are in the past. As long as they're under the blood, they no longer matter. Today, now, is what matters. Accept the gift God gave you and pray for it every day and think why you were so lucky to be blessed with such a gift."

The mood shattered at Jake's last words. "Lucky? A gift?" Maggie shook her head, pain and bitterness reminding her of just who she was and why her attraction could never go anywhere with Jake. "Thank you, Jake. I appreciate your words of encouragement."

She could tell Jake knew he'd said something to bother her. He didn't ask. Instead, after a moment he knelt near the credenza and pulled out the bottom drawer.

''Let's see what we can do with these files, shall we?''

Maggie gazed down at Jake. The shirt stretched over his wide shoulders, outlining muscles. The collar lay gently against his neck.

It just wasn't fair that a man should be so handsome. Especially her boss, her preacher, especially when she was pregnant. She sighed and turned to help him work.

She found it relatively easy to start rearranging the files with Jake's help. She also found she had a wonderful time later that day when she ran errands with him.

That night, as she lay in bed, she thanked God that she had such a good boss, and prayed that things would continue to look up.

Chapter Eleven

"He's possessed. How could I have ever thought him such a wonderful guy?"

Maggie sat on the porch, pulling off the last bandage from Captain Kat. "Tell me, Kathryn, how could I have believed it?"

The cat growled in return.

"I'm glad you agree. A town party. He expects me to attend a town party. Just because it'd be good for me to get out in—"

"That cat looks like she's had a bad hair day."

Maggie silently groaned before glancing over to where Jake was coming around the corner. He looked wonderful as usual, in a pair of jeans and a tucked-in polo shirt.

"She was hit by a car. Of course she looks like she's had a bad-hair day. She was shaved, and this is the first time most of the bandages have been off."

Jake stopped short of the cat, staying upwind, she noticed. And he said he wasn't allergic. She shook her head.

"I just came to see if you're ready. I'm really glad you agreed to help at the town party."

Maggie sighed and stood, lifting the cat in her arms.

"She's growling." The low warning in Jake's voice brought a smile to Maggie's face.

"She always growls."

Jake shifted from foot to foot, eyeing the cat as if the creature were from another planet. "It might be a good idea to think of getting her declawed if you're going to keep her."

Maggie shook her head. "She needs her claws to defend herself. I wouldn't leave her helpless."

Jake studied Maggie before nodding. "Very well. Just be careful."

"I'm always careful."

When Jake opened his mouth to say something else, Maggie decided to change the subject. "Just what is it you need my help with at the town party today that no one else can do?"

Maggie went inside, hearing Jake's steps as he followed. The sound of the door closing behind her was loud in the silence. The silence, except for the continuing growl of Kathryn as Maggie took her over and put her back in her box.

"It's a surprise."

"Oh?" Maggie went in the kitchen to dump the bandages and wash up before returning to the living room. "The job is that bad, is it?"

Sheepishly, Jake shrugged. "I suppose I could have

gotten someone else, but I thought you'd have fun. If you don't mind, let's just keep it a secret until we arrive.''

Maggie studied him, curious. He appeared almost boyish in his excitement. Why hadn't she noticed that before?

A slow smile curved Maggie's lips, and a hand came to rest on her stomach as she watched him. Finally she nodded. ''Very well. I won't ask.''

He grinned. ''Good. Let's get going.''

Jake came up and slipped a hand to her back, urging her toward the door.

''My purse, Jake.''

Jake shook his head. ''It'd only be in the way. You won't need it.''

Maggie sighed. ''If you say so.''

''Trust me, Maggie-May.''

Maggie met his gaze. Dark eyes stared deeply into her own. A current of something passed through her and she knew, in that instant, that she could trust this man. She nodded. ''I do.''

A slow smile curved his own lips. His focus dropped to her lips. Maggie felt her heart rate pick up and her breathing constrict.

Jake hesitated for a moment, then nodded. ''I'm glad.''

He turned back to the door and Maggie sagged, released from the strange spell. If she didn't know better, she'd say that was old-fashioned attraction for Jake. But as she'd convinced herself before, it would do no good to think about such things, especially since they couldn't be reciprocated.

"Sorry, but we're in the church truck again."

Maggie, her attention drawn by Jake's voice, glanced up and saw the back of the truck filled with chairs, tables and other miscellaneous stuff.

He pulled open the door for her. "You just like watching me struggle in and out," she muttered as she stepped up to haul herself into the truck.

Jake chuckled, his hands going to where her waist would normally be. "Actually, it's an excuse to get my hands on you," he joked, then hefted her up.

"Oooaaafff." Maggie hit the seat with a thud.

She scowled at Jake. He only chuckled and slammed her door, then trotted around and climbed in.

"I feel like a cow."

Jake grinned. "Best-looking cow I've ever seen."

Maggie gaped. "I can't believe you said that."

Jake raised an eyebrow. "Oh? I said you were good-looking. You are the one, my dear, who said she was a cow."

Maggie shook her head. "You're in a mood today."

Jake backed around in a large U and then took off toward town. "The annual town races are a blast. It's a day the entire town opens up for people to visit, eat, have fun and mingle."

Maggie's mind caught on the word races. "I remember you calling for volunteers for the event." Narrowing her gaze, she eyed him suspiciously. "Don't tell me you couldn't find anyone else so you volunteered me to race."

Jake glanced at her, his eyes showing his surprise. "Maggie, the only way I would have volunteered *you* to run in a race in your condition is if you were racing a turtle."

Maggie choked on laughter. "You're just full of compliments today, aren't you?"

"Well, *do* you want to run?"

Maggie shook her head. "Of course not."

Jake smiled. "I didn't think so."

She didn't like his smile. "Jake Mathison, what are you smiling about?"

"Not a thing," he replied blandly, so blandly that she knew he was deliberately lying.

"Lying is a sin."

Jake smiled. "That's right."

"So stop lying to me."

Jake's smile widened. "I'm not."

"You're not?" That smug grin made her want to wipe the street with his face. "There's a catch, isn't there?"

Jake shook his head. "I'm just joking, dear."

Maggie's heart thrilled at the endearment, then his words registered. "So what are you smiling at?"

Jake turned onto Main Street and Maggie forgot her question. Yes, indeed, she was too busy gaping at the sight before her to remember what it was she'd asked. "What in the world are all those beds doing in the middle of the street?"

Jake pulled the truck into a parking lot and several members of the church came over and started unloading it. Jake got out, came around and opened her door. "Look at that," she said and pointed, sliding out, forgetting he hadn't answered. "Brass beds, black beds, a fire-engine bed. They have homemade quilts and... Why are those people all walking around in gowns?"

Maggie turned.

Jake smiled and held up a bag. "Surprise," he said.

Dread shot through her. "Surprise what? I don't like surprises." Warily she opened the bag.

"You volunteered to be the passenger in our annual bed races."

Maggie extracted a huge, antiquated pullover gown that tied at the neck and had long sleeves, a round mop cap and... "Leprechaun shoes?"

Incredulously, she looked up at him.

Jake smiled. "I knew you'd enjoy it. Besides," he added when she didn't say anything, "I got to wear this outfit last year and have no desire to wear it again."

Maggie didn't know what to do. Something she thought long dead surfaced, and she actually laughed at being duped so easily. "You are awful," she said on a gurgle as chuckles finally broke forth.

Tenderly he reached up and cupped her cheek. "I'll be awful or anything else if it'll get you to laugh again like that Maggie-May."

Maggie's laughter died, her gaze taking in Jake's features, the gentleness of his touch, the patience in his eyes.

"There you are, Maggie!"

Elizabeth Jefferson broke the spell. With a child perched on her hip, Elizabeth said coming to a stop beside them, "I had heard you volunteered for this. I just wanted to make sure Jake here wasn't coercing you into it. Jennifer is convinced Jake threatened to cook for you or some other disastrous feat if you don't do it.''

Maggie smiled at her and the man coming up behind her, toting a child, also.

"Hey,'' Jake said amiably. "My cooking isn't that bad.''

Though he joked with Rand and Elizabeth, Maggie could still see something in his eyes. She wasn't sure what, wasn't even sure she wanted to know, but she refused to back out on him after she'd agreed.

"He didn't coerce me at all. He only had to ask.''

"Oh, no,'' Elizabeth groaned. "You'd better learn quick to change that tune or he'll have you doing all kinds of wonderful chores.''

Maggie smiled at Elizabeth, taking her ribbing good-naturedly. "That's what I'm paid for, to do chores,'' she quipped, and set to work getting the voluminous gown over her head.

She felt a pair of hands helping her and knew that it was Jake assisting her. A small shiver passed through her, one both good and bad. "Do you want to tell me just how this works?''

The gown fell down around her shoulders, and she reached up to tie it.

"He didn't tell you?''

Maggie glanced up at Elizabeth. "No.'' She eyed Jake suspiciously. "He didn't.''

Elizabeth's peal of laughter attracted attention from those around her.

"Elizabeth,'' Rand warned. He smiled sweetly at Maggie. "You'll have to forgive my wife. From what I understand, she got stuck with this three years ago. And if I understand correctly, it was in the same way you did.''

Jake smiled and shrugged. "I love volunteers."

Maggie shook her head. "No one is answering my question."

Just then a voice came over a loudspeaker.

"Come on," Jake said, handing Maggie her green shoes. "We're second in line."

"We'll be rooting for you at the sideline," Elizabeth said.

Rand slipped his arm around Elizabeth and nodded, then turned his wife and led her off.

"You are making me very nervous, Jake Mathison."

Jake touched her back, sending shivers down her spine. "I'd never do anything to hurt you, Maggie."

For some reason, Maggie believed that. He led her through the mingling people and various beds to a blue painted metal bed that had pink stripes encircling the poles. "These colors are awful."

Jake chuckled. "It stands out from the others."

"I'll say it does."

"Come on. Hop up on the bed."

Maggie gaped. "You're kidding me. You expect me to climb up on that?"

Jake grinned. "You sit on it, with or without the sheets pulled over you—that part doesn't matter. Hold on to the bars, and then we push you down Main Street here to city hall. Whoever has the fastest time wins."

"You mean they actually time you?" Maggie was

having a very hard time believing this. "Are you sure it's safe?"

Jake chuckled and patted the bed. "Come on, Maggie."

Reach out, in little steps, one at a time to trust, a voice whispered to her. Maggie hesitated for a moment more before finally deciding to go ahead and try it.

Awkwardly she clambered up on the bed. Several people were there to help push. Tyler—she recognized him—came up and smiled. "You can either sit up and grasp the bars behind you or lie down and grasp the ones at the foot of the bed. Your choice."

Maggie chuckled nervously. "I think I'd rather sit up."

Tyler nodded. "It's actually quite…invigorating."

Maggie's eyes widened. "You have done this?"

Tyler chuckled. "Four years ago."

"What does he do? Wait until someone new comes to the church and grab them?"

A slow smile curved Tyler's lips, and Maggie gaped at how handsome he was when he did that. He nodded.

"You're kidding."

"Nope. That's how he got me. That's how he got Elizabeth. That's how he got two other people. No one thought, with you in your condition, he'd ask you. Should have guessed, though."

Just then a shot sounded, and Maggie saw the bed in front of them shoot forward. That was the only word for it. Shoot—as in a rocket. "They're going fast."

"The speeds get up to almost thirty miles an hour."

Maggie watched as the team pushed until they got to

where the street sloped downward. The two people on the back jumped on the back railing. "Oh, my."

Maggie heard the cheering of the crowd, the announcer talking over the voices; saw the people pointing and clapping, the excited faces, the laughter.

"Okay, it's our turn. Hold on."

Maggie felt the warm hand on her shoulder, but it didn't change her opinion. "I'm going to die."

Jake chuckled. "That's the spirit."

"Nothing shakes you."

"Ask me that another time."

The bed jerked as it rolled forward. The vibration of the asphalt through the wheels on the bottom of the bed ran up her spine. There was a click and jerk as the bed rolled over what felt like a crack the size of New Orleans but was certainly no bigger than her finger.

Maggie had to wonder if she was going to be shaken apart going down this slight decline.

The six people from church all swarmed into place, taking what she thought of as a runner's stance. "Ready, Maggie-May?" Jake called.

The gun exploded.

"No!" she yelled, and they took off.

The wind hit Maggie's face, stealing her breath. The cap ripped from her head. Faces of people flew past, and the entire bed felt as though it were flying.

Voices shouted encouragement; cheers echoed in her ears. She was almost certain she heard Elizabeth shouting her name. The shock faded and she relaxed.

Tyler was right. This was exhilarating. When was the last time she'd done anything that had been considered fun...though she wasn't sure if she would call this fun. She still had to reach the finish line.

A huge bump jarred her, and her hands tightened spasmodically on the bars. Then the bed flew past the concession stand and announcer's podium and they were at the end of their race.

The bed jolted again, jarring her as the six men and women brought it to a stop.

Maggie gasped for breath. She looked around and saw the others gasping and laughing and leaning on the bed. Maggie couldn't resist the urge. She giggled.

Jake appeared at her side, wiping a hand over his forehead, breathing harsh, his face flushed. "Well?"

Maggie knew what he was asking. She grinned like a fool. "It was wonderful!"

Jake reached out for her hand.

Maggie met his eyes. The sounds of cheering, the drone of the voice on the loudspeaker, even the sound of the wind, seemed to fade as she stared at Jake.

Maggie placed her hand in his.

Jake smiled tenderly and tugged.

Maggie flipped her feet around and slid off the bed.

Jake continued to hold her hand, his smile fading as he stared.

"One step at a time, Maggie-May. One step at a time."

Maggie heard the echo of her heart only moments before and nodded numbly.

Slowly the voices returned; the wind whipping at her hair forced her to reach up and push it back. The others who all came running up to congratulate them had to be answered.

Jake finally released her hand. "What say we go have some fun?"

Maggie smiled. "I think I've had more fun just now than I had expected to have the rest of my life."

Jake grinned. "But, Maggie, my darling, the fun has just begun. It only gets better from here on out."

Seeing the mischievous glint in his eyes, Maggie fervently hoped he was right.

Chapter Twelve

"I really appreciate this. Shirley used to do this all the time. I wasn't sure you'd feel up to it."

Maggie listened to Jake's voice in the other room as she tied the huge white bow at her neck.

Ugh.

It was her first maternity suit, and the bow looked like something a two-year-old would wear.

The skirt was straight, hitting just above her knees, and the top flared out over her enlarged abdomen, falling midway down her thighs. It was navy blue, with white piping and large cloth-covered buttons.

"That's what you hired me for," Maggie said practically. "It's part of my job."

"Ah yes, your job." She heard Jake chuckle. Oh, how she liked the sweet rich sound of his voice. "Of course."

Maggie came out of the bedroom into the living room, where Jake stood. She sidestepped Kathryn and then leaned down to pet her. "That's a good girl, Captain Kat. You're doing just fine."

The cat made an awful sound and then wound her way around Maggie's legs before going into the kitchen toward her food.

Jake sneezed.

Maggie sighed. "You ought to go outside, where the cat won't bother you."

"That cat isn't bothering me."

Maggie shook her head disbelievingly. "Very well. The cat isn't bothering you."

After going into the kitchen, she pulled out two plates, bowls and silverware and set them on the table. Quickly she made oatmeal and toast.

"Let me help you, since you invited me to join you," Jake said, coming in and pulling two glasses out of the cabinet.

He took them to the table.

"I'd like milk, please," Maggie said, as he strode to the refrigerator.

Jake pulled open the door and looked inside. "I'll have milk, too."

Strolling back over to the table, he smiled. Maggie wondered what had changed in Jake. He'd been so solicitous to her lately, so gentle and caring.

Her mind drifted back to the bed races two weeks earlier and the look they had shared. Something had changed that day, tilted, throwing her world off-kilter.

Maggie couldn't put her finger on it, but ever since then she'd seen Jake differently, wanted more than she should, desired what she knew she'd never be allowed.

Yet she knew Jake had changed, too. At the office he held himself a bit more distant, though he did spend more time talking to her coming and going from the house. He was also much more careful about coming into her house on errands now, sending Jennifer, instead.

She missed him dropping by. It had thrilled her this morning when he'd stopped by to pick her up a little early, and she'd found out he hadn't had breakfast yet.

Mentally berating herself, she finished setting the table and took her seat.

Jake said a prayer and then Maggie opened her eyes and picked up her spoon.

Nervously, she watched Jake.

"Mmm, this is good."

Though she'd wanted him to like it, she suddenly felt ridiculous. "It's only oatmeal."

She spooned sugar and butter into her oatmeal and mixed it up.

"But I don't cook oatmeal."

Maggie paused with the spoon halfway to her mouth. "You don't cook oatmeal?"

Jake shook his head, taking another bite. He made an *mmm* sound again. "I use the little packets when I have oatmeal. Normally if I cook something for breakfast it's grits."

Maggie chuckled, watching him eat. He was gorgeous even when he ate. A hint of dark along his cheek showed that he would need to shave again that afternoon. His strong jaw worked and his Adam's apple moved when he swallowed.

A sudden dimple appeared in his right cheek. Maggie

looked up to meet his eyes, and flushed. "You should be eating, Maggie."

"I am," she mumbled, and shoved the spoon in her mouth.

"So Maggie, tell me, how is the job working out?"

Jake smiled, amused, as Maggie kept her eyes on her bowl and ate. It cheered him to know she wasn't as immune to him as he'd thought. Two weeks ago at the fair, something had happened that had knocked him off his feet. He wasn't sure what. He did know it suddenly didn't matter to him whose child she carried. He wanted her.

She fascinated him like no other woman. In church on Sundays, he found himself watching her worship and the joy on her face. Yet in the world she was so alone.

Jake shared something with her there. He loved God, had a close relationship with Him, closer than any friend. In church he had friends and people he visited, but he still felt alone in some way. Incomplete. There was more he was missing.

Jake decided it was a helpmate, someone to share with, someone whom he could talk to, dream with, be with.

"Tell me your dreams, Maggie."

Maggie almost choked. Jake frowned and reached over, patting her on the back.

"My dreams?" she gasped, wheezing, her eyes tearing.

Concerned, Jake leaned forward to pat her again.

"Please, you'll knock the vertebrae out of alignment if you whack any harder."

Jake chuckled and sat back. ''Sorry.''

Maggie dabbed at her mouth and sat back. ''No problem.''

Jake took a sip of his drink. ''I didn't mean to shock you.''

''I wasn't shocked, exactly. I guess, well, no one thinks I have dreams anymore. I mean, well, not after...'' Maggie motioned to her stomach.

She looked so awkward, as she said that. ''Everyone has dreams,'' he said softly, silently asking God to help him through this. Why had he brought this up? Or maybe, just maybe, Maggie did need to talk, to remember, to find her dreams again.

''My dreams...'' Maggie took a sip of her milk and another bite of her cereal, before answering. ''I wanted to work in my family's business, I suppose.''

''And?'' he prodded, seeing the odd look in her eye as she stirred absently at the bit of cereal left.

''And I suppose I was like any other girl. I wanted a family—husband, children, a white house with a fence and happily ever after. I wanted someone whom I could love and who would love me back.''

Maggie continued to stir, not looking up or saying anything else.

''I've always wanted the center.'' Jake shared his own dream in this quiet time. Though he'd never revealed much about his life, now he felt he could. It felt—right. ''I basically grew up on the streets. Drugs, violence, you name it. I saw my brother killed. Had it not been for someone who cared, I'd probably be dead right now. However, I swore the day I gave my heart to God that

I wouldn't stop until I had a center here in the city for kids to go to as a safe place, a refuge. The center has always been my only goal.''

Jake paused, glancing at Maggie, who still wasn't looking at him. ''It wasn't until…lately, that I started thinking I might want more.''

Maggie lifted her eyes and met his gaze. She opened her mouth to reply—or ask a question. He wasn't sure, and never would be because of one blasted obstacle to perfect peace.

''Mmmeeeooooowwwwrrrr…''

Claws dug into his leg.

''Ouch!'' Jake jumped, shooting back in his chair and upending it in his haste to get loose from the cat.

''Oh, dear!'' Maggie gasped, and shoved back, going for the cat, which was still hanging on to Jake's pant leg.

The cat hissed.

Jake stumbled and went down, sprawling.

Captain Kat ran.

''Are you all right?'' Maggie moved over to Jake.

Jake sneezed, then looked up from where he lay on the floor. ''It only hurts when I laugh.'' Slowly he gave her a somewhat pain-filled lopsided smile.

Maggie chuckled. ''You are ridiculous.''

She reached for him, and he shot her a warning look. ''Don't even think about it. You'd strain your back.''

Jake shoved up and stood, lifting the chair back up. He grabbed his bowl, rinsed it out and then stuck it in the dishwasher.

Maggie cleared the table and finished loading the dishwasher before washing her hands.

"You really should have that cat declawed."

Maggie frowned at him, then went into the living room and grabbed her purse, notebook and files.

"You sure you feel up to this? You're not too tired?"

Maggie sighed loudly. "You've been asking me that for over two weeks now."

Jake smiled and nodded. "If you hadn't pushed yourself so hard at the city celebration and gotten sick, then I wouldn't be asking you."

Maggie scowled and went to the door, digging her keys out of her purse as she did. The clicking of her heels was loud on the hardwood floor. Run, her mind told her. Get away. Get out of the kitchen, out of the house, where there's more space.

She felt sensitive, unsure after sharing her dreams with Jake. What in the world had possessed her to tell Jake what she wanted?

Maggie strode to Jake's car. That smile of his, his touch, that look that had been driving her crazy for two weeks. He was making her feel things she'd thought dead, and she didn't like it one bit.

She had vowed to survive, make it through this situation she was in. Suddenly finding herself attracted to a man, and one who touched her on some deeper level, didn't encourage her.

Jake placed a strong yet gentle hand on the small of Maggie's back. Softly, next to her ear, he whispered, "Maggie-May, did I tell you that you look wonderful today?"

Maggie turned, opened her mouth to call him on the lie, and promptly forgot what she was going to say. Jake's eyes were serious. There was no laughter in them. Only tenderness.

Maggie saw reflected in them something she felt in her own heart: temptation.

She tried again to say something to him, but her voice came out in a small quaver as she spoke words she'd never thought to admit to anyone. "I'm scared."

Jake slid his hand around to her waist and rested it there on her side. "Me, too."

A hot humid breeze wafted through the air, carrying the spicy scent of Jake's aftershave to her. Maggie inhaled, leaning forward slightly, allowing herself to enjoy the temporary feel of his hand at her waist. "Why?"

She wasn't sure he'd heard her whisper until he leaned forward and responded, "Because I don't want to see you hurt—again."

"You won't hurt me."

"I won't hurt you," he agreed, his other hand coming up and brushing a piece of hair from her face.

"But I might hurt you," she replied.

The draw of his hand on her cheek was irresistible. Maggie had yearned so long for the touch of another human being. For months now, she'd lived in a void, without touch or companionship. Jake and others had offered companionship. But the touch...

Maggie luxuriated in the rough feel of his hand against her cheek. Just for a moment, what could it hurt to give in, enjoy...

Maggie sighed.

"Oh, Maggie," Jake murmured. "If this is hurt, I'll gladly suffer."

Jake leaned forward and touched his lips to hers in a gentle, yet consuming kiss.

Maggie reeled. Her breath left in a rush. Pleasure filled her, pleasure and...fear.

She jerked back, her breathing hard. Her mind swirled with old and new sensations, until she finally looked up and met Jake's eyes.

Concern and something else shone in them. Maggie averted her gaze.

"Should I apologize?" Jake asked softly.

"No!" Maggie turned toward the car. "Not at all. I— I wanted it, too."

Why she admitted that she wasn't sure. But it was the truth.

Jake opened the car door for her, and Maggie climbed in.

He walked around the front of the vehicle, then slid behind the wheel. The sound of his door closing was loud. The engine turned over, and his hand went to the back of the seat as he looked over his shoulder to back out.

"You still have that shopping list Jennifer mentioned?"

Whatever Maggie had expected, it hadn't been that. "Yes. I do."

Jake nodded. "Good. After the meeting, we'll go shopping. How does that sound?"

Maggie thought it sounded like a long time in Jake's

company. She wasn't sure if that was good or bad. So instead of answering, she said, "Thank you."

"It's no problem."

The car turned, and they were headed into Baton Rouge.

Maggie decided it was going to be a very long drive.

Chapter Thirteen

"We're here."

Maggie groggily opened her eyes and looked around. "Wha—?"

The deep sound of Jake's sweet voice echoed in the car. "You fell asleep, Maggie."

"I what? I did not." Maggie was appalled. She never slept in the car.

"I didn't mean to," she apologized.

Jake chuckled. "Then the baby must have decided you needed it. Don't worry. You almost made it all the way to the city limits before sleeping."

Maggie's cheeks heated. "I've been out that long?"

Jake nodded. He slipped from the car and came around to open her door. "Have you been having trouble resting?"

Maggie shrugged. "Only intermittently. I have an occasional nightmare."

Maggie scooted to the edge of her seat and then stood.

Automatically, she reached up to cover her head with a hand against the misty rain that fell.

"Is this the place?" she asked to change the subject from her sleeping habits and nightmares.

Maggie looked at the hotel where they were meeting and realized it was one she had sometimes reserved for her parents when they had people from out of town coming in and were going to conduct several meetings. The hotel had wonderful accommodations and great conference rooms. The food wasn't bad, but the small Mexican restaurant next to it was great.

Maggie checked her folders, the notebook and then her purse before following Jake into the hotel. "You should have wakened me."

"You looked tired, Maggie. Don't be embarrassed that you took a short nap. I can't tell you how many times Shirley caught me snoozing in my office."

Maggie didn't like being vulnerable, and sleeping made her vulnerable. Once inside she crossed the maroon carpet with Jake, doing her best to look like a professional assistant instead of a pregnant lady who'd just had a nap. "Here are the files you needed in regard to the plans you wanted."

Jake took the file folder from her and thumbed through it. Maggie flipped her notebook open and slipped her pen in the rings, following Jake around the corner.

"Here we are," he said, going toward one of the conference rooms.

Maggie heard Jake, but her eyes were on the water

fountain just outside the doors. ''I'll be right there,'' she said, and headed toward the relief.

''I'll be just inside.''

''Okay.'' Maggie went over to relieve her thirst. Cool refreshing water filled her mouth, reviving her.

''Jake!''

She heard the male voice and Jake's good-natured response. The murmur of other voices reached her, and she still drank. After her fourth sip she forced herself to stand and take a deep breath. How long had it been since she'd done work like this? Surely not since working for her parents.

She checked her papers again and then went to the door.

Perhaps fifteen or twenty people stood around in groups, talking. All wore different styles of dress, from casual to three-piece suits. The room was set up with three tables in a U shape. Small plates and snacks were laid out on them.

No wonder Jake hadn't eaten. He probably knew there would be coffee and croissants.

Maggie should have known. If she hadn't been rattled by Jake's showing up so early, it would have come back to her. She searched the room with her eyes until she found Jake. He stood so at ease as he smiled and talked. She could see him through some people standing around him.

Their eyes met and Jake lifted a hand...just as the other person moved.

Maggie's smile disappeared. The blood drained from

her face. Black dots appeared before her eyes, and the
room swam.

The murmur of voices sounded like a sudden roar.
Maggie turned and stumbled from the room.

Blindly she reached out until she found the wall. Maggie gripped at it, leaning heavily against its cool support
against her left cheek.

*It couldn't be. She couldn't believe what she saw. That
couldn't have been...*

Strong arms slipped around her, pulling her back
against a firm steady body. Maggie jerked, gasping,
opening her mouth to scream, when the sweet warm
voice of Jake reached her.

"Maggie? What is it? Are you okay?"

Panic left. Relief filled her and she sagged against
him, her legs turning to jelly.

Jake turned slightly. An arm slipped under her legs
and he lifted her.

"No, Jake, I—" she protested as he lifted her.

"Shh. You look faint."

Maggie didn't argue the fact. She did feel faint.
"Please, I don't want them to see me," she whispered
weakly, grabbing at his shoulders.

Jake, who had started toward the lobby, turned and
walked in the direction of the service elevators and other
conference rooms, instead. Jake finally lowered her to
the soft leather cushions of a nearby sofa. Only when he
removed his arms from under her thighs and she felt the
brush of her folders did she realize she must have
dropped her supplies.

Oxygen returned to her brain and the fog slowly

cleared. When she focused clearly again it was to see Jake sitting on the couch next to her, one of her hands clasped in his as he leaned over her.

"Do you need a doctor?"

"No! I guess not getting enough sleep caught up with me."

Jake gave her a look of skepticism. But thankfully he didn't call her on the lie. "Let me get the car and I'll take you home."

"Oh, no, Jake. Your meeting!" Maggie tried to struggle up, but Jake's hand on her shoulder held her down.

"I only have some plans to present. Tyler is here. I'll have him get everything and run the meeting for me. But I'm taking you home."

Maggie felt miserable that Jake was going to miss his meeting, but she was relieved to get out of there. Her heart was still racing, and she wasn't sure if breakfast was going to stay down.

Jake stood and dug through her files, pulling out what he needed. "You don't move. I'll be right back."

"Please, don't tell anyone about...me."

Jake paused, gave her a curious look, then nodded. "If that's what you want."

"It is." Jake started to turn away, but she stopped him. "Wait." Maggie leaned over and grabbed her purse. She dug in it, retrieving a tape recorder. "If you can get Tyler to record the meeting, I'll be glad to transcribe the tape later."

"Great."

He took the cassette player. When their fingers

touched, he paused studying her. He opened his mouth, then closed it before saying, "I'm here for you."

Maggie saw the curiosity and concern in Jake's face. She wanted to reach out, to tell him everything, but she couldn't. Right now all she wanted to do was curl up and hide. "I know," she whispered.

"So is God."

"I know," she repeated.

At last, she pulled her hand from under his, leaving the recorder in his grip, and lay back against the soft leather cushions of the camel-colored couch.

As soon as Jake was out of sight, a trembling started deep down inside her. Old fears, rages, inadequacies, shame, all threatened to overwhelm her. She hadn't expected to see *him* ever again. Oh, she should have known. But in a town of over 500,000 what were the chances of seeing *him,* especially since she didn't travel in those circles anymore? And *he* had been standing there with her parents.

Maggie shuddered and wrapped her arms around herself. Slowly she rocked back and forth, trying to stop the memories. A shadow crossed over her but she didn't really register it until a gentle hand touched her shoulder.

"Jake." The whisper slipped involuntarily past her lips. Warm arms slipped around her, pulling her close. "It'll be okay."

Maggie shook her head. She couldn't talk about it. If she did, she'd fall to pieces.

He stroked her back. As he did this, Maggie felt the shudders fade. Eventually, she relaxed against him. He shifted, picked up the files and her purse, handing them to her before scooping her up.

"I can walk, Jake," she protested.

"I'm sure you can. But just let me do this. You still look too pale."

Because her legs still wobbled like pudding she didn't argue. She did note she and Jake weren't going the same way they had come. "Where are you taking me?"

"I had one of the bellhops pull the car around to a side entrance that was closer."

Maggie sagged against him in relief. "Thank you."

In what seemed like hours but was probably less than two minutes, Jake was tucking her into the car. He quickly slid in behind the wheel and left without a backward glance.

All was quiet as he pulled onto the interstate and into Baton Rouge morning traffic. He didn't ask for an explanation or ply her with questions; he simply drove.

Maggie couldn't stand it.

"It looks like the rain has stopped."

"Rainy season. Hurricane season." Jake shrugged.

"I'm sorry," she finally whispered.

Jake changed lanes before glancing over at her, concerned. "Maggie, you have nothing to apologize for. You wanted to leave so we left. Even if you hadn't been sick, we'd have left if you needed to. I'd like to know what's going on—I'll admit that. But if you don't want to tell me, I won't demand it."

Maggie wanted to confess it all to him. She opened her mouth, but the crushing weight of fear and shame enclosed her in a web, making speech impossible.

Maggie fell back against the seat and turned her head, staring out the window into the distance.

Jake's hand groped and found hers. His clasp felt warm against her own clammy fingers. But what really radiated warmth through her was when he began to pray. Maggie's heart expanded, fluttering at his words. He prayed for her joy, her day, his day, all kinds of simple everyday things, as well as for her fear. Jake continued to hold her hand and praise God for the things He had bestowed on them, the joys He gave them in the world, and on and on, until Maggie felt a peace invade the car, and her heart.

Slowly the ice within her melted, and the fear left. Jake knew that, too, for he squeezed her hand tightly, then released it.

Looking around, Maggie realized they were home. "Thank you, Jake."

Jake simply nodded.

Maggie waited until the car stopped and climbed out. She smoothed her skirt, gathered up her papers and purse, then headed toward the house.

"You didn't let me open your door, Maggie-May."

Maggie heard him following and silently admitted how very nice that nickname suddenly sounded on his lips and how much it meant to walk her to her door. "I thought you might try to make the last part of the meeting and didn't want to delay you."

Jake cocked his head to the side, eyeing her strangely. "Like I said, Tyler or Gage can handle it. Besides, I think there was mention of a grocery list earlier?"

Maggie shook her head. "It can wait. I can go later."

"You sure you don't want me to run the errands for you? Milk, bread, anything?"

"No. Really. I'll manage."

Jake walked her up to the porch and watched as she inserted the key in the lock. "By the way, Maggie, I've thought about this and I think it might be better if Jennifer helped me with the meetings. If she takes a tape recorder, then it won't be necessary for you to go."

Maggie bristled. "It's part of my job."

"Do you really want to go?"

Jake asked it softly. The sound ran through her.

"No," she finally whispered, holding on to the door. "I can't go. I shouldn't even stay here. This job is wrong. If I can't do the entire job, you should find someone who can."

Jake didn't hesitate but stepped forward and pulled Maggie into his arms. "I want you in the job, Maggie-May. Only you."

"You don't understand, Jake." Maggie slipped her arms around him, allowing some of his strength and warmth to flow into her. "Things always go wrong with me. It's only a matter of time...."

Jake rocked her, his arms like steel as they held her close. Maggie dimly wondered when their relationship had developed to hugging and holding but decided she didn't mind so she wasn't going to complain.

"Trust God, Maggie. You just believe in Him and put your trust there."

"I want to." And she did. But she just knew, if she stayed, things would eventually go wrong. If her parents had seen her today, there would be problems. They were so ashamed of her *condition*. They would raise the roof until she couldn't face Jake or he fired her.

She didn't want that.

"Just keep trying. That's all you have to do."

Maggie leaned back, lifting her gaze to him.

Jake leaned down giving her time to pull back.

She didn't.

Their lips met. No fear assailed her, only a relief and joy that despite everything that had happened, he still cared.

The baby moved, kicked, and Jake pulled back. Surprise curved his face into astonishment as he looked down. He reached out, then hesitated.

Maggie gently captured his hand and placed it on the moving child.

"Wow," Jake murmured, looking up in awe. "Is the baby always this active?"

Maggie shook her head. "On and off."

Tears filled and overflowed her eyes. Jake frowned and brushed first at one trail and then the other. "It doesn't hurt, does it? Rand never said that Elizabeth was in any pain."

Maggie chuckled and gave Jake a watery smile. "No, it doesn't hurt. It's just that until recently the child wasn't even real to me. You're the first person to share anything like this."

Maggie stepped back and wrapped her arms around herself. Jake hated seeing her look so vulnerable. He wanted to reach out and haul her back into his arms and tell her he'd not let anything happen to her. But if his suspicions were correct, his Maggie had already been through enough to last anyone more than a lifetime.

"I'm not even sure if I'm going to keep this baby."

Stunned, Jake stared. She just looked so *motherly* to him, so made for children. "It's your choice, Maggie. Just pray, seek God, see how He would lead you in this. And if you decide to give the baby up, I know a couple of good families who would be overjoyed to adopt a child."

Maggie nodded and reached for the door.

"For what it's worth, I think you'd make a good mother."

Maggie paused. "No, I don't think so."

"You were great with those kids on Saturday. Eddie is more than half in love with you. Do you know he's called the church twice this week to see if you've had the baby yet?"

Astonished, Maggie said, "But I still have a month to go...."

Jake chuckled. "He doesn't care. He's just checking up on you. And there is a tenderness in you, a softness. It's tempered with the pain of going through the fire, but it's there, strong, steady, a strength to help a child going through his or her own problems."

Maggie's hand trembled. Jake barely resisted the urge to reach out and touch it. "You might not see that strength now, but one day, you're going to see, Maggie-May, how God has sustained you through this. Pray. I'll be here to help."

Maggie nodded, and without turning went into her house.

Jake walked back down the steps thinking of this morning's events. *Oh, Father, why did you bring her into my life? Now, right when I'm about to see my dream, the dream of my entire life realized?*

Jake remembered the fear and shock in her eyes when she'd looked at him in that room. What had she seen to scare her so badly? He was dying to know but understood that if he was meant to know, Maggie would share it eventually.

Amused exasperation, Jake groaned. "Why now?"

Perhaps God was telling him there was something more for him than what he had right now.

And he hoped that the something more was the woman he'd just left at the front door of the white clapboard house.

Chapter Fourteen

"I don't want no pizza unless it's Mr. Peeper's pizza."

Maggie chuckled. "Mr. Peeper's?" She glanced down at Eddie, who was walking, chin thrust out, shoulders back, as though he owned the whole world.

"Mr. Peeper's is a new place in town," Jake explained.

"Ah, I see." Maggie nodded wisely and smiled back down at Eddie. "I guess Fair and Fun is out then." Maggie sighed. "And I was so looking forward to the rides."

Eddie's eyes lit up, before he forced the excitement away. "You're preggo. How you gonna ride those rides?"

Maggie gasped. "Well, I certainly may be pregnant, but that doesn't mean I have to give up all my fun."

Eddie squinted up at her, then nodded. "I guess if she wants to go there, Pastor Jake, we gotta take her. You

know how pregnant women get. My sister cries her eyes
out when she don't get her way.''

Jake chuckled. ''We certainly don't want that.''

They went over to the car and climbed in. Jake had
explained that occasionally he'd pick up two or three,
even all the kids for something special.

In fifteen minutes they were at the park. Amused,
Maggie watched Eddie scramble out of the car, no longer
the little man of the house but pure child.

''What are we going to do first, Pastor Jake?''

''Well, are you hungry or do you want to ride?''

''Ri—'' Eddie glanced toward Maggie. ''Women are
always hungry.''

Maggie laughed. ''Excuse me, but if I have my
choice, I want to ride the Spider first.''

Eddie's eyes widened, then a big grin split his face.
''You are one cool lady.''

Maggie gaped in surprise as he turned and ran off
toward the entrance.

''You know, Maggie-May, I think I agree with him.
You are one cool lady.'' Jake chuckled and slipped an
arm around her shoulders, hugging her to him. ''I think
you just won a place in Eddie's heart for the rest of his
life.''

Maggie thrilled at the touch, leaning into Jake. ''I'm
glad. He's a sweet kid—sometimes.''

''Hey come on, you two. Oh, yuck. You're hugging
her, Pastor Jake.''

Jake released her. ''Yeah, I am.'' He reached out to
where Eddie had run back to them and snagged him.

"And I'm hugging you, too," he said, and put words to action.

"Men don't hug men!" Eddie stated stoutly, squirming to get away, but not too hard.

"Well, I'm a pastor, so I guess I can," Jake said, chuckling and then releasing him. "Now, come on, let's go."

Jake reached out and took Maggie's elbow before sliding his hand down to her hand.

"Do you think you should..." Maggie eyed their hands.

"Unless you mind," Jake said.

Indecision warred on her face.

"Maggie, I'm only holding your hand. Would it bother you if it was any other man?"

Old memories rose, haunting her. She wanted to say yes. Yes, it would. That only Jake could hold her hand without making her squirm. "I don't mind," she said, instead. Then she smiled.

Jake felt something expand in his chest at that smile. "Come on, let's go have fun."

"I hope I'm really up to this. It's been ages since I've been on any rides."

Jake pulled out his wallet, releasing Maggie's hand to pay for three passes. "Just how long is that?" he queried, as he waited while the attendant put a bracelet on each of their wrists.

Jake glanced up just in time to see a blank stare on Maggie's face. "Twenty years?" Maggie said, her face scrunching up as she tried to remember if that was correct.

Jake shook his head. Eddie jumped in before·Jake could reply, "You're *that* old?"

Jake smothered a smile.

"Yes, I'm *that* old, Eddie."

"You sure you should ride the rides, then?"

Eddie's wide-eyed stare told Jake the kid was serious about his question. "Uh, one thing to learn, Eddie, is never to question a woman about her age."

Maggie shot Eddie a militant look. "We'll just have to see who gives out first. Now, which way to the Spider?"

Eddie looked as if he had grave reservations. However, he led Jake and Maggie over to it. By the time he reached it all worry was gone and only excitement showed.

"Come on, let's go." He reached back, grabbed Maggie's hand and dragged her forward.

Maggie grinned like an unsure kid who had been told she could walk on air and wanted to believe it but just wasn't sure.

Jake placed a gentle hand at her back. "Come on, Maggie. I'm right behind you."

Maggie hesitated one more moment before giving over. Indecision yielded to firm conviction and she went forward, almost causing Eddie to stumble in his eagerness. They climbed onto the ride with Eddie in the middle, and then slowly it started.

Jake watched Maggie's eyes widen, then she gasped. Concerned, he started to signal the man to stop. Maggie ended his concern with a whoop and laugh as she leaned over and grabbed Eddie's leg. "Isn't this great!" she cried out over the increasing noise.

"Yeah, cool!" Eddie stuck his little arms up in the air and let loose with a shout.

Maggie imitated him.

Jake shook his head and held on, laughing.

When that ride was over, Maggie led them to another and another, until they had ridden every ride in the park. Then she demanded pizza and bowled at the miniature alleys before shooting in the shooting gallery. She even challenged Eddie to a game of air hockey and played video games with him.

Jake couldn't have been more pleased. Though Maggie feared her pregnancy and had told him she wasn't sure she'd make a good mom, she was proving to him over and over just what type of woman she was.

The way she handled Eddie, even though she had no idea she was doing it. Handing him a napkin, laughing with him, treating him as though he mattered. This showed how much she cared.

Why couldn't she see it?

When Jake noted Eddie's eyes drooping he called an end to the evening. "I think it's time we go. I have to get up early tomorrow." He added the last diplomatically when he saw Eddie about to argue that he wasn't tired.

Eddie subsided. "You got to work," he mumbled, and stood.

Maggie reached out and caught Eddie by the shoulder, pulling him awkwardly up against him. Her whole posture softened when he leaned against her.

Jake helped them both into the car and dropped Eddie at home, tucking him in, then talking for a few minutes with the mother and sister.

Finally they left.

"You look tired, too, Maggie-May."

The comfort of his strong arm around her shoulders encouraged Maggie to relax against him. Warmth and strength radiated from him. Maggie absorbed it, enjoying the strength. When he stopped by the car, she reluctantly stepped away so he could open the door.

Sitting down on the soft seat, she realized suddenly she was very tired.

"Maggie?"

Maggie blinked and glanced over. Jake had climbed into his seat. "Yes."

Jake smiled and touched her cheek. "Sleep. I'll wake you when we get home."

"I'm not that tir…" Maggie trailed off, then scowled. "Fine. I'll close my eyes. Satisfied?"

"Yes."

"Don't look so smug," she warned, closing her eyes as Jake pulled out. "They may be closed, but I'm not asleep."

Maggie walked through the room, her sequined dress glittering brightly under the chandeliers. Though Maggie didn't drink, several people there did, and they all held wineglasses in their hands, laughing and talking.

Maggie searched, looking for her date. Her feet hurt. She was tired. She'd done her duty by her parents and was going home. They had these parties occasionally when her parents helped a great deal with some project.

But three hours was enough for her. Besides, it was Christmas Eve and she wanted to get home. She and Chester had plans to make. She was supposed to go over to his parents tomorrow evening and then they were going to go out and discuss the wedding plans.

May was close. They had to get those invitations sent out. And when everything had quieted down, Chester's mother wanted Maggie to finish up the invitations and get them out before the first.

Again she looked, going into the billiard room and the den and finally toward the dining room.

Finally she saw him. He stood with her parents, laughing. Maggie went over and informed her parents she was going to leave.

Her parents worried. It was raining outside and dangerous. Why not let Chester drive her and they'd see her later?

Maggie agreed. She and Chester left. The cold rain pelted her in the face, causing goose bumps to raise on her arms.

Maggie hugged herself as Chester got the car. Gratefully she accepted his jacket as he helped her into the car.

Voices were distorted as the sound of the car roared in her ears. She saw herself laugh, then Chester laugh and reach over and pat her leg.

The house, looking elongated and dark, came into view and Chester drove up to the door. After coming around, he opened her door and then escorted her in.

When she tried to give him back his jacket, he shook his head, grabbing the lapels and pulling her forward for a kiss.

Maggie giggled and kissed him, then tried to step back. He walked her backward, teasing her with words and kisses until they were in a side room.

Maggie looked around, panic building in her as she knew what was coming. She tried to reach out to the person in the dream, her own self, and warn her, but she couldn't get there. Chester pushed her down on the couch to give her another kiss...and another...Maggie watched from a camera's view as the scene progressed. She couldn't breathe. She was trapped, the world growing dark...pain...suffocation...she had to scream...to scream...to scream....

''Maggie!''

Maggie jerked up, gasping for breath. Wildly she struck out, whimpering noises rising in her throat.

Hands grabbed at her. Male hands. Strong hands. Her flesh crawled.

''Maggie! Maggie! It's me...Jake.''

Dimly Maggie heard the soothing voice. The hands grabbing at her weren't the hands of force but hands that tried to gentle.

Gasping, Maggie looked around wildly and saw... Jake.

Jake fought to keep from getting his eyes scratched out, horrified at the reaction of the woman before him.

''Maggie? Are you okay?''

He watched her heaving as she stared at him, her pupils dilated, her face pale even in the dark car. He stilled.

"Maggie, darling, it's okay. It's me, Jake. We're home."

Her eyes lost the wild look and focused on him.

"We're home," he repeated, holding on to her fingers.

Suddenly her hands moved forward, and she was doing the holding.

Jake let her. He waited. Finally she let out a long breath and collapsed against the seat. "Maggie, I'm going to let go of you, just for a minute, okay?"

Her hands tightened. Jake hesitated but decided she would understand once he took action.

Reluctantly, he released her hands, then exited the car and strode around the hood. After pulling open the door, he squatted next to her. When he reached out and touched her, she jumped again.

After only a moment's hesitation, she went into his arms. Jake willingly took her, scooping her up, then shutting the door with his hip.

"Maggie-May, darling, you're trembling like a leaf. Hold on, I'm going to take you inside."

Jake strode across the lawn and up the steps. Fumbling, he managed to get the screen open. "Dig in your purse, Maggie, and get me your keys."

Maggie moved sluggishly, as if caught between the nightmare and reality. Grimly, Jake thought the nightmare was probably reality from the past.

Slowly Maggie fumbled and found her key and shifted to put it in the lock.

Jake prayed silently. He shoved the door open, flipping on a light, and asked God for peace, protection, for

His spirit to surround Maggie. He continued to pray all the way into her bedroom, words of comfort and assurance.

"Mmmrrrroooowww?" Captain Kat lay in the middle of her bed.

When the cat saw Jake her meow turned to a growl. As Captain Kat hopped up, her hair was standing straight up. "That cat is going to be the death of me, Maggie, I swea—achhhooo!"

Jake turned his head, barely missing sneezing on Maggie. Carefully he lowered her to the bed, then sniffled.

He almost landed on top of her when she didn't release his neck. After going down to the edge of the bed, he kept her up against him, holding her, rubbing her back, praying and making soothing noises—smothering his occasional sniffle—until she calmed.

He wanted to ask her. But he felt a check in his spirit. So he simply waited. Finally, softly, in a voice he could barely hear, she confessed.

"I have nightmares occasionally, about…things. I'm sorry you had to witness it."

Knowing he had to let her go at her own pace, he replied, "Don't worry about me witnessing it. I'm simply glad I was here for you."

His heart almost broke when he felt tears wetting his shoulder. He pulled her closer, holding her, trying to give her comfort.

The baby kicked.

And kicked again.

Maggie shifted.

It kicked once more.

"Why is it kicking me like that?"

Maggie's muffled laughter caused him to lean back and look at her.

Red-nosed, watery-eyed, she smiled up at him. "It's got the hiccups."

"You're kidding."

Jake looked down at her stomach, and sure enough, her entire stomach jerked. Fascinated, he watched, waiting, and then it jumped again and finally again. "Doesn't that keep you awake?"

Maggie leaned back against the headboard and smiled wanly. "Yes and no. You learn to sleep through some of it. It's only if the baby gets really bad that you are awakened."

"I see." Without thinking, Jake reached out and touched her stomach. Immediately he jerked back. "I'm sorry—I…"

Maggie took his hand and placed it back on her stomach. He chuckled as he felt the child move, settle, then hiccup again.

"That is hilarious."

"I'll remember that at 2 a.m. in the morning when the baby is doing that, and I'm having to get up because the bouncing keeps making me have to go to the bathroom."

"Oh." Jake grinned. He suddenly realized he was sitting on her bed with her, in the middle of the night, which he felt crossed the line of propriety. And though God knew his heart had been in helping her, now it wasn't. Now it was on the way her red corkscrew curls fell around her face, the way her green eyes sparkled with residual fear as she fought and gained control.

It was on how soft she looked from the living-room light, how maternal she looked with one hand resting on top of his where his rested on her stomach.

It felt too good, too right.

Jake pulled back his hand and stood. "I'll be here for you, Maggie. All you have to do is call. I live only a few hundred yards away. If you don't want to stay alone, perhaps I can call one of the women of the church—maybe Jennifer—to come sleep with you tonight."

The smile faded and shadows resurfaced in her eyes. "No. No, I'll be fine, Jake."

Maggie struggled to get up.

"Stay there."

"I have to lock the door behind you."

Jake conceded she was right. "I don't like you staying alone after that nightmare. Are you sure—"

"I'm sure," she replied.

Jake hesitated, tempted to lean forward and kiss her. A growl came from behind him, raising the hairs on the back of his neck.

He sneezed.

Maggie chuckled. "Kathryn will protect me."

Jake sneezed again and quickly strode to the front door. Stepping out on the porch, he breathed in deeply.

Turning back, he saw Maggie standing by the door, holding the screen, the cat weaving awkwardly around her legs. He leaned forward and kissed her forehead, daring the cat to do anything about it. "Call me, any hour, if you want to talk."

He stepped back.

Maggie looked up at him, and he saw in her eyes emotions he couldn't put a name to. ''I will,'' she whispered.

''Promise?''

''Promise.'' She nodded.

''Lock the door before I leave.''

Maggie nodded, hesitated, then nodded again and pushed the door closed. The resounding click told him the dead bolt had slid home. He heard her give it a jerk and thought he heard a whispered, ''Good night.''

Reaching out, he touched the screen. *Protect her, Father, while I can't. Keep her safe, because I've decided I'm going to make that woman mine.*

Slowly he turned and walked down the stairs in a daze. Maggie.

His Maggie.

He loved her.

When had it happened?

Jake had no idea. He only knew the feeling was there and it wasn't going away.

Suddenly a grin split his face. *He loved her!*

When he got to the car he hopped in and pulled over to his driveway grinning like an idiot.

He loved her.

And she was pregnant and had been sorely hurt in her past.

Jake frowned, but only for a moment. *God, you are the keeper of our hearts. Heal her heart. Heal her mind. Give me the wisdom on how to help that healing. Show me how to offer her my love without running her off.*

He shut off the engine and got out of his car. Looking back at Maggie's house, he saw she'd left on the light in the living room. *Chase away her demons,* he whispered. *Protect her....*

Then he addressed Maggie. "And get ready, Maggie. This preacher is coming a courting."

With a chuckle, he went into his house, already planning his strategy to win the beautiful angel with eyes the color of clover.

Chapter Fifteen

"Maggie, are you awake?"

Maggie looked up from the couch in the darkened room she was lying in to see Jennifer silhouetted in the harsh lights of the hall. "Yes. Jake just insists I take this hour break every day."

Jennifer chuckled.

Maggie started to swing around and sit up.

"No, stay like that. I just brought you a snack. I thought you might like something small to eat while you rested."

"You guys are spoiling me!" Maggie said this, though she felt special, very very special. "Thank you," she added, reaching for the plate. "Oh, more broccoli."

Jennifer dropped into a chair next to the couch. "Jake doesn't have an assistant pastor. Lucky for you, huh."

"I would think Tyler…"

Maggie had discovered this office only when Jake had told her to start taking a daily break and led her to the room. It had a desk, bare walls, two chairs and a sofa. That was it.

"Tyler will help out, but he's not called to the ministry."

"I see."

"Go on, eat up. It's good for you."

Obediently Maggie munched.

"Jake said you had gone to eating six meals a day."

Maggie scowled. "I'm not surprised he'd gloat. He's been telling me forever to do that."

"One more month, right?"

Maggie nodded. "The first time Jake noticed my ankles were swollen he made me start taking these breaks."

Jennifer giggled. "That man is so besotted with you."

Maggie was glad it was dark so Jennifer couldn't see her flush. "Well, it doesn't matter. Nothing can ever come of it."

It was embarrassing and had her worried that Jake had been looking at her differently for almost a week now. Something had changed the night she'd had the nightmare.

She'd been worried the next day about how he might act. She hadn't expected the looks of interest or extra attention he spent touching her or taking her out. Nor had she realized he was paying such close attention that he'd see her swollen ankles.

"Why do you say that?" Jennifer sounded surprised, shocked.

Was everyone so dense here? For months now she'd walked around on eggshells as people had pretended her pregnancy didn't make a difference. Frustration built and exploded. "Jennifer, I'm pregnant by a man he doesn't even know about. Bad luck seems to follow me. Can you imagine what would happen if I even let myself believe that Jake could really care for me? Eventually I'll have to leave when something happens, when someone starts complaining or gossiping."

"No! Jake would never ask you to leave, Maggie. He cares for you. It's obvious."

Maggie felt a weight settle in on her heart. "He might never ask me, but he'd be relieved. Just like my par—"

Maggie clamped her mouth shut.

Silence fell. Finally, Maggie heard the squeak of leather as Jennifer shifted. "Did I ever tell you how Gage and I met?"

"Jake said he was your pilot."

"Umm-hmm," she said. "That was the most interesting trip I have ever had. Gage was a very bitter man."

"Uh, perhaps…" Maggie began.

"I don't think he'd mind me sharing this with you," Jennifer said matter-of-factly. "Many people in the church know most of the story. Anyway, he got home just in time to find out his fiancée was marrying someone while he was still engaged to her. He had to come home for his mother's funeral. You see, the entire time he had been in Korea—he was a soldier stationed there for a short tour—his mother had been lying to him, telling him everything was okay. Gage stopped trusting women completely. He was so hurt and bitter and believed nothing could be believed. He threw himself into his business. That was all that mattered. Nothing else. He was going to make his business a success—which he has. But at that time it was still shaky.''

Jennifer shifted again in the quiet room. ''Then here I come. I tend to be...optimistic. And Gage was a pessimist. He found guns in crates we were delivering to San Gabriel for a relief mission and he was certain I knew about them. But on a deeper level, as we trekked through the jungle, he had to deal with his very fears— that if he opened up, he was going to be betrayed again. He fought it, dragging me toward the closest city, determined to get rid of me so he wouldn't have to face his feelings.

''The only thing he forgot in that equation is that if God wants you to deal with something, He's going to see that you do. I think Gage getting temporarily blinded, the soldiers capturing us, the rebels robbing us, were all to keep us out there until we worked through things God wanted changed in our hearts.''

Maggie shook, Jennifer's story going straight to her heart. *But why, Father? Why am I going through this? Are you trying to teach me something? Am I running from something?*

Maggie didn't want an answer because she knew what she was running from. Memories and the pain of being hurt again. Not physically but emotionally. Tears filled her eyes. As much as she wanted to believe what Jennifer was saying, she just couldn't open up and trust Jake completely. She just couldn't. He was a good man. But when things went wrong, she wasn't going to be able to stand there and watch him suffer for her mistakes, the sorrow she would bring to him.

Trust Me.

The soft sweet voice sent chills down her arms. She shivered. *I'm trying.*

Trust Me, the voice repeated.

I—I—can't.

"Trust Him, Maggie. Let Him heal your heart. Just step out and believe that He will take care of everything." Jennifer stood. "I have to get back to those adorable little rug rats. I'll send someone by for the plate later."

"Thank you." Maggie watched Jennifer leave. Touching her stomach, she whispered, *How, Father? How can I put it all behind me? How can I trust and forget and go on? I don't even know if I can keep the baby yet? How can I heal if I haven't even made that decision?*

Maggie realized that healing and trust were going hand in hand. Despite her feelings for Jake, it could never be because of her bitterness and anger. What type of wife would she make? How could she support him in his ministry, and as a man, when she was unable to get over her own hurts?

Wearily pushing up, she went back to the office to work and think on what Jennifer had said.

The pounding on the door brought Maggie up. Heart racing, she grabbed for her robe and waddled through the house.

"Maggie! Maggie, it's me, Jake!"

Maggie jerked open the door, still pulling on her robe. When she saw Jake's face, she knew something had happened. "What is it?" She squinted. "It's after midnight. Are you okay? Is it my parents?"

"It's Eddie. He's been shot."

Maggie gasped. "What happened?" She rushed back into her room, and started pulling on clothes as fast as she could.

"Gang. Something like that. I didn't get the entire story from his sister. She was crying. He's at the hospital. I thought you'd want to go with me."

Maggie's heart beat loudly as she thought of the cute kid, and couldn't believe what Jake was telling her. "Eddie. Shot." She shook her head.

After grabbing her shoes and socks, she strode into the room where Jake was waiting. He helped her down the stairs, his face etched in harsh lines.

"What do you know?" Maggie asked, climbing into the car. Once in the car she realized she couldn't get her socks on, so she dropped them and slipped on just her shoes.

"There was a fight of some sort. Eddie got in the middle. A gun went off. That's it. Elaina wasn't making much sense at the time. Her mama was in with Eddie, evidently. Big wreck or something in town so they brought him up here to the hospital instead of one of the other ones."

Jake sped along down the highway before turning in to the local hospital. Maggie was thankful it was so close. Any farther, she would have expired from worry.

Jake let her out and went to park the car.

When she entered, she saw the sister. Mother and daughter sat weeping, holding each other. A large group of friends or relatives stood around, talking and weeping...waiting for news, she assumed. Not knowing what else to do, Maggie started toward them.

Relief flooded her when Jake came in. Touching her back, he led her forward. Elaina saw them first. With a loud cry she came toward Jake. Jake didn't hesitate but opened his arms and enfolded her in a hug. Looking at the mother, he asked, "What news?"

A woman sitting next to a middle-aged woman glanced up and said, "They got him back there now. We haven't heard anything yet."

Jake nodded. The mother, eyes red and swollen, looked up. "They shot my baby," she cried. "Came right in my house and tried to shoot Elaina. Eddie, he put himself between them. They shot him down, then ran."

The woman burst into loud sobs again. Maggie didn't know what to do. She clasped her hands, before finally going over and sitting next to the woman.

The mother cried a moment more on the woman next to her before pulling free and throwing herself into Maggie's arms. Surprised, Maggie stared, then imitated Jake's actions by enfolding the older woman in an embrace. The woman's head slipped down and her hand went to Maggie's stomach as she sobbed. Over the sobbing she heard Jake's voice as he prayed.

Maggie began whispering her own prayers and words of comfort. The people with them were all in various stages of dress. Some wore robes; others were dressed as if they'd been out for a night on the town. They stood around talking, sharing stories, relating over and over what had happened.

At one point Jake went up and spoke to the nurse and then returned. "They're still working on him," he told the group, then comforted those who needed it.

His touch, a gentle word, a look of understanding or just an ear as he listened and soothed, was all that was needed.

When Maggie saw the doctor coming, she knew. It was in his eyes, in the set of his shoulders, in the taut look of his jaw.

Eddie's mama knew, too. She stiffened. "No. Oh, no. No, my Eddie's not dead. *No!*" she wailed.

And then Jake was there along with others, surrounding her. Maggie was jostled until she was near the rear.

Stepping back, she again felt at a loss, until she saw Elaina sitting alone, curled in on herself, silent and still.

Maggie went over to her. She looked about as far along in her pregnancy as Maggie. Maybe a month or two less. Worried, Maggie awkwardly knelt in front of the girl and took her hands. "Are you okay?"

The girl looked up and the pain in her eyes broke Maggie's heart. "He was always telling me one day I was gonna get myself killed hanging around with those no accounts. He told me I didn't know Jesus and I had no business hanging around with people like that 'cause if I died, I wouldn't ever see him again."

Maggie was stunned to hear that Eddie had shared this with his sister. Eddie, who put on such a tough exterior. Eddie, who was only ten years old. Eddie, sharing the plan of salvation with his family.

"He saved me," the girl whispered. "When that boy came in and was gonna shoot me to get back at my boyfriend, Eddie jumped in front of me. Before he lost consciousness he told me Jesus loved me. Those were his last words."

Maggie reached out and stroked the girl's arms, not sure what to say. *Help me, Father,* she prayed. "He loved you, Elaina," she finally said. "Just like Jesus gave His life for us, your brother was willing to give his for you. So you'd have a chance to open your heart up to God, have a new chance at life."

"I know," the young girl said. "And while I knelt there holding Eddie, I gave my heart to Jesus. But why did he have to die? Why?"

"I don't know. But we are comforted that one day we'll see him again."

The young girl leaned forward, hugged Maggie and began to softly weep. Maggie wept with her.

Maggie wasn't sure how long she knelt there holding Elaina before a friend came over and collected her. She sat back and felt a warm hand touch her shoulder.

Looking up, she saw Jake standing there. His strong hand pulled her up, and he started toward the door. "I offered to stay with them tonight, but they have family members who will. I'll go over tomorrow to discuss the...funeral. They want me to perform the ceremony."

"How can you do it?" Maggie whispered as they made the way to the car. "During such a time, holding them, hurting with them...how?"

They approached the car. Maggie turned. Instead of opening the car door, Jake suddenly snagged her; wrapping his arms around her, he held on tight. Maggie realized this wasn't to comfort but for a need of comfort.

Maggie held him, too, stroking his back as silent tears rolled down her face. "Ten years old," she murmured.

Jake wept. Deep piercing, the choked sound rose from his chest.

Maggie rocked Jake as she held him and cried with him.

Eventually, he released her and assisted her into the car before climbing in his side. Instead of driving off, he gripped the wheel. Maggie found a tissue and wiped at her eyes.

Jake's voice when it came was so soft she almost didn't hear it at first. "My brother was ten when he died."

Maggie listened, surprised. He decided to share.

"That's why this center is so important. I want a place for kids like Eddie, kids who don't have anywhere to go and need somewhere to go. Or for kids like Elaina, who, if she'd had somewhere to go, might not have gotten involved with that boy, or for kids like the one from the gang who shot Eddie. A place that's an alternative to the street."

"She says Eddie's last words were that Jesus loved her."

Jake shuddered and fresh tears fell.

"She said, she asked Jesus into her heart right there. His death wasn't without reaping results."

Jake nodded and she had a feeling he was too choked up to talk. Finally he reached out and started the car.

They drove home with the soft music of a gospel tape

playing in the background. "You know, Jake, I'll never forget the look in that mother's eyes. The pain, fear, disbelief."

Maggie rubbed her stomach. "No matter how things were, how bad they were, she loved that child."

"Yes, she did." At the intersection, Jake turned back toward home.

"I love my child," she finally whispered.

Jake didn't comment.

"I don't think I realized until tonight. But as I watched her, all I could think of was what if that had been my child...."

Maggie rubbed her stomach. "No matter about... before. *Now* is all that counts. Here and now."

The church came into sight.

"I'm not giving my baby up, Jake. I know there are things that will have to heal in my heart, but I'm not giving my baby up."

Jake pulled into her driveway and parked the car. He came around and helped almost lift her out of the car.

But instead of releasing her, he pulled her until her belly was pressed against him. He wrapped his arms around her and pulled her even closer, then he lowered his head and kissed her.

Maggie felt the rub of his lips as he caressed hers, the comfort, the joy, the celebration of life, even a touch of grief, of loss.

When Jake released her, Maggie was breathless, staring up at him in a daze. "Wow," she whispered.

Jake cupped her cheek. "Yeah, wow."

He leaned forward and kissed her lips again with more

tenderness than passion. "I'm happy for you, Maggie. And...thank you...for tonight. For being there for me, and for them."

He pulled her back against him and gave her a long hug, then stepped back. "We should get you to bed. And I don't want you in to work until after noon tomorrow."

"But..."

"No buts, Maggie. You have a baby to think of. I shouldn't have gotten you—"

"I would have been angry if you hadn't."

"Good. Then my decision was right."

He walked her to the stairs and helped her up them. "Let me hear the lock," he said softly.

Maggie turned at the door. "Of course, and good night."

She went in, and the bolt clicked.

With a sigh and a rub of his neck, Jake went back to his car and parked it in his driveway.

After getting out, he slammed the door and started toward his house. Absently he rubbed his fingers together, remembering the touch of her cheek, the softness, the lazy glow in her eyes when she'd looked up in stunned amazement.

Oh, Father, she's the one. I love that woman. And she's going to keep the baby. Jake was happy for her. He couldn't make a decision like that for her. He would have been supportive with whatever decision she made, but the look on her face, the conviction, told him she had settled it in her mind and was certain, so he was happy.

Pausing on the steps, he gazed up at the bright starry

sky. "Eddie, not only did you lead your sister to the Lord tonight, but you just gave Maggie a new hope, a new goal. For that, I thank you."

Wearily he went up the stairs, both grief and joy warring in his soul.

Chapter Sixteen

Maggie closed the umbrella as she entered the church. "What a mess," she muttered to Jennifer, who stood there staring out the front windows.

Jennifer nodded. "Isn't it. That storm has been brewing in the Gulf for three days now. It doesn't look like we're going to get any relief from the rain for a while."

"I knew there was a reason I didn't like hurricanes. You'd think this far inland the rain wouldn't reach us." Maggie rubbed at her lower back and sighed.

Jennifer glanced her way. "Back hurting you again?"

Maggie attempted a smile. "It has hurt the entire pregnancy. I think now, though, because I've gotten so big, it hurts constantly."

"Hey, you're only two weeks from delivery. These things happen. Just think, two more weeks and you'll be out of pain and holding that precious child."

Maggie smiled softly and rubbed her stomach. "Yeah. Well, I'd better get to work. I have a ton of typing to catch up on from all those meetings Jake has been attending for the inner-city center.''

Jennifer chuckled. ''Don't you. He certainly has been busy with that.''

''That project means everything to him.''

Jennifer nodded. ''I know. Gage has worked with him some on it. He's very passionate about it.''

Maggie smiled and turned toward her office thinking that much was true. Jake lived and breathed that center. And things were coming together nicely. Maggie was thankful that he understood and didn't force her to attend those meetings.

Two months working with Jake and she had avoided her parents' detection. Maybe they believed she had left the area and weren't going to cause any more problems. After all, she hadn't run into anyone who knew them, nor had she gone anywhere near where they would be.

At one time Maggie thought she'd miss that way of life. She'd felt everything she knew was tied up in that life-style. Now Maggie found this life-style much simpler. She actually enjoyed what she did.

Ruefully she looked down at her fingers. No more manicured nails. They were cut short so she could type fast. She reached up and touched her hair, which she'd pulled back in a ponytail today to keep it out of her face. Gone was the salon cut. Her hair easily hung down to the middle of her back.

Going into the office, she uncovered the computer and unlocked her desk. She slipped off the shirt she'd put over her dress to keep the rain off her, then put the shirt and umbrella on the back of the door handle to the office door.

Maggie checked the plants to make sure they had enough water, brewed some decaffeinated herbal tea, which Jake insisted they drink because of her pregnancy, and then sat down to work.

Two hours later Jake walked in. "Get me the church directory of all our shut-ins. I need to make some calls. Looks like Sheila is turning this way and coming up the mouth of the Mississippi." His words were short, his face creased with worry.

Maggie gaped. "But…but that's almost impossible." She reached in the file and pulled out the church directory, then pushed herself up from her chair.

Jake came back out of the office. "Sit down. You're too far along to be getting up and down."

Maggie scowled. "I'm fine." Halfway up, her lower back twisted and she gasped.

Jake focused his attention on her, going immediately to her side. "Then let me help you up. Maggie-May, you're too stubborn by half. You should take it a little easier."

Maggie lowered herself back into the chair, with Jake's help. Despite what she'd said, it felt good to have his strong hands on her, assisting her. "I've not had any help my entire pregnancy except for your kindness, Jake."

Jake scowled this time. "I only wish I'd been there to help, Maggie-May."

"I didn't mean—"

"I know you didn't," he cut in, his eyes piercing her.

Maggie's mouth went dry. She tried to swallow. Her heart fluttered and her stomach turned. "I—uh—"

"No, Maggie. Don't say anything." He reached out and cupped her cheek. "I told you I wouldn't push and I won't. But it doesn't hurt for you to know I care."

Jake stroked her cheek with his thumb, then stepped back. "Now, that list?"

Belatedly Maggie looked down and realized she had the list, crumbled, in her hands. "Oh."

Jake chuckled. Leaning down, he captured her lips in a soft kiss.

Maggie felt the kiss all the way down to the curling of her toes. *Tenderness.* Oh, how that felt so wonderful. "You shouldn't do that in the office," she whispered.

Jake shook his head. "One day, Maggie, you're gonna learn to trust God and not worry about my reputation for me."

Jake took the list and, with a wink, went into his office.

Maggie watched him shut the door before going back over to flip on the radio for a weather report. It'd been at least seventy or eighty years since a hurricane had come up the river. Possibly longer than that. Maggie had heard stories in history class. But that was it.

As Maggie listened, she typed up the work that had to be done and then printed it up. She found it increasingly hard to get up and down, and wished it wasn't going to go another two weeks because of the way the baby felt.

"A lot of babies go late."

Maggie, who was half standing at her chair and waiting for the muscle cramps in her back to relax, glanced up and saw Elizabeth and Rand at her door. She blushed. "I don't think I'm going to last that much longer. I've discovered muscles I never knew I had."

Elizabeth laughed, the light tinkling sound enriching the office and putting Maggie immediately at ease.

Rand walked toward Jake's door. "Is Jake in? We've come to help with the shut-ins."

Maggie nodded at Rand. "Go on in." She went over to make copies of her reports. "Would you like some tea, Elizabeth?"

Elizabeth took the copies from her and made a shooing motion. "Go sit down and let me finish this. You look tired and don't need to be on your feet."

"Why is everyone treating me like an invalid?" Maggie muttered, waddling back to her desk.

"Because we love you," Elizabeth said. "Are you having trouble sleeping?"

Maggie lowered herself into the chair with relief. "As a matter of fact, I am. It doesn't seem I can ever find a comfortable position."

"You should have carried twins. It was just like that, except that mine were early. The last two months I don't think I slept more than an hour or two at a time. Hiccups, gymnastics, kicks, you name it, the kids were at it."

Elizabeth brought the papers over to Maggie and then busied herself pouring tea for them. "Where are the kids?"

"Kaitland is watching them. Max is doing some last-minute things at the office to get it evacuated, and Kaitland knew Rand and I wanted to come help with the shut-ins so she volunteered. Tyler is out there now, making sure the vans are ready to go.''

"Tyler is here?'' Maggie was surprised.

"Yes. We swung by and picked him up on our way.''

"What are you going to do with the shut-ins? Where will you take them?'' Maggie was curious. She couldn't remember her church ever having to do anything like this. Of course, she hadn't worked behind the scenes the way she did here.

"Well, we have families who have volunteered as adoptive families to different people who are unable to get around on their own. Jake is making sure those families are still available. Those who aren't, we'll take them to backup families to stay with. The church has a special widow's fund set up for emergencies. Helping these people during the hurricane will certainly qualify. Some have relatives whom Jake is calling to let know what is going on.''

Maggie nodded. "They haven't given a mandatory evacuation yet?''

"No. But if the storm keeps coming it'll be here in six hours. It'd be better for us to go ahead and get them out now. If you haven't noticed, the winds out there are already over fifty miles an hour.''

"You're kidding.'' Maggie stared in shock at Elizabeth.

"You haven't been listening to the radio?''

Maggie pushed herself up and came around the desk to make her way toward the front of the church. "Well, yes, but the second line has been ringing off the hook with questions. I had heard twenty-five and thirty miles an hour. But fifty?''

Dark gray clouds hung low in the sky, dropping sheets of rain on the landscape outside. The water was almost horizontal in its direction as the wind blew it off toward the north. "Look at that branch!"

Maggie pointed at a huge tree branch that went flying by.

"Yeah. It's only a matter of time before they order at least a partial evacuation or insist everyone stay inside and off the streets.''

Maggie nodded. "I had no idea. The office is very well insulated.''

Tyler came running in. "Hello, ladies," he muttered, as he jogged past.

Maggie frowned, worried. She wondered how her parents were and their business. What type of plans were they making? Was everything going to be okay?

Maggie rubbed at her aching sides and then her tummy, wishing at that moment that her parents had accepted her decision. But they hadn't and now wanted nothing to do with her.

"Come on, honey, let's go.''

Rand's voice brought Maggie's head around. Tyler, Rand, Jake and Elizabeth all stood there. It was painful to see the tenderness in Rand's eyes as he gazed down at his wife. Maggie looked over at Jake and saw a knowing look in his eyes.

Maggie glanced back out the door. "You all be careful," she said.

Elizabeth hugged her, and then they were dashing out the door to the vans.

"I hope they're okay."

Jake walked up by her and draped an arm over her shoulders. "I'm sure they will be."

The vans left the parking lot.

"By the way, the Federal Emergency Management Agency just announced a mandatory evacuation. New Orleans is already being flooded with hurricane category four force winds, and the storm hasn't even moved over them yet. They're predicting it'll be here late tonight."

"What about all the people in the hotels here?" Maggie fretted.

Jake sighed. "It looks like they'll be going farther north."

"This is just unbelievable."

"Yeah." Jake steered her back toward the office. "I want you to go home and pack a suitcase. Get everything done you need to do. Consider your day over. I'm going to finish some calls, and then some men are coming to help me board up the windows here and at the houses. I'll be ready to go in two hours at the most. Do you have anyone who can drive you somewhere or do you want to go with me?"

"I'm sure I can find someone...."

Jake shook his head. "I'd rather you go with me. Tyler has a hunting cabin three hours from here. Last time we had a bad hurricane he offered it. A bunch of us from the church met up there. Rand, Elizabeth, Max and Kaitland said they'd be there."

Relieved, Maggie didn't mention that she didn't know

anyone in the area and hadn't wanted to call her parents. Besides, if she was honest, she wanted to be with Jake. He made her feel safe. Maggie nodded. "Thank you, Jake."

"No problem. Now, get your umbrella and let's go."

Maggie grabbed the old shirt and umbrella and made her way home. The rain was falling so hard that the umbrella did no good. She was completely soaked by the time she staggered up the stairs.

On the last stair the umbrella became inverted. She grasped at it, fighting it. The wind suddenly gusted and the umbrella went flying right with her. Maggie staggered and went down hard. Panicked, her arms clutched her stomach in protection. Pain streaked through her knees and hip where she'd fallen trying to protect her stomach.

Maggie lay there panting, waiting for the pain to subside before she struggled back up. Sighing heavily, she limped to the door and shoved it open.

"Mmmmrrreeowww."

"Captain Kat! I forgot all about you, sweetie. What are we going to do?"

Maggie shoved the door closed behind her and proceeded to shed her soggy clothes. She was so wet she had to get a towel and dry herself off. The entire time Captain Kat wove her way in and out of Maggie's feet. "You're worried, too, are you, sweetie? I can't blame you there."

Maggie grabbed her "hospital" suitcase she had packed and carried it to the living room. The baby books Maggie had read told her to have a suitcase ready. It contained two little outfits she'd bought for the baby, plus everything she'd need. She went back into her room and packed a second suitcase. "Hunting cabin? What would they have at a hunting cabin?"

Maggie gathered some sheets and pillowcases. She got some toilet paper and toothpaste and washcloths and detergent. Then she added her own personal items, as well as supplies for Captain Kat.

"Now we wait." Maggie sat down on the couch. She shifted off her tender hip and ignored her stinging knees as she stared out at the bleak gray sky. "Thank you, Father, for the rain, for the beauty it will bring. Protect the people here, Father. Keep harm from them."

The cat came over and, to Maggie's surprise, jumped up in her lap.

Maggie stroked the fur. She ignored the halfhearted growl. "It'll be fine, Captain Kat. Everything is going to be just fine. Jake is going to be here to help us soon."

Kathryn growled. "You know him by name now, do you?" Maggie chuckled. "I think I trust him, Kathryn. I know I trust him," she said, changing her mind. "I just…I can't admit—"

The sound of pounding on her door caused her to jump.

"Come in!"

Jake entered, carrying an extra rain slicker. "This is better than the one you had on that day I met you. It'll cover you to your ankles. Put this on…*aaaachoo.*" Jake eyed the cat balefully. "You can't mean for that cat to…"

"Jake!" Maggie stared, appalled. "I can't leave her here."

Jake sighed, shaking his head in defeat. "Of course not."

"Maybe one of the other families can take her," Maggie offered as she watched Jake sniff.

"No. No, I'll be fine. Let me load everything and then I'll come back for you."

Maggie didn't argue. After her fall she wasn't taking any chances. She rubbed at her aching hip, then her back. Jake, who was in the process of picking up the suitcases, saw her and paused. "Are you okay?"

Guiltily, Maggie looked up. "I slept wrong and my back was aching this morning when I got up. Then on the way over here I, um…fell on the steps."

Jake dropped the suitcases and hurried over. Grabbing her hands, he lifted her arms, looking them over, turning her slightly. "Are you okay? Should we go to the hospital?"

"Jake! I just hurt my hip and pulled the muscles in my back. A warm bath will help. But when we get going, and I'm off my feet, I imagine I'll feel much better."

Jake frowned, then finally nodded. "Okay. Let me just load the suitcases." He went and picked them up, sneezed, then hurried out the house.

Maggie gathered up the cat. She slipped her under the slicker Jake had provided just as he ran back in. His hair was plastered to his head. With a shove he slicked it back, sending water everywhere. "Come on, Maggie-May."

Slipping a protective arm around her, he led her out and down the stairs. The cat meowed pitifully. Maggie made soothing noises.

Jake jerked open the door against the harsh gusts and helped her into the car. Kathryn immediately scrambled out and into the back seat in a far corner.

He hurried around the front of the car, fighting the wind as he climbed in. Jake started the car and then paused, his eyes on the church.

Maggie watched different emotions flit through his eyes. "The church is in our hearts, Jake. Even if the building isn't around when we get back, the church will still be here."

Jake nodded, turned the car and started down the road, away from their home and toward the shelter.

Maggie said a soft prayer that everything would work out according to God's will.

Chapter Seventeen

"This is the third detour we've had to make," Jake grumbled.

Maggie didn't mean to sound panicked, but she was beginning to worry. "Maybe we should have turned left back at that last highway." Maggie shifted uncomfortably and looked at the harsh rain sweeping across the small country road.

"No, this is the right way."

Maggie hoped he was right. As far as she could tell, they were in the middle of nowhere. Of course, most cabins were in the middle of nowhere, so maybe he was correct. She shifted again.

Jake noticed. "Are you okay?"

"My back is hurting from sitting in the car so long, I'm afraid. And well—" Maggie blushed "—I have to, um, go to the bathroom."

"I'm sorry, Maggie. I didn't think. We've been on the road for hours and you being pregnant and all..." Jake flushed. ''We'll be at the cabin in twenty minutes or less. However, I'll watch for something along—''

The swaying trees chose that moment to object to their mistreatment by the weather.

''Jake, watch out!'' Maggie grabbed the dash, bracing herself, and watched in slow motion as one huge branch fell right into their path.

Jake jerked his head back around. He slammed on the brakes.

The car skidded and then crashed over the branch. Maggie gasped as she was tossed up and down, then sideways.

The car came to an abrupt halt and was silent.

''Are you all right?''

Dazed, Maggie looked over at Jake, who was yanking on his seat belt. He got it released and reached for her. Maggie shakily released her own seat belt and went into his arms.

''Oh, Maggie-May, I'm so sorry.''

''It's not your fault,'' she murmured into his chest. His warmth invaded her, surrounded her, reassured her. ''I guess we shouldn't be surprised after all the downed branches we've passed on the way. No one ever expects trouble to happen to them, though.''

Jake suddenly sneezed.

''Mrreeeoooowww.''

''Oh!'' Maggie pulled back. Captain Kat sat on the seat next to Jake's shoulder, licking her paw. At Maggie's attention, she paused and meowed again. Maggie smiled, relieved. ''The cat came through it fine.''

Jake nodded. "I see that." He glanced nervously at the cat.

The cat saw his look and growled.

Jake shuddered at the sound, then turned his attention from the cat. "It appears we didn't come through it fine."

Maggie finally noticed the way the car leaned. Glancing around, she saw that the rear of the vehicle was partially in a ditch. "Oh, no, can we get out?"

"I don't know. Stay here while I check it out." Jake grabbed his raincoat from the back seat and hopped out, then slipped the coat on. She watched him go to the back and then he disappeared from view.

Absently, Maggie accepted Captain Kat's need for love and reassurance when she crawled into Maggie's lap, and Maggie stroked her. "He'll be fine. I'm sure the car is okay."

Jake stood and moved around the car. He stopped at the front and disappeared from sight again. When he stood back up, there was a scowl on his face.

Maggie shifted uncomfortably, not wanting to hear bad news. "It seems I may not get to a bathroom in the next fifteen or twenty minutes, Kathryn, if the expression on Jake's face is any indication."

The cat growled.

"Stop that, Kathryn. That's not nice."

Obviously offended by Maggie's reprimand, the cat wiggled loose and returned to the back window seat.

Just in time, too. Jake pulled open the door and slipped in.

"What's the matter?"

Jake shoved at his hair, wiping a hand down his face. "It looks like we won't be going anywhere, Maggie. The axle is broken."

Maggie stared at Jake in shock. "You're kidding."

Wearily, Jake looked at her. "I only wish I were."

Maggie suddenly giggled.

"What do you find so amazing about that statement?"

Maggie shook her head. "It's not the statement, exactly, that made me laugh."

"Oh? Then what?"

Maggie's cheeks heated. "It's that, well, despite the fact that we are stranded here and a hurricane is on the way, the only thing I can think of is that I have to go to the bathroom."

Jake stared for a moment, before his features relaxed and he chuckled. "Only you, Maggie-May. Only you."

Maggie's chuckle turned into a snort. "Only any pregnant woman who has a seven-pound baby or so sitting on her bladder. So, what are we going to do?"

Jake smiled and reached across Maggie into the glove compartment. "Cell phone."

"Oh, thank goodness," Maggie said. "I might just find a bathroom."

Jake chuckled and flipped the cell on. He listened—and frowned.

"Then again—" Jake flipped it on and off several times. "I'm afraid, Maggie, you're going to have to wait a little longer."

Maggie smothered a laugh of disbelief. "Now what?"

Jake shrugged. "Stay here and hope someone comes by?"

Maggie shifted, arching her back and trying to get comfortable. "I suppose that's one option...."

"Well, we have prayer, too."

Maggie agreed and said a quick prayer for help. Despite her words to Jake, she could not sit in this car until someone came. Her back was killing her. Her bladder was killing her. Her whole body was stiff from the fall. She had to get out, and soon, or she was going to go crazy.

Jake suddenly leaned forward, peering out the windshield into the distance. "Look, there, that looks like a possible road...."

Maggie followed where Jake pointed to a dirt track. "More like a hewn path to me."

"Exactly, which means it's not a traveled road but probably a driveway."

Just then Maggie spotted it. "Over there, almost back behind us. It curves around."

"Answered prayers," Jake murmured. Turning, he asked Maggie, "Can you make it there?"

Maggie gave Jake a long-suffering look. "I'm pregnant not—"

"Helpless. Yes, I know. You keep telling me that."

"Then let's go." Maggie picked up the cat.

Jake grimaced, then sneezed.

"You know, I think you're right. I don't think you're allergic to cats."

"I'm not."

Maggie smiled. "It's a psychological thing."

"It is not." Jake looked at her aghast. "The cat just

needs a bath. It probably picked up some pollen or something.''

''Uh-huh. Of course, Jake.''

''If we're going to take it, let me carry her. You shouldn't be walking that far carrying her.'' Jake had a stubborn little boy look, as if he were set to prove something.

Maggie rolled her eyes. ''I can do it.''

Jake shook his head determinedly. ''I'll do it.''

Maggie was certain this was tied up in some macho thing, so she let him. ''Fine. Here you go.'' She held out Kathryn.

''The cat is growling—again.''

Maggie shrugged, smiling sweetly. ''She doesn't bite—I don't think.''

''You don't think?''

''She has never bitten me.''

''Great.'' Jake took the cat, the hair on his neck shooting up.

The cat growled louder, her voice going up and down the range of sounds.

''You know, Jake, I really can carry her. You don't have to.''

Jake shook his head. ''We're fine. Aren't we, Captain Kat?''

Maggie reached in the back seat, grabbed her raincoat and awkwardly slipped it on, which wasn't any easier than having divested herself of it earlier. Finally she had it on. Glancing at the still-growling cat and the sneezing Jake, who looked as though he was afraid he was going to die any moment, she sighed. ''I'm ready.''

Jake nodded, hesitated, then shoved the cat into his raincoat. Pushing his door open, he said, "Stay right there. I'll be around."

Maggie didn't argue. She shoved open her own door and wiggled to the edge of the seat, then slowly hauled herself out of the car. When she stood, she gasped and grabbed at her back.

"I told you to wait! Are you okay?" Jake, face creased in concern, reached out for her.

Maggie willingly leaned into him. "My back is killing me. I guess when I fell I really pulled some muscles."

Jake slipped an arm around her. "Come on, let's get up there. We'll get permission to sit out the storm with these people, and then I'll come back for our suitcases."

Maggie nodded. For some reason, walking was much slower. Water soaked her feet and legs, and the baby was so low that every step seemed to take twice as long. On the driveway they had to battle the mud. "This is really disgusting. Mud is oozing in my shoes."

"You think you've got problems. I've got four sets of claws permanently embedded in my chest."

"Oh, Jake!"

"And she's still growling. How you didn't keep from having a nervous breakdown before now I'll never understand. She's making me a nervous wreck."

Maggie chuckled despite the pain in her back. "All bark and no bite, Jake."

"She's not barking, Maggie."

Maggie squeezed Jake's side reassuringly. "Just stop worrying. I offered to carry her."

They arrived at the door and knocked. Maggie stepped

away and tried to shake the water from her coat. "My stomach's wet."

Maggie looked in disgust where the coat hadn't covered her bulging stomach.

Jake sneezed, pulled Kathryn out of his own coat and handed the cat to her. "Hold her while I knock."

Maggie smiled. "Have you ever heard the saying 'Like me, like my cat'?"

Jake knocked on the door, glancing at Maggie in surprise. "Actually, the way I heard the saying went was—"

"You don't have to like my cat, Jake, to like me," Maggie hurriedly interrupted. "Not everyone is a cat lover." Maggie leaned against the wall, bending one leg as her back cramped.

"I don't think anyone is at home."

Dismayed, Maggie stared at Jake. "You're kidding."

Jake shook his head. He knocked again and waited. "I hear nothing from inside, and there are no cars around."

The pain in Maggie's back abated, but her leg was cramping from standing so oddly so she walked across the porch to ease the cramp from her thigh. "I can't wait. If they're not home I'm going to have to find a tree."

Jake chuckled. "Take your pick."

Maggie looked around at the many, many trees. "It's raining," she said in disgust.

"There's a hurricane coming, Maggie."

She heard the laughter in his voice. "Oh, is there, Jake? I thought we were just driving along for the fun of it.'' Maggie shook her head and shoved the cat at Jake.

Captain Kat meowed in objection.

Jake sneezed.

Maggie smiled. ''I'll be right back.'' Maggie shifted and rubbed at her back before going to the edge of the porch. She peered out, then carefully made her way down the stairs. ''Oh, ugh… Oh!''

Maggie froze.

Jake, who was still trying to adjust the cat and keep her claws out of his flesh, looked up.

Maggie met his eyes.

''What is it, Maggie-May?''

Dismayed, Maggie moved her raincoat to check her legs. Jake followed her gaze.

''I guess you really weren't kidding about having to go to the bathroom.''

Maggie lifted her gaze to Jake. ''I still have to go to the bathroom.''

Jake stared, then motioned to her pants, which were soaking wet.

Maggie shook her head. ''I *still* have to go to the bathroom.

Maggie watched as Jake's eyes suddenly widened and his gaze riveted on her legs once more.

''Oh, no. Don't you dare tell me that, Maggie…''

He was begging. Maggie had to smile. She had never heard that note in a man's voice before. It was edged with panic, the same panic she was feeling. *Father, we don't need two of us panicking,* she whispered. Taking a deep breath, she nodded at Jake, whose gaze was now locked to hers. "I'm sorry, Jake. My water just broke."

Jake shook his head.

Maggie nodded. "I'm afraid so. It looks like I'm going to have my baby."

Chapter Eighteen

Jake broke out a window.

"What are you doing?"

Jake didn't care that Maggie stared at him so oddly. He was worried sick. A baby. He couldn't believe it. "You cannot have your baby right now. I'll pay these people back. But we're getting in and calling for help."

Jake pushed the window open and crawled through. In seconds he was pulling open the door.

Jake took one look at Maggie standing there and reached out to guide her in. This could not be happening.

Jake ran a hand over his face. "Just sit down or something and I'll be right back." Glancing at her stomach, he thought she still seemed just like everyday Maggie. And yet her water had broken, and she was telling him she was going to have a baby. He gulped and turned toward the kitchen.

He was grateful when he found a phone in there. *Oh, Father, please don't let her have this child now. Why?*

Why is this happening? Things couldn't get any worse. *I don't understand, Father.*

Jake picked up the phone.

There was no dial tone.

Jake stared at the phone in disbelief. "God!" He actually looked up at the ceiling. "What is going on here?"

All he saw was plaster, though he knew God had heard him.

Trust me. A sweet soft voice floated to him from within. With that voice a gentle peace surrounded Jake.

"Father, Father, Father, I don't know what to do. This is just beyond belief. Please, Father, help me here."

Jake shook his head. "Tyler's cabin—it's only an hour away, maybe more...."

But Jake knew he wasn't going to take a pregnant woman in labor out into this mess.

Why? he whispered.

Jake fought and slowly forced himself to accept the situation. Then he turned and went in to tell Maggie...and found her just coming out of the bathroom.

"Maggie! What are you doing? You are about to have a baby!"

Maggie jumped and grabbed at her heart. "Don't yell like that, Jake!"

She stared at him and he felt his cheeks heat up. He couldn't believe he'd raised his voice. Wearily he ran a hand over his face, thinking panic was doing neither one of them any good.

It didn't help when Maggie laughed at him. "Jake, it's my first child. They say those labors take up to fourteen or fifteen hours—'' Maggie suddenly gasped and grabbed her stomach, her eyes widening.

Jake almost swallowed his tongue. So much for staying calm. Seeing Maggie's face contort as she grabbed her stomach like that gave him palpitations. ''What is it?''

Maggie glanced ed up. ''That one was much stronger than the others.''

Jake felt sweat break out on his forehead, even though cool wind blew in through the window. Then her words registered. ''Others?'' His voice sounded odd even to his own ears.

Maggie smiled sheepishly. He wanted to tell her not to look at him like that. That look meant trouble. No, he didn't like that look at all and braced himself for whatever she was getting ready to say.

She didn't disappoint him, either.

''I didn't know before, but now I think the pain in my back these last nine or ten hours must have been contractions. It only got worse when the water broke. I mean, it's coming all the way around—''

Maggie gasped again, her eyes widening.

''Don't do that!'' Jake reached out, paused, then reached out again for her. Watching her, his stomach lurched. He didn't like the thought that she was in pain at all.

''Do what?'' she said, panting.

''Widen your eyes as though you're about to drop that baby any minute.'' He also didn't like that he was the only person in the area and that Maggie was in labor. It hit him blindingly at that moment—the reason he didn't like it: he was so in love with this woman that he couldn't bear the thought of losing her.

Please, Father, guide me. He'd never in his life delivered a baby and here was his Maggie, about to deliver her child.

Maggie looked incredulous, drawing Jake's attention back to her. "I'm not about to *drop* this baby. Fourteen hours or so of labor, Jake. Remember?"

"You just said you'd been in labor a good ten hours," Jake reminded her. He watched Maggie as his words dawned on her.

"Oh, my," she whispered.

Jake's hope that they might get out of this without anything happening sank to his toes. But as his hope sank, a strange peace descended, too. Jake suddenly felt in control and able to cope. Maggie had no one else. God never put more on them than they could bear. God would see them through this. Jake smiled, moved forward and slipped a gentle arm around Maggie.

"So, when will the ambulance be here?" she asked, leaning her small frame against him. Jake held her, enjoying the feel of this woman depending on him.

Jake swallowed. Maggie sounded so hopeful and the cat, sitting there by her, looked expectant, too. Reluctantly, he turned Maggie toward the couch and helped her down to a sitting position.

"Well?" she asked, gazing up at him expectantly.

Gently he broke the news. "The phones aren't working."

"Don't tell me that!"

Mirrored in her eyes was the panic he'd felt only moments before. He wanted to pull her back up into his arms and hold her, tell her everything was okay. Instead he said jokingly, "The phones were taken when the people left."

"You're kidding!" Maggie glanced up, incredulous.

He watched her slowly relax as the contraction left. "Yes, I am, Maggie-May. You told me not to tell you the phones weren't working."

Dumbfounded, she stared. "You're telling me a joke at a time like this?"

Jake smiled. "Seemed the best thing to do."

Maggie fell back against the couch and laughed. "Oh, Jake. What am I going to do with you? A joke!" Wearily she shook her head.

Jake sat down next to her and took her hand. It looked so small in his larger one; it was soft and gentle. He rubbed his thumb over the top of it, noting how pale her skin was next to his darker tone. He heard her breath catch and slowly lifted his steady gaze to her fearful one. "We'll make it though this, Maggie-May. I'll go out and see if I can locate another cabin nearby and contact the authorities for help. I'll also get your suitcase so you can change."

Maggie held on to his hand, gripping it. Jake wondered if she knew how much that mirrored the fear in her eyes that she tried to hide behind a weak smile. "Thank you. I'm sorry about this, Jake. I guess the baby and God have their own time."

Jake leaned forward and placed a gentle kiss on her forehead. "I'll be right back." He stood and grabbed his raincoat. Slipping into it, he went to the door, cast one last look at her, then left.

Maggie watched him leave. When the door was closed she leaned back against the couch with her hands cradling her abdomen. So many emotions swirled through her mind. It was one thing to say she wanted to keep the baby but another to face what had happened to precipitate in the actual birth of that child.

Maggie hugged her stomach, fighting the fears of what-if....

Everything would work out fine. She had to believe that. She had to concentrate on that right now. Jake would find someone and call and they'd have help and everything would be okay.

Maggie went into the bathroom and washed her face, then braided the mass of curls to keep it out of the way while she waited for Jake to return.

When he wasn't back by the time she'd finished with her hair, she waddled into the kitchen and rummaged through the cabinets, taking stock. She was uneasy going through someone else's cabinets. But anything to keep her mind occupied was better than sitting in the living room worrying.

It was twenty-two minutes and eight contractions later before Jake returned. And of course he would walk in when she was bent over, making an awful face.

"Maggie!" Jake dropped the suitcases and rushed over to her.

Maggie, who'd had enough time to calm down, raised a hand, concentrating on her breathing.

Jake stopped and waited.

When the contraction eased she stood. One glance at him told her no help was forthcoming. "No one?" she asked, unable to believe the frustration and defeat etched deeply on his face.

"Not a soul."

Jake retrieved the suitcases, moved to the first bedroom and set them alongside the wall. He took his and went to another bedroom. "Not that I'm planning on being here that long, but you never know. Not one car passed while I was out there."

Jake returned to the living room and set up the cat's food and water.

Captain Kat walked over, sniffed the bowl, turned her tail up and walked off.

Jake plopped his hands on his hips. "I'm the one allergic, and she acts as though I've offended her!"

Maggie chuckled, dryly. "Don't worry. She'll be fine."

His exasperation faded. "Maggie—"

"I know. What are we going to do?"

"Do you trust me?"

Maggie's heart clenched. *Do you trust me?* How long had it been since she'd trusted a man? Oh, she trusted Jake, to a point. But this condition, the problem, made her so vulnerable. "I, we don't have a choice."

Jake smiled, though there was concern in his eyes. "We'll have to help each other. I've, um, well…"

Maggie's attention was caught with the way he walked over to the window and started fiddling to close and cover it.

"I've been reading up on pregnancy and childbirth.

The Lamaze method sounds easy enough, as does the delivery.''

Maggie couldn't help but stare at his back in shock. "And when did you start reading up on this?" she had to ask.

"A few months ago. With so many women pregnant at the church all the time, I found it an interesting subject."

Maggie's heart softened and melted. She walked forward and touched Jake's shoulder. "You may have just saved this child's life with that knowledge, Jake. Thank you..."

Her hand tightened on his shoulder, and she broke off as another contraction hit her.

Jake turned and cradled her until the contraction had passed. "Your suitcase is in the bedroom. Do you want to change? By the way, I left a note in the car where we were. So, if someone stops by, they'll come here, hopefully."

Maggie nodded. "I'd love to change. I'll be right back."

Maggie went into the room and opened her suitcase. Digging through it, she found a loose housedress and slipped into it. She debated underwear. "This is so embarrassing," she whispered.

Thinking about Jake delivering her baby, she wanted to groan with mortification. Of course, help still might come. Somehow, though, Maggie knew Jake was going to have to deliver this baby.

Another contraction hit just as she was turning back

to the door. Sinking down onto the side of the bed, she groaned.

Jake tapped on the door. "Maggie?"

Maggie's face scrunched up with pain. Dimly she heard the door open, but the contraction consumed her. She felt supportive hands on her shoulders.

"Breathe," the voice whispered.

Realizing she held her breath, Maggie concentrated on breathing. This contraction was worse than the others, she thought vaguely. When it faded she sat back, grateful. "That one..." Maggie shook her head. "I can't imagine them getting worse." She looked up at Jake for reassurance.

He hesitated, then reached for her hand. "Let's walk through the cabin, or maybe go out on the front porch."

Maggie nodded, thinking it a wonderful idea.

"Just how far apart are the contractions?"

"About three minutes." Maggie moved slowly to the door.

Jake opened it.

"I know they weren't this close before my water broke," she confided.

Jake frowned. "Perhaps the labor has increased, or they were that close but you just didn't notice them because they weren't as painful?"

Maggie went out on the porch and over to the railing. Rain fell in a downpour. "Sounds like someone crunching up a paper bag, doesn't it?" she said softly, soaking in the beauty of the rain.

"I don't know. To me, it sounds like a brook or a dripping faucet."

Maggie looked over to where Jake pointed and saw a large stream of water flowing. "Isn't it amazing how many sounds there are that God created?"

Another contraction hit. Maggie's hands tightened on the railing. Jake moved up and rubbed a hand up and down her back.

"Oh, that…feels…good."

Jake's hand moved back down to her lower back. "Here?"

Maggie nodded. "Yes."

The contraction subsided. Maggie relaxed and sighed. "It was raining that night…"

Jake slipped an arm around her but, she moved away. "What, Maggie?"

Maggie stared out into the rain. Her jaw tensed. She looked so alone, so lost.

"I didn't think I could ever stand the sound of rain again. But having you here with me—it makes things different."

When her hands tightened on the railing, Jake carefully moved forward and rubbed her back, offering silent support.

Maggie closed her eyes. "I'm so scared, Jake. What if… Can a child conceived in violence… Can I really love the child?"

Jake's jaw tightened and rage ran through him as his fears were confirmed. "Oh, Maggie.…"

The contraction faded and she turned into his arms, faster than he would have thought possible for a woman in labor. He didn't mind. He needed to hold her as much as she needed to be held.

They stood like that through several contractions, Jake holding her, trying to help ease both her physical and emotional pain as her contractions got closer together and her sobs continued.

Finally, Jake began to sing softly, a song of God's love as they stood there. Minute by minute, Maggie's tears quieted and Jake's anger faded.

"Please don't hate me," Maggie murmured when she could talk again.

Jake shook, unable to believe the soft words that mixed with the tumultuous sounds of the storm around them. "Hate you? Hate you! Maggie, how could I hate you for what someone did to you?"

Maggie opened her mouth to reply. A gasp escaped, instead. Here eyes widened and she looked to Jake, sudden dismay and fear in her eyes. "Oh...oh! This... is...not the time...to tell...you this."

Jake forced his anger at the unknown assailant aside, trying to hold Maggie as she sobbed and help her through another contraction. "Come on, sweetheart, let's get you inside."

Maggie groaned. "Oh, Jake...something is different."

Jake's anger fled completely, replaced by fear. "What? What is it?"

Maggie grabbed at her lower stomach. "I'm not sure. But I think, it may be time, to have the baby."

Chapter Nineteen

Jake helped Maggie into the cabin and then to the bedroom. "Lie down, Maggie."

Maggie turned and slowly lowered herself to the bed. Then she grabbed Jake's arms as another contraction hit. "Ooooh…"

"Breathe," he said gently, putting action with words and breathing with her. When the contraction subsided, he said very matter-of-factly, "Maggie, hon, I need to check you."

Maggie's face went up in flames. "This is so awful," she said mournfully. "What is your congregation going to think?"

Jake laughed. "You're worried about what my congregation is going to think at a time like this?"

Maggie's embarrassment left and she scowled. "Stop laughing."

Jake liked her anger better than her embarrassment.

Pushing her legs up, he moved her dress enough to carefully check her. "I see something…"

Maggie gasped. "Con-trac-tion!"

Jake reached out and grasped her flailing hand. "They
won't disapprove, dear."

"I…really…hate that word…*dear,*" she gasped. "*He*
used to always call me that." She surged up, grabbing
at Jake's arms. "Oh, dear—oh dear—oh, dear, this
hurts!"

"Breathe like this," he said, and took slow deep
breaths, staring at her, willing her to imitate his actions.

"He said that to me the night after he was done.
'We're going to be married, dear. What are you so upset
about?' My parents said it to me when I told them what
had happened. 'Rape, dear? You just don't want to pay
the piper now that you've gotten caught.'"

Maggie fell back, gasping anew. "They have ruined
every job I've tried to get, making sure I got fired. If
they had found out I was your secretary, they would
have made sure you fired me, too, with the explanation
'Sorry, dear, but you should really leave the area until
your little matter is taken care of.'"

Jake stroked her head, vowing to throttle her parents
if he ever met them. He was outraged, warring with his
own feelings as he listened. The only thing that kept him
from voicing his anger was his years of counseling.
Maggie didn't need his anger as much as she needed to
pour out her own anger and fears.

"I hate him, Jake. I hate him. My parents hurt me,
but I hate him."

Maggie cried. Jake stroked her forehead, her cheeks,

her hair. "Shh, Maggie-May. It's over. Let God heal you."

"I know what people think about me. I'm pregnant, single and deserved this."

"No, Maggie. Never. No one ever deserved that."

"I was taking him home from a party. He wanted to go into my house for a minute. My parents were always having him over for dinner since he's an associate. I let him kiss me...."

Jake cupped her face, then held her as she went through another contraction. While she was trying to breathe, he said, "Maggie, I don't care if you were standing before him naked. If you said no, then no is no. I don't care if you were both in bed together, no is still no. I don't care if he had been your husband. *No is still no.*"

Maggie, her gaze filled with hurt, locked eyes with him. "It was on the couch, in the den. He hurt me, Jake, and didn't care. No one cared. He kept telling me I had led him on." Maggie shuddered. "I was so helpless. He held me down. And though I had thought I was in control of my life, I realized then I had no control. I couldn't get him off me."

Jake pulled Maggie into his arms and held her while she cried. She went through two more contractions as she cried. He silently cried along with her.

"My parents have controlled my life since then, getting me fired. I'm bad luck, dangerous to anyone around me."

"No, Maggie. Don't say that."

Maggie shook her head, her face twisting as another contraction hit. Jake was certain she was in transition.

"What will I do if, when I see this child, I can't love it?"

"Take it one day one minute at a time, Maggie."

Maggie nodded, then gasped falling back. "Jake. I have *got* to push!"

Jake swallowed. "Just a minute." He checked her once more. "Give me two minutes. Breathe through the next contraction and then I'll check you again."

He checked her again and sure enough she was definitely crowning. He jumped up and raced to the bathroom to grab some towels, then went to the kitchen and found a knife.

"Jake!"

The urgency in her voice caused Jake to sprint back into the room. Maggie was trying to breathe through another contraction. Tension etched lines on her damp face, which was covered with a fine sheen of perspiration. He thought she was beautiful at this moment. "We're ready, Maggie-May."

Maggie cried out and grabbed at her knees. "Please save my baby, Jake. Don't let it die."

"God will protect it, Maggie-May," Jake whispered, and began to pray.

Checking her again, he saw a good portion of head crowning. "This is it, sweetheart. Here it comes."

"You don't, have to tell—*me*—that!" Maggie groaned and pushed.

Jake reached down and placed his hand on the top of the infant's head to steady it. Slowly the head emerged.

A tiny scrunched-up face with dark hair slicked down against the scalp slipped out into his hand. The nose was so small, and the little eyes were closed. "Oh, Maggie, darlin', it's beautiful. Push again. Let's get the shoulders…that's it…"

First one shoulder then the other came out. And finally the child just slipped into his hands. Jake took a piece of sheet and wiped at the baby's mouth. Amazingly enough, the child let out a loud squall. "Maggie, darlin', you have a girl. And she is the prettiest little girl I've ever seen…next to you."

Maggie looked up, and Jake held the baby where she could see it.

Joy lit up her face, and despite being covered with sweat and obviously exhausted, she laughed. "Oh, she's beautiful."

Maggie reached for her.

"Just let me cut the cord here." Jake tied the small pieces of sheet tightly in two spots and then used the butcher knife to slice the cord. Oddly enough, it was cutting that cord that made him nauseous. He felt faint as he severed the life supply of the child from the mother.

After wrapping the baby in a towel, he handed her up to Maggie.

"Thank you, Father," she whispered.

Jake thought she'd just answered her earlier question. Despite the circumstances of the conception, Maggie's heart had healed, and she was able to love this child.

"What are you going to name her?"

Turning back to the duty at hand, he delivered the rest of the afterbirth and wrapped it in a towel.

"Alyssa."

Jake paused in his actions to smile softly at Maggie. "That's a beautiful name, Maggie, honey."

Maggie smiled tiredly as she touched the baby's cheek. Moving up next to her, Jake wiped her face and neck with a fresh cloth before taking the baby and cleaning her up.

Maggie laughed when the baby cried. "She doesn't like that."

Jake shook his head. "No, she doesn't."

He wrapped the baby in a fresh towel.

"I have some diapers in the suitcase, as well as clothing and towels and sheets. Oh, Jake, why didn't I think of all of this before?"

"Like me, you were expecting to be rescued."

He went to the suitcase and rummaged around until he found what they required, then returned to her side. After taking the infant awkwardly, he laid her back down on the bed between them. "You know, I've handled this baby more than I've handled any other infant."

Maggie chuckled. "I wouldn't know. You handle her like a professional."

Jake put the plastic diaper on and then slipped the generic white gown with yellow bunnies onto Alyssa. The entire time Alyssa squalled. When he wrapped her back in the blanket, she quieted. He slipped her back next to Maggie.

Maggie blinked sleepily. "Thank you, Jake."

Jake smiled and touched her cheek. "My pleasure."

Maggie's eyes drifted closed.

Jake watched her for a long time and then got up and moved to leave the room. Her next words, though, caused him to freeze in place.

"I love you, you know."

They were barely murmured, but when he turned around, Maggie was looking at him.

He nodded. "And I love you."

He didn't break eye contact until her eyes shut. When she was breathing softly, he left the room.

She loved him. Jake's heart sang. *Thank you, Father, for that gift. For* both *gifts.*

In the other room he found a drawer and collected an extra pillow. He made a bed in the drawer for the baby, covered it with one of Maggie's sheets and quietly lifted the baby from her mother.

After taking Alyssa back into the other room, he slipped her into the drawer on her back. He reached out and felt the child to make sure she wasn't too cold, then sat on the couch next to the drawer, watching the baby while Maggie rested.

"Mmmrrreow."

Jake glanced over and saw the cat, near her food dish, staring at him. "Don't give me a look like it's my job to feed you and you're insulted that your food dish is empty. You positively stuck your nose in the air earlier when I filled the dish."

"Mmmrreeoooooow."

Jake sighed. He was not going to pay any attention to that cat, which had snubbed him and tried to scare the stuffing out of him from day one. No way, no how—

"Mmmmeeeeooooooow."

Except that Maggie would want the cat fed.

He stood up and walked past the cat, scowling. "Fine. Fine. But I only fed you an hour ago." Actually, Jake was glad the cat was no longer growling at him. And he was just a tad happy that she actually ate the food. Maybe he and this cat could get along after all.

Jake picked up the container of food and returned to fill the bowl. "There you go."

The cat sniffed, turned around and twitched her tail before walking off.

Jake gaped. "Stubborn cat," he muttered, then promptly sneezed.

The cat crossed the room and hopped up next to the baby.

Jake's heart tripped. He felt ill at ease that this cat was near the baby. He strode across the room, intending to shoo the cat away. But it proved unnecessary. The cat sniffed the baby, nudged her with her nose, then walked off.

Relieved, Jake sat down again next to the baby. "So, little one, I had wondered what your mommy is going to name you. I think Alyssa is a fine strong name."

The baby snuffled her face against the pillow and let out a tiny breath.

Jake melted, watching her. Reaching out, he stroked the dark cap of hair with one finger. His hand was nearly as big as the baby's head. Awed, he stroked the soft skin of her rounded little cheek and then touched the tiny hand. Five perfectly formed little fingers curled around the offering and held on.

"You're going to be a heartbreaker, sweetheart. I can already tell that."

The baby shuddered again softly, making little grunting noises.

Jake chuckled.

A sudden *thunk* outside caught his attention. He stood and moved over to the window. Looking out, he noted it was already darkening and the rain was still pouring. In a few hours the brunt of the hurricane would be there. His guess would be four or five in the morning.

Jake wondered how his little church had survived and how the people of the community who had refused to leave had fared. Worse hit was down closer to New Orleans and such.

A tree branch cracked somewhere in the distance.

A crash outside indicated a tree off in the forest had fallen. Jake stood for what surely was an hour, just communing with his heavenly Father, thanking Him, talking to Him, discussing trivial things with Him.

Finally, Jake turned his back on the storm outside, peace within him, guiding him to trust and depend on God. Realizing the electricity would certainly go out, he found lanterns and brought them into the room; they would probably need them later.

The cat followed him with her eyes, watching his every move from atop the chest in the living room.

Jake continued to sneeze occasionally but found his allergies didn't seem as bad as when he'd first met the cat. "Maybe it was psychosomatic, Captain Kat. You do have a way of doing your best to put people off. Personally," he continued as he finished up with the lanterns, "I think you were somehow behind it. You probably emitted some allergy type scent, didn't you?"

"Jake," Maggie said.

He heard the soft call and then the chuckle that followed and turned. Maggie stood, looking rumpled and exhausted, leaning against the door frame. The overhead light gave her an ethereal look. She glowed from where she stood.

"What are you doing out of bed?" Jake hurried over and slipped an arm around her.

"I've got to have a shower and change."

Jake stared in disbelief. "Surely you aren't strong enough."

Maggie willingly leaned against Jake. "If you'll stand just outside the door, I'll let you know. Would you do that for me?"

Jake debated scooping her up and putting her right back in bed, then shook his head. He was being overprotective. Of course she wanted a bath. The work he'd witnessed her put to bring forth that baby was more work than he put in during an entire month. "Okay, Maggie-May. Go on and I'll be right here if you need me."

Maggie paused, looking at Alyssa. "How is she? I noticed you had taken her out of the room when I fell asleep."

Jake felt a slight flush. "I wanted you to get some rest."

Maggie nodded.

"She's fine. Hasn't woken up yet, though she has been grunting a bit more the past few minutes."

Maggie smiled. "Good."

Jake's heart squeezed at the love in Maggie's eyes. "You'd better go ahead and get that bath before she gets hungry."

Maggie's cheeks turned pink. "I had thought about nursing her if I kept her. It looks like I have no choice now."

Maggie walked slowly back into her room and dug through her suitcase. Jake stayed back and allowed her some privacy. Then she went into the bathroom.

He heard the water run. In minutes the water was cut and he heard her moving around. "Are you okay?"

Her muffled reply reached his ears and then the door was pulled open. Dressed in a soft yellow gown with tiny rosebuds of various colors, she stood there, looking utterly exhausted but absolutely beautiful.

"You've had enough," he said, and scooped her up in his arms.

"Jake," Maggie protested.

"You just rest and let me play knight in shining armor."

Maggie subsided, laying her head down against Jake's shoulder and wrapping her arms around his neck.

"You are tired, aren't you, Maggie-May?"

Maggie nodded against his shoulder. "Some."

Jake went over to the couch and eased her down onto it. After releasing her, he grabbed a pillow and helped her adjust it behind her head, then whipped out a sheet and covered her.

"I can do this myself, Jake—"

Jake smiled and cupped her cheek. "Humor me."

Maggie nodded again. Glancing toward the window, she asked, "How's the weather?"

Jake accepted the change in topic. "Getting bad. I imagine we've got two or three more hours before the brunt of the storm hits."

A small scuffling sound and then a tiny whimper drew their attention to the tiny infant in the drawer.

Maggie pushed up and reached over to retrieve the baby. Awkwardly she held her before pulling it up against her. She jiggled Alyssa a bit to quiet her down.

Instead, the baby squirmed and the whimpering turned to small protests.

Maggie looked up at Jake. "She's not quieting down. What do you suppose is the matter?"

"Maybe her diaper?" Jake went into the other room and got one of the diapers she had brought. He grabbed the wipes and reentered the room. "Here we go. Want me to change her for you?"

Maggie shrugged. "Do you know how?"

Jake studied Maggie and realized she was nervous. It dawned on him that Maggie had never been around children. "I've seen a few changed. It's really easy. Swing your feet around here and help me."

Jake moved the drawer to the table by the couch and then sat down.

Maggie moved her feet and sat up.

After taking the baby, Jake laid the fussy child between them. "Don't worry about the cries. All babies cry."

Jake wasn't an expert, but he wanted to reassure Maggie and put her at ease. And he did know babies cried.

He cleaned the infant, finding this a totally different experience from all the other children he'd had a chance to tend to in his lifetime.

When he was done, he handed the baby back to Maggie and went and washed up.

Coming back into the room, he looked to where Maggie was trying to comfort the baby, who was still fussing. Worry lines creased her face.

Catching sight of him, she met his gaze. "Now what?"

Jake hesitated, then said, "Perhaps she's hungry."

Maggie sighed. "I didn't think about that." Looking at the baby, then at Jake, she said, "I'm not sure..."

"I can't help you here, Maggie-May. I imagine if you just put her up there, she'll know what to do."

Maggie's cheeks were bright pink. She nodded.

Jake's own cheeks were warm. "I'll just go in the other room and give you some privacy," he said.

Maggie nodded, relief plainly written on her features.

Jake turned and took one step toward the kitchen, before the lights all went out.

"Jake?" Maggie's voice cut through the darkness.

He paused. "Seems I don't have to leave after all. The hurricane took care of that for us."

Chapter Twenty

The pounding on the door woke her.

Maggie rolled over in bed and groggily looked toward the window. Gray light peeked in through the pulled blinds.

Surprised, Maggie blinked. Hadn't she just finished feeding Alyssa again?

Voices in the other room drew her attention and memories came flooding back. The hurricane. It had been awful last night, keeping them up until early this morning. Alyssa had eaten twice and Jake had finally insisted she go to bed...

Oh, no, she thought mournfully, remembering other things, too, like what she'd confessed to him about her ex-fiancé.

"Maggie?"

The tap on the door jerked her gaze to it. The handle turned and Jake poked his head in. His smile faded as he studied her.

"I'm not sure what is going on behind those eyes of yours, Maggie-May, but we'll discuss it later. Rand and Elizabeth are here. The group at the cabin was worried and each took a different road home, hoping to pass us somewhere. Rand spotted my car in a ditch about a quarter of mile up the road, where the wind blew it last night, and eventually found us."

Maggie forced a smile. "I'm glad."

"Maggie?" Elizabeth's soft voice came from the other room, then the short pert redhead was pushing her way past Jake and into the room. "Oh! You had your baby!"

"What?" Rand's voice from the living room echoed Elizabeth's and then he was pushing his way into the room.

Elizabeth moved up next to Maggie. "How are you? Any problems? How's the bleeding?"

Maggie sank down into the bed, pulling the covers up to her chin at Elizabeth's very medical attack. Rand, obviously coming to the conclusion that everything was okay, smiled apologetically and backed out of the room. "Don't hassle her, Lizabeth. Just check her out and then let's get them back to civilization."

"I'm fine," Maggie protested.

"Let her help you, honey," Jake said softly.

Maggie's cheeks turned a fiery red when Rand gaped at Jake's endearment, and Elizabeth positively beamed.

"Shoo, Jake. Let me take care of her," Elizabeth said, grinning.

Maggie watched as Elizabeth shoved him out the door and closed it.

"He's in love with you," Elizabeth said, and giggled.

Maggie shrugged, thinking of everything that had happened in the past twenty-four hours. "Not in love so much as feeling responsible after delivering my baby."

Elizabeth gaped only for a minute before she came over and started examining Maggie. As she checked her tummy and poked and prodded, she said, "Why'd the chicken cross the road?"

Maggie had heard all about Elizabeth's jokes. "I don't have to answer that, do I?"

Elizabeth chuckled. "Some chickens are just so stubborn you can't teach them to stop crossing that darned road...."

Elizabeth pulled back the sheet. "Don't be stubborn, Maggie. Accept that Jake cares for you."

"I'm not stubborn," Maggie whispered when Elizabeth reached out to help her up. "I'm scared. You don't understand. My parents will cause problems."

Elizabeth left Maggie on the edge of the bed and retrieved her robe and slippers. Then she went over to check the baby. "Your parents don't control you, Maggie. You're a grown woman."

Maggie nodded as she worked her arms into the sleeves of her robe. "I know that, but my parents are angry with me about the child. They see this as some power play or something. I will come to my senses and come home. To make sure, they have found out each place I've gotten a job and ended up getting me fired."

Elizabeth picked up the baby like a pro. Pausing, she turned to look at Maggie incredulously. "How can they do that?"

Maggie shrugged. "They hire people to find out things. My parents are stubborn. They believe I played and should pay."

Maggie motioned at the child. "They have no desire to listen to anything I have said. When they find out I've had Alyssa and plan to keep her, they'll have a fit. And they'll do anything they can to make sure I understand I have to give up my child or move out of town."

"But why?"

"I've humiliated them," she said simply.

Elizabeth wrapped the baby in a blanket, handed her to Maggie and then began picking up. "Jake won't allow them to hurt you, Maggie."

"They'll find something that matters to him, something to hold over his head. I can't let that happen."

Elizabeth finished cleaning up, then repacked Maggie's suitcase. "Maggie, hon, you've got to stop playing God. Trust Him to do His job."

Maggie didn't comment but hugged Alyssa, comforting her until she stopped crying. "How is she?" Maggie asked.

"Just fine, as are you. There's a bit of tearing, but other than that, you're fine. You'll need to go to a doctor and let him examine you."

Maggie stood and moved to the bathroom.

Elizabeth followed.

"I'm fine, Elizabeth, really," Maggie said as she ran a brush through her hair and cleaned her face and teeth.

"I'm sure you are. However, I'll just stick by you in case."

Maggie finished up and hobbled back into the room.
She went over to Alyssa, picked her up and cuddled her

"She's a beautiful baby, Maggie."

Elizabeth's soft words caught her attention, and she
glanced around to see Elizabeth staring at Alyssa.

"God gives us good out of disasters sometimes,"
Maggie murmured.

Realizing what she had said, she glanced up at Elizabeth. Instead of shock, she saw understanding. "Yes
He does, Maggie."

Elizabeth went to the door. "Okay, guys, we're
ready."

Jake came in and headed right for Maggie.

"Can you walk out to the car, Maggie?"

"I'm not an invalid," she whispered low, her cheeks
pink.

Jake nodded. "You've more than proven that, sweetheart."

Maggie silently groaned at his words.

Rand collected the suitcases and left the room, chuckling as he did. Elizabeth followed, offering Rand advice
on just where to put the suitcases in the car.

"Are they always like that?" Maggie asked, watching
the couple leave. She thought it was a good way to turn
the subject away from her so Jake wouldn't continue
with his mothering.

Jake gave her a knowing smile, indicating he understood exactly what she was doing. "Like what, Maggie-
May?"

"She's so full of energy, bouncing around him, offering suggestions. And Rand simply smiles and nods,

never getting the least bit bent out of shape over all her advice.''

Jake chuckled. ''Oh, that. Yes, Rand is pretty easygoing when it comes to his wife. Of course, I can see why he'd be that way if he loved her.''

Jake looked into Maggie's eyes.

Maggie's heart flip-flopped at the tender expression in his eyes. ''How can you love me, Jake?'' she murmured, realizing exactly what he was thinking. ''Especially after everything you know?''

Maggie adjusted the baby in her arms.

Jake cupped Maggie's cheek. ''Bad things happen to us all, Maggie-May. It's how we handle them that tells what type of character we have. You're strong. I wish the violence had never happened, but it did and you survived. I'm outraged. If I ever meet the guy, I'd liked to smash his nose for him. It's going to take me a lot of time and prayer before I can ever forgive what that person did to you. But we both have to heal. And I want to be there for you because I love you, Maggie. I love you more than I ever thought possible.''

''Oh, Jake,'' Maggie murmured, tears coming to her eyes. ''And I love you, too. More than I know how to express.''

Jake rubbed her cheek before allowing his hand to slip around to the base of her neck and urging her forward for a kiss.

Maggie leaned into his kiss, meeting his lips with her own. His were firm, strong and yet tender as they caressed her. Maggie sighed against his mouth returning the kiss.

When Jake pulled back, all the love he felt glowed in his eyes. "Maggie, darlin', will you marry me?"

Maggie stared, overwhelmed by Jake's question.

Marriage. Oh, how she loved this man. But marriage?

She thought of all the problems in the past year, of the things she'd gone through. She realized now she had never truly loved her ex-fiancé. No, she had cared deeply for him, but she had never loved him with the deep abiding love that tied two souls together under God.

She did love this man like that.

And he loved her and Alyssa, and didn't care about the past. Could she actually have found a satisfying ending to the mess of the past year after all?

Seeing the love in Jake's eyes, she melted. "Oh, yes, Jake," she whispered.

Leaning against him, she wept.

"Shh, Maggie, hon. I didn't mean to make you cry."

Maggie chuckled through her tears. "I don't know how I got so lucky."

"It's that Irish name your parents gave you," he joked.

Hearing her parents mentioned burst the euphoric bubble and brought reality crashing back in. "Jake. What will your church say? I mean, I don't have the most sterling reputation...."

Jake frowned at her. "Maggie, you have to get over that."

"But what will they say? I don't want to hurt your career."

Jake shook his head. "You have to let God take care of things, Maggie. Stop trying to control everything. If you look in the Bible, you'll discover the people in there weren't perfect. Stop examining something that wasn't your fault. If God forgave people for their sometimes bad choices and used them for His glory, how can you worry about something that isn't your fault?''

Maggie smiled through her tears, thinking Jake was one of a kind. ''Thank you.''

Jake returned the smile. ''It was a violent crime, Maggie. Violence is something we can't control. Don't ever let anyone tell you that you were responsible. You hear me?''

Maggie nodded. ''I—I'm just worried that something more disastrous is going to happen—''

Jake covered her lips with a finger, then leaned in and replaced it with his lips. When he finally broke the kiss, he smiled at her gently. ''Enough. Trust God, Maggie.''

Maggie nodded, wanting to believe what Jake was saying. Slowly she allowed her hope to build, her joy to replace her fear.

''Now, Maggie, darlin', is your answer still yes? Because let me warn you, you've already said yes and I won't let you go back on your word now.''

Maggie smiled. ''How can I refuse?''

Jake grinned, self-satisfied. ''Is that so. I'll remember that, then.''

He pulled Maggie into his arms and gave her a bear hug.

Alyssa squawked.

Jake released Maggie and looked down at the child—their child, as far as he was concerned. ''Did I hurt her?''

Maggie shook her head and glanced shyly up at Jake. "She's probably getting hungry."

A throat clearing at the door of the bedroom intruded on the intimate setting and Jake turned. Rand stood there.

"Congratulations. I didn't mean to interrupt."

Jake shook his head. "You didn't. And thanks for the well-wishes. I don't think anything could make me feel happier than Maggie agreeing to be my wife, though."

Elizabeth squealed and ran forward to hug Maggie and then Jake. Rand shook his hand and then kissed Maggie on the cheek.

Jake was the first to break up the happy scene. "Alyssa is hungry and Maggie is tired. Let's get them to the car and back to Centerton."

Rand's smile faded. "And see what is left of our town?"

Jake's own smile faded. "Yeah."

Reality impinged. However, Jake found, despite the reality, there was still a buoyancy in his spirit, a joy that knowing, no matter what he found back in Centerton, he had his future right here with him.

Chapter Twenty-One

"You look tired."

Maggie turned from the church kitchen, where she was making more sandwiches to deliver to a local shelter in the community. "I'm fine, Jake."

Jake moved over and rubbed her shoulders. "How's Alyssa?"

Maggie glanced to where the baby slept in a bassinet borrowed from the nursery. "Sleeping again."

"You should be, too," Jake murmured.

Maggie leaned back against Jake, enjoying his strength and gentleness as he held her. "I only wanted to get a few more sandwiches made before the crew gets back."

"And you have. Now, go rest. Remember, the doctor told you to rest these past two weeks."

Maggie turned in Jake's arms and hugged him. "I know. I know. And I am...."

Jake chuckled and squeezed Maggie. "You are now."

Maggie sighed, resting in Jake's arms, looking at Alyssa. She hadn't been this happy for a long time. Life was good, except for one small thing.

"Have you called your parents yet?"

Jake's low voice rumbled against where her ear was pressed to his chest.

Her parents.

"No."

Jake didn't comment, only squeezed Maggie tighter. Anxiety crept into Maggie as she thought about her parents. "I can't tell them, Jake."

"You can't *not* tell them, Maggie. You have to heal. As long as you hold on to the past and the fear, you can't heal and go on."

Maggie's chest tightened, and she pushed back. Looking up into his eyes, she whispered, "You don't understand. They don't approve. There is nothing I will be able to say that will change that. As far as they're concerned, I'm an embarrassment." They'll hurt you, she silently whispered her fear.

"They've had time, Maggie, to change their mind. However, I'm not asking you to do this for them. I want you to do this for you. Face them. See that there isn't anything they can do that will run you off this time. I'll be there with you."

Maggie's heart raced. "Why do you keep insisting I face them? Can't we just marry and...and..."

When she didn't continue, Jake cupped her cheek. "It's better to get the situation out in the open and get it over with so we can start our marriage on fresh ground. And I don't want to sneak around behind them,

Maggie. You've got to face them…and heal. Face the past and your fears, and then we can go on.''

Maggie heard his words but shook her head. ''You don't understand. We've been through this a thousand times in the past two weeks, Jake. They'll find something to manipulate us with. They're angry that I was going to have this child. I would just as soon not see them rather than risk things being—''

Jake pulled her back into his arms and hugged her. Whispering gently, he said, ''I'm sorry I pushed you. But I think you're wrong. What could your parents possibly do that could cause us problems?''

Maggie didn't want to venture a guess. Since meeting Jake she realized her parents were hurting and by forcing her away they could deny their own pain. Knowing that, though, didn't change what they'd try to do…which would be to make Maggie bend to their will again. At Jake's expense.

If only they had believed her…

''Let's get you and Alyssa back to your house so you can—''

''Margaret?''

Maggie stiffened.

Jake, hearing the soft feminine voice, stepped back from Maggie and turned in the direction of the voice. An older woman and gentleman stood before him… people who were very familiar to him. ''Henry. Mary.'' Jake nodded at the Hendersons, wondering what had brought them here. ''Maggie, this is Henry and Mary Henderson, who are on the board of directors—''

''Mom? Dad?''

Jake looked sharply at Maggie. Her eyes were wide with shock and her face pale. His gaze shot back to two people he had been working with the past year. They were pale, too, standing there staring at Maggie like—

When Mary's gaze went to the bassinet and jerked away, he asked, "These are your parents?"

Maggie nodded.

Jake reached out for her to guide her back in his arms, but Maggie pulled away. Slowly her back straightened and all emotion left her face. Coolly, she asked, "What are you doing here?"

Jake ached for Maggie. He'd seen the glimpse of fear. Silently he berated himself for not finding out sooner just who her parents were. "Maggie, your parents and I work together, sweetheart. I'm sure they're only here—"

"'Sweetheart'?"

Jake turned toward Mary, who had sounded absolutely appalled. "Mary—"

"I see she's sucked you into her lies, too, Jake," Mary said.

Oh, boy, Jake thought. Automatically, he moved closer to Maggie. "Why don't we all go into my office and sit down where we can—"

"She's good at that," Mary interrupted, overriding Jake. "How many other people have you lied to, Margaret, and told that you were leaving the area, only to turn up again? How many people did you tell lies to so you could hide around here and try to manipulate us into accepting the life-style you've chosen?"

"It's not a life-style, Mom. I told you—"

"You refused to marry Chester. What type of lifestyle

would you call that—sleeping around, getting caught and then refusing to do the right thing? And then walking around proud of the fact that you're a single parent. After all we've done for you, and you won't even leave the area...."

"Excuse me," Jake said, appalled at the attack Mary had launched against her own daughter. "Let's just go to my office." Jake hoped that once there he could calm the Hendersons down and they could all talk.

"Well?" Henry asked his daughter, ignoring Jake. "Isn't it enough your mother lost nights of sleep over your revenge as you flouted our failure? And now we find out you're hanging around this pastor, making a mockery of everything he is trying to do?"

"Just a minute here," Jake began. "Henry, Mary, I welcome you into the church, but I won't allow you to go around attacking its members or my future wife."

Shocked silence fell.

"Your...wife?" Henry sounded as if he were choking.

Mary stared aghast. "But—"

Maggie touched Jake's arm. "Jake, please..."

Jake knew he wasn't handling this well, but hearing what they had said to Maggie infuriated him. "Yes. I've asked Maggie to marry me." Jake smiled, though he was absolutely furious inside. "So, why don't we go into the office and discuss this like civilized humans?"

He immediately knew he'd said the wrong thing by the Hendersons' narrow-eyed look.

"You have no idea what you've gotten yourself into, Jake Mathison. Or maybe you do," Mary said scathingly. "This child of ours has done her best to rebel against us. We have simply been trying to practice tough love and get her straightened out. Instead, you come along and give her shelter."

"Mom!" Maggie said, dismayed.

"Is that so," Jake said mildly. "What did you think to do by banning her from your house and making sure she had no job?"

Henry moved up to Mary. "We thought to let her see what real life is like. How tough it can be. Until she recognizes what she has done is wrong and will accept and apologize to us...."

"Wrong?"

"Jake," Maggie pleaded, touching his arm.

Jake immediately turned to her. When he saw the tears in her eyes, his anger deflated and his mind cleared. Slipping a hand to her back, he rubbed gently. "I'm sorry, Maggie. Get Alyssa and we'll go to my office and all sit down and talk."

Maggie shook her head. Turning, she faced her parents. "Look, I love you both, Mom, Dad, but I don't want to fight anymore. I have a baby now and am making a life for myself. Can't you just stop?"

Henry scowled. "If you'd come home and act like a daughter and stop spreading lies about Chester, sure we could. But you keep placing all the blame for your actions everywhere else. All we want, girl, is for you to take some responsibility in this and then we'll support you."

Jake felt his temper rising again. *Father, give me wis-*

dom to know what to say, he prayed. *And peace,* he thought.

"Enough," he said in a low voice to Maggie's parents. "If you have something to say, we'll go into my office and discuss it. But there will be no more arguing in the kitchen here."

Maggie's parents stiffened up like fireplace pokers and their looks could have frozen the flames of Hell they were so cold.

"Come on, Mary," Henry said. "This is ridiculous. You were right."

"We'll just see what the board has to say about Jake's judgment," Mary hissed at Maggie.

"What do you mean by that?" Maggie asked, fear leaping to her features.

Mary smiled with smug satisfaction. "Well, if Jake can't handle his own church or what type of people he hires to work here, he surely can't be in charge of this project. We'll pull our support immediately, and after everyone else hears about his inability to judge rationally, I'm sure the others will follow."

Her parents strode out of the kitchen. Maggie felt sick as her greatest fears were realized. Jake was now going to pay the price for what she'd done. "I'm so sorry, Jake. I...I..."

Jake watched Maggie's parents go before turning to Maggie. "Why didn't you tell me who your parents were? You go by the last name Garderé."

"I didn't want anyone to know."

Jake sighed and then rubbed at his neck. "Great."

Maggie studied him, nauseated. "What are you going

to do? They're very angry and bitter and blame me for this whole situation.''

"I would have never guessed.'' Jake shook his head, disgusted. "I can tell you one thing, though. They aren't going to destroy that center. I've worked too hard for this. I don't care what it takes—I'm going to see it finished. I should probably call Tyler and Gage and let them know what's happening, just in case your parents do decide to spread slander. I'll be back in a bit.''

With a sinking feeling Maggie watched Jake stride out of the room. Jake was going to lose the center because her parents held a grudge against her and were going to use him to prove a point.

Slowly Maggie shook her head. Not this time. This time she'd let them win. This time she would leave, because she loved Jake.

Chapter Twenty-Two

Jake rubbed wearily at his forehead. He'd been at his desk for three hours going over the paperwork for the lumber prices. His figures were right. There was no way, if Maggie's parents pulled their bid, they could meet their budget and get the building done.

Why hadn't she told him?

"Knock, knock."

Jake looked up to see Tyler standing at the door. At six foot two, Tyler tended to tower in doorways. A big man, with a heart of gold. "Come on in, Tyler," Jake said, waving a hand.

Tyler ambled in and seated himself across from Jake. "So, Jake. What have you found?" Tyler made a gesture at the paperwork on Jake's desk.

"If they pull their bid, we can't afford it." Jake sighed and rubbed at his neck. "I just don't understand why Maggie didn't tell me sooner who her parents were."

Tyler frowned. Jake hadn't told him what had happened to Maggie, only that her parents had tossed out an ultimatum and she had chosen not to follow it. ''Seems to me the girl was scared. I mean, the only time you don't tell someone where you are is if you're hiding.''

Jake nodded. ''Yeah, she was hiding. She was worried that her parents would try something exactly like this if they found out where she was.''

Tyler shook his head. ''Such a shame her parents can't let go of her and let her run her own life. Some parents are that way.''

Jake straightened the paperwork and stuffed it back into the folder. ''I've counseled enough to know that. I don't understand why Maggie can't let go of the pain her parents caused and just let herself heal. You should have seen her earlier. Her whole face froze with fear when her parents showed up. And things went downhill from there.''

When Tyler didn't comment, Jake glanced up. Seeing Tyler studying him, he cocked his head curiously. ''What?''

''You know, Jake, you're taking this attack awfully personally. I realize you love the building project, but why aren't you out there with Maggie, comforting her, instead of going over these papers?''

Jake looked down at the papers and then at Jake. ''I just wanted to try to stop any damage her parents might be about to cause.''

''Why? Isn't it you who always preaches that God will take care of things if we trust Him? Why is it so important that you handle this?''

Jake saw what Tyler was getting at, and knew Tyler was right. "My brother's death."

Tyler nodded. "I know, Jake, you always wanted to do this for him. But, I think this building project has become an obsession to you, so much so that you've forgotten God is the one who is in charge of this, not you. Perhaps you should practice what you told Maggie and do a little healing yourself."

Jake felt a pang in his heart. "I just wanted to see that place built, for my brother."

Tyler shook his head. "No, Jake. I think the place is for you. You weren't there for him when he needed you and so by doing this you're atoning. Perhaps you should try forgiving yourself, since God...and your brother... forgave you years ago."

Jake's shoulders drooped. Looking back, he realized suddenly that Tyler was right. All these years he'd had in the back of his mind that he needed to get this place built for kids to go. It'd become an obsession to him, a need that outweighed everything. *Forgive me, Father, for not seeing this sooner,* he prayed.

"I even put it before Maggie," Jake whispered. Turning to Tyler, he continued, "Instead of staying and supporting her when she needed it, I rushed back here to try to save the project."

Tyler sighed. "We all make mistakes. Why don't you knock off, go find Maggie and apologize. Leave this in God's hands."

Peace flowed through Jake. "You're right. I've been such an idiot."

Healing flooded his heart as he realized that through

all these years he had been holding in a pain of loss and blaming himself. There was no reason he should have held that in the way he had. He should have let it go, let God heal him and accepted that there was nothing he could have done.

As he accepted that now, Maggie's parents' threats faded. So what if they tried to smear his name? There would be time to build this. If it was God's will, a door would open up with funds for the lumber or another place even less inexpensive to buy lumber from.

"You're right, Tyler. If Gage calls, tell him I've gone home for the evening."

Tyler smiled. "Good."

Jake nodded. "Thanks, Tyler."

Jake owed Maggie an apology for running off like he did.

She wasn't in the kitchen and Alyssa was gone. He checked the nursery, too. It was only as he approached her house that something niggled at him. Something was different.

He jogged up the steps and knocked on the door. "Maggie?"

He waited.

She didn't answer.

Jake winced, realizing his inattention might have actually hurt her. Knocking louder he called out, "Maggie-May, open up, please."

Still she didn't answer.

Worry touched his spine. He hesitated only a moment

before pulling the screen door back and checking the other door. It opened easily under his hand.

He stepped in and looked around.

"Maggie?"

He walked into the house and headed toward the kitchen. The sight in the bedroom stopped him and he backtracked.

Dread built in his chest when he noted all the open drawers and empty cabinets. "Maggie!"

He hurried to Alyssa's room and discovered the same condition.

"Her car."

He realized her car wasn't in the driveway.

Running back into the living room, he looked out.

He whirled and went to the kitchen, hoping, praying, Maggie had simply found a new place to live and had forgotten to mention it to him.

The piece of paper on the table told him he was wrong.

Jake,
I couldn't stay. I had to go. I'm sorry for the problems I've caused. When my parents find I am gone, they'll back off and the center will be saved. God bless you for all you've done. My love,
                                                    Maggie

Jake rubbed at a stain on the paper before realizing that the ink was blurred by Maggie's tears.

"Mmmmeeewww."

Jake looked down to see Captain Kat winding her way around his feet, whining at the loss of Maggie.

"Why didn't you wait, Maggie, and let me explain? Why didn't you ask me just what meant more to me?"

Fear.

That was the simple answer.

Maggie had never had the chance to heal herself. How was she to know what he felt? Maggie had had so many people put their wants and needs first that it would be very easy for her to think Jake just might do that. "But it didn't mean that much, Maggie. You mean more to me, so much more."

As he stood there and read the note, he realized that because of his own inability to let go of the past and heal, he had just lost the only woman he would ever love.

Chapter Twenty-Three

Maggie trudged along the road toward home and Alyssa. The small town of Luvilla, Louisiana, had a transportation system, but it wasn't all that great. Looking up at the cloudy sky, Maggie had to wonder if she was going to get soaked before she made it the four blocks to her home.

Maggie smiled, thinking of her three-month-old daughter and how chunky she'd gotten. It was hard to believe that she was the same tiny child Maggie gave birth to.

Thinking of that birth reminded Maggie of Jake, which reminded her of what she had left behind. Melancholy settled over her.

Jake.

Her heart felt as if there were a gaping hole where he had once been. How she missed him. She had debated only for a short while before leaving and heading north.

It had been God who had landed her the secretarial job in the small city near Alexandria.

She firmly believed that. Stopping at that diner to eat had been divine guidance. The waitress's brother was a lawyer, who just so happened to need a secretary because his was leaving on Friday.

She'd been hired within the hour.

In a way, Maggie hated how it had worked out. She had thought about going back and talking to Jake, but with the job, she hadn't had time. On several occasions she'd picked up the phone to call and explain. She'd even thought to write.

Truth was, she just couldn't bring herself to do it.

A drop of rain hit Maggie on the cheek.

Glancing up, she saw the dark skies and sighed. Looked as if she was going to get wet again. Ducking her head, she hurried along, intent on arriving home as quickly as possible to keep from getting completely soaked.

So intent was she on her path that it was a moment before she noticed the car that had pulled up beside her. Before she had a chance to look up, an achingly familiar voice said softly, "Need a ride, Maggie-May?"

Stunned, she stopped and stared at Jake. He still looked as ruggedly handsome as ever, though there were circles under his eyes. She blinked, but he was still there when she opened her eyes.

"What are you doing here?" she asked, trembling, certain he was going to disappear any moment.

He smiled. "Hunting for you."

Her heart soared. Breathing became downright hard. "How'd you find me?"

Jake's eyes twinkled. "Do you know a woman named Thelma at the local diner?"

"Yes," she whispered.

"She was nice enough to call me and tell me to get up here and heal your broken heart."

"She didn't!" Maggie said, stunned.

Jake got out, took Maggie by the elbow and led her around to the other door. "I'm afraid so, honey. I'm going to name our second child after her."

"What?" Maggie stared at Jake, wondering if he'd grown two heads.

Leaning down, he kissed her gently. "I love you. We're going to be married. But first—"

He closed the door and went back around to his side of the car; he climbed in just as it really started raining. Pulling the door shut, he turned to look at her. "I have to apologize, Maggie. I should never have left you that day to go see about the building project. I should have stayed and made sure you were okay."

Maggie shook her head. "No, Jake. I understand. That building project meant everything to you."

Jake slowly nodded. "Yes, it did. That's why I resigned as the head of the committee and turned things over to Tyler."

"You what?" Maggie gripped Jake's arm. "What did my parents do? I'm so sorry! I—"

Jake leaned over and kissed her again. Grinning, he said, "That's a good way to quiet you."

Turning serious, he continued, "Your parents opened

my eyes. That's what they did. When they came and confronted you, and Tyler made me see how worried I was over the building project, I realized I'd never allowed myself to heal. God can handle that. I am only in an advisory position now, if I decide to accept it.''

"If? I don't understand, Jake. What do you mean?"

Jake stroked Maggie's cheek. "I also told the elders of the church that I might be resigning. It all depends on you. If you don't want to go back to the area where your parents live, then we'll leave. However, before you decide, I think you should know some things."

Jake pulled out a letter and newspaper clipping and handed them to Maggie. "Your ex-fiancé was arrested the other day for attempted rape and assault. Seems he got drunk and tried to force himself on another woman."

Maggie shook as she took the article and read it. "And this?" she asked, opening the letter.

"From your parents, Maggie. It appears they are despondent over what they've done. They came to me and apologized and said that if you contacted me to please tell you that they wanted to talk to you and apologize to you for ever doubting you. They also want to tell you that they love you and hope one day you can find it in your heart to forgive them."

Maggie began to cry.

"Ah, Maggie, darlin'," Jake said softly, and pulled her into his arms. She rested there, listening to his soothing voice, and cried out all the pain, the hurt, the distrust of the past year and allowed her Heavenly Father to slowly replace the pain with peace.

When she finally pulled back from Jake, the rain was coming down in sheets.

Jake stroked her cheek. "I love you."

Fresh tears sprang to her eyes. "And I love you. I've been such a fool."

"No, never, Maggie," Jake whispered. "It took your leaving for all this to come about. God's timing, not ours. Remember that. Things always work out in His time."

Maggie nodded.

His eyes connected with and held hers. "So, do I start looking for another church or do you want to come back?"

"You'd do that for me?"

Jake nodded, deadly serious. "That and more, Maggie, if it meant keeping you at my side."

Maggie slowly shook her head. "No, Jake. God comes first. If He wants you at that church, who am I to gainsay Him? I'll go back."

Jake leaned forward. A inch from her lips, he paused. "And marry me, and live with me until we're old and gray and rocking in rockers on the front porch? And help me take care of Captain Kat, who has taken to sleeping with me every night."

A slow smile curved Maggie's mouth. "Oh, dear!"

Jake laughed. "Yeah. Oh, dear."

"I'll have fifty great-grandchildren running circles around us, and twenty cats sleeping with us, Jake, as long as I'm with you."

"Good."

With a smug smile of satisfaction, Jake sealed the bargain with a kiss.

*   *   *   *   *

Dear Reader,

Sometimes in life we feel all alone, having gone through some pain or hurt that we think no one else can understand. Or sometimes don't want to understand. Such is the case for Maggie, the heroine in this story, who has gone through a very traumatic experience and is trying to pick up the pieces of her life and go on.

It takes Jake to teach her that the love of Jesus can heal all hurts, while learning that lesson all over for himself. God loves us, wants us to heal, to let go of the past and the pain. Sometimes, as Christians, we get so caught up in what is right or wrong that we forget that we're supposed to love and help each other, be there for one another, not condemn.

I hope, if you've been hurt in the past (and who of us hasn't?) that this story will touch your heart and open you up again to God's healing love as you travel the road of rediscovery with Maggie and Jake in *A Mother's Love*. Please write me and let me know what you think. I love to hear from readers.
P.O. Box 106, Faxon, OK 73540.

In Christ's Love,

Cheryl Wolverton